PENGUIN BOOKS

The Copycat

Jake Woodhouse is a *Sunday Times* bestselling author. *The Copycat* is his fourth book.

The Copycat

JAKE WOODHOUSE

PENGUIN BOOKS

PENGUIN BOOKS

UK | USA | Canada | Ireland | Australia
India | New Zealand | South Africa

Penguin Books is part of the Penguin Random House group of companies
whose addresses can be found at global.penguinrandomhouse.com.

First published 2019
001

Set in 12.5/14.75 pt Garamond MT Std
Typeset by Jouve (UK), Milton Keynes
Printed and bound in Great Britain by Clays Ltd, Elcograf S.p.A.

A CIP catalogue record for this book is available from the British Library

ISBN: 978–1–405–92267–8

For Zara

Prologue

The candyfloss smudge of dawn.

Stars glittering up high.

The gun at the back of my head.

'I can explain,' I say. 'Just give me a –'

'What did I just tell you?' the man says as he slaps my ear. 'Maybe you need these unblocking?' He slaps the other one so hard my ear starts ringing.

We've been walking for what must be an hour now, stumbling through a wood slippery with fallen leaves. Roots snake across my path at random as if they're trying to trip me up. Water drips from branches all around. His breathing's close behind, I can feel it on my neck, and he pushes the gun harder, spurring me on. Up ahead I glimpse a break in the trees and soon the forest falls away on either side as I step into a round clearing.

Skewered on a craggy branch is a bright misshapen moon. Long thin clouds slide across the sky. The cable ties he slipped on earlier pinch my wrists.

For the briefest of moments I think about running. I shake it off. Back at the academy they teach you what to do if you're ever held at gunpoint, and it sure as hell isn't run. Lesson number one: you can't outrun a bullet, movies notwithstanding. The preferred route is to shut the fuck up, do what you're told, try not to anger them until you can work out a better plan. Or backup reaches you.

As backup isn't even aware of me, I'm left with the first. And I failed the not-angering-him bit before we even started the forced march.

'Stop,' he says as we reach the centre of the space.

What choice do I have?

Muscles ache from the march. My right heel, rubbed raw with each step, feels like it's bleeding. And it's all my fault.

'Undress,' he says.

Oh fuck. I know what's coming now. I thought, given he had the gun, he'd use it. At least that would be quick. But if he's asking me to undress . . . My pulse techno-beats in my ears. I need to think of something, fast, but he hits me across the back of the head with the butt of his gun and my thoughts scatter again. I start fumbling with my belt to bide time.

'Faster,' he growls.

Jeans pool at my feet with a soft exhale.

'Everything,' he whispers into my ear. 'Take off everything.'

Socks come off slowly, giving me time to think. Underwear. My balls shrink and shrivel – the cold air's like a caress from a dead hand.

'T-shirt.'

'My hands are tied. How can I –'

Another blow to the back of my head. The exact same spot as before. Everything sways, narrows sharply, but I just cling on to the thin, fragile thread of consciousness, forcing myself back into the world. He grabs my T-shirt, lifts it away from my back, and I hear the soft hiss of fabric being cut. Which means as well as the gun he also has a knife. Of course he does. He has a fucking knife and I'm naked with my hands tied in front of me in a wood in the middle of nowhere and no one knows I'm here and –

I try to ground myself, slow things down. I've two enemies right now: the man behind me, and panic. I can't defeat the former if the latter takes hold.

'Knees,' he says once the T-shirt drops away and I'm shivering hard. I hesitate and feel his grasp on my shoulder. He pushes me down. My knees strike the ground and something scuttles away from me. I listen to it escape into the night.

I smell earth, rotting leaves, my own fear. *The black wolf raises its head, nose to the wind.*

I glance up at the sky, the immensity of it all striking me for the first time. *I was part of this,* I think, *but soon I won't be.*

Because I know how this is going to end.

Panic hits and questions fly at me: how did I end up here, how did it come to this? Thoughts rush and tumble over each other until it comes, the memory of how it started just days ago with a woman's scream. I hear it again, the piercing intensity of it, which I now recognize as a signal to stay away. If only I'd realized that at the time.

I'm breathing fast. *I feel the black wolf shudder.*

'You don't have to do this,' I tell him.

All I get in response is a laugh. And a cold blade against my throat.

A cloud crosses the moon, cutting out the light.

The stars flicker downwards.

Towards the raw, bloodshot dawn.

Four Days Before

Visiting the graves,
the old dog
leads the way.

Issa

'I told you to never contact me on this number unless it was absolutely *necessary*.'

'Yes, sir, but we may have a situation on our hands.'

'You mean Marianne Kleine?'

'I spoke to her father not long after she . . . she was found. He told me how she had been killed and it reminded me of Koen Muller's daughter.'

'I am aware of the similarities. The main thing is, are the police?'

'Well . . . I've been doing some digging through my connection there, and so far it seems they aren't. Whoever clean-swept the original case did a good job. Their system didn't alert them to the similarities. And it turns out, of the three cops on the initial investigation one is in a coma, and one has disappeared from the face of the earth.'

'You said three, what about the third?'

'He's alive, but he's no longer a serving officer. He had some kind of psychotic breakdown last year. Thing is, because the details of how Kleine died haven't been released to the press he wouldn't have any way of connecting the dots, even if he reads about her death.'

'Still, he's the biggest threat in all this.'

'Are you saying what I think –'

'What I'm saying is this, you keep monitoring the situation for now. I'll want reports every day and I'll text you a new number to get me on.'

'Yes, sir.'

'One last thing, the cop that had the breakdown, what's his name?'

'Uhh . . . Rykel. Inspector Jaap Rykel. Or ex-inspector I should say.'

9

Sour Hound

I hear it as I turn the corner, dazzled by the canal blazing gold in the setting sun. At first I think it's the shriek of brakes and I take a pull on my vape, savouring the taste, the little head rush, and look around, searching for the source. It comes again, only louder, clearer, a long soprano note swooping through the air before sliding down to a choked-off finish. This time I work out what it is. It's a scream.

I'd been out at the lock-up working on the Mustang and decided to get off the train two stops earlier, walk back to my houseboat through the canal district. Sure, it'll take me twenty minutes or so longer, and I'll have to contend with all the tourists, many of them in Halloween gear, but I could do with the walk. And anyway, I've been an Amsterdammer all my life, I don't even *see* tourists any more. Except when they wind up dead and it's my job to step in and sort it out.

Was, I remind myself. *Was my job.*

And now this, a man, less than thirty metres away, with his hand round a woman's throat. She tries to scream again, though this time it's quickly muffled as his grip tightens. I start forward, taking another hit from the vape before sliding it into my pocket.

The woman tries to wriggle free. They're face to face now, arms flailing like fighting crabs, and she shifts round into profile. For a split second I think it's Tanya – her hair the same shade of red, held up in a ponytail with the exact same bounce – and a deep sadness washes over me as I relive in a single moment all that went wrong between us.

Another cry snaps me out of it. The man grabs the woman's hair, jerks her head back and starts whispering in her ear. They're by a cluster of shiny metal tables. Steps behind them lead down into a bar, the glass doors of which are crammed with Halloweened faces peering out. I note that none of them are rushing to get involved.

'Hey! Let her go!' I call out when I'm close enough.

'Fuck off,' he says without even turning round to see who it is. He's wearing a grey suit, his tie loosened, the top buttons on his shirt undone, tails hanging loose. He sticks his pale tongue in her ear where it darts and writhes like a hungry, slippery eel. The woman's trying her best to fight him off, but he's bigger and stronger than her and she just can't break free.

I reach them and swing my arm out round his throat, hauling him back hard. He tries to fight but I just tighten even further, closing off his airway. A few more seconds of that and he can see he's not going to win. He stops struggling and releases her, though I can feel he's still tense, still amped up. The woman stumbles away, hands at her throat, each gasp for air a saw through wood. A couple of spectators, finally deciding it's safe enough, stream out of the bar towards her. He's dressed in a skeleton suit. She's got yellow skin with a cobweb creeping across her face. They flank her and all three move down the steps.

'I'll release you,' I tell him once they're safely inside. 'Don't make me regret it.'

'All right,' he says, voice tight and breathy. 'All right.'

I loosen my arm, allowing him some air. But he's quick, one step ahead of me, and he stamps down hard. My left foot explodes with pain as he slithers out of my hold, grabs a bottle off one of the zinc-topped tables and smashes it on the edge. I try to duck as he spins round but the bite of jagged glass lights up my arm. *The black wolf shudders.* I stagger left and he takes advantage, charging me like a bull. I've no time to dodge and he rams his shoulder into my stomach. It knocks the wind out of me and still he keeps on coming, feet slipping and skidding until my heel catches a ridge at the top of the steps. Then there's weightlessness and pit-of-the-stomach fear as I'm launched backwards into space. He starts to run away as I fall, gritty footsteps receding fast as I hit the ground hard. My hip and shoulder take the brunt of it. My head whip-lashes down.

By the time I scramble up, the shock of the impact still reverberating through my body, the wound in my arm pulsing and the rush of blood loud in my ears, I can see he's long gone.

I'm sat in one of the bar's semicircular booths staring at the shard of glass in my arm when two uniforms finally saunter onto the scene, closely followed by a paramedic. A muted trumpet melody haunts the space and the air is warm with exhaled alcohol. I move and light flashes across the surface of the glass. It's got an elegant shape, curved like a sail catching the wind. Or a fang. I reach out to grasp it.

'Don't,' calls the paramedic, striding towards me with

a kitbag. He's young, sleeves rolled up, and has the air of a man who can deal with a situation. He snaps on some gloves, does a quick visual.

'Nasty,' he says. 'Looks like it's gone deep. Should probably get you to a hospital.'

It's that soft time between afternoon and evening, and I'm pretty sure the wound isn't life-threatening. Meaning I'll be back of the queue at A & E, most likely oversubscribed because it's Halloween and people have started drinking early, despite the fact it's a Wednesday. Do I want to spend hours under fluorescent lights waiting for my name to be called, surrounded by sick people and relatives desperately hoping for the surgeon to stride out and tell them everything's going to be okay? Or by drunk people sobering up after their friend got so roaringly drunk they'd put their head through a shop window and were right now being stitched up so their face will be a permanent reminder of Halloween?

'Can't you just pull it?' I ask as he's about to make the call.

'Problem is, if it's hit the brachial artery and I pull it out then you will bleed.'

His radio bursts on, a priority-one request for another incident not far from here. I know priority one is only used for injuries deemed potentially fatal if not treated swiftly.

'That sounds more urgent. Just pull it. I'll be fine.'

He frowns, but allows his eyes and fingers to rove, assessing damage, checking angles of entry and possible exit.

'Squeamish?' he asks.

'No.'

He reaches into his bag and pulls out a miniature torch, then pinches a bit of flesh, opening up the side of the wound to see how deep the glass goes. I glance down into all that glistening pinky moistness. Well, maybe I am a little squeamish after all.

'I dunno . . .' he says, clicking the torch off and stowing it away.

He looks at me and checks the shard again, frowning to himself whilst probing round it gently. His hair's close cropped with a widow's peak pointing to an oddly flat nose. He's also drenched in a strong aftershave which is giving me a headache. Or maybe that's from the fall.

'Honestly I'd be happier taking you in. I don't want a bleeder.'

'Just do it,' I tell him.

The paramedic weighs it all up for a moment then nods. 'You just can't help some people,' he says with a shrug.

He starts assembling what he needs and I take a moment to look around. The place was full when I'd been helped in by the barman, but most of the people have cleared out, not wanting their evening to be disrupted with answering tedious questions posed to them by the police. Major buzzkill when all you'd wanted to do was leave the stresses and strains of the day behind you and party into the night as if morning's never coming round again.

The only people left now are the woman, the barman and the manager who'd come down from the office upstairs, wringing his hands and fussing like an old woman with unexpected guests. Further afield severed heads, crooked-winged bats with glowing eyes and alien autopsy jars hang from the ceiling. Filaments glow dimly in over-sized bulbous glass retro bulbs imitating the Edison originals. I find myself staring at one.

'Hey, second thoughts?'

'Ready,' I say. A ghost of the filament stays with my eyeballs, merging two realities into one. It dances as I watch him pinch the shard delicately between thumb and forefinger, the blue gloves wrinkled as if they're just a bit too big for him. He gives it a little wobble first, just check-ing how well embedded it really is. Pain shoots right up my arm and into my neck. He catches my eye and nods. I nod back and blow air out of my mouth three times in quick succession. On the third he yanks it out. Blood wells up in the shard's wake. The sting's sharper than I'd thought it would be.

He's quick, lost in the flow of work, and soon has a folded swab pressed hard against the wound, which he asks me to take charge of. After thirty seconds or so he checks it, gives a satisfied nod, and sprays the cut.

'Not a bleeder,' I say, more relieved than victorious.

'Lucky for you,' he says, dressing it. 'Seriously, though, me? I'd want it stitched.' He packs up swiftly and dashes off.

The uniform taking the woman's statement finishes up and walks over with his hands in his belt like he's John Wayne. Typical patrol. Overinflated sense of self-importance. He asks for my details.

'*Inspector* Jaap Rykel?' he asks when I give him my name.

I think of the letter in my pocket.

It'd come earlier in the week, forwarded by my lawyer, Pieter Roskam. I've still not signed it. Every time I go to pick up a pen I find something better to do. I've been carrying it around for days now, hoping that maybe I could somehow sneak up on myself and sign it whilst I wasn't paying attention. So far I've not managed.

'Used to be.'

'Right.' The uniform nods. 'Thought I recognized you. You worked with Inspector Jansen for a bit, didn't you?'

'How's he doing?'

'Seven shades of hell I think. He's on that big case, the Marianne Kleine murder? Pretty nasty from what I've heard.'

He says it like I should know who Marianne Kleine is, and maybe I should, but I don't follow the news. Part of my treatment plan is to avoid triggers wherever possible. And the news is definitely a trigger. Despite that, I find I'm about to ask him, and catch myself just in time. *I'm done with all that*, I tell myself. *None of my business now.* I need to focus on me, getting better, getting away from everything that screwed me over in the first place.

I give him my statement, and then ask about the woman perched on a bar stool. She's in tight jeans which show off the curves of her legs, and a loose black top, which has slipped down, exposing a creamy, freckled shoulder. A glass of water stands untouched by her elbow. She shifts in her seat and pulls the top back up, as if she can feel our eyes on her.

'Bit shaken up, but okay. Knows the guy apparently, had trouble with him before. Sounds stalker-like if you ask me, but she says she's not pressing charges.'

'What's her name?'

'Sabine Wester.'

I look across at her. It's easy to see why I thought she was Tanya, even if it was only for a brief moment. It's been over a year, but from the sting of it you'd think it was yesterday, and clearly the mere thought of Tanya is another trigger of mine.

'I'll talk to her,' I say.

He snaps his pocket book closed. 'Knock yourself out.'

She turns to look at me as I slide onto the stool next to her. *Blue eyes, not green*, I find myself thinking.

'Hey,' she says. 'Thanks.'

Her voice is smoky going on hoarse, probably an after-effect of the screaming and the hand clamped across her throat. She gives a little cough, reaches for the glass and takes a sip.

'You're welcome.' The wound in my arm throbs like someone's just turned the pain dial right up. 'You know the guy?'

Sabine winces and looks away. Her top slips over her shoulder again. She pulls it back up. 'Sadly I do,' she says, turning back to look right at me. 'What you might call one of life's mistakes.'

'Let me guess, he doesn't see it that way?'

'Something like that.'

She picks up a beer mat. On it a grinning white squid wraps its tentacles round a glass of foaming dark beer. She turns it over and over, hitting it against the bar and sliding her fingers down before flipping it and starting again. Bruises are already starting to form on her neck. By tomorrow they're going to be very visible.

And I've seen all this before. Enough times to know

how it usually ends. The muted trumpet breathes its last. The piece segues into a more upbeat sax number.

'You need to press charges, stop him doing it again.'

She's still working the beer mat. 'He showed up outside my flat the other day so I called the police. You know what they said?'

I can probably guess. Truth is we, *they*, only have limited powers until a crime has actually been committed. Unless there was a restraining order and the man had breached it, there'd be little they could do.

'I was told to stay inside,' she says. 'They didn't even send anyone. So I press charges against him? He's only going to get more angry. And it's not like he'll be locked away forever.'

Realistically he would probably only get community service. I don't tell her this.

'Where do you live?' I ask just as someone, presumably the barman, cuts the music. My voice booms in the sudden silence.

She glances up. For a moment my surroundings blur away and I experience an internal, expansive whirl I've not felt for a long time. I wonder if she felt it too. I guess I'm *hoping* she did, though I'm not sure I can see any sign of it.

'On Nassaukade,' she says. 'By the park?'

I take the beer mat off her, borrow a pen from the uniform now talking to the manager, who is still wringing his hands. If he carries on like that he's not going to have any skin left. I write on the mat, along one of the straighter tentacles.

'You see him again? Call me.'

I tap the mat, turn and walk out. Not a bad exit if I say so myself. For some reason I hope Sabine was impressed. I get that giddy little whirl again.

It's dark now, colourful lights streak across the canal's black surface, and I stand for a moment breathing in the city I know so well. The city that made me.

And then tried its best to break me.

The earlier warmth left with the sun. A shudder trembles my spine.

I pull the hood over my head with my good arm and slip off into the neon night.

Just before I reach Bloemgracht, the canal where my houseboat is moored, I pass a newsagent's board screaming the headline 'No leads in Marianne Kleine case'. Inside I pick up a copy of *De Telegraaf* and take it to the counter.

'Anything else?' The bored guy's question brings me back to myself. *What am I doing?*

'Uhhh . . . no. Actually I don't need this either.'

A bell tinkles as I open the door and leave. I'm shaken, but also pleased I didn't fall back into the trap. These days I have to celebrate the small victories. I turn off Prinsengracht and my houseboat swings into view. I stop for a moment and admire it.

In its day it hauled freight, coal I'm guessing, until a fire in the mid-sixties took out a large part of the upper deck. Headed for the scrapheap, or whatever the marine equivalent is, someone snapped it up at the last minute and repurposed it as a houseboat. They rebuilt the deck and reconfigured the inside into liveable space. I bought it eleven years ago, just when my career in the police was really taking off and it seemed like the future had open arms.

Now, standing here remembering the past, I think of the letter in my pocket. My current future. Which doesn't seem like much of a future at all.

The gangplank sways and creaks underneath me. Odd. I notice the motion sensor light above the door hasn't come on. I reach up and wave my hand. Nothing. I tap it a few times. Darkness reigns.

The lock yields to the key and I'm trying to remember if I've got a replacement bulb somewhere. I step inside and flip the switch on the wall. No light here either. The circuit board's tucked at the back of a cupboard in the old engine room and I follow my phone's light through the houseboat right to it. The board itself is a mystery. I start randomly flipping switches in the hope something will work. It doesn't. I should really be able to do something like this myself, go the DIY route, but whenever I try that sort of thing I step into a parallel world where I'm Wile E. Coyote and everything I touch is made by ACME. And in this case I'd be dealing with live electricity, so on balance I decide the situation warrants a professional. Which is going to cost. I think of the letter, the offer they've made. Truth is I could use it. But by signing I'd be out forever, with no chance of going back.

As I exit the utility cupboard my shoulder knocks something off a shelf. Illuminated in the phone's beam is a round tin, with the most kitsch hand-painted Virgin Mary you've ever seen. Added to that, the painter wasn't actually that skilled; an unfortunate smudge makes it look like the Virgin Mary has a moustache. I pick it up, remembering the day Tanya and I bought it out at the flea market at Waterlooplein. It was one of those spontaneous purchases you make when you're high on another person; at the time we thought it was hilarious, but in the end it was just a stupid tin which never had any use and quickly got lost in everyday life.

Now, though, it reminds me of it all, of how it ended between us and I start to feel the deep pull of loss and regret. I think back to that night, to the things I had to do to keep her safe, and which meant that in the end I lost her.

I shove the gun right into his face. The barrel pushes his lip up.

The flashback's brief, a split second, but still so disorientating. And I know that it might return at any moment. I stumble back into the main area, reaching for my sealed glass stash jar on the shelves behind the sofa. They are ferocious beasts, the flashbacks, and the only thing that even has a hope of taming them is cannabis.

Inside the jar there's only a single nug left, a rare strain called Sour Hound which I got from Joel. I break up the sticky bud with shaky fingers and put it in the grinder, twist it, then load up the vaporizer with the ground herb. It's taking an age to heat up. I find myself staring at the red light, willing it to turn green. C'mon, c'mon. I feel the deep, sucking groundswell telling me there's another one coming. The space is closing in around me. I'm having trouble breathing. For some reason I can feel the back of my neck more than anything else. My arms feel four times too long. I wonder if I'm going to throw up.

The light turns green and I inhale fast, pulling the vapour deep into my lungs.

*

I caught it in time. It's five minutes or so later and I'm melting into the rug, my back against the sofa. From my shifted perspective the flashback seems inconsequential, not something that should hold any power over me. And yet at the time they grab you and don't let go. They're part of the condition I've been diagnosed with, Uncomplicated PTSD, and they seem more real than real itself. And what's so scary is the speed; it's like a switch's been flipped, changing the channel of your world. There's no way of telling how long it's going to last either. It could be seconds, it could be minutes. The worst episode happened mid-afternoon, just as I was leaving my therapist's office; by the time the switch flipped back it was dark and I was halfway across town slumped behind a row of dumpsters with no memory of how I got there, a large scratch running down my left calf.

Now I'm just grateful the cannabis has worked, and I become fascinated with ripples on the water, visible through the large pane of glass running along the entire living area. They're tinged with the street lights' glow, and appear random at first, but if you really watch them you start to see there *is* a pattern; it's just hard to work out exactly what it is. I get caught up in them for a while before realizing I'm settling in nicely, time relaxing its frantic grip as I slide into the everlasting present, and the thought of food is just emerging when my phone lights up the ceiling. The number on it is one I know well, the station. My *old* station. I don't want to take it, but call it force of habit.

'Yeah?'

'Sir? It's Arno Jansen. Heard you've turned into a vigilante.'

Inspector Arno Jansen, closest thing I ever had to a protégé. Before I was forced to knock him out with a rock in a quarry just outside Amsterdam. I'm not sure he's ever forgiven me for that, even though he knew it was done at the behest of a psychotic killer who was holding Tanya hostage and would have killed her if I didn't follow his orders.

'Just a bit of fun. Haven't beaten anyone up for a while.'

'Well, glad you weren't hurt too badly.'

I take another pull from the vape. 'How's things?' I ask after exhaling.

'Well . . . been meaning to call you actually. Wondering if you can help me with something?'

'If it's itchy, I'd see a doctor. Better safe than sorry.'

'The old ones are always the best, sir.'

Truth is, I've hardly spoken to anyone in months. Since the diagnosis I've been doing my best to get better, but I learnt early on that being around other people wasn't helping. Now I'm starting to see the result of shielding myself, walling myself off from the world. And yet it's worked. I'm better now than I've been at any other time since I was diagnosed. Better, but still not fully there. And I don't need anything to knock me back. Which is why I'm starting to feel nervous about this call.

'So what is it then?' I ask.

'I've just been helping out Marit De Jong. He arrested someone earlier who he thinks is the guy who broke into a Rashid Benkirane's coffee place, stole a machine and beat the owner up. Apparently Rashid's a friend of yours?'

'You've got the guy?'

'Marit did. Been trying to get hold of Rashid but his

23

phone's off. I believe you helped him when he made the original report and I was wondering if you knew where he was. You live right by him, don't you?'

I get up and step over to one of the windows. Rashid lives above his business just across the canal and I can see lights on in the two-room apartment.

'Looks like he's around.'

'Don't suppose you could nip over there, pass the message on? Maybe even bring him in if he is?'

'Is it really that urgent?'

'Kinda is. I'm up against it at the moment. Big murder case and I'm only on this as one of Marit's kids was taken to hospital, and we'll have to release the suspect soon if we're not able to charge him. Honestly I just want it off my desk so I can get back to what I'm really supposed to be doing. Please?'

'Why do you need me to bring him?'

'Marit said Rashid's really nervous of police, and that you'd gone with him all the previous occasions.'

Which is true. Rashid comes from a culture where you fear the police, and, whilst he's adapted well to life here, some feelings run too deep to ever entirely eradicate. But I don't want to go to the station; I want to sit back and watch the ripples and let the Sour Hound ease that tension away. I look down at the grinder only to discover I'm out. And the Sour Hound I've already inhaled has fled, tail between its legs.

I'm just about to say no when the idea hits: if Joel's around I could drop in on him on the way back. I don't buy from coffeeshops if I can help it. All that low-grade stuff they produce for the tourists is covered in pesticide residue and half the time grown so poorly they have to drench it with illegal research chemicals bought in bulk from China just so it has some nominal effect.

That's junk. I need medicine. Which is where Joel comes in.

'Call it repayment for the rock thing,' Jansen says, breaking into my thoughts.

'Well, shit, if I'd known you'd be so bitter . . . All right, I'm on my way.'

I fire off a text to Joel and get ready to leave. As I shrug on a fresh hoody, my arm still sore, I remember the letter. I pull it out of my jeans and drop it on the table.

Despite the darkness I can't help but notice a few drops of blood on it.

I don't know why, but I bend over and sniff it.

Sucked Back In

'Seriously, *how* much?'

I'm with Rashid, we're walking down Marnixstraat, the station less than two minutes away, and I'm listening to the electrician reel off his fees for an out-of-hours call. Out of hours? The way I see it, it's dark, the most likely time you're going to need light. Try telling the station chief that you're not heading out to the crime scene because it's out of hours and see what happens. I ask what the in-hours rate is and just as he answers a tram judders past and I have to get him to repeat himself. I settle for an appointment tomorrow morning. By the time I hang up my phone's like a hot coal.

'Will I have to see him?' Rashid asks. He's in jeans and an Ajax sweater, a team he's embraced with a fanatical zeal that some of his countrymen pour into headier philosophies than football.

'Most likely he'll be in a room. You'll be able to see him but he won't be able to see you,' I reassure him.

I can understand his hesitation. Rashid came to the Netherlands to escape conflict. I don't know the full extent of it because he's never told me, but from what I've managed to piece together he's the only survivor from a large family. He'd run the usual gauntlet of immigrant jobs until he'd struck lucky, a boutique roastery out in Haarlem. He started off as floor sweeper but whilst there had discovered a love for coffee and had eventually persuaded the company owners to give him a chance at learning to roast. Which turned out to be the best move ever, because Rashid found he was an artist, his medium the bean. Less than six years later he'd opened his own place, complete with two very expensive coffee machines. The Van der Westen Speedsters, he'd told me many times, are like the Bentleys of coffee making. He doted on those things, cleaning them up each night with a spit polish so they started the next day with a gleam.

A gleam which had caught someone else's eye, because one night he'd heard noises, sneaked down the steep, twisted stairs from his flat and got knocked unconscious by the man who'd broken in. Rashid woke on the cafe floor with a cricked neck, a bad concussion and two spaces on the counters where the Speedsters had been. He's been battling the insurance company ever since.

'This will help with insurance?'

'Hard to say. But maybe.'

'Hope so. I had to get loan to buy new machine.'

'How much did that cost?'

He tells me. Jesus. I hope for his sake the insurance comes through, and fast.

The station's just up ahead now. Apart from a couple of secondments to Haarlem and Den Haag early on, it's been my home for the best part of eleven years. And like any home, the people there became like family. As in, we bickered, talked behind each other's backs and held on to resentments long enough to forget what we were actually resenting in the first place. In between that we managed to solve a few murders as well, so it wasn't all bad.

A desk sergeant I don't recognize is busy processing two arrests as I step inside so I take a look around. There are framed photos on the wall, previous station chiefs, all in full regalia. One of them makes my stomach flip. Station Chief Henk Smit. His unexplained disappearance last year was a major embarrassment to the force.

He's laughing. I shove the gun right into his face. The barrel pushes his lip up. There's a rough band of yellow plaque on his canine. My finger's on the trigger and —

The flashback cuts out, jarring me back into reality. The curse of PTSD: the flashbacks which seem more real than real.

'Jaap Rykel?'

The source of my name is the desk sergeant; he's giving me an odd look.

'Sign here,' he says, holding out a pen. 'Inspector Jansen told me to look out for you.'

I get my signature on the page. It's shaky as hell.

We're just being handed our VISITOR badges, which feels strange and sad at the same time, when I spot Jansen. He's about my height, short blond hair, and always looks like he's ready to spring into action at a moment's notice. Since I last saw him he's obviously been working out. His shirt sleeves are tight with pumped muscle, though his face is maybe gaunter than I remember.

'Sir, thanks for coming in. This shouldn't take long.'

'Seriously, what's up with the "sir"? You never called me that when I was actually your boss.'

'New regime.' He rolls his eyes. 'Just got into the habit I guess.'

'Yeah, it all seems a bit different around here.'

'You don't know the half of it. Beving got promoted to station chief.'

'Whoa.'

'Tell me about it.'

I make the introductions, and Jansen takes us through the airport-style security, another new addition, and into the building itself. Jansen's talking to Rashid, explaining what's going to happen, and I lag behind, shaken by the flashback, already regretting my decision to come here.

We turn the corner, past the first of two main incident rooms, and down the corridor to the stairs which lead to the basement, where the main interrogation suite is. Jansen and Rashid are ahead of me, their heads just disappearing down the steps when the lift door opens. Lazy man's option. Two uniforms get out and I duck in and hit the basement button. The lift pings, and the doors slide shut. Next to me a female officer holds a large pile of papers. The top one catches my eye – a crime-scene photo. In it a naked body is kneeling on the ground in a pool of blood. The tag across the top reads MARIANNE KLEINE. I stare at it and all of a sudden *I'm stepping into a room in another time, another place. The victim, Lucie Muller, is naked, kneeling on the ground in a pool of blood, her torso bent forward over her knees. Her forehead touches the ground in a weird parody of worship, and her arms are straight by her sides, hands by her feet. I move forward on weightless legs, moving round to try and see her face. But her hair is covering it, falling down into the blood, spreading out like roots.*

'Sir, you all right?' The voice jolts me back. I'm standing in the lift, the officer with the photo gone, another one holding the lift door open and looking at me with concern.

I can't believe I've had a second flashback within minutes of the first. That's unusual. And doesn't bode well. I need to get out of here and get to Joel's as soon as I can.

'Yeah, fine,' I say, taking a couple of breaths. 'Never been better.'

I catch up with them in the basement, after another uniform has scrutinized my pass to make sure I'm not a terrorist, or worse, an undercover reporter.

'There you are, thought I'd lost you.' Jansen's just opening the door to interview room number five.

'Listen, there's something I need to tell you. That case you're working on, is it the Kleine case?'

He stops and turns, hand on the door knob. 'Yeah, why?'

But suddenly I don't know what to say. Or rather, I know what to say, I just don't want to say it. I feel as if I'm perfectly balanced between two worlds. Jansen's looking at me with raised eyebrows.

'Look, we're on the clock here,' he says. 'I've got less than twenty minutes before I either have to charge the guy or release him so . . .'

'Okay, let's get this over with first.'

He gives me a sceptical look, then nods. 'Rashid's in the viewing room.'

I join Rashid and we watch through the two-way mirror as Jansen enters the interview room. Gangsta-slumped in a chair is a North African man, Moroccan most likely. The suspect's wearing a white tracksuit, with double gold stripes snaking down the arms and trouser legs. He's got tramlines buzzed into his hair and a single stud winks from his ear when he moves his head.

Jansen steps into the room, pulls out the chair and sits down. He flips open a file and after quickly scanning it starts talking. Almost immediately the Moroccan shakes his head in response.

We've got no sound so I find the audio switch and flip it on.

'So then what?' Jansen's saying. 'Then you just happened to be there? Right at that moment?'

'Bro, like I told you already.'

Jansen nods slowly, a sage pondering great insight. A good interviewer is like an actor, the role you play dictated by the situation, by the suspect themselves. Sometimes it takes playing several roles before you find the one that unlocks something in them.

Jansen pulls out a couple of photographs from the file and slides them across. He taps one of them with his forefinger.

'See, the thing is we've got these images of you less than two streets away from the place where the burglary and assault took place.'

Tracksuit refuses to even look at them. Suddenly Jansen jumps up from his chair, shoots his hand across the table, cups the man's skull and forces his head forward so his nose is millimetres from the images. Fair to say Jansen's just switched roles to bad cop.

'And you see that time stamp?' he shouts at him. 'Can you see that? Huh? It fits exactly. Ex*a*ctly.'

He releases him and sits back as if nothing's happened, flips further through his file.

'And the money that was found at your flat . . .' Jansen is all calm business now, as if he's a civil servant rubber-stamping traffic-light legislation. He finds the photo he's after and slides it across. Rashid and I lean forward, just enough to catch the image of two evidence bags with fat rolls of notes. 'This money, where did it come from?'

Tracksuit sucks his teeth, but just stares at the wall behind Jansen.

When it's clear Tracksuit has nothing to say, Jansen exits the room and pops his head into ours.

'Okay, zero hour. I've got to charge or release. But what we've got is pretty circumstantial and without something else I'm most likely going to have to release him.' He gives Rashid an expectant look.

'If he convicted, do I get money back?' Rashid asks.

'That's hard to say at this stage, but to be honest it will take a while for this to get to court and –'

'Yes,' Rashid says, still staring through the mirror. 'It is him. He is man who assaulted me and stole my coffee machines.'

Rashid seems to have gone from unsure to very sure in a quick space of time. Jansen throws a questioning glance my way. The only answer I can give is a shrug.

'Okay. We'll charge him now.'

By the time it's all wrapped up and I've sent Rashid off into the night Jansen suggests we get a drink. Up in the deserted canteen we grab a seat by the window overlooking the intersection. The glass is frosted with condensation and changes colour with the traffic lights just outside.

'So . . .' Jansen says as he blows on his coffee.

The Red Bull hisses as I pull the ring. I take a couple of large gulps. Tastes of chemicals, but they're always promising wings, and right now I need all the help I can get; flashbacks and a lack of the one thing capable of stopping them, cannabis, is not a good combination. Coming here was a mistake, and I should have left just now with Rashid. But I can't unsee what I saw.

'The case you're working is the Marianne Kleine case?'

Jansen nods and very discreetly checks his watch.

'Yes, sir.'

'Have you heard of Lucie Muller?'

'No, should I have?'

One of the canteen staff drops a tray, and cutlery jangles and clatters to the ground.

I suddenly feel split in two: one part urging me on, the other telling me to get up and walk out, leave all this behind. Because the last thing I want is to get sucked back in. But I think of Lucie Muller, and the man I put away for her death, Sander Klaasen. I take a breath, then I begin to talk.

Lucie Muller

'Fuck,' Jansen says as I finish. He breathes out, shaking his head and grimacing all at the same time.

The canteen staff are clearing out the last plates of unwanted food and a man in a dark blue boiler suit is mopping the floor morosely. Jansen leans back in his chair and stares at the ceiling, trying to take in all that I've just told him. My throat's dry and I shake the can, upending it for the last tiny warm dribble. The window cycles between green and red.

'How sure are you?' Jansen finally asks.

'About the way she was killed? Hundred per cent. The victim in that case was found exactly as your victim was, naked, same posture, and I'll bet all the blood came from a cut across the throat?'

'Yeah, it did. So the first question's going to be has the man you put away been let out of prison?'

'He got thirty years, so it's unlikely. I guess if he'd been on best behaviour, there's an outside chance he might just have got an early release. But the victim in the case was the daughter of a judge, and I doubt there's a parole board anywhere in the country he couldn't influence, if it ever came to that.'

'Who's the judge?'

'Koen Muller.'

Jansen's pensive, processing the info I've dropped into

his lap. Which on the one hand is potentially good, a lead in a stalled case. On the other, the implications are anything but.

'So what have we got on our hands here, a copycat killer?'

Copycat. Not a word anyone wants to hear in relation to a murder. People kill for all sorts of reasons, usually money and sexual jealousy of one type or another. But killing just to imitate another murderer indicates a special kind of warped mind. Not one I want anything to do with. I'm about to tell him I need to go when he speaks again.

'Listen, I'm working this case with Inspector Vermeer. She needs to hear this –'

'But not from me. You can look up the case to get the full details.'

'It's so weird we didn't get any red flags; we ran all the details through the system and no match came up. I can't believe no one here remembers the case either. Surely someone would?'

I don't know about that. I worked it with my friend and colleague Hank de Vries, and later on in the investigation with Station Chief Smit. Right now, the only thing keeping Hank breathing is a life-support machine at the AMC, the Academic Medical Center, and Station Chief Smit . . . well, he isn't breathing at all. I brace for another flashback which thankfully doesn't come.

'Because of the bizarre way she'd been killed the circle was kept very small,' I tell him. 'There were probably only a handful of us who knew the full story. I imagine Judge Muller had a hand in that as well.'

'Makes sense. Vermeer's managed to keep the details

of Kleine's death out of the press so far. How long that will last, though, I don't know.'

'Good luck with that. We managed it back then, but seven years ago was like a different age.'

'The system, though, that should have alerted us. That just feels wrong . . . like someone was trying to hide it.'

'And I thought *I* was paranoid. You know what systems are like, someone didn't enter the details correctly or screwed up some field or other.'

Jansen rubs his hands over his face before breathing out another long sigh. I wonder how much sleep he's been getting.

'You're right. Fucking overworked is all. But I really need to get Vermeer; she'll want to hear this.'

'First thing I'd check is if there's any link between Lucie Muller and your victim.'

'Yeah, I'll look into that. Unlikely, though. Marianne Kleine would still have been a teenager during your case.'

'How old?'

'She was twenty-five. And she was already the founder of a tech start-up that investors have put millions into. Kids these days . . . If you haven't made yourself into a billionaire with some world-changing idea by the time you're thirty, then you're basically a total loser.'

'If you haven't managed that you can always become a cop.'

We both do the mirthless laugh at that one.

'My dad told me not to,' Jansen says. 'Maybe I should have listened . . . Anyway, Vermeer. I'll go get her.'

'Listen, there's a bit of paper at home waiting for me to sign,' I tell Jansen. 'Once I do I'm out, for good.'

'All the more reason for you to stay now and speak to her.'

I should walk out now; my arm's throbbing again, I've just had two bad flashbacks, and unless I get going soon Joel will have gone to bed. So I open my mouth to tell him no, only to hear it betray me. 'You've got ten minutes.'

Every investigative cop gets one.

One case that seeps into you like a devastating chronic disease. For some reason I got more than one, but of those Lucie Muller's death was probably the worst.

The case broke just after three p.m. The station was quiet and I was engaged in a classic bit of work avoidance. The work I was avoiding was a final report on a pointless theft case I'd been assigned, which I had no hope of ever resolving, and the avoidance consisted of scrunching up bits of paper and trying to lob them into the bin three desks away. My score at the point the call came in was zero, paper balls scattered far and wide, everywhere but the bin itself. So I was all over the new distraction.

The body of a young female had been found in a flat in the Nieuw-West. The officer on scene gave me the run-down: a neighbour had noticed blood seeping under the door to flat seven on the second floor of a four-storey block. I got there less than twenty minutes later.

She was lying in a misshapen pool of her own blood, slumped in the pose that, when it'd been described to me over the phone hadn't made any sense, but which made even less when I actually saw it. The reason for all the blood became clear when the forensics arrived and lifted her body – the slit across her throat like an awful

37

grin. I kept thinking of abattoirs and couldn't get the word 'slaughter' out of my mind.

I called into the station, spoke to Station Chief Smit, and he put Hank de Vries on it with me. We were young, we were outraged, we were the Gods of Righteousness and we worked the case like it was everything.

But right up front we hit a complication: the victim turned out to be Lucie Muller, daughter of the prominent judge, known for his hardline attitude to criminals in a system that was famous worldwide for its softer approach, favouring rehabilitation over incarceration. Such a cruel death as Lucie Muller suffered doesn't leave any room for irony, but still.

The first question to tackle was why Lucie would be living in an area better known for immigrant unrest than housing the well-heeled offspring of a rich and powerful man such as Judge Muller. After a bit of digging it turned out the answer was she'd rebelled against her privileged upbringing by slumming it the way only rich kids can. A rebellion that brought her into contact with the kind of people she probably had no real idea, ironically given her father's occupation, of just how dangerous they were.

One of whom, the man we suspected was her killer, had been caught on CCTV entering the building prior to her murder, and leaving not long after. But as he'd taken the precaution of wearing a cap and hoody, and knew exactly where the cameras were angled, we had no image of his face.

So we started with Robert Huisman, Lucie's on/off boyfriend and rising star in the local heroin scene. At one point we found evidence she may actually have been involved, playing bagman, or bagwoman, for him on occasion. Needless to say that never made it into the trial documents. It didn't take us long to establish that given the height and build the hoodied man could easily have been Huisman.

Only Huisman himself seemed to have skipped town, and he proved hard to find, further upping him on our list of People We'd Very Much Like To Talk To. In the end it took us two days to track him down and by the time we had him in custody we were sure we'd have the case wrapped up in a matter of hours.

Which is when Huisman kicked back in his chair and slapped down his alibi with a smirk on his greasy low-browed face.

He claimed he'd been spending a few days with a mate of his down in the countryside just north of Maastricht. Now I'm not saying that inspectors have a monopoly on sniffing out bullshit, but over the years your nose gets pretty attuned to it. And his alibi was filling both our noses with that pungent, freshly laid scent that often permeates suspect interviews. But process dictates, so we followed up, driving all the way down there and locating the friend in question.

Which is where things got tricky.

The friend, a vermin-like creature called Jan Akkerman, swore Huisman had been with him the whole time. We applied pressure, telling him about things such as Obstruction of Justice and Perjury and Accessory to Murder, but Akkerman didn't budge, wouldn't change his statement, and sat there like a self-satisfied Buddha grinning down on our folly from the fucking Bodhi tree itself.

Because, he'd said, he could prove it.

He unearthed a video, complete with time stamp, which was subsequently checked and verified. On it, and at almost the exact same time that Lucie was bowing her head into a pool of her own blood, another woman was bowing her head, only this time the destination was Huisman's dick. As Lucie Muller slipped out of this world her boyfriend was getting sucked off by one of two young women 200 miles from the crime scene. Turned out both men pulled a scam several times a year where they held auditions for women to 'star' in their latest porn films. They claimed to own an online portal for which the lucky candidates would make videos and receive a share of any profits. Of course, to get the job all candidates would have to get past the interview stage. The men saw to it that the interviews were rigorous, interactive and in-depth, filmed by one whilst the other took a more hands-on role in the process.

We had no choice but to hand it over to Vice and move on. The old cop cliché of the first forty-eight hours being crucial is sort of true, and we were well over that. The case started floundering. We felt like fish in a drying riverbed. First there were leads that went nowhere, then there were just no leads. Desperation started to grip us. We were inching closer to the unthinkable, an unsolvable murder. And the pressure weighing down on us from above, pressure that was undoubtedly initiated by Judge Muller himself, was increasing exponentially. It felt like gravity itself was suddenly no longer obeying its own law.

'Finished with that?'

I look up to see mop man pointing to the can in front of me. I pick it up and toss it into the black bag he's holding open. He ties it up and shuffles away.

We'd had to go back to the drawing board. Alternative theories were tossed around, some plausible, some just about possible, some utterly preposterous. We pushed ourselves to think outside whatever box we were obviously trapped in, but still we were going nowhere. Joel once told me it's hard to see what's on the label when you're in the jar itself. Then Station Chief Smit, under pressure himself, took the unusual move of joining our investigative team. We didn't like it, but then again it was clear we needed help.

No one who worked with the man would ever have characterized his presence as a good omen, and yet in this instance, soon after he joined us we got lucky, a phone call that changed it all.

A man called Burt Dankert who'd been working a few streets away around the time of Muller's death, part of a crew digging up the road to lay fibre-optic cable, was on a break when he recognized a man walking past in a hurry. The name of the man, Dankert claimed, was Sander Klaasen. They'd worked together on a building site up in Alkmaar the previous summer, Dankert explained. Klaasen had quickly gained a reputation for being an outsider, not fitting in with the crowd, moody and just about cooperative enough to keep his job, but nothing more. So he wasn't that surprised when he called out to him only to have Klaasen blank him completely. Dankert shrugged his shoulders and went back to work, thinking nothing more of it until a couple of days later he caught sight of a newspaper with stills captured from the footage we'd released. What he saw stopped him dead; the man we were looking for was wearing the exact same hoody and cap Klaasen had been when he'd walked right by him.

Now we had a name. But running him through the system gave us no less than seventeen Sander Klaasens in the Netherlands, and a further two in the Dutch Antilles, none of which, after a gruelling process involving coordinating teams in several different provinces, was the one we were after. It was starting to feel like Klaasen was a ghost, or, at the very least, an assumed name. Which of course only made us even more keen to talk to him.

By getting Dankert, and five of the other people who'd been on the building site in Alkmaar that summer, to sit down with a police artist we came up with an image of his face which was widely circulated. And the next morning we got a result, a keen young officer in Haarlem spotted a man crossing the road who she thought resembled the image she'd been shown in her morning briefing. She got out of her car and approached him. He took one look at her and legged it. The chase lasted ten minutes, and she finally apprehended him, earning herself a nasty black eye and the respect of all. Hours later he was turned over to us for questioning.

He wasn't fully convincing, giving only rambling stories which didn't address our specific concerns, though he repeatedly denied killing anyone. Further background checks revealed nothing. That is, there was no record: of him being born, of being in school, being in care.

Nothing. Hank and I pushed him hard, but he didn't give us his real name. His DNA wasn't on the system. I contacted mental health units up and down the country but no one recognized him. It's like he'd come out of nowhere.

Even so, with no confession, all we had was circumstantial, and we were nervous about putting the case forward to the prosecutor. There were another seventy-two hours before I'd have to release him, at which point he'd probably disappear.

Pressure mounted from above. An informal chat with the prosecutor confirmed my suspicions; she couldn't recommend I put the case forward based on what I'd presented. With two hours to go I got a call from an officer up in Bergen who had seen the alert we'd put out on the internal system, saying there'd been a man who looked like our suspect who'd been living in a holiday cabin in the woods. Normally it wouldn't have warranted more than a note in the file, but if there was a chance she'd be able to fill in some of the background on the man, then we were prepared to take the drive up north. We were set to leave just as Station Chief Smit called us into his office and told us, very specifically, to go back to the building Muller's body had been found in and show Klaasen's mugshot around. I countered this had been done, no less than twice already. Three could often be the lucky number, I was advised.

With one hour to go a man looking like a serial heroin user positively ID'd the man in the photo as having left Muller's flat about the time of her death. The phrase 'reliable witness' and the man propping himself up on the door frame in front of me, scratching at his elbow pits and avoiding any kind of eye contact, didn't seem a natural fit. And yet he was confirming just what we needed. Just in time.

On the ride back to the station I became more and more convinced that the witness was a plant. Had it come from Muller himself? It was all too neat, all too just-in-time for my liking. But I had no proof, and wouldn't get any either. Of that I was sure. So we had no choice but to submit the case.

The trial was swift, the three judges – in the Netherlands we don't trust the general population to sit on juries, so we entrust the whole thing to judges – handed down the maximum penalty allowed, and did it in record time to boot.

And now this.

An identical killing.

A copycat killing.

It can't be, I think, it's got to be Klaasen. The double buzz of my phone brings me back to the canteen, empty now except for the man with the mop. Jansen's still not back. I check the message, relieved to see it's from Joel. Even better he's in Amsterdam and will be home in about ten minutes. It'll take me twenty to walk. I check the time; it's been way longer than the ten I'd promised Jansen. Fuck it. I've told him everything I know anyway. He and Inspector Vermeer can wrestle with it, not me.

The moon's up as I step out of the station and the air has that cool autumn moisture which hints at the winter to come. I head north towards the Jordaan, the sound of traffic humming by me, a plane groaning overhead on its final descent to Schiphol and the muted thump and pump of bass from a club nearby.

And yet, for some reason, all I can really hear is Jansen's voice saying *like someone was trying to hide it* over and over again.

White Wolf, Black Wolf

It's past ten by the time I reach Brouwersgracht, probably one of the most expensive bits of real estate in the country. Despite this, a bunch of drunken tourists cluster at the canal edge, braying and throwing things in the water. The canal I live on is much less famous, and as such doesn't attract anywhere near the same level of fuckwittery as this one.

Still, Joel's flat, the entire top floor of a double-fronted seventeenth-century merchant's house, is pretty damn nice. I press the bell just as the braying behind me turns into shrieking. I turn to see one of their group hit the water with a tulip-shaped splash, tinged orange in the street light. I'm tense suddenly, primed for action, but there's been enough heroics for one day. The door buzzes open and I head up the stairs, leaving them to it.

He's at the door as I reach the top of the stairs.

'Just the man,' he says, ushering me in. 'Got something really special for you.'

Which, after the last few hours, is *very* welcome news.

Joel bought the two flats three years ago, gutted them, and knocked through to create a huge gleaming open-plan space that could hold its own as the centre spread of any property porn magazine.

I flop down on the enormous L-shaped sofa and watch

the writhing flame in the globular fireplace. It's suspended off the floor by its own flue which juts right through the ceiling. Joel's getting something from the kitchen area when my phone buzzes. It's a text from a number I don't recognize.

THANKS FOR EARLIER ☺ DRINK SOMETIME? SABINE.

I put my phone away as Joel walks over, handing me a beer-like bottle.

'Christ, you're almost smiling. Sure you're feeling okay?'

'What's this?' I ask, ignoring him. Truth is, after my time down at the station, an unwelcome taste of my old life, Sabine's text does make me want to smile.

'Kombucha, some fermented tea thing. I was seeing this girl for a while and she loved the stuff. I've got a fridge full of it. Haven't got round to chucking it yet.'

Joel and women. I'm not even going to start on that one. I sniff the bottle's neck; it has a faint vinegary smell which isn't exactly enticing. I take a sip.

'You really should have chucked it,' I tell him.

'I'm getting notes of camel piss and sweaty socks, what about you?'

'Rotting vomit and vinegar.'

We spend a few minutes catching up before we ditch the kombucha altogether.

'Let me show you something,' Joel says, moving over to a sealed humidor on the kitchen countertop. The countertop itself is made from cast concrete, and has hundreds of tiny LEDs embedded in the surface in a pattern reminiscent of a galaxy. I get lost in it for a few moments. Joel opens the humidor, an intoxicating aroma infusing the room.

He finds what he's looking for and hands it over to me. It's a couple of really frosty-looking buds, more so because instead of the usual green colour the buds are almost pure white. They glitter as I turn them, the trichomes containing all the goodness sparkling in the light.

'What's this?'

'This is what I was telling you about.'

Joel's a smart guy; he left university with a degree in research pharmacology and worked for a big pharma company for several years before deciding to go back to study for his PhD. Which was a surprise to everyone because he switched disciplines, working on some obscure aspect of plant phenology. His move made a bit more sense when, on completion, he went to work for one of the major cannabis seed banks where he was in charge of the breeding programme for over ten years. His brief was to constantly develop new strains for a hungry worldwide market. With increasing legalization in the States, and decriminalization in some parts of the old continent, more and more people were saying no to dealers and growing their own. And it was Joel's job to make sure his employer had a steady supply of new and exciting strains. But just over a year ago he decided he'd learnt enough to leave and start his own company.

Now his time is split between Amsterdam, the operation he set up down in Spain where the bulk of the commercial breeding takes place, and twice-annual trips to places all over the world looking for wild strains with which to enliven his already lively gene pool.

'The one from Ecuador?' I ask.

'Yeah, took the cutting two years ago and we've crossed

48

it with about ten other varieties. All of them were good, but this particular cross is something really special.'

We sit back down and Joel fires up the Volcano, which has pride of place on a short side table. Joel has a vast collection of smoking apparatus, but in the end prefers, as do I, the Volcano. It's a classic, designed by two Germans back in the day but which has stood the test of time. It forces hot air, the exact temperature of which the user can set, through whatever herb you have into a bag which collects the vapour. Joel grinds up the nug, and we watch the bag fill with milky-looking air. He hands it over to me once it's full.

'Haven't got a name for it yet. We're provisionally calling it Skywalker, but I'll need to come up with something better.'

Like Obama, I inhale. Tastes good. Very good. Spice, berries, diesel and something I can't quite place.

'So, you finally out?' Joel asks as I hand the bag back to him. I notice my shoulders drop, making me aware of just how tense they'd been.

'Got the papers, just haven't signed them yet.'

'Seriously, what you've gone through over the last few years.' Joel shakes his head. 'You're kind of due a break, y'know?'

I suddenly notice the flame's hypnotic dance. I feel drawn into it. There are so many colours, constantly changing, shifting. So-called primitive cultures all over the world shared a remarkably similar belief that everything is alive. Sitting here watching the flame, cruising high on Skywalker, I'm starting to think they may have been onto something.

'I know. It's just . . .' I finally say, eyes still on the fire.

'Yeah?'

My phone buzzes. I should leave it, I know I should, but something makes me think it might be Sabine again so I pull it out. It's not, the message is from Jansen.

SORRY, GOT AMBUSHED BY BEVING AND COULDN'T
GET AWAY. NEED TO TALK ASAP.

Luckily there's still some Skywalker left. I inhale again, trying to put the text message out of my mind.

'Bad news?'

'Kinda. Old case of mine seems to have blown up. I feel like I'm being drawn back in.'

Joel takes a big inhale, tips his head back and blows a stream out towards the ceiling.

'You're going to do it?'

I shake my head. The flame's still dancing, but now it's starting to look like something automatic, lifeless. Mechanical, almost sinister.

'Fuck. I don't know.'

'There's life outside of the police.'

Bag. Inhale. Exhale.

'Maybe that's what I'm afraid of.'

'How d'you mean?' he asks.

'I dunno. I was so *into* being a cop; it seemed the most important thing I could be doing, you know? Now I'm starting to wonder why I was so caught up in it . . .'

Joel shifts, stretching his legs out onto a furry cube footstool.

'Look, it's a cliché, I know, but it's never too late to change. And,' he says, his voice shifting gear, 'I think you should find yourself a woman. Maybe two. You can't let the whole thing with Tanya ruin the rest of your life. Go out, have a bit of fun. I mean, you're fugly as fuck, don't get me wrong, but I'm sure there's some cock-starved old crack-whore out there that might still be up for –'

Stoned I may be, but I still manage to kick his leg from where I'm slumped on the sofa.

Joel laughs. He sucks down the last of the vapour, the bag crinkling like static as it's emptied.

He's probably right, I think. I should text Sabine back, meet her for a drink.

'Seriously, though, I'm glad you came round. There's something I've been meaning to talk to you about.'

'It's all right. I don't mind if you're gay. It won't ruin our relationship. Just as long as you're happy.'

I'm really out of practice. I need to get out more. No point meeting Sabine if I can't even hold an adult conversation.

Joel gives me the middle finger. 'So you know I just got back from Canada? Well, I was there having a meeting with the largest producer of medical cannabis in the world. This company is massive – they're listed on the Toronto Stock Exchange, and they've recently opened grow facilities in Denmark and Portugal and have just been granted a licence from the German government for two in Germany. In three years' time they'll have opened more in Italy and Poland as well. And this stuff here is exactly the kind of strain they're looking to grow. They analysed it and the THC/CBD ratio is spot on, plus the terpene profile is highly favourable for a medicinal strain. Their head of production said it was the best-looking profile they'd ever seen. They're on the hook, basically.'

'How would it work?'

'We'd license the strain to them, so once we've signed we wouldn't need to do a thing. Basically for every plant they grow we'd receive a small fee, but given the scale of their operation we're talking a renewable gold mine.'

I notice how the word 'we' has snuck into all of this.

'Are you offering me a job?'

'Well . . . I'm offering you the opportunity to buy a share in the business. The thing is, to make sure we're fully protected we have to apply to the EU for Plant Breeder Rights, and that costs money . . .'

'Uh-huh.'

'And, as you were saying, you'll get a payout when you sign. I thought this could be a good opportunity to invest it.'

At the moment Joel has his production facility down in Spain where he employs five people full-time. They breed new strains and produce seed to sell, mainly to hobby growers all over the world. He's done well out of it; I'm pretty sure he's already on his way to being a millionaire. But he's clearly got a much bigger vision. One I could be part of.

We talk some more before I finally decide to call it a night.

Just as I'm leaving Joel takes a few more buds out, slips them in a bag and hands it over.

'This'll help,' he says. 'With your decision.'

On the way back I think about the message from Sabine. I gave her my number, not really expecting anything. It takes me most of the walk back to my houseboat to decide that I *am* going to text her back. My phone's battery has other ideas, though; it's fully dead. Having no power in the houseboat means I can't charge it up now, so I'll have to text her tomorrow.

As for Joel's proposal, that's going to take a little longer to respond to. Despite the coolness of the night, intensified by being on the water, I take out one of the white buds only to find my vape has gone the way of my phone. I don't know why people are so afraid of technology rising up to take over mankind: Skynet initiating nuclear war to clean the planet of the human virus, marching armies of robots strafing us with lasers as they crunch over the burnt-out husks of our civilization. What'll *really* happen is that technology will run out of battery once we've delegated everything over to them, leaving us in a kind of helpless chaos. Mankind's more likely to become extinct poking each other's eyes out with sticks over the last pack of triple-A batteries, than fighting robot overlords. At least in my view. Though I have to concede it could be the Skywalker talking.

I'm looking for rolling papers when I pass the letter on the table, now highlighted in a round beam from the street light streaming through the porthole. It's glowing orange and spots of dark blood dapple the surface like mould. I get a pen and stand over it, almost like I'm watching someone else, waiting to see what they'll do. The pen's rolling back and forth between my thumb and forefinger, the ridges hard. I think about Klaasen, about what Jansen had said. I think about Joel and Sabine and before I can stop myself I think of Tanya. I think of the black wolf. *A snarl, the flash of teeth. Eyes glowing amber.*

And then, the night deep and full and momentous all around me, I reach down and sign my name, the scratching nib the only sound I hear.

Feeling better than I've felt for a long time I climb up onto the houseboat's roof, flop down in one of the pair of deckchairs I have up here, and roll a joint, my fingers revelling in the familiar, delicate movement. Once done I hold it up to the street light and am pleased to see it's a perfect cone. Next up, flame. It dances into life – those ancients really were on to something – and I guide them together until the little twisted curl of paper at the very end takes light.

I blow smoke at the cloud-smudged moon, imagining it might move a little. After the harshness of the first few pulls I find the world softening, but at the same time becoming more real, more solid, more full of meaning. The events of the evening start to seem distant, unimportant somehow. It was my old life, reaching out to me, a hand from the past trying to pull me back. But as the cannabis starts to work I feel a kind of strength, one which will allow me to resist the pull.

A few minutes later, how many I'm not sure because time seems less important now, I find myself wondering about the air: where it came from, where it's been. How far round the world has it travelled to get to me? What mountaintops has it brushed against, what swirling eddies has it been part of, what people has it caressed, blown a full gale at, what lungs has it already seen the inside of? What death and life has it touched? Where will it go next? Have I ever breathed it in before, will I again? Or is this it, our one contact, a single moment never to be repeated?

Water laps the hull, and I spiral off into what might be.

There's an old story about the mind. They say it's formed of a white wolf and a black wolf. The white is love, joy, the best of what makes us us. The black wolf is anger, jealousy, hate, the worst things a human mind can imagine. They're locked in battle; neither has an advantage.

Unless you feed them.

And whichever one you feed is the one that will grow strong and win.

I've lived for years dealing with the results of others' black wolves, the death and pain and suffering they caused. And in doing so, unknown to me, my own black wolf quietly feasted in the shadows, growing stronger and stronger, waiting for the moment to pounce.

And when it did, it nearly won.

But I survived, am *surviving, now that cannabis feeds my white wolf.*

Feeds it so it can be strong and flexible.

So it can overcome.

The gangplank separating the houseboat from the shore rings out with footsteps. Whoever it is reaches the deck and stops, as if considering what to do next. There's a brief pause before three sharp knocks sound at my door.

'Who is it?' I croak down, the return to smoking having roughed up my lungs and throat.

'Inspector Rykel? I'm Inspector Katja Vermeer. I need to have a word. I tried to call you but your phone was off.'

'If you want to talk to me, you'll have to come up here.

Go to the aft and step on the wooden box. There's a bit of rope you can use to pull yourself up if you need.'

I listen to her progress, and soon she's hauled herself onto the roof and is walking towards me. I almost double-take; in this light she's the spitting image of Diana Rigg playing Emma Peel in *The Avengers*. Minus the leather cat-suit, of course.

I'd actually heard of her before tonight. She's risen far and fast, partly because she's reputed to be smart and tenacious, partly because she's also known for being tougher than most of the other inspectors here. One story doing the rounds says she single-handedly took down three bikers who decided that they didn't like her asking questions about their probable involvement with a people-smuggling ring, and wanted a little playtime before they acted on their plan to hoist her off a bridge, most likely with a bullet in the back of the head. All three of them woke up in hospital, hands cuffed to the bed frame, wondering just what the fuck happened to them. Reput-edly one of them actually cried when Vermeer walked into his hospital room, though I don't know if I believe that bit.

'Nice,' she says, looking around. 'Quirky.'

'Good to meet you,' I say. 'But I told Jansen everything I know so I'm not sure why you're here?'

'We need to have a chat.'

'About?'

She sniffs the air a couple of times. I'd tossed what was left of the joint a few minutes earlier, but I'm sud-denly paranoid that it's clinging to my clothes. Not that it really matters; having signed the letter I'm no longer officially a cop. Just a regular citizen medicating. Nothing to see here.

'We checked up more closely on Sander Klaasen. He's still in prison.'

Her words are like a jolt of reality, not what I want to hear at all. My brain looks for a way out.

'He could have told someone about what he did, the exact way he killed her. Then whoever he told kills Marianne Kleine the same way to confuse the police.'

'Aside from that being a pretty far-fetched theory, it's not actually possible.'

'Why not?'

'Because it turns out the day he was convicted he was put in a van and transported from the court to Bijlmerbajes prison. Only he got in a fight with another prisoner during the journey, and when he arrived he was in a really bad state. Had to be loaded into an ambulance and sent straight to the ICU. He was in a coma for a few weeks, and when he finally came out of it they found he was severely brain damaged. He can move around, but he can't talk, can't write, doesn't seem to remember anything or anyone.'

For the second time tonight I find all the mellowness draining away. The breeze brings me a cloud of Vermeer's perfume; it's rich and spicy and floral. It's a strong contrast to the taste of combustion in my mouth. The boat rocks gently and the gangplank creaks with it.

'So what are you saying . . .?'

'Klaasen had been kept in solitary from the time he was arrested right the way through to his trial. He had no contact with other prisoners.'

I don't like where this is going. I should tell her to get off my boat and leave me alone. But I can't help myself.

'You're telling me that Sander Klaasen didn't have the opportunity to tell anyone about how he'd killed Lucie Muller?'

'That's *exactly* what I'm telling you. Which starts to make it look like it wasn't him after all, and the real killer is still out there.'

Three Days Before

Crumbled Away

He's laughing now, and before I know what I'm doing I have the gun in my hand. I shove it right in his face. That shuts him up. There's a flash of fear in his eye. The barrel pushes his lip, revealing teeth so it looks like he's sneering. A night insect buzzes by. I can feel the trigger, the tension of it against my finger. His Adam's apple bobs and I . . .

. . . wake on my back, heart thudding, hand clasped tight round something. I lift it to see it's not a gun but an empty cup. A boat glides past and I lie gently rocking in its wake, the subtle movement gradually slowing my heart and breathing down.

In the kitchen I take the letter off the table and stuff it into an envelope whilst trying to avoid looking at my signature. I spend a few moments puzzling over why the kettle won't fire up before I remember about the electricity. My body's aching a bit from the fall, the wound in my arm feels hot, and I *really* need some coffee. The electrician said he'd be round at ten, and, checking the time, I see I've got enough time to get out to the lock-up and finally finish the work I'd started months ago. But first I need to medicate.

I collect the prescription every month at the pharmacy on Spuistraat. The paroxetine is blue and was the first one prescribed. Unfortunately it comes with side effects; it gave me the runs. And really, Uncomplicated PTSD is bad enough without the feeling that you're going to shit yourself the whole time. In addition, it never seemed to do anything for the flashbacks and it only improves the hyper-real dreams by about five per cent, which is hardly a stellar job. So I was then given another, a pink pill to try and negate the bowel issues. Only there were side effects to that as well, and on and on, until one morning I was staring at a pyramid of pill bottles on my kitchen table towering over me ominously. At which point I claimed to be side effect free because I couldn't face any more. So, all told, there's a rainbow of them: blue, pink, yellow, white, round, lozenge-shaped, ones that need to be cut in half, others that need to be taken in multiples, some with enteric coatings, some that dissolve right on your tongue.

I prep them all, opening each one in turn until I have the required daily dose, and put the bottles back. Next I take the pills themselves, cradled in the palm of my hand, to the bathroom, lift the toilet seat and drop them in. They look pretty in the bowl, and when I flush they bob and swirl around and disappear in a most therapeutic manner.

There, much better already.

I gather up my stuff: vape, rolling paper and, a last-minute decision, my old glass pipe. Just in case. To get to Rashid's I need to walk south-west along the canal, cross at the Lijnbaansgracht bridge, and then double back up the other side. The movement seems to shake loose the thoughts that I've been doing my best to ignore since I woke; Inspector Vermeer thinks I might have sent an innocent man to prison where he ended up with permanent brain damage. Worse, if Klaasen was innocent then I let the real killer walk free to kill again. On the bridge the breeze rolls a can towards me. I stomp on it until it's completely flat. A couple of tourists, wary of me, cross to the other side.

I'm first in and Rashid waves me over. He's excited. In fact, he's beaming from ear to ear. He points to the reason: a new coffee machine glinting like some alien spacecraft that came in to land during the dead of night.

'They paid up?'

Rashid's still grinning, unless he's had a stroke and his face is now paralysed. He grabs a cloth and fusses over the machine, rubbing off an imaginary smudge then standing back to admire it again.

'No, I told you, I took a loan. This was delivered first thing this morning. Is beautiful, no? Is Elektra Belle Epoque,' he says as if that means something, before taking me through the highly technical features. When he's finished I ask him how much. He tells me. Now I *really* need a coffee. I hope the insurance company pays up in full, and soon.

I take a table by the window and find a socket in the wall. There's a moment of indecision: I've only got one charger cable and both a phone and a vaporizer that need electrons pooling inside them. Reluctantly I choose the phone. Rashid's already at it, the hiss and scream of the new machine even more serious than the previous models. Once my phone's live I pull up Sabine's text. I hesitate for a moment, then fire one back. I find my heart's beating a little faster as Rashid brings over the coffee. He hovers whilst I take a sip.

'It's like engine oil,' I say.

Rashid looks worried. 'You don't like? I can –'

'Rashid, I'm kidding. It's the best cup you've done me yet.'

I need sunglasses for his smile. He goes off to serve a couple who've just stumbled in looking even more in need of coffee than me. I check my inbox, and buried in the usual onslaught of junk there's one from Jansen, saying he's following up my discussion with Vermeer last night and he's getting someone to drop the full Kleine file at the houseboat this morning. Before I can stop myself I've tapped out a quick message telling him to leave it behind the cluster of flowerpots on deck if I'm out. Whereas I should have told him not to bother. *Was Sander Klaasen innocent? Is Marianne Kleine's death my fault?*

I finish up and leave a large tip for Rashid. To exit I have to step under a ladder which has appeared over his front door. I hope it's not bad luck. I turn to see a man at the top of it fixing a CCTV camera to the wall. It's good he's getting it done, but really Rashid should have had one before.

Now I'm on foot, forging through the city towards Centraal station. Bikes whizz, trams clang. I pass through pockets of air scented with coffee, pizza by the slice, sewage, before stopping off at a bank to pull some money out of the wall. I type in my pin then request 200 euros. The machine gives me a large frowny face and a message saying there's not enough in the account for that. I try for one-fifty and this time get a smiley. Infantilized by a machine, this is what it's come to. The 08:12 to Haarlem's on time, so I optimistically buy a single, jump on, watch the scenery, before jumping off at Sloterdijk. From there it's a short walk to the lock-up that holds the thing that has been keeping me sane these last months, and today is the day when all that work is going to pay off. I hope.

It's a 1969 Mustang SportsRoof in matt black, which I bought for next to nothing and have been trying to get roadworthy ever since. When I say kept me sane what I really mean is that it's driven me crazy, but at least it was an externally focused crazy. I've scraped knuckles raw whilst trying to unscrew bolts deep in the engine cavity; I've banged thumbs and sliced flesh. I've also waited weeks for a part to arrive only to discover it's not quite right, or opened up a pipe to have disgusting, and clearly dangerous, fluid seep over my fingers.

It's really my therapist's fault. She'd been urging me to take up a hobby, something using my hands, something to get me out of the houseboat at least once a week. Which all sounded like a pretty tall order, and the thought of trying to find an activity that would fit all those criteria was starting to stress me out, until I passed a used-car place near Stadionplein. I spotted it almost immediately and had a weird out-of-body experience, a kaleidoscopic mash-up of every car ad cliché I'd ever seen. I cruise curvaceous mountain roads with snowy peaks and blue skies, I zoom across a never-ending bridge with a woman sat beside me, hair blowing in the wind, I park with a flourish in front of a modernist building in an impossibly beautiful setting. Of course the woman bears a distinct resemblance to Tanya.

Before I knew it I found myself walking up to the salesperson who'd obviously clocked my altered state and was mentally limbering up for the kill.

Sure it needed some work, he'd said with a car sales-man's smile, a little TLC to get it back on the road. And sure, it's a little effort now, but it will be worth it, cars like this are becoming rarer and rarer, he said. Also, and here he dropped his voice and took a quick look around to make sure we weren't being overheard, he could envisage a not-too-distant future where a car such as the very one I was looking at, properly restored, would be worth con-siderably more than the minuscule asking price.

'Can I do this myself?' I asked. 'Given that I don't know anything about cars.'

He didn't even miss a beat. I got the feeling he never blinked.

'Sure,' he'd said. 'Sure, sure. All the information's online. You can find second-hand spares there too. And you don't need a raised ramp or anything.'

I called Mark Sattler who runs the car pool back at the station. He came out later that day, eventually agreed that it was probably doable, and grudgingly said he may, and he stressed the may, be able to help out occasionally if needed. Two days later I had it delivered to the lock-up I'd rented off the Marktplaats website. When the truck pulled away I wondered just what on earth I was doing.

The lock-up door rattles as I haul it open and flip on the light. The bonnet's up, a patient waiting for the surgeon, and I take a minute to check over everything I'd done yesterday. Satisfied that it was all good I turn to the final job: I need to attach the throttle body to the air induction system, and attach the air induction system to the air fil-ter. Then it should be good to go. In the end the therapist was right, there's something about working with your hands that changes your perspective. She'd said that it can actually alter your brain chemistry in such a way that old patterns can be disrupted.

'Nice car. Rent please.'

I turn to see Mark Liu silhouetted in the doorway. He's second-gen Chinese, his parents fleeing the Cultural Revolution to scrape a living with one of the first Chinese restaurants in the city. How he's ended up renting out these places is a mystery, but not one I've been overly inclined to delve into, not least because the rents he charges are well below market rate. As long as payment's in cash. My wallet splits open, and I count the notes and hand them over.

'So, how far off are you?'

'I reckon about half an hour. I just need to connect up the throttle body.'

I marvel at the fact that five months ago I didn't know what a throttle body was. In fact, the words 'throttle' and 'body' usually had a whole other meaning for me.

'Nice, but I still don't know why you didn't just buy a normal car.'

'I'm not normal.'

This seems to satisfy him, like he'd known that all along but just needed to hear it from me.

Once Liu's gone I stash next month's rent in an old paint tin in a pile of old paint tins and fish out a can of Red Bull. I keep a few here for when I'm working on the car, but notice I'm down to my last three. I crack one open and get back to work.

I'm done in twenty, with only a minor bruise to the back of my hand. I stand and look at the engine before taking out the keys, opening the driver's door, and inserting them in the ignition. If this thing blows I don't want to be inside it. I take a breath – this is months of work – and turn the key.

The engine makes a series of choking noises before dying off.

Fuck. At least it didn't explode, though. I go back to the engine cavity and it takes me another ten minutes to see what I'd missed: two 8-mm bolts that hold the induction tube on to the throttle body weren't properly tightened, allowing air to escape. I fix it and try again.

This time it comes to life with a meaty roar. I can hardly believe it. I've done it. I get in and gun the motor. Oh. Yeah.

I take it easy at first, but once I hit the A10 northbound I squeeze down the pedal and she responds beautifully. I'm pretty sure I hit warp speed before I realize that my exit's flying towards me. I slow down and take the ramp on to the A5, curling back round the city in an elegant arc. This is the long way, and thirty minutes later I'm pulling up outside the houseboat completely exhilarated. I park, get out and take a moment to admire my work. Who'd've thought?

As I step onto the gangplank the Westerkerk bells start ringing ten. On deck I notice Jansen's package hidden poorly behind the flowerpots, which I keep meaning to plant up but never seem to get round to. I pull it out to see whoever addressed it to me misspelt my name.

First thing I see on board is the envelope with the signed letter dominating the kitchen. It's like a sign. I suddenly get the feeling I've been waiting for, the reluctance melting away. Why has it taken me so long? I wonder. The drive gave me time to think of Joel's proposal, and I'd come to the conclusion that really the only thing I had to lose was the money. And if it paid off I wouldn't have to get some shit security job, which is what retired inspectors usually ended up doing if they'd not made pensionable age, which I'm very far off. I put it by the front door, so I remember to post it next time I go out.

I'm still holding Jansen's file. Really I should just call him now and say I'm not going to look at it.

Sander Klaasen could be innocent. You're responsible for Marianne Kleine's death.

I sit down at the kitchen table and take a deep breath. Then I open up the file. The more I read the more my stomach drops away.

Footsteps clatter on the gangplank just as I've finished going through it. At the door is a man so unabashedly unconcerned with the fact that I've been waiting around for him that he must be the electrician. I lead him to the circuit board, which is located in the former engine room at the aft of the boat. Back at the table I realize I'd left the photos out. Which probably has something to do with the strange looks he gave me on the way down.

There's a box under the sink unit in the kitchen where I keep copies of a few old files. Only those that were either unsolved, or which were solved but that just never felt right. Lucie Muller's one of latter. Back at the table I clear Vermeer and Jansen's file away and start reading through the Muller case, and I'm struck all over again by the similarities. It's uncanny – there is no way this is a coincidence. None at all.

I take a quick break on deck, rolling a joint with Joel's white cannabis. Smoke curls up in the strangely still air. I watch a seagull cruise out of the sky, wings hooked, orange feet splayed out haphazardly, adjusting as it comes in to land on the water.

Back at the table, reading faster now, seeing how Hank and I tackled the investigation, watching it unfold on paper. I take the photos of Lucie Muller out, compare them to Marianne Kleine. This can't be coincidence. It just can't. I read on, flipping between the two, hoping to find something, some detail which could explain the similarity away, all the while the air around me thickening with dread.

Ten minutes later I find it. There's a bit of paper stuck to the back of one of the Muller case photos and when I peel them apart I find it's the tech report on the video itself, the one that featured Huisman and the two hopefuls. I place it in the pile and start putting the whole lot away when something makes me stop and go back to it. I read it through properly. The name of the requesting officer is de Vries, and the technical officer who did the report is Joos Wilders. The report says, in the stiff formal language these things are always written in, that the footage had definitely been taken from the video camera recovered at Akkerman's house. I turn the sheet over, expecting more, but the other side is blank. There should be more to this, specifically a check that the time and date displayed on the camera were actually correct, the whole point of getting the report done. I search through the rest of the file. Nothing. I search again, my heart beating faster this time. Again, nothing. I tell myself to calm down. I get on the phone to the department responsible, ask to speak to Joos Wilders.

'He retired,' the crackly voice tells me. 'About four, maybe five years ago?'

I give the voice the report reference number and tell him to pull the file and email it over to me. I give him my personal address, saying there's something wrong with my work one. He doesn't even bat an eyelid; I wonder if I should tell someone about the lack of security. On deck I go through another joint. Just a small one this time.

'Mate?'

'Yeah?' I turn to see the electrician poking his head out of a porthole.

'I need to show you something.'

Down in the engine room the circuit board looks like a terrorist bomb mid-manufacture, a multitude of coloured wires spilling out of the box. It seems very far from being fixed. I tell him this.

'Gonna be a while,' he says. 'This thing was wired up by a monkey. You're lucky it didn't catch fire.'

'Fucking monkeys, they're everywhere.'

I'm not sure he hears me.

'So I need to get a few extra parts. These bits here are screwed, probably what tripped the whole fhing.'

'When will you be back?'

'Later today, tomorrow at the latest.'

'So what am I supposed to do in the meantime. If it is tomorrow?'

'Well, you see this switch here?'

He's pointing to a black plastic switch, the type that flips up or down. I concede that I can see it.

'Good, so whilst I'm gone, don't touch this, okay?'

I let him out and find myself back in the engine room.

The electrics haven't been touched since the boat was converted, so I'm not really that surprised. I find myself reaching out for the switch and I wonder why I've never been very good at doing what I'm told.

The phone saves me, snaps me out of it. The buzz is an email which turns out to be the report I'd asked for. I go back to the table, ready to compare it with what I've got, but when I open the attachment I see there's only one page, the same one as in the file. There's no second page, nothing to indicate they performed the most basic of tests. Hank de Vries had been in charge of that; he was a good cop – there's no way he'd've made such a mistake. Mistake being code for Monumental Fuck-up.

I call them back. Same voice as before.

'Is there any way there's a missing sheet?'

'No, I checked. Each page is given a unique reference which is logged on the system. This report only ever had one page.'

'So whoever did it didn't check the time on the camera itself?'

'If they did, they didn't make a note of it.'

Deck again, another half-joint, and I find my hand shaking a little as I light it. More birds. I look across at the Mustang; one of them's Jackson Pollocked the bonnet – a massive splodge of white shit, bright and watery against the matt black.

Back inside I stare at the table, the papers spread all over it. I'm overwhelmed by jittery coldness. I go through it again, and again. The feeling only gets worse. I know what it is; I've felt it before. It's denial.

Because from what I can see, Huisman's alibi, the one that meant he didn't go to prison for the murder of Lucie Muller, has just crumbled away.

Bit of a Punk

Once I've calmed down I get on the phone to Vermeer. Only her phone's off so I have to settle for Jansen.

'We need to meet,' I tell him.

'What's this about, sir?'

I'm beginning to think this whole sir business is him being sarcastic.

'It's about a unifying theory of everything, which manages to finally bridge the gap between general relativity and quantum mechanics. What the hell do you think it's about?'

'I –'

'Where are you now?'

'Den Haag, I'm down here with Vermeer.'

'When are you back?'

'We'll be at the station around three or so. But what's this –'

'Call me when you're close. I'll meet you there.'

I hang up before he can say 'sir' again.

The more I think about this, the more I know something's not right. But calling Jansen was maybe premature. I get on the phone to Gert Roemers, head of the computer crimes unit at the station.

'I thought you'd left,' he says once I've got hold of him and made my request.

'Sort of. But I'm thinking of writing my memoirs and

I wanted to speak to a couple of people involved in old cases.'

Roemers makes a noise like liquid's shooting out of his nose.

'Memoirs? Jesus. You're not putting me in them are you?'

'No, you're not interesting enough.'

'Good. All right, give me the names; I'll call you back.'

'First is Robert Huisman. He's on the system already, should be easy to trace. The second is Joos Wilders, who used to work in tech, retired about four years ago.'

I stuff the letter into my pocket and go to the houseboat moored next to mine. Leah answers the door. She's seventy-ish, grey hair and piercing eyes the colour of which I've never quite been able to fathom. Atlantic Ocean in winter might be close. Leah's been living here since the early seventies when she emigrated from New York to pursue her art, abstract sculptures made from pieces she finds on her frequent wanderings round the city: scrap metal, bits of bikes, plastic bags, branches from trees, used syringes. She finds a use for everything. Her deck has a constantly changing array, and so many tourists stopped to take photos that she eventually bent her artistic principles enough to actually contemplate selling the odd piece. Now if you catch her on a good day she might even take cash. As to men, there've been many over the years, but none of them for long. She once told me she felt stifled, suffocated even, if one of them stayed more than four or five days. None of them ever reached six, as far as I could tell.

I give her a spare set of keys – they were Tanya's and have a ghost of her scent, even just holding them brings back that gnawing regret – and ask her to look out for the electrician.

'That yours?' she asks, pointing to the Mustang.

'Yeah,' I say and for some reason feel a slight swell of pride.

'Shame . . .' she says, staring at it wistfully over my shoulder.

Back on board the houseboat Roemers calls. He's got Wilders' address, which I scribble down quickly. Huisman, though, is going to take him a little longer, he tells me. I ask him how long. He says something smart about a bit of string. I tell him to get on with it.

I'm just getting ready to leave when my phone goes off again. Nellie de Vries, Hank's wife. I debate not answering for a moment, but we've not spoken recently so . . .

'Jaap, there's something I want to talk to you about.'

She sounds different to usual, flatter somehow.

'Sure, what's up?' There's a stab of fear in my gut.

'It'd be better in person, maybe we could meet up?'

My antennae are twirling at this point, but I know not to push it over the phone. We agree I'll drop by her place in IJburg later on today. I hang up feeling queasy, because I've got a terrible feeling I know what she's going to say.

Joos Wilders is first. I check the address, which seems like a retirement complex out near Kasteel Brederode, a building that was of strategic importance in the Hook and Cod wars of the fourteenth and fifteenth century, but has now been relegated to a national monument.

I lock up, get in the car. Then I get out, clean the shit off the bonnet. Leah's still on deck and I wave as I go past, but I don't think she can even see me, her focus entirely on the vehicle. It's like she's deconstructing it in her head, working out which bits she could cannibalize for the sake of art. I'm going to have to watch her.

My route's the A10, then A4, before I swing onto the A9 northbound, which funnels me up through expanses of reclaimed land. The sun's out, and it's an almost perfect autumn day with a fragile light blue sky and seventeenth-century clouds. My interior weather is not as good; it feels tense like the gathering of a storm. It's not long before I spot the sign for Sunrise Homes, an arrow pointing to the next right. Sunrise. Who are they kidding? It should be Sunset. I take the turn and motor down a lane that ends in a parking space next to a field. On the other side, buildings are dotted around some manicured grounds, and there are old people everywhere: gardening, sitting on benches, chatting in groups. They don't look all that unhappy. I resolve not to mention the Sunrise/Sunset thing to anyone.

The reception desk has one of those old-fashioned bells that looks a little bit like a breast, and you have to hit the nipple with the palm of your hand. Next to it a vase oozes with obscenely voluptuous tropical flowers. A stack of leaflets promise a wonderland of fun for anyone lucky enough to live the Sunrise Lifestyle. There's a distinct lack of receptionist, though, even after I've slapped the bell up a bit.

'She might be a while,' croaks a voice from behind me. I turn to see an old woman, wrinkled, bent, a half-smile and eyes which, whilst watery, hold a certain power still. She shuffles towards me like a penguin, bringing with her

76

an aura of powdery lavender. She's wearing a taupe bath-robe with a purple waist tie, and slippers which each have two pink furry balls stitched to the tops. They flop around as she moves.

'Someone died about half an hour ago,' she says by way of explanation. 'And they're short-staffed today.' She moves closer and adopts a conspiratorial air. 'It's because of the laxative I put into the staff breakfast; two of them have gone home already. Good to keep them regular.'

She chuckles, her shoulders keeping time.

I'm about to ask her if she knows Joos Wilders when we're interrupted by a voice.

'Elsie, there you are,' says a harried-looking woman in uniform heading towards us, a Stepford grin on her face. 'I've been looking all over for you. You didn't take your medicine this morning; it was found hidden in the flower-pot again.'

'It's not medicine,' Elsie stage-whispers to me. 'It's poison. They're trying to poison me. All of them are.'

'I'll be with you shortly,' Stepford Receptionist says, leading away Elsie who is protesting verbally but comply-ing physically. A few minutes later she's back.

'Sorry about that,' Stepford says, inserting herself behind the desk, her walk oddly stiff. She's wearing a light blue polo shirt with an embroidered rising sun, shooting rays all over her left breast. 'What can I do for you?'

'I'm looking for Joos Wilders, I believe he lives here?'

'Are you the dog warden?'

'What? No, I'm . . . an old friend of Joos, I was passing and thought I'd drop in.'

'Oh, I'm sorry,' she says, tempering her forced smile a

little. 'Joos Wilders died earlier this morning. That's why everything's a bit chaotic here at the moment. And I've got two staff off sick as well, both gone down with a stomach bug, so it's hard holding it all together today.'

I start to understand her pained grin, and I suddenly wonder about what Elsie said.

'How did he die?'

'Probably just old age. It's not uncommon. He adopted a dog only last week and it was barking really early this morning. That's how we found him. Anyway, I don't mean to be rude, but I really need to –'

'I'm actually from the police,' I tell her, hoping she's not going to be officious and ask for some ID. 'I needed to talk to him about an old case but that's obviously too late. I would like to see where he lived, though.'

Chances of me finding something important, like a memo from him saying he had actually verified the time stamp are infinitesimally small. But I'm here, and what else can I do? Her grin's getting ever more pained.

'Look, if you point me in the right direction I can let you get on.'

She thinks it over. Her stomach gurgles. Then she tells me how to get to Joos' bungalow and swiftly disappears behind a door marked STAFF.

I walk through the grounds. There are probably forty or so small bungalows spread out, each with their own little garden. Some are vegetable plots, others are more ornamental. One is a square of grass trimmed to precisely 2.5 millimetres; I'm guessing the occupant used to work in government or for a local council. I'm a rare beast in this terrain, and the local fauna check me out, mostly with friendly smiles, though I spot a few pairs of medicine-dulled eyes.

Joos' bungalow is easy to spot. A cleaning crew is hanging around outside with mops and cigarettes and slumped postures.

As I step closer I hear muffled barking from inside. The door opens and a man, who must be the one Stepford mistook me for, steps out with a dog on a leash. I've seen enough police dogs to know what it is, a Malinois, though it doesn't seem fully grown yet and it's almost entirely black. It looks like a black wolf. *Oh god.*

The Malinois abruptly finishes barking, and decides it would like to sniff pretty much everything in the world. The man holding the leash is in danger of having his shoulder dislocated.

'Are you a relative?' he asks me as the dog lunges forward and sniffs my shoes.

'Of the dog or the dead man? Neither.'

'You don't want a dog, do you?'

'Why, what's wrong with it?'

The dog's moved on from my shoes and is exploring my leg.

'There's nothing wrong with it – it's just in all likelihood it'll end up being put down. The shelter's already oversubscribed. I took seven dogs in yesterday, know how many of those are alive today?'

I don't know because I'm not a mind reader. I hate being posed rhetorical questions, so I don't say anything or give any indication that I care about the answer and yet he makes a zero with his thumb and forefinger anyway.

'Sorry, I can't.'

The dog's worked his way up my leg and is now poking its snout right at the pocket where my vape is, making a series of loud snorts.

'He likes you,' the man says. 'First time he's stopped moving since I got here.'

'I'm sorry,' I tell him again.

The man shrugs. 'C'mon boy,' he says, gently tugging the leash to get the dog moving. The dog's less than keen, but the man ends up dragging him behind him. They pass another man, in a uniform similar to Stepford's, who's heading in my direction with righteous purpose in his step.

'Can I help?' he asks in that way people have when what they really mean is *who the fuck are you?* but don't have the balls to actually say it. He tacks a little forced laugh on to the end of it.

'No, I'm fine,' I tell him as I step past the cleaners who seem in no hurry to get into the bungalow.

'You can't go in there,' he calls out to me, though it sounds more of a squawk really.

I turn to look at him; he's short and stocky and doesn't seem to have much flexibility in his spine. His smile is a masterclass in insincerity.

'I'm an old colleague of Joos',' I tell him. 'I just need to see inside.'

'You're police?' he asks, less squawky now, but still suspicious.

'Exactly.' I step through the front door.

The first thing that hits me is the heat. The radiators are on nuclear meltdown setting. The space is decent, though: a large living room looks out onto a garden at the back. Beyond that a field filled with small clouds fallen from the sky. Sheep, on closer inspection. The kitchen's tiny, the bathroom has a sit-in bath, and the bedroom has a floor-to-ceiling bookcase and a single bed. The cover is pristine white and the whole thing looks unslept in. There's a round white mat on the floor which is covered in black dog hairs. Thankfully, though, it's cooler in here – the window's half open. I scan the bookcase, mostly technical volumes and a shelf devoted entirely to the works of Ursula K. Le Guin. Moving on I find two entire shelves crammed tight with spiral-bound note-books. I take one down and find it's a diary of sorts. Flipping through it I can see the man was obsessive; there's an entry for every single day, the writing cramped but precise.

'Do you have some ID?'

Doorway. Mr Sincere. Behind him a security guard. Notebook back on shelf.

'Yeah,' I tell him, running my finger along the spiral spines, trying to work out which one I need. I pull one out, find I've miscounted, and try another. This one's right, the date range covering what I need.

'I really would like to see it,' he says, taking a step into the room, the forced laugh at the end of each sentence really starting to grate now. He's positively vibrating with some pent-up emotion.

'It's in my car,' I tell him. 'I'll take you there once I've finished here.'

He snatches the notebook from me and puts it back on the shelf.

'I don't believe you,' he says. I can see his inner child. And it's a petulant snot-nosed little brat who would have benefitted from some boundaries being laid down in early life. The security guard steps in, his inner child's the none-too-bright sort who hang around and protect people smarter than themselves. *My* inner child reckons it's getting a bit cramped in here.

'Bit cramped in here,' I tell them. 'Let's move out.'

I step towards Mr Sincere and he decides to retreat, the security guard turning round and moving through to the living room. The second Mr Sincere's through the doorway, I slam the door shut, lock it, and quickly find the notebook again. There's a barrage of banging. I toss the notebook out of the window, then unlock the door.

'Tripped,' I say by way of explanation. 'Fell against the door.'

Two pairs of suspicious eyes. I grimace and rub an elbow, just for show.

I'm escorted back to reception by both of them, one either side of me.

'Did you eat breakfast here?' I ask.

'No.'

'I've heard it's good. Maybe there are some leftovers you could get.'

I feign heading back to the car park, but as soon as I'm out of their view I double round and find the notebook where I threw it. It's splayed open on the grass, a breeze flicking pages as if it's being speed-read by an invisible man. I pick it up, skim through until I find the date I'm looking for and start reading.

It starts out with a description of what he had for

breakfast, details of a strange-shaped puddle he spotted on the way to work, and various other bits of minutiae that he seemed to think were worth recording. Then, right at the end of the page, I find it. Just two sentences. I read them several times, just to make sure I'm not misinterpreting them.

But unfortunately I'm not. I close the notebook, as if that will make what I've just seen disappear.

The dog warden's van is parked next to the Stang. The man himself is leaning against his vehicle, sucking something strawberry-scented out of a vape pen, and playing a game on his phone. I've been trying to get hold of Jansen but his phone's off. I try one more time as the dog explores the rim of the front tyre with his snout. Still no Jansen. I give the dog warden a short wave, get in and drive away. Then I stop, throw it into reverse and pull up by him.

'Is that dog really going to be put down?'

''Fraid so,' he says. 'There are just so damned many of them, and no one wants a dog like this.'

I get out and check my phone for Carice's number. She runs a hugely profitable business training police dogs and selling them to forces around the world. It can cost upwards of thirty thousand euros to train a top-level bomb-detection dog, and she's damn good at it. She's only five foot, but has a way with hard-bitten working dogs which doesn't just border on the supernatural – it's downright surreal.

'Wassup?' she asks in American, as I knew she would. Carice spent time in the US, somewhere in Michigan is as about as precise as I can remember, studying with one of the foremost working dog trainers in the world. Since then she's always done a faux-American thing in the way that only a European can, dripping with irony and superiority. None of which hides the strong undertow of longing.

I tell her, exactly, wassup.

'You with the dog now?'

'Yeah.'

On the phone a riot of barking starts up. Carice yells *No!* and silence reigns.

'FaceTime me; I'll have a look.'

I get it going and show her the dog.

'Move towards him,' she tells me.

I move forward. The dog stops being interested in the tyre and turns to look at me, ears alert. But he stands his ground, doesn't back away even when I'm up real close.

'He's fine,' she says after a few seconds. 'Bit of a punk, but not too bad. Confident body language. It's the nervy, neurotic ones you need to be wary of.'

'So you'll take him?'

'Take him? I thought this was about *you* taking him.'

'Me? I don't know anything about dogs.'

'It's easy. Just remember not to treat him like a furbaby, and don't let him get away with anything you don't want him to do. If you get really stuck, you can bring him out to meet me. Gotta go, I've a bitch in heat and one of the young males is getting a bit fruity.'

She's gone, leaving another very loud *No!* ringing in my ear.

The guy hands me the leash. 'Thank you,' he says. 'You've just saved a life.'

He's in the van and away before I can change my mind. The dog's nosing at my pocket again. Seems like he might make a natural drug dog. Maybe he'll come in handy.

I open up the passenger door and the dog jumps in without me having to prompt him.

'Good boy,' I say.

He gives me a look which says don't patronize me. Or maybe I'm misreading it. After all, I don't know anything about dogs. As the Stang's engine bites and we're both pushed back in our seats I wonder just what it is I've got myself into.

As I hit the A9 again I find out. Apparently the dog likes to bark at cars as we pass, and as I tend not to be a slow driver there are a lot of cars to bark at. Carice had said not to let him get away with anything I didn't want him to do, and this barking is driving me insane. Not to mention the very real threat of permanent hearing loss. So I try out my best *No!*, which only results in him barking more. It worked for Carice, but clearly I'm missing something. This is not good.

I try Jansen again. This time his phone's on and he answers.

'Back yet?'

'Yes, sir, just walking into the station right now. What's that noise?'

'It's a pet cat.'

'I didn't know they barked, sir.'

'Neither did I. Maybe I should take it to a vet. Listen, I've got something for you. Don't go anywhere. I'll be there in half an hour.'

Halfway through the journey, just as we're pulling into

Amsterdam, the dog gives up looking out of the window and curls up on the seat. His ribs expand, then he lets out a massive sigh.

I might have just saved a life, but does that make up for my mistake?

Because from what I can see in Wilders' notebook, the odds that I did are starting to look overwhelming. A mistake that has had deadly consequences and could have led directly to the death of Marianne Kleine.

Disturbance in the Force

'That's not allowed in here,' the desk sergeant tells me as I'm trying to sign in.

'He's a highly trained dog,' I tell him. 'It'll be fine.'

'Yeah? So why's he peeing on that chair?'

I turn to see the dog cock-legged. He swings his head round. From the way he's holding his mouth, teeth visible, I swear he's grinning.

'I dunno. I don't know anything about dogs.'

Jansen saves the day and this time we go to the canteen, leaving the desk sergeant muttering that the last time he checked his contract it didn't say anything about mopping up dog piss.

'What's this about, sir?'

'I'm not going to tell you unless you stop calling me "sir".'

'Okay, s—'

'There, not too hard is it?'

Once I've taken him through everything he gets his phone out.

Five minutes later we're in the incident room upstairs and I'm telling the story again, this time to Vermeer. The dog takes a liking to her instantly, rubbing against her leg and nuzzling her hand. She pushes him away.

'So Robert Huisman's alibi could be false?'

'It was never corroborated properly; doesn't actually

mean it *is* false. But given how Marianne Kleine died it's starting to look like a very strong possibility.'

'You liked him for it at the time?'

'Look at it this way, on character alone you've got a small-time dealer funding his own habit, and he and a friend tricking women into having sex with them on camera. What's not to like? I was sure he was the one, until the alibi surfaced. At which point there wasn't much we could do.'

'So this all hinges on the report not being done properly. Any evidence of that?'

I pull out Wilders' spiral-bound diary, open it to the right page and slide it across the desk in a rather showy way. She reads it then passes it over to Jansen.

'So the day Wilders was doing his report on the video tape happens to be the very day he gets a call saying his sister was rushed to hospital and he left early. And as a result he didn't complete the full report, like the verifying of the time stamp?'

'Yeah.'

'Lucky for him he died this morning, otherwise I'd have him brought up on a disciplinary.' She picks up the notebook again. 'What did Wilders die of?'

The chances of his death being related to this crime are slim to none, but I'd checked anyway. Seems Vermeer has as suspicious a mind as I do.

'Heart attack apparently. I did ask for the full report, just in case.'

'Jansen,' Vermeer says, turning to him, 'run Huisman through the system. I want to know everything about him.'

'And Akkerman too,' I tell him. 'You potentially fake

an alibi for a friend, starts to make it look like you might actually be involved yourself.'

Vermeer gives Jansen the nod.

Once he's gone Vermeer cranks up the charm.

'If this turns out to be significant, it's a pretty major fuck-up.'

It's hard to disagree with her assessment. And it happened on my watch. Though it's not strictly speaking my fault. Hank de Vries was the one in charge of that particular piece of evidence, and he reported to me that it was solid. I didn't go and check his work; we were equals, and he was a good cop. I can't believe this is happening.

Jansen walks back in with a laptop. The dog, which has been lying at Vermeer's feet, gets up and wants to check out what Jansen is carrying. It jumps up and puts its front paws on the table. Vermeer brushes it off without even looking at it. Claws hit the floor.

'Nothing on Akkerman, but I've got Huisman's file. Arrest for heroin possession two years ago, then nothing.'

'Known address?'

'None.'

'Get Roemers onto it,' Vermeer tells him. 'I think it's time we had a chat with Messrs Huisman and Akkerman.'

'When you find either of them I should be there,' I tell Vermeer as Jansen disappears again.

'Why?'

'Because I've interviewed them before, and it'll unnerve them if I suddenly turn up on their doorstep.'

Deep in space planets spin and photons speed through nothingness and black holes suck matter into their mysterious cores. And still Katja Vermeer stares at me.

'I don't think that's necessary,' she finally says. 'Thank you for your help, though. It's appreciated.'

She gets up and heads for the door.

'C'mon. You wouldn't have this if I hadn't brought it to you. I can help.'

She stops and stands with her back to me for a few seconds, as if trying to make up her mind. She turns and looks at me.

'Before I let Jansen contact you I read your file.'

So it's come to that, has it? People reading my file before dealing with me. And I'm not even sure just how much is in there. Though I'm sure there's enough.

'Then you'll know I'm serious.'

'I know you're trouble.'

'Is it true you made a grown man cry?'

A flicker of a smile. It's not much but it's something I can work with.

'You want me to beg?' I ask.

There's that flicker of a smile again. Or maybe it's an unconscious twitch.

'No. Wouldn't make any difference anyway.'

'Look, if this turns out to be related to the Muller case, then I want to be involved.'

'I thought you were about to officially leave the police? You've cut your deal, you'll get your early retirement and you can go off and do whatever it is you do. We asked you to go over the file, but that's it. Leave this to the professionals.'

The door closes behind her and the dog stands watching it in case it opens again, his tail gradually winding down from a full wag to being still. I think of the interviews

Hank and I had done with Huisman, the feeling we'd both had that he was the killer, then the alibi which made it impossible, even though it went against our instincts. Something I've learnt over the last year is that ignoring your instinct occasionally isn't going to do you any harm. But ignoring it again and again and again can land you in a very dark place. And right now my instinct is trying to tell me something. I'm just not sure what.

'C'mon,' I tell him. 'We're not wanted here. Let's go and see Nellie.'

Nellie de Vries turns her head to look out of the window onto the IJburg, the vast waters separating Amsterdam from Amsterdam-Noord. I follow her gaze. A cargo ship looms on the horizon, dwarfing the ferry that runs between IJplein and Centraal station. Above it all a plane dives fearlessly towards a bank of cloud. I watch as it emerges unscathed on the other side.

At my feet the dog stirs as if he's just felt a disturbance in the Force.

Which he probably has, given what Nellie's just told me. The words she'd uttered creep through me like a kind of cold death.

She still lives in the same house she and Hank bought back in the early 2000s, when they both knew the future held nothing but joyful opportunity, a place where nothing bad would ever happen. It's a floating structure, purpose-built and tethered to a quay at IJburg, part of a range of artificial islands constructed to ease pressure on Amsterdam's ever-expanding housing crisis. We're in the large downstairs, an open-plan area with views out over the water, sitting at the table where Hank and Nellie had eaten for years, where now she eats alone.

On the kitchen surface behind her is an empty bottle of wine. If you stare through it, the tiles beyond become curved, magnified. I suddenly *know* that in the bin there are going to be many more bottles. Some inspector I am, I think to myself, not having spotted that earlier. I'd always thought she had the kind of fragility only the truly strong allow themselves to show the world. Now I'm not so sure.

'When?' is all I can manage, the word catching in my throat, the cold creeping further through me.

'They said it will be put before the committee and I'll have an answer the next day. If it's approved, then it has to take place within four days or another application will have to be made.'

Jesus. I've lost people; it feels like more than most. But their deaths all happened. I've never had to face the decision Nellie's been wrestling with for months now. I wonder about the first time the idea popped into her head. Did she hate herself for even thinking it? How did she gradually come to decide it was time?

Nellie's a paediatric neurologist, working with the worst cases of childhood epilepsy, including two of the most devastating, Lennox-Gastaut syndrome and Dravet syndrome. We're talking kids who have twenty to thirty fits a day, kids for who the standard medications simply don't work. Frustrated, she researched heavily and has for the past three years been treating with a phenomenal success rate. The prescription is cannabis, small doses of which reduce the frequency of episodes down to a couple a month, sometimes less. Say you have the choice of watching your child fit upwards of thirty times a day, or a couple of times a month, what are you going to do? Unsurprisingly her waiting list is over a year long now, with desperate parents bringing their children from countries all over Europe.

Her main clinic is at the same hospital Hank lies in. She has lunch with him every day, where she talks to him, tells him about what's going on, about her patients, her life without him. When she'd first told me she was doing that I wasn't sure it was a good idea, but I've changed my mind. I think it's brought her to this point now, which although terrible, is maybe for the best.

I reach down and scratch behind the dog's ear. It would have been easier if the shots had killed Hank outright, but instead they hit his leg, and I'd staunched as much of the bleeding as I could until the ambulance got there. But by the time he arrived at the hospital he'd slipped into the coma he's lain in ever since. I've often wondered if I should have left him to bleed, if it would have been better that way. But hindsight's always twenty-twenty.

And irony on top of irony, we were busting a grow room.

It's been years now, and there's never been any change in his condition. Nothing that hinted at a recovery. Whoever said hope's a cruel mistress was understating it. Hope will tear you apart, prey on your nerves till you're a wreck. I can only imagine what it must've been like for Nellie, second by second, waiting for the call telling her that Hank's woken up. Or that he'd died.

This isn't what anyone signed up for.

'Will you be here when –'

The emotion takes over, forcing the tears she's been holding in for so long. I reach out for her hand and she grasps it tight. We sit like this until she's cried it out. The dog makes his move, pushing into her leg. She reaches down, strokes him and he lets out a low growl of pleasure.

I'm feeling sick now, and guilty too, because this isn't really the time to ask, and yet I need to. She takes it well, though, and tells me Hank's old case notes are up in the spare room on the first floor. I leave her with the dog and go upstairs.

The room looks back towards the shore, a narrow window framing the golden minaret on top of the turquoise-tiled Elmouhssinine Mosque. The walls are covered with framed photos; one of them is of Hank and me the day we graduated posing in our uniforms. It strikes me that we look like kids. If only we knew what was coming, we probably wouldn't be grinning like idiots. It prompts one of those moments where I don't even know who I am, how I got here. The rest are of Hank and Nellie, their story played out in pictures from when they first met to their marriage at De Koepelkerk, and beyond.

Until that day.

The black wolf shudders. It's hungry. It needs the anger and the sorrow and the pain.

I turn away to the boxes and I find what I'm looking for quickly. There's a desk and chair by the window and I take the book of Hank's notes on the Muller case over and sit down. They're handwritten, the letters slanting forward as if leaning into the wind. A few pages in I decide I'm going to need more time. Back downstairs

94

Nellie's sitting on the sofa, looking out at the water. The dog is right next to her, head resting on her lap. She's gently stroking him and he's lapping it up.

'He's nice. What's his name?'

'So far it's just "dog"; haven't really had time to think.'

She strokes him a little more before she speaks again. 'I saw Tanya the other day.'

Words which suck all the air from the room.

'How is she?' I finally manage.

'I'd like to say she's fine, but really she's not. I can tell.'

All I'd ever tried to do was the best for her, and yet somehow I ended up hurting her, the last person in the world I'd want to harm. How did it get to this? Why was I such a fuck-up?

'I think you should talk to her, Jaap. I know things were bad, especially after the miscarriage, but I'm seeing you both, and you're both miserable. Being apart clearly isn't working. For either of you.'

The reality is I tried, though. Tried several times but she wouldn't see me, said that it was over, we were done. I'd got angry, which hadn't helped. And then I began to wonder if she wasn't, in fact, right, that maybe it *was* over and I just had to accept it and move on. I think of Sabine.

'Did she say anything?'

'She didn't have to, but it's clear she's hurting and I think she regrets how it ended.'

Regret is such a small word for how I feel about it all. Regret doesn't even come close. On the kitchen table Nellie's phone rings and she gets up to answer it. I feel like I need some air, so I walk over to the door, which leads to the balcony overlooking the water. Seagulls mock me with their cries as I step out. My fingers tremble when I'm filling the vape, and I lose some of the bud over the rail.

I hear Nellie's footsteps behind me. 'Feeding the ducks?'

I take a couple of draws, and it starts to dampen the swelling wave of anxiety I'd felt inside. It strikes me that without this stuff I might not even still be alive.

'You think if I tried to contact her she'd respond?' I finally ask.

'What have you got to lose? At worst she'll just ignore you. But I think it's time.'

I take a few more inhales just to steady me off. Several ducks float by, though they don't seem interested in what I'd dropped. Probably just as well. They seem pretty stress-free; don't look like they need it. Suddenly I hate myself for being weak, for having to medicate just to survive. Another swelling wave: this time it's self-pity.

'Jaap, I really think you should call her. Before it's too late.'

Too late. The saddest words in any language.

As we walk to the door I ask her if I can take Hank's notes and she agrees. She opens it and we see a harried-looking courier racing back to his white van and speeding off.

'I feel like I'm failing,' she says.

I hold her for a few moments. She seems so delicate, even though she's probably the strongest person I know.

'You're doing the right thing. Hank would say the same.'

'So you'll be here if it happens?' she finally asks.

I tell her I will. Even though I can't think of anything worse.

Knocking the Walls Off

I can't stop thinking about it as I drive through the tunnel under the IJ heading south. Hank's life ending at the flick of a switch. Alive. Click. Dead.

As the narrow sides open up and we shoot out from under the NEMO building, Roemers gets me on the phone. I feel a quick rush of relief before I realize this all seems so familiar, distracting myself with work. Not good.

'Remember the guy you wanted me to find, Huisman?'

'You know, those Alzheimer's meds must be working. What about him?'

'You didn't get this from me, all right?'

'I don't even know who you are.'

'Promise.'

Next to me the dog barks.

'Will that do?'

He gives me an address and hangs up. I should really call Vermeer or Jansen. But I find myself making a U-turn and heading towards the address. On the way I pass the Boerejongens coffeeshop on Baarjesweg. I've never been in, but it's supposedly got the kind of stuff most of the tourist-focused places don't; all their cannabis is organically produced, for starters. The bud Joel gave me yesterday isn't going to last long at the current rate so I pull up outside and leave the dog in the Stang.

A few minutes later I'm back in the car with three little

bags, a Krystal Kush, NYC Diesel and a Sweet Cheese. My phone goes off, the electrician, so I put the bags on the dash and answer. But he's rung off. I call him back. Answer machine. I tell him to call me just as a text message from him comes in. How hard does this have to be? His text tells me he has the parts and is on his way now. About bloody time. I text him back telling him to get the keys from Leah.

As I'm slotting the key in the ignition, some sixth sense is nagging me that something's wrong. I glance up to see there are now only two bags on the dash; the Krystal Kush is missing.

Quick look at dog. Mystery solved.

He has it in his mouth. I make a grab for it, and he ducks his head, eyeing me suspiciously. Luckily he's not chewing. Yet. I try again, and he ducks his head the other way. Then he starts mouthing it. It's in thick plastic, but it's not going to take him long before it rips . . .

'Give it to me,' I say in a sweet-toned voice.

Nothing.

I try again, more authoritarian this time, trying to channel Carice. The dog just looks at me, though I'm sure there's a challenge in his gaze now. I try again and fail. He's starting to mouth it, still staring at me, and I'm frozen because I don't know what'll happen if he manages to break through the wrapper. I'm steeling myself for one last desperate grab, when a cyclist whizzes past. The dog swivels his head round and barks. The bag drops and I grab it, checking that it's still sealed. It is, though the paper label is dripping with saliva. Jesus, that was close.

I'm just pulling up at the address Roemers hadn't given

me, when it comes in one of those startling flashes of clarity you get where everything meshes together in a whoosh.

'Kush,' I tell the dog. 'I'm going to call you Kush.'

He gives a single bark; I wonder if that's a no.

'Well, it's either that or Krystal.'

This time he stays silent.

'Good, Kush it is.'

There are no more spaces left outside the address so I have to hunt for one in the next street, just managing to squeeze between a monster SUV with blacked-out windows and an old Ford propped up on bricks. I stash the three bags in the glove compartment, which piques Kush's interest. He keeps nosing it. Hopefully he can't get it open.

I reach the entrance just as a woman in jeans and a shiny green bomber jacket is backing out of the door with a pushchair in tow. I hold it open for her and then slip inside. On the left wall is a bank of mailboxes, stairs on the right. I work out from the address Roemers gave me and the number of mailboxes that Huisman's flat is most likely on the top floor, a calculation that turns out to be correct.

It's number twenty, at the end of a corridor under a light which isn't working. The doorbell doesn't rouse anyone, and knocking doesn't either. I try the handle gently, but the door's locked. I'm just thinking that once upon a time this would have been easier. I could have simply kicked the thing in and claimed I'd heard a scream or a cry for help. I check the door sill, running my finger along just in case he's left a key. All I get is a thick layer of dust obscuring the swirl of my fingerprint. Once again I think

99

a well-aimed kick will sort it just as I think I hear some-thing for real. I put my ear to the door and listen. There it is again: a faint noise I can't quite make out. It's like fabric moving. Maybe Huisman is in there and trying to hide behind the curtains? I kneel down and try to peer through the keyhole. It's dark, though, so I pull out my phone and hit the torch app. It's tricky to line up, and I'm struggling to get the angle right, which is maybe why I don't see or hear them coming until it's too late. I sense a presence and turn just as they see me. They stop dead.

'Sir, what are you doing here?' Jansen asks.

'What he's doing is sticking his nose in where it's not needed,' Vermeer says, walking swiftly towards me.

I put my finger to my lips, pointing to the door.

The look on Vermeer's face is anger, but she stops and beckons me to her.

'No one answered, but I heard a noise in there,' I whis-per to her when I'm level.

'Okay, you go downstairs and wait –'

'I –'

'*Downstairs. Wait*,' she hisses at me.

Turns out it's not for that long.

And they don't come down with Huisman, or anyone else. Vermeer spots me sitting on a low concrete wall, the surface of which is layered with the work of generations of young taggers practising their craft. Her phone goes off before she gets to me.

'Wait,' she tells me, answering her phone and walking out of earshot.

Jansen walks past awkwardly.

'Huisman in?' I call out to him.

'Hasn't been seen for several days, sir. At least according to the neighbours.'

'Let me guess, since Kleine was killed?'

The twitch tells me I'm right.

'You think it's connected?' he finally asks.

'You think it isn't?'

Jansen shrugs, and he looks over to see Vermeer deep in conversation, then joins me. 'I dunno,' he says, shaking his head.

'I heard something in there, though.'

'There was a blind hanging by an open window; could it have been that?'

I concede it could.

'Something weird, though,' Jansen says.

'Yeah?'

Jansen glances at Vermeer again, who's still deep in conversation. He sits down.

'We spoke to Huisman's boss earlier. Turns out he works shifts up at the docks. Just manual stuff, hauling around boxes in a hi-vis, that kind of thing. But his boss says that Huisman had been acting strange the last couple of weeks.'

'Strange how?'

'Apparently he was usually pretty quiet, kept to himself. But there were a couple of incidents recently when he got into arguments with other people on the crew.'

'Arguments over what?'

'Just stuff, nothing out of the ordinary. But here's the thing, he had some leave owed to him and he booked it off a week and a half ago. His boss assumed he was going on holiday and asked him where and Huisman got uncomfortable, couldn't give a straight answer. So I checked it out and apparently Huisman doesn't actually have a valid passport; his ran out six years ago and he never renewed it.'

'So he didn't go abroad, but plenty of people holiday here.'

'I guess . . . I was hoping we'd find something up there to tell us where he'd gone but there was nothing. No computer either so can't get his emails.'

Vermeer finishes up and heads our way. Jansen takes this as his cue to stand up.

'I thought I made myself clear yesterday,' Vermeer says when she reaches me, 'but obviously I didn't. So let me be clear now: you are not to get involved with this investigation, *unless* we specifically ask you to look at something for us. If I find you poking round again, I'll have you arrested for impeding an active investigation. Clear?'

I nod. She holds my gaze a beat or two longer, before walking back to the unmarked, Jansen in tow. She's right, I should drop it now, walk away. It's not going to do me any good. But I'm finding there's a part of me that doesn't like to let go.

'So what's next?' I find myself calling out.

Vermeer stops, then turns back. 'Next? I don't think you've understood. There is no next.'

'Are you telling me Huisman's not connected?'

'I'm telling you it's none of your business.'

Funny, I've been told that my whole life. Somehow it's comforting to hear. Vermeer and Jansen disappear into their car. Again I tell myself I should just let it go. But I slip off the wall and step over quickly to knock on the car's window. It slides down.

'Yes?' she asks in a sweeter-than-sweet voice.

'You came to me, insinuating that I'd got the investigation wrong and sent an innocent man to prison *and* possibly left the real killer free to kill again.'

'Yes?'

'And I brought you Huisman. Without me you wouldn't have discovered his alibi was probably worthless.'

'Again, yes. Your point being?'

I think of the letter in my pocket. I think of Joel's proposal. I also think of Lucie Muller, and of a man in prison, put there by me, who may not have been her killer after all. I think, even though I'm trying hard not to, whether it's possible that a mistake I made years ago has caused Marianne Kleine to die in a pool of her own blood, her last seconds spent watching her life seep right out of her.

'My point is this case is clearly connected to the Muller case. Which was mine and –'

'Exactly. *Was*. It's called the past tense.' Her finger stabs a button and the car comes alive.

'*Is* my case if it's reopened. I can put a request in, and given what I discovered about Huisman I think there's a very good chance it will be reopened.'

She reaches out and turns the engine off.

Jansen's sitting in the passenger seat. I think he's on my side. But who knows?

'It might get reopened,' she concedes. 'But given your record, and the fact that I'm investigating the Kleine murder already it'll come to me.'

'Maybe. Or maybe they'll want a larger team on it, maybe they'll bring in someone else because the only break you've had so far has come from me, not you.'

'I don't think that's likely.'

'You want to take the risk? Go for it.'

She smiles again as the window glides up. The engine roars, the tyres bite hard and I'm breathing fumes. I watch them go. As the car disappears round the corner I decide it's probably for the best. Going down this path is only going to end one way.

And now I've decided, I'm walking with purpose, my intention to get into the Stang and drive away from all this, dive headlong into the fear, start living my new life outside the police. Up ahead a postman turns into the street pushing a mail trolley. The idea comes out of nowhere and before I can stop myself I've pivoted round back towards the building. Standing by the mailboxes I time it perfectly, dropping my keys just as the postman opens the door. I pick the keys up and pretend-hunt for one, before advancing the smallest key I have towards box number twenty.

'Here you go, mate. Twenty, yeah?'

I turn, look surprised, then grateful.

'Thanks,' I tell him as he hands me a couple of letters, delivers the rest and heads out.

Back at the Stang I find it's surrounded by kids. The reason, I see as I get closer, is Kush. He's sitting in the driver's seat, chewing the top of the wheel. The kids are loving this; at least two of them have got their phones out and are filming it. YouTube fame at last. It'll probably go viral and have five million views by the end of the day. I guess I'd need to own it, though, to get the ad revenues. Maybe I should confiscate their phones.

I settle for disbanding them and get in, ignoring Kush and turning to the letters instead. The first two are circulars, but the third is a credit card statement. I scan through it; it's mostly small purchases, until on page three there's a payment for nearly two thousand euros. I check the date: a week and a half ago. Ties in with the last-minute holiday story. And yet . . . That's a lot of money to pay for a holiday if you're not going abroad. It's also a lot of money for someone working shifts at the docks.

I stare at the paper a little longer, before folding it up and starting the engine. As I pull away I wonder why I'm feeling so uneasy all of a sudden. I pull over and get Roemers on the phone. He answers on the third ring.

'What now?'

'I need you to check something for me.'

The six towers of Bijlmerbajes prison stand stark against the sky. Built in the late seventies the blocks look more like social housing than a prison complex. They're mostly empty now, and by next year the whole complex will be closed, refurbished, then reopened as a refugee centre. Welcome to the Netherlands.

I dropped Kush off at the houseboat. The bathroom has a sunken bath so I slipped a bath mat into it and coaxed Kush to clamber inside. He sniffed a bit but then settled down on the mat. He seemed happy enough until I tried to leave and he started barking like crazy. I hope Leah doesn't mind. I park and turn the engine off, letting the silence surround me for a moment, soothing the kernel of dread that has been creeping up on me during the drive. I stare at the towers looming over me, and feel that pit-of-the-stomach dread increasing with each passing thought. Was I part of putting an innocent man in there? Did the real killer get away, only to kill again? Is Marianne Kleine's death on me?

The black wolf's got his nose to the wind, sensing the anxiety, feeding on it, waiting for a chance to strike.

My thoughts are starting to speed up, a tell-tale sign. I wonder about having a quick hit before going in, and even pull out a bag from the glovebox. I stare at it, torn. No. I can do this. I can conquer this feeling on my own. I stash it and reach for the door.

The guy on reception remembers me from last time I'd been here and doesn't even suspect I may not be on official business. As he leads me down brightly lit and eerily quiet corridors he tells me exactly why my trip will be a wasted one.

'Don't think you're going to get much out of him,' he says. 'Guy's fucked in the head.'

Sometimes I wonder if that doesn't just sum up the human condition. He motions me into a viewing booth and tells me Klaasen will be brought in shortly. I suddenly find the room seems slightly off centre, like the angles aren't all straight. My hands are cold now, palms moist. I think of the glovebox. Damn. I should have had a pull. The anxiety's definitely kicked up a level. In fact, it's knocking the walls off. My thoughts are speeding up. I try to slow them down to manageable levels.

I don't know why I've come.

To apologize? Or to try and make myself believe he really did kill Muller all those years ago?

It's time to go. Doing this is only going to feed the black wolf. I stand up just as the door on the other side of the cramped space opens and a man shuffles in: prison PJs, hands cuffed, head down. He seems lost for a moment, then shuffles forward and sits on the chair opposite mine. I'm swimming, treading water. My breathing's ramping up. I get the weirdest sensation, like I want to laugh. He brings his head up, eyes settling on mine.

I stare at the face in front of me.

More racing thoughts. The whole investigation in a mad jumble, a shifting collage of facts, images, feelings.

'Nnnnnnnnnngh,' he says. 'Nu . . . nu . . . nnnnnnnngh.'

The urge to laugh has gone.

Because Jansen hadn't been kidding, whoever beat him did a thorough job of rearranging his features. He's practically cubist now. I don't recognize him at all. My hands are drenched. Trembling. The room's breathing. I'm not. I can't.

He leans forward, as if he's trying to whisper something to me.

I instinctively lean closer to the Perspex dividing us. His tongue's pushing out his bottom lip.

'Nnnnnnnnnnnnngh.'

He pulls his head back like a horse rearing up in slo-mo, the whites of his eyes weirdly visible. Then things switch to double time as he slams his face right into the Perspex. Again and again and again.

Fuck. I . . . Am I responsible for this? Is this my fault?

There's blood spouting from his forehead, splattering everywhere.

I should call out for the guard, but I'm paralysed.

He rests his palm against the Perspex, then slowly slides it down, leaving a bloody smear.

'Nnnnnnnnnnnnnnnnnnnnnnnnngh.'

He's drooling now. Eyes focused on me like a rattlesnake about to strike.

No. God no. No, no.

I can see he's accusing me, just like he did in court that day when he'd been sentenced and he glared over at me and I felt the hatred being transmitted through the air like electricity.

I can't breathe. I get up and stumble out. Corridors, security gates, startled receptionist, car park. The Mustang's a million miles away, tarmac stretching out with every step I take. I'm walk-running, then I'm just running. (*Nnnnnnnngh.*) Keys. Fumble. Scratch the door. Shit. Slot. Open door. Fingers scrabbling at the glovebox. Bag. Rip open. Fingers trembling. Crumbling the bud. Dropping half of it. Stuff a little in the vape. Wait for the light. Taking forever, forever. Vape dies before it reaches temperature. Roll a joint instead, fingers enduring their own personal earthquake. That's not good. Fuck it. Have to resort to my glass pipe. Fill the bowl, lighter, touch with flame.

Inhale.

Inhale.

I*nnnnnnnnnnnnnnnnnnnnnn*hale.

It's been back-to-back meetings so far today and there's a little pulse at his temple which he knows can get worse quickly. He reaches his office, his PA on the phone but waving to him in an I-need-to-talk-to-you way which he ignores, and goes inside, closing the door behind him. At the back of the drawer he finds a packet of painkillers, only to discover it's empty. Damn. There's a faint buzzing from the drawer two down, a drawer that remains locked, the key kept taped to the back of the drawer above. He unlocks it and pulls out the phone.

'What now?' he snaps. He finds himself massaging his temple with his finger. Got to get a painkiller, he thinks. The headaches have been getting worse, and if he doesn't get the drug in his system soon it'll blow up into a migraine, which will most likely leave him incapacitated for several days. And he can't afford that. Not in his position. Not now.

'Thought you should know Rykel visited the house of one of the cops on the original investigation. I saw him leave with what looked like a file or folder. I'm guessing they're notes to do with Muller's case. He's also just visited the prison.'

He stares out of the window across the car park to the motorway beyond. Dear God, he thinks. How much more of this can I take? For a moment he feels as if things are spiralling out of control. There's also, and he doesn't want to admit it to himself but it's there nonetheless, a snaking, twisting surge of fear.

'I'm going to have to talk to someone, work out what our next step is. Meantime you just keep on him, understood?'

He kills the call, puts the phone back in the drawer, locks it, retapes the key, and heads out of the door, ignoring his PA again. The pain in his temple's gone. Or not gone, but no longer relevant.

He's got a much bigger problem now. One which, if not sorted out, is going to make a migraine look like a fleabite at Chernobyl.

Don't Call Me, I'll Call You

Roemers gets me just as I arrive back at the houseboat. I'm attempting to parallel park into a space I'm not entirely convinced is actually big enough. My hand hesitates over the phone, the panic which had engulfed me at the prison now largely gone, but the memory of it a warning nonetheless. A warning I should probably heed. Then again, if there's even a chance that what I fear might be going on here is true, I can't just walk away.

'Got what you wanted,' Roemers says. 'Payment was made to a charitable foundation.'

'Not a holiday company?'

'No.'

'So what sort of charity is Huisman giving two thousand euros to, then disappearing?'

'That is exactly the question *you* should be asking, because I've got some other stuff to do which has been deemed urgent.'

'Can you send me what details you've got?'

'When I get a minute.'

I finish parking, just managing to squeeze in without any damage, and turn the engine off. Part of me had been hoping Roemers would get back to me with something straightforward, something that would mean I could just forget about it. Instead it's just provoking questions, reigniting old paths in my brain, the investigative mind probing, constructing scenarios. It almost feels good. Which, I reflect as I reach for the door handle, isn't good at all. I pass the postbox and before I know what I'm doing I pull the crumpled letter out of my pocket and jam it in the slot.

'Jaap, we need to talk!'

I'm crossing the gangplank when Leah emerges on deck, waving her arms to get my attention. And she's having to shout just to be heard above all the barking.

'Sorry, Leah,' I yell back. 'I'm sure he'll settle in soon. He's just got to get used to it.'

'He's been doing that since you left; it's driving me crazy.'

'I'll get it sorted.'

Though how, I've no idea. Kush explodes from the bathroom in a frenzy when I open the door; he almost seems pleased to see me. I take him up onto the roof and flop down in a deckchair. I'm finally starting to feel normal again. Going to the prison was a pretty good reminder of why I'm getting out. Clearly I'm still prone to stress reactions which can escalate way too quickly. Just as well I posted the letter.

But Klaasen.

I barely even recognized him, that's how bad his injuries were. And if he wasn't responsible for killing Lucie Muller, then . . .

Here was a man who'd always protested his innocence and I was finally starting to believe him. Only that line of thought would quickly lead back into panic; if he really is innocent, then I'm responsible for what happened to him. And what about Huisman? Why is he giving large sums of money to charity – and given what he must earn two thousand euros is a very large sum – then disappearing on holiday? And . . .

I breathe out a long slow breath. I tell myself none of this is my problem, that I need to relax, put it out of my mind. I shift my focus to the leaves shimmering over the canal water. They're already starting to colour and the occasional one breaks loose and flips its way down to the water's surface. But before I know it I've got my phone out and I'm googling the charity Huisman gave the money to. Roemers had sent me a text with the details, the name of the charity anonymous, 'FZC International', and Google comes up with nothing, apart from the register of companies and charities, showing that it was registered in Den Haag over ten years ago. But there's nothing else, no website, no contact details other than a PO box in Haarlem, no explanation of what the charity exists to do. Ten minutes later, with me none the wiser, I start to wonder how it is they solicit donations like Huisman's if there's absolutely no information about who they are or what cause they represent. How would Huisman even know about their existence? I spend a few more minutes trying to convince myself it has nothing to do with the case, with Huisman's disappearance. But I fail miserably. And despite my earlier resolve I realize this isn't going to leave me alone. I clamber down from the roof, the dog jumping down to the deck with more grace than I manage.

Hank's notes are there on the kitchen table and I sit down and open them up like they're a holy text which will furnish me with all the answers I need.

*

Words can eat away at you like a virus. There's no vaccine, you can't unhear them, and once they've registered in your head there's little you can do to stop their relentless march. At least I think that's what's happened in Vermeer's case, because my phone went off as I was taking a break and we're now talking. She's covering herself, though, playing up Jansen's involvement.

'Jansen has convinced me that you could be an asset on this case. So here's what I'm going to do. I'll talk to my station chief and, assuming he agrees, I'll find a place for you on my team. Purely in a consultancy role. But you've got to be clear on a couple of things.'

She reels off the usual: I work for her, I don't do anything without her say-so, chain of command, blah, blah.

'Agreed?' she asks when she's finished.

'Agreed.'

'You'll get a call. Until then you are not to do anything in connection with this case. Understood?'

'Understood. And there's something I think you should know.'

I tell her about Huisman's money and the payment to the mysterious charity which doesn't seem to promote itself.

'I'll get Roemers onto it; he's good at following trails. Anything else?'

'Not so far.'

'Good. Like I said, wait to hear from me. And, Rykel?'

'Yeah?'

'Don't make me regret this.'

I head back into Hank's notes, which are detailed and more orderly than mine tend to be. I follow the investigation through, all of it chiming with my own notes and I start to think there's nothing here. But as I'm reading I start to wonder about Jan Akkerman. If it turns out that he was covering for Huisman by fabricating an alibi, was that just to help a friend out? Or was he also involved? Were there, in fact, two killers? I run through it all again, focusing on Akkerman, though initially I don't find anything.

Three rings and Roemers picks up. I ask him to run a current location for Jan Akkerman.

'This is for your memoirs I take it? Because I had Vermeer down here chewing my balls off for giving you Huisman's details.'

'We've made up; I've joined the investigation now.'

'Really? So you won't mind if I check with her first?'

'Not at all.'

'Just fucking with you, Rykel. Give me a minute . . .'

I hear the furious staccato tap of keys. 'And . . . there are quite a few Jan Akkermans.'

'Scroll through, one of them should be tagged from an old investigation.'

'Nope, they're all clean.'

'What, all of them?'

'Well, there are a few speeding tickets, one of them's got a caution for chopping down a neighbour's fence, some kind of boundary dispute. It's all pretty hardcore stuff. Oh, here we go, there's one here who was accused of groping a woman at a night club. Police were called, but in the end she didn't press charges so he was just given a talking-to.'

'When and where?'

'Club 57, twentieth of Feb. this year. Isn't that the place Ron Koopmans works at?'

'Does he? Since when?'

'Yeah, must have been when you were . . . off sick. He took early retirement. Pretty sure he's now head of security there.'

I thank him and hang up. Club 57 is about ten minutes' walk away, west of Centraal station. I think about it for a few moments. Kush is busy excavating soil with his snout from one of the flowerpots. He keeps flicking his head up, causing sprays of dirt to cascade everywhere. Vermeer was pretty clear about not doing anything before I heard back from her. But the way I see it is this: Kush could obviously use some exercise, and if we just so happen to stroll past Club 57, then what of it?

Just over ten minutes later I reach the building. Despite the early hour the heavy thump of bass is audible way down the street. The guy on the door – black jeans, black shirt, a curl of white snaking out of his ear – stops me.

'No dogs allowed.'

'Ron Koopmans in?'

The guy's neck is almost as thick as his head, which is shiny-bald.

'Who wants to know?'

'Jaap Rykel.' He stares at me. 'Inspector Jaap Rykel,' I clarify after a few more moments.

He looks me up and down once before raising his arm and talking to his cuff.

A few minutes later Ron steps out through a fire door further down the building, and waves me over whilst he holds it open. He's a good head shorter than me, allowing me to see he's starting to thin on top. As if to make up for it he's wearing a beard, which I'm sure he never used to.

'Jaap, how are you? Long time no see.'

'Yeah, good.'

He looks at me as if he can see the lie, but doesn't comment. 'Come in.'

'What about him?' I point to Kush. 'Your guy said no dogs.'

Ron gives him the once-over, then shrugs. 'Frankly he looks more civilized than most of the customers here. Anyway, I'm head of security. Shall we?'

We catch up whilst he takes me through a series of corridors to his office, a room with a massive bank of computer screens covering just about every angle in the club's multiple rooms. A woman with spiky dyed-blonde hair and large hooped earrings sits in front of them.

'So, what can I do for you? Assuming this wasn't all social.'

I tell him about the report of a Jan Akkerman caught groping a woman.

'Honestly, it's not that rare an occurrence sadly. When did you say it was?'

'Twentieth of February.'

'Claudia, you remember that?'

Claudia turns to look at us. She's older than I assumed from the hairstyle; she must be well into her fifties.

'So many creeps,' she says. 'What was that date again?'

Ron tells her.

'You can look it up in the dailies then,' and she turns back to the bank of screens.

For some reason I get the sense there's something between these two. More power struggle than anything romantic, though. Ron rolls his eyes, sighs, mutters something about doing stuff yourself being the only way to make sure it's done right, and opens a laptop. As it's booting up he points to one of the screens on the bank, a bird's-eye view of one of the largest rooms in the club. The wall is made entirely of glass, opening onto a view of the IJ's waters. I realize I could probably see Nellie's house across the water if I were to go and stand in the room and look north.

'That's the one,' Ron says.

'The one what?'

'The window Tanya shot. It's like a legend down here, cost the owners *a lot* of money to repair. They weren't happy; their insurance only covered part of it. In fact, we've got it here somewhere. Claudia, can you put it on?'

Tanya had told me about this, but I didn't realize there was footage of it. It happened just a few days after we'd met, the separate cases we'd been working on crossing like fate. So much has happened since. All I can think is, I wish it hadn't.

She'd come to the club in search of a suspect in a child-kidnapping ring we eventually brought down. The suspect in question decided he didn't want to talk to her, however, and had assaulted her instead. Tanya was forced to pull her weapon, which would have put an end to it except the suspect had an accomplice who'd tried to take the gun off her. Which is when the shot was fired.

Claudia points to a screen, which was blank but now flickers on to show the main room, a few people in it. There's movement in the bottom-left corner, and my heart thumps as I recognize Tanya, her face visible for a split second as she wrestles with the man trying to take the gun off her.

'And . . . boom!' Ron and Claudia say in unison like an old couple just as a spark of muzzle flash appears, and the massive wall of clear glass frosts over in an instant. Then the whole thing falls away, the view restored. Tanya's no longer on the screen, but I remember that she'd managed to fight the guy off and single-handedly arrest both men.

'I love watching that,' Ron says as the image cuts to black. 'Awesome woman. You got yourself a good one there. Okay, here it is,' he says, having spent some time navigating various menus, clicking ever deeper into the belly of the beast. 'What do you want to know?'

What I want to know is why it's all so difficult, why I ended up hurting the only person I'd ever truly loved. Why I'm such a fuck-up. Why the black wolf is inside me and won't leave.

But all I say is, 'Everything you've got.'

'Not much, but . . .' He hits the enter key and a printer across the room whirrs into life just as my phone goes off. Vermeer.

'I've got something I need you to do,' she says. 'Marianne Kleine's sister Cheryl is landing at Schiphol airport just past midday. Jansen's going to talk to her and I want you with him. He'll pick you up.'

'I can do that,' I tell her. 'Does that mean I've been approved?'

'Not quite. There's something else you're going to have to do first.'

'Which is . . .?'

'Frank Beving wants to have a chat with you; he'll be the one with the final say.'

'When?'

'Soon as you can make it to the station.'

Ron hands me the paper and as he escorts me back through the building I ask him about civilian life.

'Thinking of getting out are you?'

'Might be.'

'Well, my advice to you is this, make sure you've got a proper job lined up before you send your resignation letter in. Otherwise you might end up doing something like this.'

'Can't be that bad, can it?'

Ron mimics hanging himself, head lopsided, tongue out of the side of his mouth and a strange gurgling sound which makes Kush perk his ears up. As I feel the draught of air from the security door closing behind me I see my hand slipping the letter into the postbox, a flash of white disappearing into the darkness.

Appropriately Medicated

'Obviously it's great to see you again.'

At the station I was directed to the third floor where I'm now enduring Station Chief Frank Beving's patented brand of deep sarcasm.

'Likewise, Frank. Likewise.'

'Of course, though, if I can be honest here, I wasn't that thrilled when Vermeer told me she'd like some help from you.'

The very definition of an oxymoron is Frank Beving being honest. And that's easy on the oxy bit, with a heavier emphasis on the remainder of the word. Though I'd never tell him that, of course. I'm also suspicious of people who tell you they are being honest, because in my experience they *never* are.

'I wasn't that keen either.'

Beving runs his tongue across his top teeth and studies me as he relaxes back in his chair. I've always thought he looks like Rutger Hauer in *Blade Runner*, probably helped by the electric-shock hairstyle he's worn ever since I first met him back at the academy. We didn't like each other then, and the years haven't done much to improve the situation. No softening, no *rapprochement*, just good old-fashioned smouldering antagonism.

'No, I can see that,' Beving is saying when I tune back in. 'After everything that happened I wouldn't blame you for walking away from this for good. But it's our duty to serve, is it not?'

His grin has a canine quality to it. Or lupine. Deep shudder up spine.

'It most certainly is.'

I get the feeling he's waiting for me to say 'sir', so I hold off on that, even though I want to get this over with as quickly as possible.

He finally gives in, his too-light-blue eyes with their yellow ring round the iris freaking me out a bit.

'So,' he says, tapping a closed file on his desk like he's sending out Morse code, 'I asked for a report from your therapist, and although she's not one hundred per cent keen for you to be back in action she did mention that you are being appropriately medicated?'

I think of the rainbow of pills swirling round and round the white porcelain before disappearing forever, maybe to be gobbled up by some daring, or just plain hungry, fish. I hope they're better for them than they were for me. Otherwise they'll be floating around in a daze with shit dribbling out their asses. I can picture it now, each squirt propelling them forward into another location. Those fish must be bewildered . . .

'Did I say something funny?'

Quick snap back to reality.

'Er, no. I *am* being appropriately medicated so I think I'll be fine,' I tell him, suddenly paranoid he can smell cannabis on me. I use it so much I've noticed it sometimes comes out in my sweat, a deep herbal odour which is pretty much unmistakable. I wonder if that means I should cut back a little. Then I think of what happened at the prison.

'You *think* you'll be fine,' Beving is saying, nodding his head gently whilst continuing to stare with his freaky eyes.

'I'll be fine. Really.'

He takes a few more moments as if to emphasize the gravity of the whole situation before speaking again.

'There's one thing I'd like to discuss with you before I consider allowing you back on. Whilst you're on this case I need you to report directly to me, is that understood?'

So that's what all this has been about. I knew it had all felt way too easy.

'Not to Inspector Vermeer?' I ask in my best puzzled way.

'You will of course be reporting to Inspector Vermeer on a day-to-day basis, yes. But you will also report to me.'

I'm getting a significant look. *Very* significant. Even a dullard would get his message; he wants me to spy on her. The question is, why? Is Vermeer plotting to take his job? Or is he just paranoid and wants to be prepared? She's smart, much smarter than he is, and also ambitious. Beving has every right to be worried.

'Is that understood?'

It seems like I don't have a choice.

Back at the houseboat I go through Hank's notes again, this time focusing not on Huisman but Akkerman. I find what I'd missed the first time, on page forty-three in the margin. An address is scrawled followed by the name 'Akkerman' and a question mark.

I do a mental check. Nope, don't remember that address. I cross-reference with my own notes, finding that my memory was correct – my notes have no mention of this address; the only one we had associated with Akkerman was down near Maastricht where Huisman had claimed to be when Lucie Muller was killed. So I'm not sure why Hank scribbled it down. Could Akkerman have owned a second property, or maybe it belonged to a relative?

A few minutes on my phone tell me that, according to the land registry, the property was bought in 1979 by a Marit Berkhout. Berkhout sounds familiar, only I can't place from where. I quickly go back through my notes and find the section on Akkerman. And there it is, buried in the background profile every major suspect has done: his mother's maiden name is Berkhout. Now that's what I call police work. The doorbell goes off, and I open it to two middle-aged women, one Dutch, one African. They're both holding glossy leaflets in their hands and the love of Jesus Christ in their hearts. Luckily Kush comes running, barking his head off at them.

'Satan,' I growl. 'Satan, down boy.'

Kush, bless him, stops barking and plays along almost as if he understands.

The two ladies are clearly appalled. They snatch glances at each other and one of them nervously fingers a cross dangling on a chain round her neck.

Once they've left my soul to eternal damnation I give him a bit of cheese from the warm fridge.

'Sir?'

Above me branches sway back and forth, micro-glimpses of sky in between. My back's cold from lying on the houseboat's roof. It's not the most comfortable thing I could be doing but the discomfort is grounding somehow.

Kush's tied up to the non-functioning chimney stack, and whilst he didn't appreciate it to begin with he has now settled down.

'Up here.'

A speedboat roars up the canal, making the houseboat rock just as Jansen gets to his feet on the roof.

'I see what Vermeer means; it *is* quirky up here,' he says, taking in the deckchairs and odd assortment of flowerpots, some of which actually contain plants. 'Ready?'

After my chat with Beving I'd been told to go back to my houseboat and wait, then Vermeer had called ten minutes ago saying we were on and that Jansen would be round to pick me up soon. I spent the time looking at the report Ron Koopmans had given me. It was just a single sheet of A4, a standard incident report someone knocked up in Word with printed boxes, some of which are filled in by hand. The handwriting itself is on the edge of being illegible, but I could just make out the sequence of events which ended with Jan Akkerman being expelled from the club. There was no photo of him, but the sparse description – male, average height, tattoos on both arms – fits with my memory, though it could equally apply to hundreds, if not thousands, of people in that area of Amsterdam alone. It did say he'd been with two other people, one of whom didn't have a name, but was just referred to as 'Snake'. I'd put a call into Ron asking who that was but was told he was out and would get back to me.

Jansen's ready to go, so I throw some food in the bath and Kush hops in.

'Where was her sister?' I ask as Jansen gets us moving south towards Schiphol airport.

'Bali apparently. She'd gone with her fiancé and a few days in they get our call. Best holiday ever.'

'She as high-flying as Marianne?'

'She's a journalist, freelance. Got the impression she's struggling, though. Her father told me there was a chance she was going to be joining Marianne's business at some stage; she's got a degree in biology, and the business was something to do with microbiome research, so makes sense.'

I'd read the file. Marianne and Cheryl's father is pretty high up in a large pharmaceutical company, so the old thing about apples not falling far from the tree seemed to be true in this case.

We reach Schiphol, park and are soon being ushered into a room by an immigration officer. Moments later the door opens and a woman is brought in. She has that slenderness I often associate with models, one which suits the camera but in real life can appear almost too willowy, too thin, giving her an aura of fragility. Mind you, having just got off a long-haul flight with nothing to do but come to terms with the death of your sister isn't going to be doing anyone much good. Her dark hair is tied up in a high bun. We'd been told her fiancé had to get a later flight.

She shakes hands with us both as Jansen does the intros and invites her to sit. The room has been designed to sniff out law-breakers; it's stark, the lighting's harsh, and there are no windows.

'Tell you what, how about we give you a lift home?' I ask once Jansen's sat down opposite her.

I'm rewarded with a grateful smile.

*

Traffic's picked up, and we end up crawling on the A4 back into Amsterdam. So far we've not spoken much, left her to her own thoughts. I know from experience how the death of someone close to you is an almost psychedelic experience; the whole world looks the same but different, as if you're viewing it from a millionth of a degree off centre. It's one of the most disconcerting feelings you can have.

'You never told me how she died,' Cheryl's saying to Jansen.

On the way down I'd asked Jansen if Cheryl had been told about how Marianne had been killed, but he told me they'd kept that from her for now. He and Vermeer had decided the shock of Marianne's death was enough without adding details into the mix; they could do that when they met face to face. Somehow I don't think this is quite the moment, though.

Jansen glances at me in the rear-view mirror. I shake my head.

Cheryl's place is the top two floors of a red and white brick house which is actually closer to a mansion. She may be struggling as a journalist, but from the looks of this I guess her father must have picked up the bill. He's obviously *very* high up in that company. We help her up the stairs with her suitcases and soon we're sitting in the living room with views over the green expanse of Vondelpark. It's a large space which looks to have been decorated by an interior designer; rich fabrics, vintage furniture and an array of abstract ornaments remind me of a boutique hotel Tanya and I stayed in just off Steinplatz in Berlin.

It'd been a rare Friday when both of us had finished cases and hadn't yet been assigned another. Tanya had the weekend off anyway, and I called in a favour and got someone to cover for me. We were lucky enough to get last-minute tickets for the seven-hour train journey and a late booking at a hotel we'd not normally be able to afford. We'd spent the nights pulsing to music in a club housed in an old brutalist power station and the days walking through the Tiergarten, trees ablaze with colour, exhausted but exhilarated too. We slept the entire journey home.

Jansen has the file with him and he hands it over to her. We sit in silence as she looks through it. A bird flickers past the window, casting a quick shadow across the room. She starts crying, tears dripping on to the photo clasped in her hand. Jansen shifts in his seat. I've found over the years that watching other people's grief can affect you in one of two ways; the first is empathetic, but I've also experienced the opposite, where grief can cause a sort of disgust. I don't know if it's a sort of defence mechanism, or something else. But I do know that if that hits you then you're not going to be able to talk to them effectively. Something about Jansen's face tells me he's experiencing the latter. I catch his eye, motion for him to leave. He's startled for a moment, perhaps that he can be read so easily, then nods, gets up and leaves. Cheryl doesn't seem to notice his departure.

'I've only just joined the investigation,' I tell her when I judge the moment's right, 'and I'd really like to get a feel for what Marianne was like.'

Cheryl wipes her eyes with a tissue then blows her nose. There's a ring on her finger: rose gold with a large oval diamond which catches the light. I've no doubt it's real. She takes in a deep shuddering breath then lets it out again.

'Marianne was . . . she was very single-minded. Even as a kid.'

'You grew up in Den Haag?'

'Until I was thirteen, then we moved to Haarlem because of Daddy's work. I remember Marianne kicking up a fuss about not wanting to move.' A little sad smile at the memory. 'She had her friends and didn't want to go.'

'She was shy?'

'Shy? No. It wasn't that; it was more like she just didn't see the need. But she didn't sulk like a normal kid did; she just threw herself into convincing Daddy that we didn't need to move. So she prepared a whole argument which she presented to him one weekend on bits of paper, all reasons why we shouldn't move. She was driven, I guess, is what I'm trying to say, didn't like to be told what to do.'

A quality which I know all too well can be a double-edged sword.

'But when Mummy died a few years later she changed, became more . . . Well, she became different. A little harder maybe. But I suppose we all did.'

Jansen had filled me in on the mother's death. Ovarian cancer, nothing relevant to the case. And yet sometimes these things are very relevant, just not in an obvious way.

'Tell me about her business.'

Her eyes flick towards mine for the first time, then away almost as quickly. So quick I wonder if I didn't just imagine it.

'I was due to be joining it in six months' time, but I can't really discuss it.'

'Why not?'

'Because like everyone else I had to sign a non-disclosure agreement.'

'Even being a family member?'

'Doesn't make any difference. Once she took the investors' money there was no question of me not signing. Not even she could force something like that through.'

'Why all the secrecy?'

'The company is focused on some research which could lead to a very significant breakthrough. And that breakthrough could make a lot of money. So no one who is involved with the company can say anything.'

'Any competitors, people who didn't want your sister's company to succeed?'

She shakes her head.

'What about her boyfriend?'

'Ruudy? Oh god,' she says as if she'd forgotten about him. 'He was devoted to her. I don't know how he's going to cope.'

She starts crying again. The thought that this might have been stopped if the investigation into Lucie Muller's death was handled differently needles at me. As we leave I can't help thinking that this is all on me.

Friends in Common

Jansen drops me off outside the houseboat.

I've lived here for eleven years and have been through so much during that time, it's like a floating memory bank, good and bad. In those shapeless days and months after the diagnosis it became both my refuge and my prison. And yet I still love the place, love the scuffed paint on the hull, the rich wood of the front door.

Which, as I'm standing here getting all sentimental, suddenly opens and a man I don't know steps out.

'Who the fuck are you?' I call across.

The guy squints up, puts a hand over his brow as if I'm blazing light from my body.

'You the owner?'

'Whaddya think?'

He nods like a puzzle's just been solved. 'I work with Willem; he couldn't make it so he sent me. Your neighbour gave me the key.' He points across to Leah. She has a welder's mask on and is attaching spent nitrous oxide canisters to an upturned bath in a brilliant shower of sparks.

'You're an electrician?'

'Yeah, yeah. Of course.'

I step over and give him a Rykel Special Stare, Popsicle Edition. It's cold, hard and long.

'I mean, I'm not actually *qualified*,' he says, his Adam's

apple bobbing a couple of times. 'But Willem told me exactly what to do.'

Great. So my real electrician outsourced the job to someone who isn't.

'All fixed then?'

'Good as gold now. All you have to do is turn on the main switch on the board and you're good to go. Willem said you'd pay cash?'

I'm not about to walk in and get myself electrocuted because some amateur doesn't know his live from his neutral.

'Show me first.'

He's as good as his word, though. He flips the main switch and I hear the fridge judder as it starts up. Kush barks from the bathroom.

'What about the cash?' he asks as I escort him off the houseboat.

'I never said I'd pay cash. Get him to send me an invoice. And tell him there's no urgency.'

I close the door and let Kush out of the bathroom. Far from being pleased to see me he nearly knocks me over as he rushes to the kitchen where I find him paws up on the counter nosing around. I suddenly realize I don't know how much a dog is supposed to eat. I consult the food packet I'd bought earlier, which helpfully gives me the number of grams per day per kilogram of dog. There are two problems with the instructions that I can see. The first is that I don't know how much he weighs and don't have a scale so I'll have to guess. But say I get it wrong and give him a little too much? Surely we'll get into a positive feedback loop? If I feed him a certain amount and he gains a little weight, then according to the feed chart he should get more food, which will then in turn . . .

I tip a load into his bowl and leave him to it. I'll sort out the exact amounts another day.

I do a quick check through the houseboat, flicking switches on and off, and, satisfied, make my way back to the kitchen where Kush is still deeply involved with nosing the bowl. It's like he believes by licking it more food will magically appear. He's got this technique where he'll gradually edge clockwise with his back paws whilst keeping his nose buried in the bowl itself. Round and round, the bowl slipping on the wooden floorboards.

'I think that's it,' I tell him.

I drag him away for a quick walk up and down the canal, then I pop him in the bath and close the wooden door. I'm preparing to leave when Kush starts howling and scratching at the wood. I can still hear him as I'm getting into the car. Leah's back on deck giving me evils. Two minutes later Kush's jumping into the passenger seat with a wagging tail.

Dog one, human zero.

Thing is, it was either piss off Leah or piss off Vermeer. Neither's really an option but Leah's the more immediate threat, not least because of the welding torch's blue flame, so I'll just have to think of something on the quick drive over.

The duty sergeant is on an intense-sounding phone call, undoubtedly being dumped due to his personality, and I manage to sneak Kush past him, who then proceeds to drag me up the stairs and direct to the incident room.

There are at least eight people at computers, and one wall is taken up with the murder board itself. Which doesn't have a whole lot on it, other than the photo of Marianne Kleine, which I wish I *hadn't* spotted the other day.

Jansen waves me over to his desk. He's looking tired, head resting on one hand whilst he scrolls through what looks like a never-ending bank statement.

'Kleine's bank account,' he says. 'Already been through it once . . .'

Vermeer walks in a few minutes later as we're discussing the case.

She's wearing jeans, a shirt undone enough to catch a glimpse of some sort of pendant, and a jacket that fits her like it's tailor-made. My hoody starts to feel a little scrappy. Jansen's got a shirt on too, I note. Maybe I need to dust off a few items from the back of the wardrobe, though I'm not sure there's much there apart from even older hoodies.

'Remember that thing I said yesterday about you doing exactly what I said?' Vermeer asks when Kush bounds up to her like a long-lost friend, trying to get her attention by any means necessary.

I just about manage to pull him off her. 'Look, I know. I'm trying to work out somewhere he can stay, so it's just for today.'

'Better be.'

She guides me to a table and sits down opposite me.

'So I spoke to Beving after your little chat, and he's willing to allow you to work under me until the case is closed, or I deem you're no longer needed.' She pauses like that last bit's significant. 'Here's the paperwork.'

I glance at the document she's just slid over the table; it's many sheets thick.

'You will need to sign it and adhere by it.' Another significant pause.

'Understood.'

'You know what the word "adhere" means?'

'I'll google it later.'

'Good. Google "appropriate clothing for a police inspector" whilst you're at it.'

I again wonder why Beving wants me to spy on her. Is he scared she's going for his job? She's certainly confident, and if her reputation is anything to go by, more than competent. Or could it be something else, something to do with the deep current of misogyny that some men swim their whole lives in? Knowing Beving the latter wouldn't be a total surprise.

Vermeer spends twenty minutes taking me through the major points of the investigation so far, mostly a rehash of what I already read in Jansen's file, before asking Jansen about his work on links between the two victims.

'The only things they have in common are that they're both female, and both relatively young when they died. Muller was brought up in Amsterdam, Kleine in Den Haag, then Haarlem. They didn't go to the same schools, they weren't Facebook friends, they never worked for the same companies, nothing.'

'There has to be something connecting them,' Vermeer says. 'And so far we've not come across anything that would suggest Marianne Kleine had anything to do with Huisman, and yet I think his disappearance, especially given his alibi for his whereabouts at the time of Lucie Muller's killing isn't as rock-solid as it was believed to be, is suspicious.'

'Did Roemers ever get anywhere on the charity he donated the money to?' I ask.

'Not yet, and we've come up with no holiday destinations either. He's vanished. No one knows where he is. Jansen, you were checking up on his property, I assume it was rented?'

'Sort of. It's actually council-owned. I got the name of the people it's supposedly being occupied by, a couple called Sharon and Gerard van Baalen. Turns out they split up and she got another property. I can't find any trace of Gerard.'

'It's an old game: get a flat with a wife, pretend to split up so she gets a separate property, both move there whilst renting out the first.'

'Thank you, Rykel. It's a wonder any of us have been able to do anything without your wisdom and perception. So we should probably talk to them. Don't know if they're going to know where he is right now but I'm not sure what else we've got. Jansen, address of the poor battered wife's property?'

'Not yet, working on it.'

'I've been thinking maybe there's someone else we should be talking to, his old friend Jan Akkerman.'

'I already thought of that,' Jansen says. 'But I can't find any trace of him.'

'Which in itself, given the circumstances, is also somewhat suspicious,' Vermeer says.

'About that . . .'

'Is there something you'd like to tell us, Rykel?'

I tell them about my visit to Club 57, and pull the report out from my pocket.

Vermeer picks it up and reads through it.

'So this Snake, who is he?'

'I asked, just waiting for a callback.' She looks at me with eyebrows raised. 'All right, I've been busy. I'll do it now.'

Ron is there now, I discover when I ring him, so I'm not sure why he didn't return my call. Not like he's rushed off his feet at his job. I put him on speaker.

'The report mentions someone called Snake. Any idea who that is?'

Ron laughs. 'Snake? Yeah, I know who he is. Guy practically lives here.'

'What's his real name?'

'Don't actually know. Claudia, what's Snake's real name? No? Really? No, she doesn't know either.'

'We need to speak to him.'

'Well, like I said, he practically lives here. He's in the lower bar mid-afternoon most days.'

'Do me a favour, call me when he turns up.'

'Anything else?' Vermeer says once I've shut down the call.

I get the uncomfortable feeling she can read my mind.

I tell them about Akkerman's mother's address. 'If anyone knows where Akkerman is, it's a good bet his own mother does.'

'And Akkerman might know where Huisman is.' Vermeer looks round. 'Anyone got anything better?'

It seems not.

'Let's do it then,' she says. 'We've got a few hours before "Snake" is supposed to appear anyway.'

I'm up already, Kush leaping into action, followed by Jansen, when Vermeer speaks.

'Wait,' she says to me. Then she turns to Jansen. 'I'll go with Rykel; you carry on working on a connection between the two victims.'

'But I –'

Amazingly she actually silences him with a stare.

Just before I leave I lean across to Jansen. 'Check friends in common.'

'What?'

'Facebook. You said they weren't friends, but did they have any in common?'

'I didn't check that.' Jansen's cheeks colour. 'I'll do it right now, sir.'

As Vermeer and I exit through the front reception area I hear an angry voice.

'Oi, I said there were to be no dogs other than official police dogs in here. My job's bad enough as it is without having to sit here smelling dog piss all day.'

I turn to see the same duty sergeant as yesterday. He's got the gaunt look of the long-distance runner, and the clamped jaw of a pedant.

'Look, I'm sorry, but he's young and I'm sure –'

'He's doing it again!' the man screams.

I turn round to see that Kush has returned to the scene of the crime and is wantonly committing the exact same offence in the exact same spot.

Once outside I give him an ear scratch. 'Good boy,' I tell him.

'That's hardly responsible dog ownership,' Vermeer points out.

'No, but the guy's a bit of a dick. Drama queen. Should be made of sterner stuff.'

'Agreed. He *is* a bit of a dick.'

She mimics his pissy reaction so well I can't help laughing.

'By the way, *I* do the driving,' she tells me.

'Whatever you say, boss.'

According to Hank's note the house number is twenty-seven and we're currently sat outside three. A short walk down the street shows us we may have a problem. There's a gap in the row of houses, from twenty-one to twenty-nine, a canal glittering beyond. I check the address; this was definitely it.

'What the hell is this?' Vermeer asks.

'Crane fell on them,' says a voice behind us.

We turn to see an old couple who've just squeezed out of the door of number twenty-one. They're ruddy-cheeked and sparkly-eyed with the kind of grins you usually associate with the criminally insane. Break out the pointy hats and you'd have a perfect pair of garden gnomes.

'What? The houses?'

'Flattened them completely,' the man adds, nodding his head a bit too fast. There's a fixed quality to his gaze which speaks of some inner pain, despite the grin.

Now that they mention it there's a ghost of a memory, from maybe last summer. Not that I can remember much. Things were at their worst. The black wolf fully in control. I lost days back then. Weeks. The anxiety ferocious, unrelenting. Sleep a thing of the past. I'd had flashbacks. I'd also had periods of time unaccounted for, complete blanks in my memory. I'd suddenly find myself somewhere with no knowledge of how I got there, or what I'd been doing. In a way those were even more scary than the flashbacks. I feel like those days were stolen from me.

'There were two cranes lifting a huge steel plate to fix the bridge,' the woman says, pointing across the water. 'The first one fell, and it took the second one with it. Totally destroyed the houses.'

I turn to look at the gap again. The ground hasn't been completely cleared. A loose layer of rubble is accumulating wind-blown rubbish. A seagull lands and starts jabbing at something I can't see.

'We're looking for Marit Berkhout,' Vermeer tells them.

'Hers was one of them,' the woman replies with grim satisfaction. So much for survivor's guilt. 'She'd just got back from the doctors. I was talking to her not five minutes before it happened.'

'That must have been terrible. Did you know her well?'

The woman looks at both of us in turn, suspicion in her eyes for the first time. 'Who are you?'

'Police.' Vermeer shows her badge. 'Did you know her son?'

'Jan? Never met him, but we *heard* about him a lot, didn't we? She was so proud of him, never talked of anything else. Jan this, Jan that, Jan's getting big in the film business. I never believed her, and he never came and visited. Must have been too busy making a name for himself.'

'Do you know where he lives now?'

'No idea.'

Back in the car Vermeer again takes the wheel.

'That was a bust,' I say as she pulls out into traffic. 'What now?'

'If she left a will, there's a chance she named her son in it.'

'Doesn't necessarily mean there'll be contact info in it, though.'

'No, but I'm not sure what else we've got.'

Alphen aan den Rijn is a small town, and as such it takes us just over an hour to find the firm of lawyers who'd dealt with Marit Berkhout's affairs. Vermeer has sent me in on my own, saying she had some calls to make.

From the outside it looks imposing, a double-fronted unit with smoked-glass windows. Inside the carpet is threadbare and there's a hint of damp or mould in the air.

'How cute,' says the receptionist as Kush gives her proffered hand a thorough forensic analysis with his nose. She'd come out from behind her desk the moment we walked in, and squatted down, waiting for Kush to approach.

Soon there's baby talk and stroking, Kush lapping it up like he's been starved of affection his whole life.

'Hi,' I say.

She reluctantly leaves Kush and goes back behind her desk. 'How can I help?'

I explain that my colleague had called less than twenty minutes earlier.

'Oh, you're the police?' She seems dubious, but picks up the phone and has a quick conversation with someone.

'Henny Beernink can speak to you. Thing is, he's scared of dogs but you can leave him here with me if you want?'

A good liar she is not. But it's kind of sweet she'd go to

such lengths so I hand Kush over and follow her directions to Beernink's office, which I find at the end of a corridor where the smell of mould is even stronger.

By the looks of things Beernink's overdosed on whatever supplement gives you an abundance of jovial bonhomie, and before I've even sat down I know the name of each of his three kids, his wife, and that he enjoys windsurfing at the weekend. What an exhausting amount of effort for him to go to just to get me to like him. Especially as it was doomed to fail right from the start.

'So you'd like to make a will?' He finally gets down to it and I see all the bonhomie was pure salesman. As is his suit, tie and side-parted hair, which he keeps sweeping back with a nervous hand. I also see that the pretty receptionist was so busy plotting out how to get some quality time with Kush she'd clearly not given this man the full story. I lay it out for him now. He listens, adopting a more sober mask as I go through exactly what I want.

'Of course we can get the files for you. I will need to see some ID, though.' He flashes me a pained smile, which tells of a world of rules that he'd love to be able to break because what a pain in the ass they are, but his hands are unfortunately cable-tied behind his back by the system.

When I go back outside, Vermeer's deep in conversation with someone on the phone, so much so that she doesn't see me until I'm right close by. She covers her discomfort well once she spots me, holding her hand over the phone's mic whilst she talks to me.

'Lost your dog?'

'They definitely handled her affairs, but they're not going to give them up without a bit of badge waving.'

She rolls her eyes. 'All right.' She tells whoever's waiting on the line she'll get back to them and follows me inside where she duly slaps her badge down in front of Beernink.

'You got it from here?' she asks me, but heads back out before waiting for an answer. Whilst Beernink taps away furiously on his computer – Vermeer seemed to have quite the effect on him – I think of Beving and his demand that I had to keep tabs on her. Once again, I wonder why.

'Okay, got the file references here,' Beernink says, hitting the enter key with a flourish. 'Oh.'

'What?'

'They've been archived.'

'So unarchive them.'

'They're actually kept off-site. We have secure storage for all our clients' documents and –'

'Surely you've got something on the computer?'

Beernink shakes his head. 'We only keep files we're currently working on on our servers, though it's true that if the client corresponds with us via email we'll have more. Many of our elderly clients don't use email, though, and from what I can see here Marit Berkhout was one of those.'

'It's really important we see those files; how long is it going to take to get them?'

Beernink checks his watch. 'I'll try for today but it may be first thing tomorrow.'

'It's going to need to be quicker than that,' I tell him.

Back at reception Kush is lying on his back, front paws praying mantis style, having his chest rubbed by the receptionist.

'He's so cute,' she says, not even looking up. 'Cute, cute, cute, cute, *cuuuute*,' she says, rubbing his belly some more.

Kush lets out a low groan of pleasure.

Vermeer, on the other hand, lets out another type of groan when I tell her where we're at. She's leaning against the car, arms crossed, a frown on her face. Beernink walks out of the building and across the car park to a silver Lexus. He does a half-wave to me as if he doesn't know whether it's appropriate or not.

'Looks like you've got a new friend,' Vermeer says.

'We bonded over legal stuff.'

'He's going to the archive now, is he?'

'That's what I told him to do.'

The Lexus reverses out in a smooth arc as Vermeer's phone goes off. Kush strains at the leash, trying to sniff a patch on the ground, darker than the surrounding asphalt, which is just out of reach.

'What have you got?' Vermeer asks. 'Really? Okay, send it to my phone.' She hangs up. 'Get in.'

'What is it?'

'The couple who sublet the flat to Huisman? Jansen's found the poor battered wife's new address. They might be able to shed some light on Huisman's disappearing act.'

Lifestyle

We pull up to find the street itself is actually blocked off to traffic. A team of workers in hi-vis are clustered round a mini digger, so we have to park right at the end and walk. Kush stays in the car; Vermeer is quite clear on that point. I hope he doesn't try the chewing-the-steering-wheel trick again. We reach the house number Jansen had got for us, the place the couple who'd illegally sublet their council house to Huisman were now staying. The small digger starts tearing at the road with its mechanical claw; it's almost poetic in a primal machine kind of way.

'According to Jansen, Gerard and Sharon van Baalen got divorced and this is the property Sharon was subsequently assigned.'

'How much you want to bet they're both living there now?'

As we pass the mechanical claw it scrapes along the concrete. The noise is ear-splitting.

'I do the talking, got that?' Vermeer shouts at me as we're reaching the front door. She keeps her finger on the bell until there's movement. The man opening the door is classic benefit cheat; it's written all over his tracksuit bottoms, the bulge of his stomach, the piggy eyes, the food stain on his T-shirt, and the shit-faced attitude. To say nothing of the expensive trainers.

'Gerard van Baalen?'

The acknowledgement is minimal so Vermeer invites herself in. The man looks for a second like he's going to complain but then steps aside. At the back of the house a living room is dominated by a massive TV screen. I've never seen one so big. On it some kind of zombie video game is paused, a head just in the first stages of what is going to be a gory, messy explosion. By the sofa opposite it are a few empty cans of Amstel in a thicket of bottles which once contained much stronger stuff. Breakfast of champions. Paid for by the state, no less. There's an over-powering scent of chemical air freshener. All the electronics are plugged into an extension cord that snakes across the scuffed lino floor.

Vermeer pulls out a photo of Huisman and holds it up for the man to see.

'You know him, right?'

You can tell he's used to dealing with authority; his stare's a bit zombie-like itself. And he can hold it for an impressive amount of time, especially given Vermeer's intensity. Or maybe he's just very well medicated. Finally he breaks his eyes away and glances at the photo, but remains silent.

'Let me put it this way,' Vermeer says when it's clear the man doesn't think he has to talk to her. 'I know you know him, I know that you and your wife have screwed the council out of two properties by going through a fake sep-aration and that you now rent out the flat they gave you to fund your *lifestyle*. And I also know that the person renting it is this man, who has, it seems, disappeared. So I'd like you to take this conversation a little more seriously.'

Gerard shrugs. 'Never seen him.'

'In which case I'll be forced to make a phone call to the council and let them know about your little scheme. Fair to say, I don't think they'll be that pleased. You'll probably lose both properties. Then where will you sit around and jerk off to computer games?'

Upstairs there's the sound of a door opening, footsteps, a toilet lid being raised. Whoever it is vomits hard, the heave and gush following a hard night's drinking. Must be the lovely lady of the house, Sharon.

'What do you want?' He's got a sullen look now.

Toilet flush, footsteps retreat.

'What I want is for you to spill your guts as effectively as that.' She points to the ceiling. 'You know this man, and I want to know how to contact him.'

'Like I say, I don't know him. It was done through a guy; he handles the clients and takes a cut of the rent.'

So Gerard has an agent in the middle.

'We need to speak to him,' Vermeer says.

But Gerard, having just admitted to defrauding the government, and therefore his fellow citizens, slumps down on the sofa, picks up the console control, and starts wasting zombies like Vermeer and I don't exist. Time for a tried and tested psychological approach. I step forward, slap the controller out of his hand and drag him to his feet.

'Did you not hear what she just said?'

He looks at me like I've just swiped his last candy.

'I can't tell you that. People like him don't like to be found.'

I release him and he bends down to pick up the controller again.

'What about this?' Vermeer steps up to him, all reasonable, cajoling almost. Then she screams in his face. 'Where is he?'

Shocks the guy. Shocks me too. But it gets through to him.

'All right, fuck. No need to shout. I don't know his name and I've only ever seen him a couple of times.'

'Description.'

'My height, average-looking really. Head's shaved, though. And he wears glasses.'

'He sounds like a demigod. How do I get to meet him?'

'I've got a number on my phone.'

On the way out I accidentally stumble over the extension lead. Just hard enough to yank it out of the socket. Back in the car there's a strong smell of dog, but I'm pleased to see the steering wheel's still attached and doesn't appear to have too many tooth marks. Kush's actually curled up asleep on the back seat.

'So we've got the middle man's number,' Vermeer says. 'He'll have had direct contact with Huisman. How best to approach him? If we call and ask to speak to him, he's just going to disappear, given that what he's doing is illegal. Right now he's our only link to Huisman. I don't want him doing a runner.'

One of the men in hi-vis steps up to the hole and suddenly starts waving frantically to the digger driver. The claw stops moving. More men cluster round to peer at whatever caught the first man's attention. One, the leader I guess by his slightly more upmarket hi-vis, gets on the phone and starts gesticulating a bit manically. Something's clearly up.

'Give me the number.' I pull out my phone.

'You're not going to call him?'

'Yeah. As a prospective client.'

She looks at me then shrugs. 'All right, go for it.'

On my phone I punch in the number and compose myself. Then I place the call. Someone picks up on the fourth ring.

Who?

Incident room, late afternoon. Those present: Vermeer, Jansen and a bunch of junior staff I've been introduced to but whose names are going to take a little while to get straight in my head. The mood: sombre. Vermeer's briefing everyone, and her clear and professional delivery makes me wonder if the reason Beving wants me to spy on her is purely because he's afraid. Aside from the strangely private phone call she was having outside the law firm, from what little I've seen she's more than competent, and a better cop than he'll ever be. And really, wanting to keep a conversation private is hardly suspicious behaviour.

She raises a laugh when she recounts to the small team an account of my impersonation of a would-be benefit cheat, telling them that it was Oscar-worthy stuff. Whatever. She can scoff – it got a result.

The man on the phone had been monotone and guarded. Nonetheless, after having told him I had a council property which I wanted to sublet on a long-term basis he was interested, and he agreed to meet. Which we're doing this evening.

Kush, I notice, is not much of a team player. He's the only one in the room not paying attention, instead exploring the space with his nose. He seems particularly entranced by the open bin close to the door. Vermeer finishes up and throws it open for questions.

'You checked they didn't have any friends in common?' I ask Jansen.

'Nothing.'

I glance at the map on the far wall, the location of Kleine's death marked by a red dot.

'We need a map of the entire country.'

'What are you thinking?' Vermeer asks.

'Apart from both being killed in the same way there's so far been no link discovered between Muller and Kleine. And the person convicted of killing Muller is not only in prison, he's incapacitated. And yet someone killed Kleine in exactly the same way. So far the only possibles have been Jan Akkerman and Robert Huisman. Huisman has conveniently disappeared and we're still trying to locate Akkerman. But assuming that either he or Huisman, or both of them, *are* responsible for a moment, we've still got the question why? Why these two victims? They're both young women, but neither showed any sign of sexual assault, and they both look different – different hair colour, different style, different body shapes – so they're not an obvious type. So why did he pick them?'

'Could just have been opportunity, sir?' says one of the bright young things, a woman with dark shiny hair tied tight in a bun and quick, focused eyes.

'Could be, but the way of killing seems so specific, so planned, that I can't help think there's more to it than that.'

'Do you think they knew their killer, sir?' Jansen asks.

'I've got no evidence to say they did know their killer. It's just a theory, which is our job to prove or disprove. And part of that is ruling in or out any connection between the victims. Let's get a map of the whole country up and track their movements on it.'

'How far back?' Jansen asks.

'Couple of years before Lucie's death at least. Maybe more.'

Jansen nods, though I can tell he's sighing inwardly; what I've just tasked him with is massive.

'And we also need to keep in mind that this may not stop with Marianne Kleine.' I look around the room, making sure everyone's tuned in. 'Two identical deaths, what's to say there won't be a third?'

'What, in another seven years?'

'Seven years, seven months, who knows? But it's our responsibility to make sure it never happens.'

The team gets to work, Vermeer disappears, and I decide to drop in on Roemers, to see where he's got on the payment Huisman made just before Kleine's death. I head to the tech department, an airless room in the basement where Roemers is king, only to find the chair at his desk is empty. When I ask the nearest person, a middle-aged man who blinks a lot and never quite looks you in the eye, where Roemers might be all I get is a shrug and something about Roemers keeping his own counsel.

Back upstairs I get a call from Ron.

'The Snake is in the nest,' he says. 'Repeat, the Snake is in the nest.'

I'm not sure Ron's coping that well with leaving the police force. I try not to think what that bodes for me. Am I really ready to give this up?

I call across to Vermeer, letting her in on the news.

'Right, back in the car,' she says. 'Oi, what are you doing?'

Everyone jumps, but it turns out she was directing

herself at Kush, who now has his head deep in the bin. When he pulls it out he has a *stroopwafel* wrapper in his mouth. In the car pool I load him into the vehicle, having divested him of his prize.

'Tomorrow you need to find somewhere for him to stay,' she tells me as we head off.

'Might not be a tomorrow.'

'I know you had a breakdown but, damn, that sounds pretty pessimistic.'

'No, what I mean is, there might not be a tomorrow because if we get lucky the guy we're meeting will be able to tell us where Akkerman is. And I'm starting to feel he's just as involved as Huisman. And if *that's* true, we find one, we find the other.'

'We can hope,' she says, nosing out into traffic. 'We can hope.'

The walls are vibrating, Claudia has been replaced with a young man who looks like he's severely hung-over, and the club itself is fuller than it was earlier.

'Do none of these people have jobs?' Vermeer asks.

'It's bewildering, right?' Ron says. He's been drooling over Vermeer since we stepped in a few moments ago, and isn't showing any sign of letting up. 'I mean, just who the fuck are they? It costs a fortune to get in, the drinks are massively overpriced, it's not even five o'clock on a weekday, and yet here they are.'

We all marvel for a minute at how the other half live before I ask where the man we're interested in is. Ron speaks to the hung-over man who points to a screen marked LOWER BAR, LEFT CORNER. There are a series of semicircular booths all facing a stage. There's a shiny pole in the middle of it, though as of yet the act hasn't started. There are people in each booth, and the man points to one with three figures.

'Snake's the one in the middle.'

By the time we make it down there the show's started. A woman in sparkling bright green high heels, red hair that's got to be a wig, and a few scraps of fabric the same colour as the shoes strategically dotted around her body, is listlessly going through her act. Her eyes, when you glimpse them, show just how far away she is. Not that the punters seem to notice, they're still drinking and cracking jokes with each other, all the while allowing their eyes to feast on the woman's body.

We walk up to the table where the man known as Snake is and stand right in his view.

'Fuck are you?' he asks. 'Out the way, babe.'

'I haven't been called that in a long time,' I tell him. 'What's your name?'

He looks me up and down with a curl of the lip. Doesn't respond.

'What's your name?' Vermeer repeats.

'Snake.'

'Your real name.'

'Didn't you hear?' says one of his companions, a man in a patterned shirt, enough buttons undone to show the tattoos rising up from his chest to his neck.

Vermeer flashes her badge. 'Get lost,' she says without even looking at him. 'You as well.'

Snake stares at her, picks up a toothpick out of a little ceramic holder on the table and tries to dislodge something, probably imaginary, from between his teeth. Finally he nods and both men get up and walk away, taking their tall glasses of beer with them. The tattooed one glares at her as he goes past. Vermeer gives him the best fuck-you smile I've ever seen.

Once they've gone Vermeer speaks again. 'Bit too seedy in here. Let's go outside.'

Snake blinks in the light. The lighter flicks on with a chirp and he brings the writhing flame to the cigarette end dangling from his mouth. He takes a big draw. A long reverberating ship's horn blares across the water behind him. I look up to see the same cruise ship I'd seen from Nellie's gliding along the IJ, heading for open water. People on the deck wave towards land even though no one's returning the greeting.

'Yeah, I remember the guy,' he's saying. Now he's away from the others he hasn't exactly become cooperative, but there's a little less bravado in his manner. 'He was really aggressive, basically kicked off and got us all thrown out.'

'And that wouldn't be anything to do with you dealing drugs?' Vermeer asks.

'I'm not dealing anything, just there enjoying the show with a couple of mates.'

'Every day?' I ask. 'Doesn't it get a bit boring?'

'I like watching women dance, what can I say?'

'Did he ever buy from you before?' Vermeer asks.

'Like I said, I don't know what you're talking about; you can search me if you like.' This was directed to Vermeer. 'Don't forget here.' He grabs his crotch.

'If you're searched it'll be back at the station by a couple of my male colleagues,' Vermeer says. 'They don't really have a soft touch, and they're *very* thorough. So, tell us everything about him.'

'I've seen him around a bit. One night he got rowdy with us and got us all chucked out. Not seen him since, lucky enough for him.'

'We need to speak to him. Any idea where we can find him?'

'No idea, hardly knew the guy. And like I said already, pretty sure I've not seen him since then.'

He resists all further questioning and eventually we let him go. As we're walking away he calls out to us. 'Hey, wanna know why I'm called Snake?'

'No.'

He sticks his tongue out and waggles it around. And there it is, a split making his tongue slightly forked.

'Botched tongue-tie operation when I was a kid,' he says. He sticks it out and waggles it again, before walking away, his fist raised, middle finger pointing right at the sky.

Back at the station we each go our own way, frustrated that yet another lead has just crumpled. But a couple of hours later Beernink comes through for us. He gets me on the phone, telling me he's pulled the files from his off-site storage and is now sitting in his car in the car park going through them.

'Anything which might tell us of Akkerman's whereabouts?' I ask.

'We've got a correspondence address which was in use just over nine months ago when Akkerman's inheritance was finally settled. Do you want it?'

'Phone number, email?'

'Not so far. I'll carry on going through, if you need . . .?'

I get the feeling he wants to go home.

'Give me the address, and if you get anything else then call me back.'

He tells me and I relay it to Vermeer who punches it into her phone.

'Look at that, less than ten minutes away from the flat Huisman rents. Didn't you say he used to live in Maastricht?'

'Yeah, and now he's moved close to his old buddy's place.'

'And then someone else dies in a way which perfectly matches a murder Huisman only got off from because of an alibi given to him by his BFF.'

I check the time; we've got a little over thirty minutes till I'm supposed to be meeting the man who handled the sublet.

'Think we've got time to check it out?'

'Let's do it,' Vermeer says.

Soon we're turning into a street west of the Jordaan. The house we need is one of a row of council houses, many with Turkish flags hanging limp in the windows. Last year the Netherlands government turned away a series of Turkish politicians who'd come to the country to whip up support in their up-coming election, causing the then Turkish prime minister to compare the country as a whole to Nazi Germany. Unsurprisingly there's been tension here ever since.

'Not the kind of place I'd expect someone like Akkerman to live,' Vermeer says as we near the number we're looking for.

'Because he's not Turkish?'

'Because he's surely got more money than this, what with his inheritance.'

We find the number. No Turkish flags on the property, which is a good sign.

Vermeer presses the doorbell and steps back.

Footsteps in the hallway, the gravelly slide of a chain, the creak of the door. The woman standing there is my age or older with long brown hair tied up in a loose bun, a harried look about her face. She's holding a wooden spoon in one hand and a bouquet of supermarket flowers, dead but still in the wrapper, in the other. She also has eyes the same colour as Tanya's. But I'm not thinking about Tanya. I'm just not. Maybe I should be thinking of Sabine instead.

'Yes?' she asks, looking between us.

'We're looking for Jan Akkerman,' Vermeer says, holding out her ID.

'Who?'

Vermeer pulls out a mugshot I recognize from the Lucie Muller file.

'Oh, *him*. He died four months ago. Didn't you know?'

Oscar

The street lights are flickering on as I walk onto the small triangle of grass. The man I'd spoken to earlier about subletting a flat had chosen this place to meet. I'd tried to suggest somewhere but he'd been adamant: his rules or not at all.

We'd hardly spoken on the drive, the frustration at finding we'd been chasing a dead man keeping us both self-contained. It also threw into stark relief just how much we've got riding on this meet yielding results; if this fails, then we've got pretty much nothing. Also, I've not been able to sneak away and top up today, and I'm starting to feel a little jittery.

Which is bad because now all I have to do is wait. I choose a bench and try to look the part. Vermeer had earlier critiqued my attire, but as I'd stepped out of the car she'd commented that I actually looked the part. I gave her the middle finger, which just made her smile. All told, I'm starting to like her.

The air seems to be thickening around me. There's an overflowing bin nearby and something's rustling inside it. A young couple stroll hand in hand, oblivious to anything but each other. It reminds me I'm due to meet Sabine in a couple of hours. Which leads me on to Tanya, what Nellie had said earlier. I shouldn't be feeling guilty about meeting Sabine, and yet there it is: guilt in all its ugly self-torturing, gut-churning glory. It swirls around me, swirls inside me, and before I know what I'm doing I've pulled my phone out and am thumb-typing a message to Tanya, which, once started, never seems to end. I read it back, then delete it all. My clammy hands shake as I put my phone away. An old man carrying a crumpled plastic bag shuffles painfully past and a young woman on a moped drones by.

A few minutes later a man slides onto the bench next to me. He's short, wearing a similar tracksuit to the man Rashid had ID'd. He smells like he hasn't washed in a while. He's got a black string bracelet and doesn't look at me when he speaks.

'Help you?'

'We spoke earlier about the flat.'

'What you need?' he asks.

'I need to rent my flat,' I tell him.

'What you need, heroin, crack, meth?' he says again.

'I'm good,' I tell him.

'Heroin?' he asks one more time.

I shake my head.

He finally takes a long, disappointed look at me, then gets up and walks away.

Half an hour later I send the man I'm waiting for a message, asking where he is. The little bubble pops up so I know he's typing a response. It seems to take an age before disappearing again. I wait for the message but none comes. I wait a few more minutes, the jitteriness increasing with each passing moment, before deciding I've waited long enough.

I reach the car, parked three streets away to avoid

detection, where Vermeer's just finishing yet another phone conversation. She hangs up when she spots me, and, seeing the look on my face, gets out. Not for the first time I wonder who it is she's always talking to.

'No show?' she asks.

I shake my head.

'This case,' she finally says. 'Jesus. What now?'

'I don't know. I feel like we're hitting a wall here.'

'There must be a way to find this guy. He can't have just disappeared –'

My phone goes off.

'Hang on, maybe this is him.' I pull it out to see it's a message from the man. It's almost eloquent in its simplicity.

FUCK U COP

It's followed moments later by a second message, a smiling turd emoji.

It starts as a simultaneous pressing in and a swelling up from somewhere deep inside. *My heart's racing, I'm freezing hot, I feel sick as the raging black wolf erupts inside me. The jitteriness goes into overdrive. My vision clouds as I blaze to black . . .*

I'm trembling, sitting on the kerb. I can hear barking. My heart ramps up again, before I realize it has passed. The barking is Kush in the car.

'Jesus,' Vermeer says.

She's sitting beside me, and she removes her arm, which I now sense was over my shoulders. 'You okay?'

There's a weird taste in my mouth, sour and metallic.

'Yeah . . . I'm all right.'

She looks at me. There's concern there. Doubt too. She

hands me my phone, the corner dented, the screen snaked with jagged cracks.

'You threw it at the ground,' she says in explanation. I press the home button and the screen still lights up, the messages still just visible.

'Guess that Oscar isn't in the running after all,' Vermeer says, having looked at them.

I take a big, long breath in. I put my head back and stare at the sky.

Police Brutality

I'm sat on a bench up by the Lekkeresluis waiting for Sabine to turn up. For some reason I keep thinking that Tanya will appear and see me with Sabine. I try to shake that thought off, but before I can I hear Nellie's voice in my head telling me to contact her before it's too late.

Earlier Vermeer dropped me off at the houseboat and the first thing I did was to go on the roof and roll a joint. Being unable to medicate during the day meant I'd succumbed easily to the rage, the black wolf, the thing that isn't me but seems to be trapped inside. The darkness within. If I'd been able to keep my cannabinoid levels up during the day it wouldn't have happened with such severity, and the come-up would have been long enough for me to have done something about it. But I'd been caught up in it all, the investigation taking over my mind, and I'd welcomed it, felt good about doing the work again. Part of me thought that I was strong enough now, that I could do this on my own. Seems that part of me was wrong.

Up and down the canal, elm trees are scattering leaves, their delicate forms picked up by the street lights, and Kush has been amusing himself by staring at the water-birds that float past every so often, their jerky head movements contrasting with their stately glide. He freezes when he spots one and I notice his legs tremble a bit, as if he's holding himself back from jumping down the metre or so into the water, swimming over and tearing them to shreds.

'Hey . . . Jaap?'

Kush explodes into an orgy of barking and I turn to see Sabine. She's in tight jeans, a long-sleeved tunic which hangs down past her knees and has a scarf wrapped round her throat. Those bruises must have shown up. She looks worried by the ferocity of Kush's reaction. Strange, I've not seen him like this before. Maybe it's just because he didn't hear her coming either. I manage to calm him down a bit, though I see Sabine's still nervous. Whether about meeting me or because of Kush I can't tell. But then she was the one to contact me, so I just need to get out of my head and say something before she thinks I'm an idiot.

'Sure you haven't been followed?'

Sabine laughs and it's like a musical scale rising up and down. It all seems so surreal. Yesterday I was hauling a man off her and today we're out on a sort of date.

'Could all be a plot. First I'll seduce you and then get you to kill him for me,' she says.

'Been done before. Many times.'

She sits down next to me. Kush eyes her suspiciously, then goes back to scanning the water. We chat for a bit, and it seems surprisingly easy given how out of practice I am.

'So, is it exciting being a cop?' she asks.

I watch a few more leaves tumble through the air as I think of everything that has happened today, every glimmer of hope fading away to nothing. The knowledge that a man we suspect of being involved in two separate murders has disappeared and we've so far been unable to find him is not exactly exciting. Intensely frustrating would be a better phrase.

'I'm not a cop any more.'

'Really? You look too young to be retired.'

'Hormone treatment. Amazing what you can buy off the internet from dodgy Russian websites.'

'Trouser trouble?'

'Not those kind of hormones.'

She gives me a playful nudge. God, how I've missed this. I manage to stop myself from telling her that. We've only been here twenty minutes or so, bit too early for that sort of thing. *Just hold off*, I tell myself.

A slight breeze blows her hair across her face and she flips it away with a brief shake of her head. Exactly like Tanya used to do. I suddenly wonder how I've ended up on a date with a woman who is so similar.

'Something wrong?' she asks. 'You're looking at me strangely.'

'Nothing, it's just . . .'

'Just what?'

It would take so long to explain. And I don't really want to. I'm sure she doesn't want to hear it anyway. Talking about your ex on a first date isn't the smoothest of moves.

'Never mind. Wanna do something fun?'

'As long as it's legal.'

'I'm a cop, remember.'

'Ex-cop, I thought?'

I think about that for a moment. Kush's nose is leading

him over the canal edge, a floating bird the target. I tighten the leash.

'It's complicated. Shall we?'

The resonant, jangling Westerkerk bells strike one in the morning.

'You mind?'

Sabine pulls a cigarette out of her jeans, now a crumpled heap by the bed. She props herself up on the pillow.

'Go for it.'

I wonder about joining her with a joint, but I'm startled to realize I don't feel I need one. The power of a good evening out with an even better end. The only downer was Kush, who'd been in a stroppy mood all night, to the point when we'd got back here I'd put him to bed in the bathroom and closed the door. I wonder if dogs get jealous. He certainly hasn't taken to Sabine. Well, tough. He'll have to cope.

Next to me Sabine's lighter flickers to life briefly.

'Never slept with a cop before. Not bad.'

Earlier in the evening I'd found out she was ticklish. I apply that knowledge now until she's squealing for me to stop.

'That's police brutality,' she finally says when she can talk again. 'I might have to report you.'

'Good luck with that.'

She finishes her cigarette, taking the butt to the kitchen, and I notice as she steps out of the room a mark on her lower back I'd not seen earlier, a line of raised scar tissue. When she's back in bed I ask her about it.

'That guy, Tom.'

'The one I met?'

'Yeah.'

The mood's changed now, and I regret asking.

'It's funny,' she says after a while. 'When I first met him I had this strong sense of him being the one, y'know? And it *was* good. We were good together, for the first six months or so anyway. You'd think that would be enough time to get to know someone, but it clearly wasn't.'

'What happened?'

'It was weird. The change came so suddenly. We'd gone to the beach at Zandvoort, you know it?'

I'd been there with Tanya, and I remember with crystal clarity. It was the last time we'd gone anywhere together. 'Yeah, been there a few times.'

'I liked it there. I used to go as a kid, and I wanted to share that with Tom. I remember we had grilled fish for lunch, and a beer. In the time I'd known him Tom never drank, said he didn't like the taste of alcohol. But he didn't mind if I did, and I was feeling great; here I was on a sunny day, out by my favourite beach with the man I was starting to think I loved. So I had a beer with lunch, and he joined me. I didn't think much of it, but then he ordered another one, and another. I was a bit surprised, but he seemed happy and we were talking about the future and . . . Well, you can probably guess what happened. We were heading back. I was a little tipsy but it had hardly seemed to touch Tom. At the station we bumped into an old colleague of mine, a guy I'd worked with a few years before and we'd chatted for a few minutes whilst we waited for our train, just the usual kind of thing. Tom changed during the ride back; he got quiet, sullen almost, and I wondered if he wasn't feeling well. Maybe the fish, or just the fact he'd had a few beers and wasn't really used to it. So anyway, later that evening, I was getting a glass of wine from the fridge, and I closed the door and got a real shock: he was standing in the kitchen doorway and there was something different about him, about his face. I asked if he was all right, and he just lost it. I mean full-on-crazy lost it. He started ranting and raving, accusing me of fucking the old work colleague. That's not normal, right? You might say "seeing" or "sleeping with", but he was insistent that I was "fucking" the guy behind his back. So we argued. I told him he was just being paranoid, that he needed to calm down, but of course that just made him madder. But he didn't hit me that night. The next morning he was so sorry, apologized over and over, begged me to forgive him. He blamed the alcohol, said that he couldn't handle it, which is why he didn't drink, and that I wasn't to let him drink again.

'If I'd known about alcoholics then I would have got out right away, but I didn't. I told myself he was sorry. I believed him when he said it wasn't going to happen again, that it was going to be okay. Stupid. But it was okay for a couple of weeks, and I was almost forgetting it when he came home later than usual one night. Which is when this happened.' She reaches her hand round to her back. 'I threw him out after that, but he kept coming back late at night, banging on the door. I had to call the police, your lot. Have to say I wasn't that impressed; this guy just told me to stay inside. So I terminated the rent and got another place. Seemed like the only thing to do.'

'But then he found you again.'

'That was just bad luck. I was walking home from work

and I heard someone call my name. He was at that bar, standing outside on his own, having a drink.'

'You think it was?'

'Was what?'

'Bad luck?'

'Well, it wasn't good luck. Unless you mean because we got to meet . . .'

I agree with her. But what I really meant was, was it simply bad luck Tom had been there on her route home? Or something else. Something more akin to a plan?

I fall asleep thinking I might just look him up on the system tomorrow.

The whiskey started off rich and full and peaty. A whole world to dive into after the long day. Now, at the bottom of the second glass, it just tastes harsh, tastes like alcohol and little else. He knows he should be going to bed; he has to be back in the office first thing, but with all that's going on he's not been able to sleep. The whiskey had seemed like a good compromise. He's just considering popping a couple of painkillers, the ones he swallowed earlier to stave off the migraine not enough to see him through the night or fend off the assault the single malt is going to mount in a few hours, when his phone lights up.

'Bad news. My source there says he's actually on the team now, officially.'

'Where is he now?'

The words feel a little off in his mouth, not exactly slurred but just . . . off. He hopes it's not obvious.

'He's been out all evening with a woman, but he's back at his houseboat now.'

'I'm beginning to wonder if we shouldn't act pre-emptively. I've been told we can send a little message.'

'Thing is, the woman's still with him. At this stage it's fair to assume she's staying the night, which kind of complicates things.'

'Keep watching. There'll be an opportunity; you just need to be ready to take it.'

He washes a couple of pills down with the last of the liquid and goes to bed, where he finally drifts off right before the alarm sounds, bright and jangling and painful.

Two Days Before

Sorry

Morning. Consciousness unfurling like a sticky tentacle. It takes in my body, the smooth warmth of the sheets; it takes in sound, the hum of the fridge, the cry of seagulls; it takes in that Sabine is no longer here, though I can still smell her perfume on the pillow. It also takes in the fact that I only had one dream where I heard footsteps on the roof and the wail of sirens.

Which overall is a massive improvement. There was a time when I barely slept for weeks on end, days merging into night and back again until I thought it would never end. Those were the months after I'd been put on medical leave, months of emptiness which somehow still managed to be full of angst. Some days I paced round the houseboat for hours on end, unable to leave, unable to make a decision on anything. I thought I was going crazy. And whenever I did finally manage to drift off through sheer exhaustion I'd be treated to a Technicolor mash-up of every dead body and every crime scene I'd ever attended. I remembered details I didn't even know I knew with startling clarity, and when I checked old crime-scene photos I'd find that, sure enough, my mind wasn't making this stuff up. I felt the cumulative shock of each murder like sickening body blows, my heart rate constantly high. I lost track of the times I woke up sweating and screaming and shuddering.

It's ironic that the only thing that helped lessen the

frequency and intensity of those episodes is a plant that is only semi-legal. What the tourists don't realize is that although the selling of cannabis in coffeeshops is tolerated, the supply chain behind it all is still a criminal enterprise. Growing it, curing it and transporting it poses a real risk of prosecution, and it's only once the package is dropped off at the coffeeshop itself that you're in the clear. The whole thing is beyond insane. I'd busted enough grow rooms in my time before making inspector on the homicide squad, and it'd been done with a sense of righteousness which now makes me cringe. Many times the grower had claimed it was medicine, believing that their drug was actually helping, not hindering them, a claim I'd dismissed as addicts in denial. Now I wonder how many of them were like me. I marvel at the fact that life has a startling tendency to switch up on you. Or a tendency to be just plain perverse.

I get up and open the bathroom door. Kush clambers out of the bath and follows me through to the kitchen where he stretches, front paws out, back concave and head down as if he's praying to some kind of doggy deity. Which he kind of is, because I Am the God of Food. I dispense some in a suitably grand manner and leave him to it. I check my phone, and there's a text from Sabine saying she had to leave early, and that she'd had a great night.

It's misty outside, and the thick black paint coating the deck is slippery with moisture. Silver with it too. Tram bells clang over on Rozengracht and cyclists glide in and out of the mist. There's a strong smell of tar which I think must be coming from Leah's boat. I lean against the side rail as I take my first pull of the day.

*

174

Contrast with the station. Bustle, noise, chaos and stress.

Turns out the sirens of my dream might have been real. A man had sprayed a liquid into a crowd of revellers at Rembrandtplein at just past two in the morning. The liquid has yet to be fully identified, though clearly from its effects it was a strong acid, and the whole incident has been declared terror-related. Which means Vermeer's team has been pruned back to the bone, the bone in this case being Vermeer, Jansen, myself and just two junior officers. And Kush. Because I can't leave him on board all day, and don't know what else to do with him.

Vermeer raised an eyebrow when I walked in, but I notice that just ten minutes later he's positioned himself next to her and she's absent-mindedly stroking him whilst she works on something on her computer. Jansen has joined us in the meantime; he'd been out for a run and had walked into the office in socks, carrying a pair of expensive running shoes and huffing and puffing like he'd just completed a twenty-four-hour Iron Man. A wedge of sweat darkened his T-shirt. Vermeer took one look at it and told him to clean up, and quick.

With the numbers so low the project of tracking the two victims' movements over the last couple of years has ground to a halt, though I note that they'd got a few points up on a map before they'd been reassigned last night. I stare at it, trying to see something, a pattern that's so far been missed. But nothing leaps out at me.

I remember my resolve from last night, and access the system, intending to search for Sabine's ex. But I don't have his surname, and the incident report from the bar the other night makes no mention of it either. I debate texting her and asking for it but decide against it. Then I dial down to Roemers; I want to see if he's got anywhere with the charity Huisman had donated to.

'What charity?' he asks when I speak to him.

'The money Huisman sent to the charity. We talked about you finding out more about it? Remember?'

'Yeah, I remember now. Got sidetracked. You still want me to look into it?'

I tell him I do want him to look into it. Preferably right now. I put the phone down to find Vermeer looking at me.

'You okay?' she asks.

'Fine.'

'You'll tell me if you're not, right?'

'I will.'

She takes a few moments as if to assess whether she can trust me or not, then seems to come to a decision.

'All right, got something for you. We've not yet spoken to the chief operating officer at Marianne Kleine's start-up, but given how stuck we are I think it's probably worth doing. You up for it?'

'Sure, when are we going?'

'We're not, you are. I've got a few things to do. Here are the details.' She hands across a sheet of paper. She pauses at the door, looks on the verge of saying something, but then leaves.

With the meeting set up in half an hour I'm quickly going through what I can find on Kleine's start-up when Roemers calls back.

'Not much to report. Whoever set up the charity did it in such a way that it's hard to find out anything about it.

The only concrete thing I've got so far is their correspondence address, which is a PO box. Anything else is gonna take quite a while to unpick.'

'There's no phone number? No way to contact them?'

'Only thing I can find is the PO box.'

We seem further than ever from finding Huisman, and this is pretty much all we've got. I tell him to do it. He sighs and tells me there's no way he has the time or resources.

'Where's the PO box?'

'Why, you gonna stake it out?'

'No. I'm not.'

But Jansen is. At least that's my plan. He doesn't sound thrilled when I swing the idea past him. He suggests a uniform instead. I tell him to do whatever he needs to do. He agrees, and leaves to sort it out.

Before leaving, I speed-read what I'd managed to find on Kleine's start-up, the main point of note being that two months earlier she'd raised 1.5 million euros in VC funding. From all the press releases it was quite hard to work out what the business was actually for, and the website didn't help much either. It did have lots of cool sliding animations and pictures of impossibly happy people doing everyday things: a large wristwatched man plays golf, an old couple hand in hand are caught mid-skip on a tropical beach, a woman with arms raised hits the finishing-line tape whilst a blurred crowd go wild. None of which really tells me anything. The only constant between all the images that I can make out is their dazzling white teeth. Maybe it's a dental start-up? Jansen had said microbiome, maybe oral microbiome?

'Right, let's go and find out what they're all grinning about.'

I'm expecting Kush to leap up at my words, maybe even bark, but all I get is silence. I look around; I can't see him anywhere. Where's he got to? There aren't any females in the room, just one guy plugging away at something on his laptop in the corner.

'Have you seen my dog?'

'Err . . . no, sir. What's he look like?'

'Albino, three legs, no tail. Teeth like a walrus.'

'Sorry, sir.'

I'm starting to wonder about the hiring policy. A quick search in the outer office reveals I may have a problem. I'm standing by a desk, the bottom drawer of which is open. Inside is a very expensive-looking running shoe. Just the one.

I eventually find Kush in the far corner, tucked behind a trolley of water-cooler bottles, doing his best to utterly destroy the missing shoe. He's actually got his front paws pinning it to the ground whilst he tugs at the fabric with his teeth. I have to say he's doing a pretty good job. I take it off him and make threatening gestures but he seems completely unconcerned, simply jumping up and trying to reclaim his caught prey. Back in the incident room I drop the ruined shoe on the table in front of laptop man.

'I'm going out to chase down a lead. I need you to get another pair of these. Identical size and colour.'

'I'm not sure I understand, sir.'

'Just Do It.'

He looks at me blankly. Christ, does nobody know their corporate slogans any more?

'Just Do It. Nike.'

Blank stare.

'Never mind. Just make sure they're identical.'

'Yes.'

'Yes?'

'Yes, sir.'

'Be quick.'

As I've not yet signed the papers Vermeer gave me I don't have any ID which would ordinarily be required to sign out a car. I'd rather take the Stang, but it's back at the houseboat and I don't really fancy the walk. So I try going down to the car pool anyway and am rewarded for my positive thinking, because who should I meet but Mark Sattler. We go through the long-time-no-see routine, then he asks me about the car.

'Yeah, I bought it.'

'Let me guess, still in pieces.'

'You're such a downer, you know that? I actually got it working just yesterday. Been driving it quite a bit since then.'

'Really? Good on you.' He slaps me on the arm. I think the wound opens up again. 'Like to see it sometime.'

I tell him any time, but that I need something from the pool just now. He sorts it out, overriding the sergeant's objections and signing for it himself, then tossing me the keys. I press the button and the car that beeps turns out to be a cruiser with POLICE DOGS written on the side and a cage in the boot space. Kush is hesitant, but I finally get him in. The look he gives me as I lock it shut is the worst kind of emotional blackmail, but as there's been little in the way of contrition over the Eating of the Shoe I ignore it.

*

Amsterdam's Silicon Valley is what the press call it. Which says something about the standard of journalism these days, because when I pull up in the valley I find it's nothing more than a fairly average street where a few old houses have been converted into spaces with blond-wood floors, glass walls and huge whiteboards, and then rented out to a range of hopefuls, none of whom look like they've even left school yet.

I'm here to meet the chief operating officer, Patrick Wust. But he doesn't appear to be anywhere around when I reach the front of the building. A young intern, dressed in what I guess is geek chic, is working his phone hard, eyes glued to the screen, thumbs a blur. I look up at the building: typical merchant house, five storeys of red brick with a stepped gable and pulley system jutting out of it. I was once called to an address on Herengracht where a naked man had been found hanging from one almost identical. I met Tanya for the first time during that case, an investigation which ended up with both of us kneeling on the deck of a container ship with a bent cop called De Waart about to blow our brains out. No wonder I got sick.

'You okay?'

I look up to find the geek has momentarily suspended his thumbs and is looking across at me, concerned or puzzled it's hard to say.

'Yeah. Just waiting for someone. Patrick Wust, you know him?'

'I do,' the geek says. 'Are you the police?'

I see him looking at my Baja hoody with frank scepticism. Though it is the predominantly grey one, I suddenly realize I look like one of those painfully obvious undercover narcotics officers. Jesus. All I need is some dreads and some out-of-date street slang and I'll be good to go.

'Yeah, I am.'

'Oh, r*iiiiiiii*ght. Undercover.' He nods like he's digging it. 'I'm Patrick.'

Chief operating officer. Unbelievable. At his age I'd just finished at the academy and still had to wear a uniform.

He leads me into the building and up the stairs to the top floor.

'We closed down when we heard . . . the news,' he says as he fishes out a key chain. 'But we're planning on re-opening the office tomorrow. I . . . oh.'

He's seen what I've just spotted, that the door is open a crack.

'That's odd.'

I motion for him to step back. Whoever opened the door did so without a key. They used a well-aimed kick. I suddenly wish I hadn't left Kush in the car. I toe the door open. No gunshots ring out. I step into the room and my heart's pounding but it's soon pretty clear that there's no one hidden inside. The place has been trashed, though. Tables overturned, chairs jumbled up, a water cooler on its side, a large puddle darkening the floorboards. There's also a ping-pong table which has been split in half, and a series of beanbags have been slit open, tiny white polystyrene balls dancing in the draught I've created.

'Don't think you're going to be reopening tomorrow,' I call out to Patrick who appears in the door frame. 'You've had visitors.'

*

The coffee place has a mix of Patrick-lookalikes and serves a range of rare coffee from minuscule plantations in far-away and, I'm sure in some cases, made-up countries. The walls are plastered in sepia maps, the current bean menu is chalked up on a large blackboard behind the baristas, and filling the air there's that jaunty anonymous jazz usually reserved for when you're stuck in a lift with someone you don't know who has clearly just farted.

Compared to Rashid's, this place feels like it's trying too hard. Especially when the relaxed vibe is shattered by a bearded barista telling me that no dogs are allowed inside, but we're more than welcome to sit outside. Normally I'd take that to mean I'm more than welcome to spend my money elsewhere, but this is work so I let it slide. We grab a table and order our drinks from a waitress who's bright and bubbly and probably cries herself to sleep at night, whilst Kush sniffs the ground and ruminates on the inequality still present in twenty-first century Holland.

Across the street there's a dirty white delivery van, the driver of which looks familiar but I can't place him. Was he someone I'd arrested back out on the streets? Or was he just questioned in relation to a crime? Or . . . maybe I'm just being paranoid.

After seeing the state of his offices Patrick had got jumpy, making several calls in quick succession, and talking to me didn't seem top of his list. I'd had to insist, just after I'd made my own call. I had to go through Jansen to get uniform out to secure the offices. Now, here in the cafe, I turn to Wust and spend a few minutes getting his background, before asking how long he'd known Marianne Kleine.

'Just over two years. I met her at one of those network-ing events they put on for start-ups and we got talking. Next morning I get a call offering me a job.'

'And what was the business doing, something to do with the dental industry?'

'Dental?'

'Your website . . . It's full of smiling people with very white teeth.'

'Oh, yeah. It's just a holding page; we're getting ours developed, should be ready soon. But to answer your question it's not dental. We're doing microbiome research.'

Which doesn't really answer my question at all.

His phone is on the table face up and he keeps checking the screen. I reach out and flip it over. The look on his face says he can't believe I've just done that and for a moment I think he's about to react. But it passes. I'm starting to see glimpses of the future COO he's going to become. Most people are intimidated in a situation like this, but he seems to be holding his own. Mind you, maybe if I'd dressed up a bit things might have been different. Tomorrow I'll def-initely pull out something a tad smarter.

'Which is?' I ask him.

'The thing is, I can't really go into details. We've all had to sign a pretty strict confidentiality agreement so that nothing leaks before we're ready to launch. But essen-tially, we've got more bacteria in and on our bodies than we have cells. Traditionally medicine has viewed them as nothing more than a nuisance, unless they get out of balance and an infection occurs, in which case you kill them with antibiotics. Thing is, that model was so overly simplistic it looks barbaric now, because it's caused almost as many problems as it solved. Kleine saw this and started to think of ways to manipulate the microbiome in far more subtle and precise ways. A few years later here we are.'

'What exactly did she discover?'

'That's as much as I can disclose.'

'I get that, but your founder has been murdered, and your office has just been turned over. Maybe that changes things?'

His phone buzzes twice. The shake of my head stops his hand.

'Honestly? I don't know. I'd have to talk to my lawyer. I'm pretty sure the agreement stays in place, not least as we're most likely going to carry on.'

'You can carry on without Kleine?'

'The investors put a lot of money into this; they're not going to want to see that disappear.'

'So the break-in doesn't worry you?'

'All our computers and servers are safeguarded; the information on them would be overwritten even if someone tried to clone the hard drives, so I'm not worried.'

'Whatever Kleine came up with, did it have the potential to upset more traditional lines of treatment?'

'Disrupt? Obliterate more like.'

'So anyone invested in the old way of doing things wouldn't like to see this succeed?'

'You tell me,' Wust says.

Kush is bored, so he rolls over onto his back and squirms around, trying to reach his own tail. When he fails to catch it he stands up, shakes his whole body, then lies down again and rests his chin on my feet.

'What about enemies, anyone she'd clashed with recently?'

'She could be abrasive, but you have to be to get something like this going. And the pressure increased with the funding she'd got. All those investors were suddenly interested in what's going on, and some of them would drop in unannounced. That really hacked Marianne off, but there wasn't a lot she could do about it. I know she spoke to her father about them. I think he just advised grinning and bearing it for the moment. If anyone knows how to weather a shit-storm it's him.'

'What do you mean?'

'The company he worked for, DH Biotech, went through a rough patch years ago. Something went wrong, I think, and he'd been on the front line. Marianne mentioned it once. Something like that would normally put an end to a career, but Pieter-Jan Kleine's a fighter and now he's really high up in the same company. She looked up to him, wanted to have that kind of fighting spirit. And she did, until . . .'

I show him a photo of Huisman I'd pulled from the file.

'Recognize him?'

Wust looks but shakes his head. 'Don't think so. Who is he?'

His phone's buzzing again, a call this time. The noise sets Kush off.

'Look, I really need to . . .'

'Get it, but we may need to talk again.'

As he answers his phone I scribble down my number and hand it over. 'In case you think of anything,' I tell him. He takes it and nods, listening intently to whoever's on the other end of the line.

There's something in what Patrick's said which has set off a small jolt somewhere in the back of my brain, but I can't quite work out what. As I'm pondering this, walking back to the car, a man calls out to me. I turn to see the bearded barista taking a break, cigarette in hand.

'What sort of dog is that?' he asks, as if trying to make up for earlier. The cigarette hangs precariously from his lips whilst he lets a little bit of smoke escape like he thinks he's Bogart or something.

'Chihuahua,' I tell him. 'Pure-breed chihuahua.'

I step across to the offices, which have already been taped off, a lone junior officer standing guard. A quick glance around doesn't reveal anything that looks significant, and I'm just about to leave when it hits me, that little jolt I'd felt when talking to Wust. Marianne Kleine's father works for a pharma company called DH Biotech, and it strikes me that I have some distant memory of Lucie Muller's father being on the board of a large pharma company as well.

I drive away with the question buzzing round my head: was it the same one?

Back at the station I find Vermeer in the incident room alone.

'Lonely at the top.'

'Hey, Kush,' she says, ignoring me.

Kush rushes to her and she fusses over him for a minute. He laps it up, a big doggy grin on his face. It's amazing how quickly he's wormed his way into her affections; she's gone from a strict no-dog policy to this in no time at all.

She finally acknowledges my presence. 'So, what have you got?'

Well, two can play at that game.

'In a minute.'

I locate a laptop, pull up a browser and launch into cyberspace. By the time I find what I'm looking for the room has a couple of extra people in, some I recognize, and Vermeer looks like she's calling a meeting. I join them at the round table in the centre.

'Any updates?' Vermeer asks me.

'How about this? A link between the two victims which –'

'Who has my shoe?' Jansen demands from the doorway.

Uh-oh. We all turn to look at him, standing there with one shoe in his hand and a bereaved look on his face.

'What shoe?' Vermeer fires back, visibly annoyed.

'The other one of these. Someone's gone into my desk and taken it and I want it back.'

For some reason he sounds just like a child on the verge of a screaming tantrum. Looks like it too.

'I'm serious,' Jansen says. 'Who's got it?'

For a moment I wonder if he's going to burst into tears. I look around to find the man I'd tasked with buying another pair, but he's not here.

'Really, we've more important things to discuss than your shoe. Sit down and we'll get on.'

Jansen sits, but it's with considerable bad grace. He places the shoe on the table in front of him.

'Rykel, carry on.'

'Up until now the only thing the two victims had in common was their mode of death. But I've got another connection here. Marianne Kleine's father was involved in a pharmaceutical company, DH Biotech. The thing is,

I remembered that name from somewhere. Took me a little while to track it down, and, sure enough, Judge Muller was –'

'Rykel!' I look up to see Frank Beving's at the doorway. 'You've not been here a day and you're already starting to piss me off.'

I have that effect on people. But in this case I've no idea why. Beving steps into the room and tosses a box onto the table we're sitting round. His aim's good, and it slides across, spinning as it does, and hits me in the chest with a sharp corner. It's plain white with the black swoop logo.

'You are not to get junior members of staff to run personal errands. You want to buy some running shoes you can damn well go and get them yourself. On your own time.'

Once he's left I push the box across to Jansen, now glaring at me.

'Sorry. From Kush.'

He takes the box and opens it up, checking them over with frank suspicion.

Vermeer clears her throat. 'If everyone's happy now, let's hear what Rykel has to say.'

'Yes, let's,' Jansen replies, glaring at me.

I don't like the accusatory tone. Neither does Vermeer it seems.

'About the case,' she clarifies.

'As I was saying –' I avoid Jansen's incendiary gaze. '– Marianne Kleine's father was involved with DH Biotech. Now if you look at these company records you'll see a familiar name, Koen Muller, also known as Judge Muller, Lucie's father.'

I let that all sink in. Here I am, less than a day in, and I've found the link between the victims. Vermeer must be impressed.

'Oooookay,' Vermeer says. 'And?'

Well, if so, she has a funny way of showing it.

'There is no "and". Yet. But here is a possible connection between the victims: they were both the daughters of people involved with DH Biotech. I think that warrants a little more excitement.'

'All right, look into it. Jansen, I need a word. If you've got over the shoe thing?'

Heads swivel. We all wait.

'At least they're the right size,' he concedes, pulling one out and inspecting it from various angles. 'But the colour's different.'

'What about the PO box?' I ask him. 'Any movement?'

'I've got someone waiting there,' he answers, still stroppy. 'I told them to call me if anyone comes to collect.'

He puts the shoes back in the box, gets up and walks out.

Client Confidentiality

Despite Vermeer's lack of excitement about my theory, I decide to tackle Judge Muller, but he takes some tracking down. First I try the courthouse on Parnassusweg, but I'm told he'd retired nine months ago. The address they give me out towards Amsterdamse Bos turns out to have been sold to a developer who'd taken the large double-fronted red-brick pile and turned it into a warren of tiny flats, presumably with an eye to housing midgets. A call-back to the station and a helpful junior officer puts me right, working out that he'd bought a property in Purmerend, a half-hour north of the city.

I'm driving the police dog cruiser again and wish I was back in the Stang, though Kush is much quieter when travelling caged in the back. I start to think the Stang's maybe not the best car to have if you own a dog. Thing is, I worked so hard on it there's no way I'm giving it up now. Kush'll have to adjust. The E22 is relatively quiet and as I drive I think about the best way to approach the judge.

Throughout the investigation into his daughter's death Muller stepped well over the line multiple times, and yet, because of who he was, got away with it. The pressure had started off a light trickle, but as the days progressed it turned into a torrent, which made Hank and me feel like salmon swimming upstream. His daughter had been killed in an horrific way, so it was in many ways understandable, but the constant meddling with our investigation, the phone calls, the chance meetings, the outright interference got old, fast. At one point he'd even threatened to have us both removed from the case as he felt it wasn't moving quick enough. I told him, to his face, to do it. Funnily enough he didn't follow through.

I pull off the main road and within ten minutes I'm turning on to a private drive lined with trees. The house zoetropes in from my left through the trunks as I navigate the long curving driveway deep with gravel. Reaching the house I park and wonder how he's going to react when I walk back into his life.

The house itself is impressive. Big bay windows, ornate stonework and a Virginia creeper creeping over large sections of the brickwork, the cooler evenings having turned the leaves bright red. As I get out of the car I accidentally knock the siren and lights on, startling several crows which explode into the air from a large beech tree. It takes me half a minute to work out how to turn them off again. Not that I try that quickly. Petty, I know. I get Kush out of the crate and clip his leash on.

After the sirens the doorbell seems distant, ringing somewhere in the depths of what is an enormous property. Kush decides to mark one of the box balls planted either side of the entrance. He lifts his leg and squirts out a long jet of pee, most of it missing the bush and hitting the wall behind just as someone who clearly isn't ex-Judge Muller opens the door.

'Yes?' she says in an accent heavy with decades of Soviet repression.

I tell her I have to see Judge Muller. She eyes me suspiciously, then throws a look over my shoulder to the car. Finally she looks at Kush, who for some reason is being well behaved for once, sitting by my side like a fully trained dog.

'Judge Muller doesn't like dogs.'

I tell her that Kush isn't a dog – he's an officer of the law.

She gives me a hard look, then shrugs. 'Follow.'

We do, through a hallway with chessboard tiles, a large living room with Dutch masters hanging on the walls and a musty air, another hallway smelling of wax, and finally a wooden door at what must be, by now, the back of the house. She knocks, then goes in, closing it behind her. A minute later I'm ushered into the room.

At the far end a figure sits in a wheelchair, silhouetted against one of the three large windows looking onto a formal Italianate garden beyond. Bookcases line the walls, right up to ornate plasterwork, and a Persian carpet lies on wooden floorboards, dark and shiny with age. In the space above a gaudy chandelier hangs, and a clock on one of the shelves ticks a dry metronomic beat. I notice on a separate set of shelves a series of framed photos of Lucie Muller, starting with her as a baby and sequencing right up to her early twenties.

The figure in the wheelchair turns laboriously, inching one wheel forward and one back, and I see he's hooked up to a grey metal canister, the clear tube snaking up to his thin nostrils held in place by straps stretching behind his ears. He's dressed in mustard cords, a checked shirt, and has some kind of tweed jacket complete with elbow patches. To go with that he's also wearing a blank expression, making me think he doesn't recognize me. Maybe something to do with the clothing. And thinking about it my hair's a bit longer than it was when we last spoke. His own hair's cut the same as I remember, but the blond has lightened to almost complete white now.

'Was that you making all that racket?'

'The dog knocked the siren on when he was getting out of the car.'

Muller peers over his glasses at Kush but doesn't say anything.

'You are? The stupid maid didn't catch your name.'

'Inspector Rykel. Amsterdam Police.'

'Undercover division I see. Right, take a seat.'

He clearly runs his house like he ran his courtroom. I find a leather armchair and once I'm in it he wheels closer, bringing his canister with him. At one point it nearly tips over and Kush lunges for it. Luckily I have the leash held tight so I just about manage to stop a major incident. I go to help right the canister but Muller waves me off and I'm forced to watch his slow and laborious progress.

What a change grief can make. Before, he was a powerful man, the type who have a density about them capable of pulling together whole rooms of people. Now he's shrivelled down, whatever illness landing him in his wheelchair undoubtedly induced by the stress of his daughter's murder. I've seen it happen before, the death of a loved one like the first domino to fall.

'So why are you here?' he says once he's finally finished.

I sit forward in the chair and tell him about Marianne Kleine's murder, how the particulars match exactly that of his daughter's death. He listens with an intense stare which makes me think his eyesight's deteriorated.

'I know you, don't I?' he says when I've finished.

For a moment I wonder about brazening it out, but decide it's probably not worth it.

'I was the investigating officer in the case of your daughter's murder, yes.'

There's a long pause whilst he nods his head ever so slightly, eyes fixed on me.

'Yes, I remember now. I didn't think you were doing a very good job at the time. You and that other one.'

'Hank de Vries —'

'Yes, that's the one —'

'— is in a coma, injured in the line of duty.'

'Well, sorry to hear that,' Muller finally says with a distinct lack of real feeling, at least to my ears. 'But I still don't understand why you're here.'

Before coming I'd done a little digging on DH Biotech. The main thing I'd discovered was that the man in front of me and Marianne Kleine's father had both been there during a two-year period before Muller left. What my digging didn't tell me is what contact they may have had during that time. So I start by asking him about the company.

'What about it?'

Am I imagining it, or has he just sharpened up? I tell him about Kleine's father, Pieter-Jan.

'Never heard of him,' he says. 'I was on the board. The only people I dealt with were the COO and the CFO.'

'He was head of research; he never presented anything to the board?'

'Maybe, I can't remember. It was years ago after all, and a lot has happened since.'

'Tell me about the company.'

'Why? It has nothing to do with anything.'

'Just indulge me.'

We have a little staring game, which I obviously win, as he draws a breath in and starts talking.

'DH Biotech was formed by Didier Hoffman with the intention of finding a cure for MS. Over the years they did a lot of research and got several drugs into stage-three clinical trials. Unfortunately none of them passed. It's a rigorous process and the fail rate is high across the board. It can take years to get a drug to market; the amount of testing that has to go into any drug is phenomenal, and costs considerable amounts of money. Each new compound you're testing is a lottery, because it can fail at any stage during the process. Obviously the further through the process you are the more has been invested. Failure can therefore be *very* costly.'

A brief look at their accounts had shown they were a very profitable business, with the exception of one financial year where they posted a loss of several million euros. Which was presumably linked to the shit-storm Patrick Wust had mentioned.

'And that's what happened?'

Muller looks out of the window, though I can't see what it is that's suddenly caught his eye. On one of the shelves I spot a series of photos of him. One in particular strikes me. In it Muller stands wearing an expensively cut pinstripe suit, his hair blond and cut short. He's shaking another man's hand whilst accepting a small trophy. The other man is the old mayor, Sven Nuis. Both of them have politicians' smiles plastered all over their faces.

'I don't know. If you'd done your homework, then you'd know I left the board a year or so before that.'

'You left one year *after*.'

Yeah, I *have* done my homework. A silence settles into the room. I'm comfortable with it, but I think Muller's less so. Because by lying to me he's opened up a crack which is now impossible to close.

'Well, what does it matter? And once again you seem to be floundering, just like you did when you were in charge of investigating my Lucie's death. I've half a mind to throw you out right now.'

I shift in my seat and wait for him to see the reality of the situation: he's in a wheelchair and I've got a large dog. Throwing me out is not on the menu today. I notice he's gripping the arms of his wheelchair with scalloped knuckles.

'I'm just trying to get to the truth, sometimes that takes me on tangents. But sometimes those tangents are what get the case solved.'

'What are you trying to say?' he finally asks.

'The details of your daughter's death were kept out of the press, only a handful of people knew them, aside from the killer himself.'

'So?'

'So we now have a second killing which exactly matches the first. How did they know?'

'Coincidence.'

'How many times did you accept a coincidence like that in your courtroom?'

'There are a million ways I can think of. He could have told someone. He could've bragged about it in prison for a start. Seems to me you should be checking anyone he might've been in contact with there.'

'We've done that, and it turns out Klaasen can't have told anyone because he was beaten to a pulp the very day he arrived in prison. Brain damage. Very bad brain damage. Vegetable-type brain damage.'

'What a terrible shame.'

Deadpan.

It's like he already knew.

I'd long wondered about the sudden appearance of the heroin addict witness at just the moment we needed him. It had bugged me so much that a couple of weeks after Klaasen had been convicted I was passing by the building where Lucie had been found and on a whim I went to the heroin addict's flat, only to find a family of Sudanese immigrants who had no idea what I was talking about, blank faces staring at me.

But now I'm wondering could Muller have had something to do with it? A grieving father making sure the man he thought responsible was put away? It seems like a stretch, and yet . . . Could it be? And if so, if he had that kind of power and reach, arranging Klaasen's beating wouldn't have been too difficult.

He is staring at me. I get the sense he's almost willing me to accuse him of it, daring me to. Or am I misreading him?

Somewhere in the house a phone rings, an old-fashioned mechanical chime, and something streaks across the lawn behind Judge Muller. For a second I think it's Kush, but I can feel him resting his chin on my foot.

'Something up, inspector?'

I suddenly get the feeling he knows everything, knows

that *I* know that he arranged Klaasen's beating. The room starts closing in, paranoid thoughts kicking off, the voices coming to life. I need to get out of here. I need to move now. But before I can Kush raises his head and lets out a long, spine-tingling howl, like a wolf standing on a ridge in front of a rising moon. I listen to it as it tails away, and realize the panic is subsiding now too. Kush rests his head back down on my foot.

A moment of weird reality – did that just happen? Muller is giving no indication anything out of the ordinary took place. The clock ticks like it always has, like it always will.

Was that just in my head? Did I imagine it?

I blink and carry on. Because really, what else can you do?

'I'm still not clear on –'

'You don't look like the sort of person who likes to be given advice,' Muller says, still staring at me intently. 'But I'm going to give it to you anyway. Sander Klaasen killed my Lucie, no one else, do you get that? No one else but that evil bastard, and it has nothing to do with DH Biotech or this Kleine you think I knew, or anyone else, and, I swear, if you're going to carry on, then I'll . . .'

It costs him, but he manages to cut himself off. He knows threatening a police officer is not a smart move, even if there are no witnesses. I guess he could be worried I'm recording him.

'Go on.'

'I think it's time you left,' he says, the anger reined in. But it's still there, underneath, hidden like the disease slowly eating him from the inside out. 'Go back to your houseboat and drop all this.'

Outside I let Kush off the leash and lean against the car. In a way I can understand Muller's anger and reluctance to have the case brought up again, and maybe my earlier thoughts were wrong, maybe it's as simple as him having nothing left except the certainty of knowing his daughter's killer is in prison paying some kind of price. To entertain the thought that the killer may still be out there would take that certainty away. Grief can be irrational. I'm suddenly not quite sure why I'd come, and yet as I drive away, the house flickering between the trees again, glimpses of a parallel universe, I get the feeling there was something in what he'd said that was important. Only I don't know what it was.

'What do you think?' I ask Kush.

As reward for breaking me out of the rising panic, and I don't know if *that* was a coincidence or it was something he did on purpose, I'm letting him ride up in the front seat with me.

He just looks at me, panting, tongue hanging limply from his mouth. He stays silent all the way to Amsterdam.

Back at the station I delve deeper into DH Biotech, Muller's outburst having the opposite effect on me to that which he'd intended. And yes, he *had* meddled with the investigation the first time round, and on the drive back I'd come to believe that he'd somehow got to Klaasen in prison, but that's not going to stop me. He was once a powerful man, but I doubt he retains enough of that to interfere with this investigation. But then again, how does he know I live on a houseboat? Odd, to say the least. I shake it off and turn to the papers in front of me.

'You Rykel?'

I look up to see a young uniform standing in the doorway. He's eating a packet of crisps.

'Me Rykel.'

'Beving wants to see you.'

Upstairs Beving tells me to close the door behind me.

'I get the feeling you've been avoiding me,' he says.

'Been busy. On the case.'

'You've not forgotten our agreement then? I was thinking maybe you had.'

'Not forgotten, just nothing to report.'

He eyes me suspiciously, before reminding me that it's only because of his good grace that I'm here at all. Once I get out of there I head back to what I was doing before being interrupted.

DH Biotech was formed in 1981 by the Swiss biochemist Didier Hoffman. Hoffman, like his far more famous namesake and discoverer of LSD, Albert, had initially worked for Sandoz. But, for personal reasons, he'd eventually left to strike out on his own. There'd been a lawsuit at the time, his old employer saying he'd taken research that they owned with him, but a court of law found in favour of Hoffman. After that the firm grew rapidly, partly because Hoffman had set up a division to oversee clinical trials for other pharmaceutical companies and help them navigate the FDA approval process – necessary for access to the very lucrative US market – which allowed him to continue his research, the reason he'd become a biochemist in the first place. When he was twelve his father had been diagnosed with multiple sclerosis. Watching the pain and deterioration over the next fifteen years was probably what drove Hoffman towards investigating novel ways to at least slow the disease's progress, if not halt it entirely. His area of research was based on a particular part of the immune system, the over-activation of which held, he believed, the key. None of which is really making anything clearer for me. I'm starting to think Muller was right, it is a coincidence. Just one that's hard to swallow. I turn to Marianne's father, Pieter-Jan Kleine, and start reading up on his background when a voice startles me from behind.

'I've got the culprit, sir.'

I turn to see Jansen standing at the door, pointing to Kush who I see has wandered over to Jansen's desk just on the off-chance. I call Kush over, and he reluctantly stops sniffing around the closed drawer and comes across with a very teenager-like slouch. He glances at Jansen as he passes him but doesn't stop.

'Look, about the shoes, I'll –'

'It's all right, sir. I got over it. But I wanted to say I just had a phone call. Someone did pick up some mail from the charity's PO box.'

'Did they follow them?'

'Got an address right here.' He hands me a slip of paper. It's some kind of clinic on a street in Amsterdam-West, an affluent neighbourhood.

Vermeer walks in. I bring her up to speed.

'Think we should check it out.'

'I agree,' she says.

We pass some kind of political demonstration outside the Taibah mosque. A small group of neo-Nazis are holding up placards, the general gist of which isn't what you'd call welcoming. One says FOREIGNERS GO HOME, another is simply a picture of a turban with a lit fuse poking out of the top. Some of them look round at the sound of the siren.

'What is wrong with these people?' Vermeer asks.

I don't really have an answer for that.

We forge on, passing the AMC, the hospital Hank's in. I try not to think about that. Two minutes later we're parked across the road from a two-storey structure, all steel, glass and angles jutting into the sky. It contrasts with the other plots which have single-storey houses, all blocky and identical. There's no name plaque, nothing to indicate what's inside.

'What is that?'

'I don't know. But Huisman gave them what must have been a huge amount of money for him, so let's go and ask them.'

'Wait a minute.' Vermeer gets Jansen on the phone and puts him on speaker. He'd been tasked with running the address whilst we headed over, and it seems he's had some luck.

'It's a private rehab clinic. Basically a front for a Hollywood religion, the one with that actor? They prey on the needy and sick, bring them in, and induct them into their belief.'

'Why is Huisman donating to them?' Vermeer asks.

'I don't think he's donating.'

'So what?'

'When I knew him Huisman dealt heroin, but also used it himself. I reckon it's become a problem in the intervening years. What if the money wasn't so much a donation as a fee?'

'You think Huisman kills Kleine then checks into rehab? He goes on a self-improvement kick right after killing someone?'

I look at the building again. Hiding in plain sight is usually better than running. I should know. If I'd run after Station Chief Smit's disappearance, it would have been like raising a massive red flag. As it is, I stayed and so far no one's come knocking. Though I can't share this with Vermeer.

'Could be. Or he just worked out a secretive rehab clinic would be the perfect place to hide out. Worth paying money for. In either case, I think there's every chance he's still in there right now.'

Just as I get out of the car my phone rings. Nellie de Vries. Oh god. I can't deal with this now. I'm about to leave it when I think about her sitting at home calling me, willing me to pick up.

'Uhhh . . . I'm going to need a minute.'

Vermeer looks at me like, *Really? Now?*

I nod, my pained expression not all fake.

'Meet me in there when you're done,' she says as she walks off across the street.

I answer the phone. 'Hey, what's up?'

'Jaap, they've approved my request.'

She doesn't need to say what that request is. The ground doesn't feel stable and my throat's tight.

'When?' I finally manage.

'Don't know yet. They have to set a date, which they'll let me know in the next couple of days.'

She sounds oddly emotionless but I know that's just because she's holding it all in. Not least because one of the emotions she has swirling around is probably a tiny sense of relief, even if she's not admitting that to herself. Yet. I tell her I'll be there, and that we can meet later if she wants. She says she'll let me know.

Vermeer returns. 'They're insisting on a warrant.'

'On what grounds?'

'Client confidentiality. Which is bollocks. And the thing is, it's going to take hours.'

She gets on the phone and starts the process. I glance across at the building and wonder if there's another way. By the time she's finished on the phone my plan has been worked out.

'How about we get something to eat whilst we're waiting?'

Glass

The place is busy, a blur of talk, the clatter of an open kitchen, and a mix of smells which make me realize just how hungry I actually am. Vermeer's choice, a place on Cornelis Schuytstraat which I'd never been into before. On the outside it looks tiny, but once inside you notice it stretches all the way to the back of the building and spills out into the courtyard as well. A small army of waiters and waitresses wheel platters of food and trays of drinks around at a startling rate. Right now one of them, a girl with a severe undercut, deposits our food in front of us with surprising grace and is gone before we can even thank her.

I'd opted for the burger made from some rare-breed cow, which had been, according to the menu, massaged daily and had Bach's Forty-Eight played to it during the day and the Goldbergs every night, whilst Vermeer had ordered a pot of mussels. The menu had given a choice, native or Scottish. Being a good Dutch woman she'd gone native.

'You don't want any bloody foreign ones,' she says as she lifts the top off and releases a cloud of steam. She waits till it disperses and starts picking through them, slurping the yellow-orange flesh out of each shell and discarding them into a rapidly growing pile.

'I still think we should dig a bit further into DH Biotech. Seems too much of a coincidence that both the victims' fathers have links there.'

'Coincidence? From what I've seen so far I think Huisman's much more interesting. He was Lucie Muller's boyfriend, he's clearly a shitbag, and you yourself said you'd liked him for it at the time.'

'I know, it's just . . .'

Vermeer's phone rings. She wipes her hands before answering.

'What do you mean delayed? That's not good enough. I need it now. Yeah? Really? How about this, I don't care. I need that warrant and you'd better get it to me.' She hangs up and goes back to her mussels.

'They're saying another couple of hours.'

Which gives me the opening I need.

'How about we go and see Marianne Kleine's father in the meantime?'

She slurps down another couple of mussels, discarded shells tinkling as they hit the bowl.

'All right, anything to make you happy.'

'It'll make me ecstatic.'

When we get back to the car we're met with the sorriest dog in the world, sitting in the back seat with a mournful look which could haunt even the stoniest soul. He perks up when I let him out and toss the remainder of the burger I'd slipped out of the bun onto the ground. On its way down I notice it has a slice of gherkin stuck to the charred flesh. It's gone in a flash, a greasy stain on the concrete the only evidence it'd ever existed at all.

I let Kush into the back and slide into the passenger seat, only to find Vermeer wiping down the steering wheel. She looks at me like it's my fault. We move off and Kush sits up, his head almost between ours. He's panting, then stops suddenly. I turn to look at him just as he burps loudly. The car smells of gherkin the rest of the way.

The doorbell rings and rings. Vermeer turns and shrugs. We're at Kleine's property in Vinkeveense Plassen, a massive lake turned into a water sports complex just off the A2. Sporadic plots of land on the shore have been built on with the kind of properties only affordable to those living off the interest of their interest of their interest. To get to it we'd had to abandon the car and walk across a vast flat lawn dotted with large specimen trees, their leaves yellow against a grey sky. Eventually the house itself appeared, a two-storey oblong much like a gigantic shoebox, clad with wood silvered by the weather.

'I'll walk round,' I tell Vermeer.

She nods and keeps her finger on the bell.

I skirt the building. The path is laid with woodchips and lined with grasses and clusters of late-flowering plants. The place is immaculate, nothing is out of place, not even a leaf or petal. He must have a team of gardeners to keep it like this. But it also seems empty somehow, lacking. I turn the corner and reach the long section facing the water. The side of the structure we'd approached had the odd window and an imposing front door, but this side is pretty much just glass, massive panels two storeys high giving Kleine views over another lawn which stretches away until it reaches the water itself. A flagpole stands naked right at the water's edge, and a wooden jetty juts out over the water, which today is as steel-grey as the sky. At the end of the jetty the two curved metal poles of a ladder arch off the wood and into the water below. They're like smooth slinkies caught in motion.

Turning back to the building it strikes me that with the lights on inside at night you could sit out on the water in a little boat and see pretty much everything that went on inside. As I walk round I wonder if that ever bothers him. Or did, before his daughter was killed. I can't imagine this overt luxury is bringing Kleine much pleasure now. I step closer to the glass to take a look inside and see a moving head. My heart goes into overdrive until I realize it's just my reflection. *Stupid*, I tell myself as I try to slow my heart back down. I can faintly hear the bell still ringing inside, an on–off rhythm which tells me Vermeer is a) stubborn, and b) still round the other side. I take the opportunity and reach for my vape, wandering across the lawn down towards the water's edge.

A breeze flutters my face. When I look down the water's surface is choppy. Further out I can see a lone windsurfer standing on his board, hauling the sail out of the water. I hit the button on the vape and wait for it to warm up, watching as he gets the sail upright. It bulges with the wind and he's off, leaning further away from the board as his speed increases. I check my vape. It's not hot. I hit the button again; the LED telling me it's heating up comes on, then turns off. Battery dead. At this rate I'm going to have to go back to smoking joints, but not only would that mean burning through roughly four times the amount of cannabis, because combustion is so wasteful, I really hate walking around with my mouth tasting like an ashtray. I pocket the damn thing, noticing the windsurfer's nowhere to be seen now, and head back to the building, the sun choosing this exact moment to break out from the cloud and light the glass up. I reach the window and cup my hand to kill the reflection when I'm right by it.

I'm looking into a large open-plan living space flooded with the warm late-afternoon light. An L-shaped sofa, which could probably seat twenty. Rugs on the polished concrete floor. But it's not immaculate like the grounds. In fact, it's kind of a mess: sofa cushions thrown all over, some ripped apart, foam oozing out of their innards; a painting, a massive canvas, which appears to have been painted just black, has three large cuts in it, revealing the white wall behind. First Marianne Kleine's start-up offices, now her father's house. What is going on? I start moving along the glass and see the kitchen section has suffered the same treatment: knives and forks scattered, shards of plates. A large tin on its side with spaghetti shooting out of the top looks like a quiver spilling arrows. And beyond that something on the floor I can't quite make out. I edge to my left, trying to work it out, get a better view.

'Rykel?'

She must've got bored of ringing the bell and come to find me.

'Over here!' I call out, unable to take my eyes off it. Because I can now see it's a massive red stain seeping out from behind an enormous kitchen island. Worse, I'm pretty sure that slumped on the floor I can see a body.

Chateau Lafite 2000

We've got an ambulance on the way, the dispatcher had said eight minutes, and a scene of crime team scrambled from the local station in case we're too late. Breaking one of the large glass sheets would be devastating, even if we managed it. The front door is similarly out; it's wood but solid enough to withstand a tank. Which leaves us with one of the round windows on the first floor.

'It's too high. We need something to stand on,' Vermeer says.

'You can give me a leg up.'

She looks me up and down, then pulls out her gun.

'How about *you* give me a leg up instead?'

I'm not about to start arguing with a woman holding a gun. I lean against the wall, position my hands and lock my fingers together. Vermeer flips the gun round so she's holding the barrel then raises her boot.

'Ready?' she asks.

'Go.'

The grip on her sole is chunky, and it bites my fingers as I take her weight. She launches up, puts her other foot on my shoulder. Soon she's standing with one foot either side of my head, and I'm grasping her ankles to keep her steady. My leg muscles are already starting to shake.

'Close your eyes,' she says.

'Don't worry, I'm not going to up-skirt you.'

'You're not, mainly because I'm not wearing a skirt. Ready?'

'Do it.' I scrunch my eyes up.

I hear the impact. Glass tinkles down around me and I hope I'm not about to get another one stuck in my arm. When it's safe I open my eyes to see a nasty-looking shard, the brother of the one I met the day before yesterday, sticking into the ground just by the toe of my shoe. Vermeer knocks a few more pieces out before declaring herself ready. Here comes the really hard part. I let go of her ankles and hold the palms of my hands flat. She steps onto the right hand first, then the left. I push upwards, my arms straining so hard they're trembling. I can hear the ambulance in the distance. Just as I think I can't push any further I feel the pressure ease off. Vermeer must've got hold of the sill. She hauls herself through and I'm free to drop my arms.

I'm by the front door well before Vermeer, and I'm starting to wonder if she's got lost inside. The ambulance is closer now. The door swings open.

'You okay?' I ask Vermeer. 'You've got blood on your face.'

'Just my hand,' she says, holding it up to show a swooping gash. 'Must've wiped it.'

The ambulance has stopped, the siren cut out. We rush through the house and entranceway leading directly into the vast space. The kitchen area's off to the left and we run over. There's a strong smell of alcohol.

The body's lying in a dark pool.

It's not blood though. It's red wine.

'It's him,' Vermeer says.

I get close and reach over to feel the man's throat. He groans when I push in for a pulse, and raises an arm to try and swat my hand away.

'Fuck,' Vermeer says, shaking her head.

'We're going to look like idiots,' I confirm.

Running footsteps behind us on the tiled floor.

'Well, this is embarrassing. For you two.'

I look up to see one of the two paramedics staring down at the scene. He's got short ginger hair and black-rimmed glasses and I'm sure he spends his spare time conversing on conspiracy theory forums on the internet. He doesn't look particularly amused.

'The thing is . . .' Vermeer says.

'. . . it really looked like blood from outside,' I finish. 'With the sunlight and . . .'

He shakes his head like he's never had to deal with such a sorry bunch of fuck-ups in his whole life, then moves closer to the body with a deep theatrical sigh.

'You dead, sir?' he asks, prodding him. 'Dead, or just very, very pissed?'

Pieter-Jan Kleine groans.

'Well, my work here is done,' he says, standing up.

'You could look at her hand before you go. Make the trip worthwhile.'

He glares at me, but then nods to Vermeer who shows him the cut.

'Nice,' he says. But he drops his kitbag and gets to work.

I get on the phone and cancel the scene of crime team. By the time Vermeer's cleaned up and bandaged another call's come in so the two paramedics have to run back to the ambulance, leaving us alone with Kleine.

I walk over to the bottle smashed on the tiles. Part of it is held together by the label.

'Chateau Lafite 2000,' I read as I pick it up. 'Looks expensive.'

'About a grand and a half a bottle,' Vermeer says, adding, 'My soon-to-be ex is a wine broker. Tosser.'

I'm stunned, both at the price, and that Vermeer has offered some personal information. But before I can follow up on the tosser wine broker soon-to-be ex she gives me a look that makes it clear nothing else is going to be forthcoming.

'That *was* embarrassing.'

'I know, but from outside it really did look like blood.'

'Let's get him sobered up.'

I haul him over to the sofa and wedge a large glass coffee table up against his legs to stop him moving, whilst Vermeer gets him a glass of water.

'Two bottles of Jenever in the sink,' she says. 'He must be wasted.'

The wine had just been an afterthought it seems, a little tipple just to round things off after he'd downed the Jenever and tried to wreck his own home.

Vermeer walks over and Kleine holds his hand out unsteadily to reach for the glass. She throws the liquid in his face. He groans again. She gets another glass and this time hands it to him.

Whilst he's sipping I take a quick look round. It's even bigger once you're inside it, the double-height ceilings reminding me of airports or warehouses more than somewhere you'd want to live. I roughly calculate I could fit four of my houseboats in here and still have enough left over for a small circus top.

Over the next few minutes he gradually comes round, to the point where he looks well enough to answer a few simple questions. He's mid-fifties, lean, and if you gave him a black polo neck and some round glasses he could pass for a Steve Jobs lookalike. As it is he's wearing jeans and a dirty orange sweat top, the arms of which are a little too short. His face is so pale he looks like someone's siphoned off a few litres of blood. On the table are a variety of coffee-table books – a large volume on contemporary architecture in Chile, one on the steep-sloped vineyards of the Rhine – and a large conch shell, mainly white but with apricot tinges here and there.

I ask him about DH Biotech.

'Why?' he says, his voice croaky.

'Just background really.'

He's still feeling the effect of the alcohol, but is it just me or do his eyes narrow as he looks at me?

'What do you want to know?'

What I really want to know is what his connection with Muller might be. But given his delicate state I decide I need to warm him up a little before getting to the important question.

'Tell me about the company. It seems they'd been working on a cure for MS but it didn't work?'

He winces and rubs his left temple as if it's hurting bad. Which it probably is. He picks up the shell.

'Marianne loved this,' he says, turning it over in his

hands. 'She was only twelve and we'd gone on holiday to Zakynthos in Greece and she'd been so excited about diving in the sea that she'd talked of nothing else for weeks before we even got on the plane. We'd got her goggles, flippers and a snorkel, and the minute we arrived at the hotel she was itching to get in the water. Of course, she'd been imagining this rich underwater world for so long that the reality was a huge disappointment. There were no bright coloured fish, or beautiful shells. It was mostly sand and the odd bit of rubbish which had got stuck on the seabed. She was so upset that I found a tourist shop and bought this, and the next morning I went down to the beach before breakfast and hid it by some rocks so I could find it later. She was pretty reluctant to go into the water again, but I persuaded her and made sure we swam near the rocks. She saw it of course and dived for it. At first she seemed really happy, but by the next day she'd lost all interest in diving and didn't go in the water again for the rest of the week. As we were leaving the hotel I was checking her room and saw she'd left it on the bed. I packed it, and when we got back here I showed it to her, saying she'd almost left it behind. I'll never forget the look she gave me. "It's not real, though, is it?" "Of course it's real," I told her. "You put it there, didn't you?" she said. I said no. She got her phone out, typed something in and showed me a Wikipedia page on this type of shell, which it turns out is slightly different from any found in the Mediterranean.'

He holds it up for us to see, turning it slowly in his hands. There's a shiny curled inner lip and a spiky outside.

'*Lobatus gigas* it's called, and it's only found in the north-west Atlantic. I lied to her, and she knew I was lying. The same way I'd held her whilst she was growing up and told her everything would be okay, reassured her that life was wonderful and that she was going to do great things. And all I can think about is that whilst she was . . . was being killed she must have known I'd lied again. Do you know what that's like, to lie to your own child?'

He's still staring at the shell when I prompt him on my original question, why none of the compounds the company was studying worked.

'You want a lecture on biochemistry?' he asks, placing the shell back on the table. 'They didn't work. I'm not sure what else you need to know. At that stage none of the costs were recoverable.'

'What sort of costs?'

'Millions. Forty, fifty. Does it really matter? Marianne's dead, and I don't know why you're here asking me questions about something so far in the past.'

He suddenly looks even paler than before, as if all this talk is painful. Which, of course, it is.

'I know it seems odd,' Vermeer says, 'but we are doing everything we can, and we could really use your help in answering just a few more questions.'

He doesn't take his eyes off the shell, but he finally nods.

'The offices Marianne rented were broken into. Can you think of why that might be?'

'When?'

'Most likely last night; it was discovered this morning.'

'I . . . no. Not anyone specifically.'

'What about in general? Would your company be interested in the research she was doing? From what I hear it could be the start of a medical revolution.'

'Not without Marianne it won't. But anyway, no pharmaceutical company is going to raid their offices – that's just crazy.'

Patrick Wust seemed to think otherwise.

I show him the same photo of Huisman I'd shown Wust.

He hesitates for a moment before shaking his head.

'I don't recognize him. Is he the one you think killed her?'

'Just someone we want to talk to,' Vermeer says.

'Did you have any dealings with Koen Muller?' I ask him, changing tack. 'He was on the board of DH Biotech around about that time the trial failed.'

Do I imagine it, or does something in his posture stiffen at that name? I'm just about to push for an answer when he leans forward and vomits onto the glass table in front of him, hitting both the books and the shell. Vomit runs across the table surface, and then over the edge.

'You see his reaction before he threw up?'

'He's lying,' I say as we walk back to the car.

'It could have been because he suddenly felt bad, but . . . I'm inclined to agree. Pretty sure he knows Koen Muller.'

'When I spoke to Wust he said that Marianne's discovery could obliterate more traditional forms of treatment. And her own father works for a company that could be seen as a competitor.'

'What are you saying?'

I shake my head. 'I just don't know.'

'So where does that leave us?'

A question to which I haven't got an answer. I glance out over the water. The sun's setting, fattening up as it slides towards the horizon. The silhouette of a bird streaks across it.

I haven't got an answer.

But I *am* going to get one.

There's a Man With a Gun

'Move it!' Vermeer's leaning out of the window yelling at the white delivery van blocking our entrance onto Bloemgracht. Result, nothing of note. She slides back and flips on the siren and lights. Two seconds later the van starts with a jump, then gets moving.

We're here because at the same time Kleine was hurling wine onto the table, Kush was testing out the seat fabric in the car, checking it met with his stringent durability tests. Unfortunately the fabric failed, as did the foam inside, the seat belts and even the faux leather on the gearstick handle. From about fifteen metres out the whole thing looked like a snow globe just after it's been shaken.

Result: strained relations. After we'd cleared up the worst of it into a bunch of large evidence bags which had been in the boot, I'd floated the idea of dropping Kush off at the houseboat for a while. Vermeer concurred. We're expecting the warrant to come through soon, and we can't leave him in the car again whilst we're searching the place. The journey hadn't mellowed Vermeer's mood, not least because, as she'd loudly proclaimed when we'd gone over a speed bump in Amsterdam-Zuid, 'Great, now I've got a spring up my ass.'

'We'll get out here,' I tell Vermeer.

'See you back at the station,' she says as I take the disgraced animal out of the back. 'If the warrant's issued in the meantime, I'm not waiting for you.'

As soon as I shut the door she reverses hard, the engine's high whine drowned out by the bells of Westerkerk striking the hour. We turn into Bloemgracht and I let Kush off the leash. Which is when I see a figure wearing jeans and a hoody step off the shore and onto the gangplank which leads to my houseboat. There've been a couple of break-in attempts over the last few years, but they usually wait until the early hours. In both cases they were heroin addicts, looking for items that could be converted into cash. The first was unlucky. Whilst trying to prise open a porthole – a move that wouldn't have got him anywhere because there was no way he'd've been able to squeeze through it even if he had got it open – he'd sliced open his wrist. I'd come back late from a case and found him slumped on deck, minutes from departing the world. If I'd been a few minutes later, or the ambulance hadn't happened to be close by when I put the call in, he would have died there. The second attempt was when I was on board, and a man had crashed through the front door. I ran at him screaming and the thin weasel-faced addict legged it fast. And now another.

'Hey!'

The figure freezes, shoulders rising. Then he turns, his face difficult to make out as the hoody's low over his eyes, his face in a dark pool of shadow. After a moment of indecision he legs it even faster than the last one. Kush is off after him before me, giving chase and catching up with the man just as he skids round a corner out of view. The last I see of them is Kush jumping up, a flash of white teeth clamping round his left arm.

I spend twenty minutes walking the streets searching for Kush or the man but don't find either. Eventually I give up and head back to the houseboat.

The kitchen light flickers when I flip the switch and for a few seconds I think it's going to blow. I try a few more lights and each one does the same. Something's not right, I'm going to have to call that damn electrician again.

I'm just pulling out my phone when I spot movement outside. It's Kush, I find when I'm back on deck, standing by the gangplank. I call him over and he trots across. He's panting hard, but otherwise appears fine. I reach out to try and stroke his head but he flicks his snout up so it catches my fingers. It feels wet. I bring my hand up so I can see it better.

My fingers are slick with blood.

'Fucking unbelievable,' Vermeer's saying as I step into the incident room. I raise an eyebrow, which sets her off, telling me the whole story that she's clearly already told those present several times already. Not ten minutes earlier her warrant request had been turned down because of lack of evidence that it would 'further the investigation'. After she's vented, she decides to speak to Beving, and orders me along.

'And so you agree that Huisman is potentially a person of interest?' she asks him after barging into his office.

I like her style. Beving does not. But he seems oddly subdued. Anyone else entering his office unbidden would be instantly reassigned to a community liaison support role deep in the countryside on a permanent basis. But Vermeer seems to hold some sway over him.

'Possibly,' Beving concedes.

'Then I'm not sure what else we need? This was a simple, routine request, and it's been rejected for no reason that I can see. Sir.'

Beving takes a moment before speaking.

'Rykel, wait outside.'

'Rykel, don't wait outside.'

I like Vermeer even more. Beving throws me a death stare before turning his attention to Vermeer.

'Look . . .' he starts before trailing off. He's flicking the corner of a bit of paper with his thumb. He tries again. 'The place you want to search has . . . Well, it's possible they have friends in all walks of life, all professions and –'

'You're telling me they have someone in the police?'

'I'm not telling you anything. I'm merely thinking out loud, wondering about possibilities. Maybe it's all a coincidence.'

I don't like coincidences like this. Neither, it seems, does Vermeer. She's opening her mouth when Beving cuts her off.

'But for the moment this discussion is over.'

'Who is it?'

'Like I said, I was just speculating. But I don't think there's anything I can –'

'You mean you won't do anything.'

'*If* you'll let me finish. What you need to do is go out there and find enough evidence that the warrant *can't* be turned down. And you, Rykel, where's that paperwork you were supposed to sign?'

I feign puzzlement.

'I handed it to the desk sergeant, told him to get it to you straight away. Are you saying you haven't had it?'

The incident room is winding down, the acid attack still a drain on staff numbers. I keep thinking of Kush, the blood on his muzzle from the man he'd chased and bitten.

'So what do you suggest we do?' Vermeer asks me.

I don't have an answer for that. Not yet, anyway. Jansen's taken over the map showing Muller and Kleine's movements and I step up to it. He's been hard at work. Last time I'd looked there'd been only a few dots, black for Kleine, red for Muller. Now there are many more, but surprisingly none where they overlap. It looks like that was a waste of time, nothing in this case adding up. And yet, I think of the two dead women, two fathers who, despite their grief, are hiding something.

And a man we need to talk to hiding out in a cult-run rehab who have just used some of their power to stop us from getting to him. And then there's Klaasen. Could he actually have been telling the truth? Could he be innocent?

'We haven't really talked about Marianne's start-up offices being trashed,' Vermeer says. 'Could there be a link with the company her father works for?'

'From what I can gather there's no link at all,' Jansen says. 'Marianne Kleine owns fifty-one per cent and the investors she brought on board own the remaining forty-nine per cent. I've checked the investors out; none of them have any obvious connection to DH Biotech.'

Vermeer shakes her head. Jansen looks apprehensive. Vermeer asks him something else, but I don't hear it, a sudden thought crowding out all the space in my head. It's about Judge Muller. Has Muller still got enough power left? Could it be that this is his doing? I share it with them.

'He threatened you?' Vermeer asks when I've finished.

'He was worked up but managed to stop himself. Seems reasonable to expect that as a judge and a father he'd want to find the truth, but I don't think he has much time left. He didn't look that well and he has nothing to live for. I reckon he wants to go to the grave with the knowledge that his daughter's killer was punished. He doesn't want that messed with.'

'Surely if there's a chance the earlier conviction wasn't right then he'd want to find the real killer?'

'I don't think he's thinking straight; you could see it in his eyes. He wants to die knowing someone was punished for his daughter's death. Say we were to find out that, in fact, Klaasen didn't kill her and it was Huisman, then a trial's still going to be a year, eighteen months away. I don't think he has that long.'

'That's crazy,' she says, shaking her head. 'Fuck!'

She sweeps a whole load of paper and a laptop off a nearby table. The laptop crunches against the wall. Paper flutters wildly like a flock of disturbed birds. She storms out of the room.

I wonder about picking it all up, but decide I can't be bothered. I nip outside, round the corner, and take a few pulls instead.

'Is that . . .?'

I turn to see the officer who'd bought the wrong colour shoes, eyes squinting with suspicion. He's holding a large coffee in one hand and an even larger bagel in the other, two bites breaking the perimeter.

'Yes. It is.'

'I don't think you should be –'

'Fuck off.'

He does, and I finish up and go back to the incident room where a calmer Vermeer is present.

'So, what do we do?' she asks.

'Give me ten minutes, then I'm taking you for a drink.'

I track Jansen down and tell him what I need.

'But what exactly?' he asks.

'Everything about DH Biotech: company accounts, people involved with it, everything.'

'Right,' he says, shaking his head like I've just asked him for the impossible. 'Anything else, sir?'

There is actually. The first step of the plan I've been concocting.

'Is there a phone shop around here?'

He tells me where the closest is. Just as I'm out the door he calls out to me.

'Oh, thought you'd like to know. Patrol picked up someone breaking into a building right next door to Kleine's offices. Turns out it was the same guy.'

'How do you know?'

'He confessed to it and they got some CCTV footage of him.'

'Do we need to talk to him?'

'From what patrol says he's just a low-grade criminal, bad one at that. Doubt he has anything to do with anything.'

I'm at the wheel this time and we move off into the night. I don't know if it's because Amsterdam's special, or that I've lived here so long that I'm just somehow tuned in to

225

it, but there's a definite change in the vibration of the city as it shifts gear, from the grind of the working day towards the promise of evening play. You can feel it in the air, a crackle of energy that feeds your imagination. Though I get the sense that Vermeer's *not* tuned in to it. She's pensive, an echo of her earlier outburst hanging around her like a shroud.

Turning on to Eerste van der Helststraat a street light's flickering, like we're celebretards and it's a paparazzo. She breathes out and suddenly clocks our general direction, surfacing from whatever deep place she was in.

'What, we're going to stake the place out?'

'Such a bad idea?'

'Maybe not.'

But I turn onto Gerard Doustraat, past the tattoo parlour I'd once had to arrest someone in. They were eventually convicted of murder, but at the moment I'd burst in he was having a swastika inked onto his left arm. Only I didn't let him finish, so now he's in prison with a nonsensical tat and probably about fifteen years before he can do anything about it.

At the far end of the street there's a little bar Tanya and I used to go to when we first started seeing each other, those deliciously expansive days when we were falling in love. Days I try not to revisit too often.

The bar itself is a rabbit warren of a drinking hole, started by an old American lesbian who decided there weren't enough bars in Amsterdam that celebrated 1920s swimsuit porn, and so decorated the place with blown-up scratchy black and white images of women in less-than-revealing one-piece swimsuits. Luckily for her a young crowd had decided the whole thing was unbelievably cool, and the place had rapidly acquired a steady stream of clientele. Then the inevitable, some hack working for a travel guide stumbled across it and within a year the place was filled with tourists congratulating themselves on being just so goddamned hip. The old lesbian died, and the place has been preserved like a museum piece; it's all there, but something's missing.

But for my purposes now it's almost perfectly located. Jansen had directed me to the phone shop and I bought one, all ready to go in my pocket. The bar takes up all four floors of a late nineteenth-century house, and tonight we're in the basement, which has all of twenty seats in various little alcoves. The light's low, the music's soft, and the atmosphere is . . . I suddenly wonder if Vermeer thinks I'm trying to hit on her. Which reminds me I'm supposed to be meeting Sabine tonight, but that's looking like it might be unlikely. I debate texting her to put it off, but decide that, as we're not due to meet for another couple of hours, I might as well keep my options open for a little longer.

A Latin-type waitress in a strappy top which shows off her tattoos and two thick bushes of underarm hair arrives to take our order. I plump for a Coke whilst Vermeer's going through the cocktail menu. Because I don't drink it hadn't occurred to me that Vermeer might. Which is a problem because I really need her *not* to have had a drink for what I've got planned.

'The cocktails aren't that great,' I tell her, earning me a pretty feisty look from the waitress. 'How about a Coke?'

'Hey, you invited me out for a drink, and a drink is

what I'm going to have. In fact, now I'm going to have two. And you can drive me back.'

She's really not that different from me. Taste of my own medicine.

Once the waitress has gone and Vermeer's off finding the toilets I look around and realize I'm unprepared for the rush of memories this place is bringing back, like they'd been stored here rather than in my head, and I'm only accessing them now through proximity to the source.

Tanya and I had met when a case of hers had crossed over with one I was working on, and she'd travelled down from Friesland to Amsterdam. I remember seeing her the first time we'd met and the feeling I'd got. There was something there right from the start, something that felt light and weighty at the same time. And that was pretty much our relationship summed up. There were light times, times when we felt giddy with it all, with each other, with the world we'd fashioned around us. There were the weighty times too, moments when I suspected there was something Tanya was keeping from me.

Of course I eventually discovered what she'd been carrying round with her, the years of abuse she'd suffered at the hands of a man who'd been tasked with protecting her, her foster father. It was a discovery that led me on a path to doing something I'd never have believed I was capable of. But I've heard it said love can be like a kind of sickness, one which can take over your mind, make you do things you'd never otherwise have thought of. In a way I can believe that now. It *was* like a fever, my efforts to do what was best for Tanya, trying to protect her from further harm, made me neutralize a threat who turned out to be Station Chief Smit.

Fevers break, though, and the very moment when I pulled the trigger to protect Tanya it was like I'd not only killed Henk Smit, I'd killed hope as well. Everything we'd had shattered into so many pieces it wasn't even worth trying to fix.

And all the while the black wolf ate in the shadows gathering strength.

'Cliché I know, but you look like you've seen a ghost.'

Man, how long have I been gone?

'I . . . yeah. Something like that.'

'You're not about to have one of those PTSD fits, are you?' she says, sitting down.

'They're not fits.'

'No? I saw you when you lost it after that guy didn't turn up. Looked like some kind of fit to me.'

The waitress brings our drinks. She puts down the bottle for me, and in front of Vermeer places a clear cocktail in a martini glass with rose petals scattered on the surface, and one in a shot glass which is virtually black. Vermeer chooses the martini glass and raises it.

'*Proost.*'

'*Proost.*'

I take a sip, Vermeer takes a couple. Her shoulders drop a little and she sighs as she puts the glass on the table.

'So?'

'So . . . I actually don't know what they are, but they're not fits. And I'm not just about to have one.'

'Your face said otherwise.'

My face. That traitor. Always the same.

'Just thinking,' I tell her, taking a sip of Coke to help me along.

'About?'

'The past, what else?'

'The past? I thought you were supposed to live each day like it's your last. Isn't that what they say?'

'Yeah, and it's terrible advice. You do that and you're constantly under pressure, to get things done, get more, squeeze it all in.'

'So what do you suggest?'

'Live each day like you're going to live forever. That way you can just relax into whatever you're doing, without worrying that you should be doing something else, like you're missing out on something.'

'That's what you do?'

'Well, turns out it's easier said than done . . .'

'You're not trying to hit on me, are you?' she asks. That breaks it, and we both laugh, relaxing a little, getting us off the awkward track of conversation we'd somehow got on to. We talk about the case, but when we get on to the topic of the warrant Vermeer gets angry again, more animated. For a split second she turns into Tanya before reality flickers back in.

'We're supposed to be servants of the law, but do you ever get the feeling we're actually just servants of the powerful?' she asks, accompanying the word 'powerful' with a wide sweep of her arm.

'It's taken you this long to work that out? Maybe you're not as smart as I thought.'

'All right, Mr fucking-know-it-all, so why are you still here?'

Yeah, that's really the question. Vermeer has a knack for asking difficult questions. Sadly, though, for this one I have an answer.

'Same as you. We're still here because we can't help ourselves. We're addicted to it.'

'Maybe,' she says. The music's turned up a notch, the evening's softening. I notice the first cocktail is gone. We really should get going before she moves on to the second one.

'Maybe we should call it a night?'

She gives me the sweetest smile and a middle finger, then reaches for the next, the liquid blacker than night.

'Smoking gun,' she says. 'Six parts gin, one part vodka, smoked chilli syrup, squeezed lime and charcoal. That's the colour.'

'Sounds deadly.'

She offers me a sip. I decline. She shrugs and downs it in one.

'Now let's call it a night. You're driving, remember?'

I pay at the bar and we're just reaching the car when I stop and pat my pockets.

'Damn, I left my wallet.'

Vermeer rolls her eyes. 'I'll wait in the car then.'

She heads off and I duck back inside, make for the toilets and pull out the pre-pay mobile I'd bought earlier. It turns on. Though it has trouble finding reception. The one part of the plan I hadn't really thought of was that I was going to have to make this call from a basement. There are four cubicles and I notice one of them has a street-level window. I close the door and step up onto the porcelain rim, a dinosaur spine of shit riding down the back of the pan into the water. I hold the phone up . . . no bars . . . no bars . . . yes! Three bars. I place the call, my thumbnail ready against the phone's speaker.

When the call's answered I talk in a breathy whisper, scratching at the phone's mic with my thumbnail. I manage to get the message across, though, and hang up when he asks for my details. SIM down the toilet, battery out of the phone. I'll dispose of that later.

'Got it?'

Vermeer's sitting on the car's bonnet, legs crossed.

'Yeah, left it by the bar. So where do you want me to drop you?'

But before she can answer the police radio crackles into life, and we listen to dispatch: reports of a man with a gun, possible hostage situation. He gives the address. Vermeer and I look at each other like *What the fuck?*

Vermeer picks up the radio and signs in. Five seconds later we're accelerating hard away from the kerb, blue lights flashing on, the sirens screaming into the night.

'Looks like we may have just got lucky,' she says.

I don't say anything. Because sometimes you just have to make your own luck.

For Your Own Safety

What I hadn't counted on when formulating my plan was for dispatch to over-react and send a fully armed response unit who arrive just as we get there, blue lights flickering in the dusk. There are six of them, including the leader, a short man called Mark Rutte who makes up for his lack of height by spending time in the gym. Rutte takes one look at us and decides we're nowhere near hardcore enough for this kind of thing.

'Let us handle this,' he says whilst his team are prepping with military precision.

'We'll go in after you,' Vermeer tells him. 'Cover your back.'

Rutte stares at her for a moment, then tosses us each a bulletproof vest.

The man at the front desk's eyes pop out of his head as we storm into the building, weapons drawn, Rutte yelling for him to stay where he is. His team spread out just as a door opens and a woman steps through. She's tall and thin, with cheekbones you could slice meat on. For some reason I can see her in an eighties exercise video, neon tracksuit with a matching towelled headband. The real version, in a black suit, doesn't look happy. Vermeer steps behind me, trying to keep out of view.

'What is this?' she demands of the room at large.

Rutte steps up. 'We received reports of shots being fired.'

'Here?' She's incredulous.

'The caller said they were here for treatment and one of the other patients has gone crazy with a gun. They said there were shots fired. Have you not heard anything?'

'No. That's . . . No one here has a gun. We wouldn't let a bunch of druggies . . . patients walk around with guns.'

'So you've heard nothing?'

'No, and they're not allowed phones either. So I don't know how they could have called. Seems to me you've been the victim of some kind of joke.'

Rutte stares at her for a few seconds. Then he gets on the phone and has a quick conversation with dispatch. I'm hoping he doesn't decide to pack it up and I'm just wondering what I can do to influence his decision when he turns and addresses the team.

'Right, we're going in. Be prepared.'

'No, wait, you can't do that.'

'I suggest you both wait outside, for your own safety.'

She looks like she's going to argue, then gives in. As she and the male receptionist walk past Vermeer moves so that her face is out of view.

We're soon on the move through the corridors, following Rutte's team, which is a precision-engineered machine, and we make progress clearing the building. Halfway through we reach a door with TREATMENT ROOMS written on it. We go through to another corridor with doors on both sides. Each door has a clipboard hanging from a hook, and on each clipboard is a name. Rutte's team clear the first room, checking the patient over for guns or a gunshot wound.

I spot, further down the corridor, a door with Huisman's name on it. I catch Vermeer's eye. She nods. By the time the team are at Huisman's door, one officer each side of the door frame, I'm starting to sweat.

They do their countdown hand gestures, then one of them reaches out and turns the handle. Ten seconds later one of them yells 'Clear' from inside and they exit and move on to the next. Soon the FRU are moving round the corner like a human millipede.

'I think I heard something suspicious in there, did you?'

'I did indeed,' Vermeer says.

I close the door behind us. It's sparse inside, with only a small window set high in the wall. There's a toilet and washbasin in a corner, and a table with a book on it, and a single bed with a man lying on his back.

By now I recognize him.

It's been years, and the years haven't been kind, but it's definitely him.

This is the Huisman we've been looking for.

We've found him, I think to myself, the thought repeating in an ever-spinning loop.

I find myself soaring, giddy with it all.

'Did you send the message like we discussed?'

'Uhhh . . . You're not going to believe this. I got all the gear together, went over there, but . . .'

'But what?'

'It was already done. It's burning right now.'

'What? How can that be?'

'I don't know, I just don't know.'

'Don't tell me you don't know. Jesus. Are we still in control of this thing?'

'Right now, I'm not sure.'

He hangs up and puts the phone back in the drawer. The desk tilts, the room spins. He picks up his desk phone, takes a few deep breaths, then dials a number. One he'd hoped he was never going to have to call.

Fire

It's definitely Huisman, the man we've been chasing all this time.

We step towards the bed and he lets out a low groan before his head jerks up suddenly, as if an electrical current's passing through him. He's held there for a few seconds before his muscles go slack and his head drops back down. He groans again and I realize he's strapped down with thick fabric bands.

'He looks like shit,' Vermeer says. 'Not sure he's faking it.'

Heroin withdrawal's no joke. I once sat with an ex-colleague who'd had to shoot up undercover and just couldn't seem to kick the habit once he returned to desk work. The withdrawal itself broadly fits into three stages. In the first eight hours after the final dose the craving starts to take hold, and people often seem to get irritable at even the smallest things. Then it starts to go downhill in stage two. The stomach cramps, the profuse sweating, the desperate desire to move increasing in intensity over the next day or so, the unbearable knowledge that there's a simple remedy to stop all this just a needle prick away. The third and final stage can last for days: muscles spasms, diarrhoea, vomiting, your body alternating between a high fever and a death-like chill till you'd claw your own eyes out in despair. Some veterans add in a fourth phase: relapse.

From the looks of it, though, Huisman's in the second. I step closer and see his T-shirt and tracksuit bottoms are dark with sweat. He also smells like he's been sweating for some time. He turns his head and opens his eyes slowly like it's a struggle. The whites of his eyes are heavily bloodshot and have the manic quality of a person seeing things.

'No . . .' he says, his voice like paper sliding off paper. 'No more.'

You can see from his eyes we're not getting anything out of him for a while. Maybe even days. Days he's going to have to spend in the drunk tank, which is a far cry from here. In any other situation, if we weren't here to arrest a man we suspect of brutally killing two young women, I might even feel sorry for him.

'You want to do the honours?' I ask Vermeer.

She reads him his rights, though it's clear he's not really taking it in. Once done we loosen the straps, and help him upright. He's groaning, but compliant. But as Vermeer pulls the cuffs out a change comes over him.

'No!' he screams and lunges at me. I sidestep, only my foot lands on something and shoots out from under me. He takes advantage of my loss of balance, coming at me hard, the impact knocking me down. Vermeer reacts fast, grabbing him from behind in a chokehold. He reverses direction, slamming her back into the far wall and then elbows her in the stomach. She gasps and loosens her grip, and he slips out of her grasp and turns to her. I'm scrambling up from the floor as he throws the first punch right at her face. But Vermeer ducks, his fist hits the concrete with a sickening crunch, and she's already grabbed his wrist and is twisting it down behind his back. It's swift and clinical. She has him cuffed and on his knees in seconds.

'You all right?' I ask.

She shrugs, like it was nothing. 'More worried about you.'

'Yeah, just . . .' I look round to see what I'd slipped on. It's a clipboard, the type that hang on the ends of beds in hospitals. I pick it up just as Vermeer's manoeuvring Huisman to the door.

'Let's get this fucker booked in,' she's saying just as my heart detonates hard in my chest. The room starts to spiral very, very slowly.

'Oh shit . . .' It can't be true.

Vermeer stops. 'What?'

I hand her the clipboard over a vast distance.

'What am I looking at?'

I point to the date of admission.

It's two full days before Marianne Kleine was killed.

It takes less than ten minutes to confirm that Huisman checked in when the clipboard said he did, and hasn't left the property since. In fact, he'd not even left the room, and the CCTV footage the woman in charge had shown me, since Vermeer had decided not to be seen by her again, confirmed that. Huisman is categorically off the hook.

I walk out of there and feel like the world's dropping away from me. All this work to get to Huisman, only to find he can't have killed Marianne Kleine. Which in turn means he most likely wasn't Lucie Muller's killer either. I feel a deep cold creeping through me. Because we've now got two murders, two young women whose lives were taken from them, and no idea of who or why.

Vermeer lets me drive, and we don't talk. Because what is there to say?

A few minutes out from the station Vermeer finally speaks.

'You covered yourself, right?'

'How do you mean?'

'I mean, they're not going to be able to trace that call to you, are they?'

I needn't have worried about her being able to handle the situation after two cocktails. Seems it takes far more than that to reduce her performance. I wonder just how experienced a drinker she is. Then I think of my voice, converted to a series of 1s and 0s, there for anyone to listen to, analyse. The scratching and whispering should be enough. Should. But there's always a chance some hotshot audio engineer has developed a new technique for clearing up recordings. But I can't think of that now.

'No,' I tell her. 'Because that would make literally no sense.'

'It would literally make a *lot* of sense.'

'Something I've learnt over the years is that the odds are so stacked against you most of the time –'

'You make your own odds?'

'– that when you do get a break, sheer good luck, you have to grasp it.'

She stares at me as if by doing so she can reveal the truth.

'I hope so,' she finally says. 'I really, really hope so.'

My phone goes off. I check the screen. Leah. Kush

must be barking again. She'll have to cope. I'll be back there soon. I let it ring out and it starts again. Again I let it ring, again it finally cuts off then starts afresh.

'Oh for fuck's sake.' Vermeer grabs the phone off me as I'm taking the third exit of a tricky roundabout.

'Who's Leah?'

'My neighbour. She doesn't like it when Kush barks.'

'Rykel's phone,' she says, imitating a bored secretary. 'How may I help?'

She listens for a few moments then, 'What? Say that again.' She listens then hangs up.

'What is it?'

'She said . . .'

'What? What did she say?'

'Your houseboat,' she says, turning to look at me, her face flicking on and off in the passing street lights. 'Your houseboat's on fire.'

Stark Night

I can smell it before I even turn into Bloemgracht, that rich, dry rasp of woodsmoke cut with something more unsavoury: plastic, paint, unnatural things. I run down Bloemstraat, unable to see my houseboat yet, but Rashid's coffee place across the canal gives me a taster, its windows ablaze with reflected flame. Blue lights flicker too, catching tree trunks and highlighting faces in windows as they watch the firefighters battle from the shore.

I'm running hard into the heavy, ballooning heat and a fireman sees me coming, throws an arm across my chest, stopping me getting any closer.

'Have you seen my dog?' I scream over the noise. 'That's my boat – have you seen my dog?'

The fireman just shakes his head and holds fast. I can see Leah on the far side of the fire engine, the heat distorting the air between us so she looks wobbly, unreal. I can't see if she has Kush with her. I think of the electrics, and for a crushing moment realize it's my fault. They'd been faulty and I'd left them on. With Kush inside. Two men direct the hose, strafing the aft of the boat. The flames roar and crackle, and when the water hits them they hiss too. But the water does little more than dampen the flames down; they seem to come back with increased ferocity. I turn away, back off from the fireman and run behind the fire engine towards Leah's boat. But as I round the truck I can see she's standing there alone, Kush not with her, watching my boat burn and hoping the fire doesn't reach hers. She looks so old suddenly, so old and alone, like she's the last human on the planet, staring into the cataclysm which took us all.

I step beside her and she turns to look at me and just shakes her head. After a few moments she reaches out a hand and clasps mine, holding it tight. I look at the flames and see something, a shape in the darkness between two flames dancing on the roof. It's gone in a flash, but it appears again. Then again and again.

It looks like a black wolf, head thrown back, fur standing proud on the back of its neck, as if howling at the moon.

A spark becomes its eye, before it's gone in an instant.

'Jaap?'

I don't know how long I've been here. The firefighters left, the fire engine groaning away into the night, Leah back on board her boat, safe as the flames were doused before they got there, and the faces in the windows gone back to their lives, their beds, their dreams. And I'm here sitting on the concrete edge of the canal, my feet hanging over dark water. I notice suddenly I'm shivering. I turn to see Sabine standing close by.

'Jaap, oh my god. Are you okay? I was calling and you didn't answer . . .'

I feel her arm round my shoulders as she sits next to me. We sit there for a long time and eventually my shivering stops. Later, back at her flat, I let the water from the shower pour over my head as I think about what I've lost, about how Kush must've died in agony – the panic, the fear. I screw up my eyes but the images get worse so I keep them open. I end up counting the number of tiles on the wall, over and over, like I'm stuck in a loop. Finally, when the water's run cold, I get out and dry myself. I'm in a daze, my movements automatic. Next thing I know I'm standing, staring at myself in the mirror when the door opens and Sabine steps in naked. She kisses me, and yet all I can think about is the shape I saw in the flames.

Sabine's caressing me now, kissing my neck, my chest. She sinks to her knees and sucks me into her mouth and I try to fade away, lose myself in it.

But as I close my eyes I can still see my houseboat, the flames dancing accross it with glee.

And, worst of all, the eye, staring right at me, a dot of fire in the vast dark of my mind.

Later I wake in bed, the thud of my heart so loud for a moment I think there's someone hammering on the door. I get up slowly, I don't want to disturb Sabine, and creep through to the bathroom. There's a window there, looking out over the rooftops, and I open it and let the night in, hoping it will calm me down. The air's cool and smells of the city I know so well, the city I've always called home. *But now?* I wonder. *Can it be again?*

I must be imagining it but I catch the scent of burning and close the window. I go back to bed, where Sabine is mumbling something in her sleep. I gently get in and lean closer, holding my breath. It takes me a while to work out she's saying something over and over again.

I'msorryI'msorryI'msorryI'm . . .

I lie here in the stark night and wonder if it ever ends.

One Day Before

The Day Before

Green

The cold water's like a stun gun to the face.

I crank the tap off, grab a towel and dry myself. Then I step over to the window, open it and lean out. Grey clouds like a lid over the city, gentle rain. I listen to it trickling in the gutter just below the window and wonder if it would have made any difference. If it had rained yesterday, would it have stopped the fire?

Here I am again, I think.

I was so close to being out, turning my back on the police, the person it'd made me become. But I got caught up in it again, giving in to that part of me that can't let go, the part of me which has to know, has to find out who killed Lucie Muller and Marianne Kleine, who it was who'd stripped them naked, slit their throats and let them bleed out like beasts in an abattoir.

And now I've been punished for it. Punished for being who I am. The darkness within. My mouth's dry.

I find the note in the kitchen, held down with a set of keys. Her handwriting's bold, fluid, and reminds me of old parchments and quill pens. It tells me she's had to go to work but that I can stay as long as I like. There's not much else around. Sabine had said she was only here temporarily whilst she looked for somewhere more permanent; her stuff is all in storage. I'd found a charger plugged in next to the toaster, so I drift around the place aimlessly whilst I wait for my phone to charge, and try not to think of what I've lost. I flick the radio on, voices arguing about the acid attack, which a fundamentalist group has now claimed responsibility for. Click. Silence. Which gets drowned out by the noise inside my head. I don't think I can cope with it right now.

I wander around looking for something to distract myself with. In the living area, a small space with little more than a TV on the wall, I move a cardboard box off the sofa and a photo falls out. In it Sabine's sitting on a stone wall somewhere out in the countryside, her hair flapping about in the wind. I wonder who took the photo. Was it her ex, Tom? The one who'd stabbed me in the arm and shoved me down the steps?

Despite the transience of the place, it still seems like hers, and it starts to feel like an intrusion, more intimate an act than sleeping with her. I force down a coffee laced with sugar, and some sliced cheese I find in the fridge, which I roll up like a cigar before biting off the end. It tastes old. I spit it out and chuck the rest. Next I try to compose a note to Sabine, but after several false starts scrunch it up into a ball I put in my pocket. There's a first-aid kit under the bathroom sink. I clean off the wound and use a plaster which is only just big enough. I drop the old dressing into the bin. It lands face down, white fabric with a large circle of blood dried in the middle.

Just as I've locked the front door I suddenly realize I've left the bathroom window upstairs open. Earlier I'd noticed that if someone was able to get onto the roof just below it they could easily reach up to the sill and clamber in. And given Sabine's ex's temperament I decide to go back in and shut it. There's a puddle on the floor, the rain must have shifted, and I mop it up and then make my way out into the city.

I keep expecting to feel anger, but everything around me is distant somehow, like I'm not part of it. Shock can be like that, a cocoon that separates you from the world. As I walk to the station the city seems alien. Another time, another place, but with me as spectator. Raindrops prickle the skin of my face. I've been through this before, though, and I made it out. Just.

The question is, do I have enough left to do it again?

It's not long before I'm soaked to the bone. I think I should go home and change, before the thudding reality hits me that I now have no home. I've lost everything, clothes included, and for a moment I'm caught in a vortex of dizziness.

Once it's passed I buy some clothes and a raincoat, stuffing my wet gear into the plastic bag offered, and then duck into a small coffee place on Runstraat. Once I've drained half the cup, the hot liquid only partly warming me up, I start to feel a little better, so I pull out the phone and make the call I've been putting off. But the electrician doesn't answer. I leave a message asking him to call me urgently. Then I tackle my voicemail, of which there are plenty. The last is from someone called Theo Veldt. He's the fire investigator assigned to the case and says he'll be there at midday, if I'd like to meet him there. I'm not sure I can face it. I know that he's going to find it was the electrics. I must have left something on and condemned Kush to his death.

I turn on to Keizersgracht, past all the fancy houses,

and then turn right into Leidsestraat. It's busier here, two tramlines and people on bikes streaming in both directions, spray spinning off their tyres in elegant arcs. A man in work boots, hard hat and an orange hi-vis steps out of McDonald's taking large bites out of a burger, and knocks into me. Further down a shop window is full of TVs, a jumble of different-sized screens. They're all tuned to the same channel, a news programme; there's a talking blonde head, and in the corner of the screen a small rectangle with a scene I recognize. The rectangle zooms out till it takes up the full screen. It's shaky mobile-phone footage of my boat burning in the dark. From the angle I can work out roughly where it was taken from, a house across the canal in the opposite direction to Rashid's. I watch it for a bit, the flames being tickled by the jets of water before it ends and the talking head appears with the next news item. I'm starting to think the electrician's not answering my calls because he's seen this and skipped town. I walk on quickly, my heart punching my ribcage. All of a sudden I know what's coming. I can feel it, a presence behind me, gathering strength, a sense of darkness sucking at my back, sucking at my feet, sucking all the air out of the world.

It hits when I'm crossing the next bridge. At first I think there's an earthquake. But it's not; it's the anger, the black wolf. I stumble to the rail and grab it as the rage ignites inside. People cycle by, no one stops. I get my vape out, press the button. It's taking too long, and I feel myself start to slide. My fingers fumble and the vape falls into the water below. Splash. A tram rumbles. The bell clangs once. Reality fragments into static scenes. Time loops.

Traffic. Horns blaring. I stumble into someone. *Hey-watchout*. Clouds. Spires. Circling birds. Voices coming in and out of focus. Hands in front of me. My hands? Opening a gate. Rain rain rain. Back of my neck. Coin on the ground. *Black wolf's eye*. More horns *speeding* past and dropping in pitch and another one and *another one* and a . . . Wait here for a while, maybe it'll pass. Walking now, *feet* distant; they look miles away. Better not look down. Time speeds up, *blur of people*, too fast. *Black*. *Faces*. Faces. *Faces*. Station Chief Smit, gun wound. *Faces faces* faces. *Shoe in my hand. Throw. One. Two. Screams. A woman's face. Fear on it. Move. Move now. Wet grass* against my *soles. Eyes. Eyes everywhere. Mouths muttering. Soft* whispers building *to a* deafening *roar. Hands clamped on ears. Heart thudding.* A man taking something out of a bin. *The eyes are looking at me. Sodden cigarette butts clustered round a lamp post. There's something I . . . On the move again. Where am I?* Where are *we? What* are *we? Our head's turning, a million freeze-frames one after the other.* Metallic taste. *Wet grass on my cheek. Something crawling in my ear. There's something . . . Time stoooooooooooooooooooooooooooooops.*

What – do I . . .

The call had not gone well. Which was hardly a surprise. He's driving home from the office, having told his PA he had a last-minute doctor's appointment. Only the doctor is waiting for him at home, inside a bottle with a fancy label. The traffic lights up ahead turn red and he slows to a standstill. Another car pulls up alongside him and he feels jumpy all of a sudden. He glances over and sees a couple of young men, mid-twenties most likely. They have the windows down, music blaring, the driver smoking a cigarette, the passenger upending a bottle of something. They're pumped up and he suddenly zooms back in time to twenty years earlier when it could have been him in the car. He finds himself wondering what happened. How did he end up where he is now? What would his younger self do if he'd known the route he was travelling down would land him here? The light changes and the car roars away, but he just sits there, unable to move, unable to press the accelerator until the next light cycle comes round.

It's Not The World – It's How You Look At It

'Rykel.'

I look up to see Vermeer behind bars. For a moment or two I wonder what she's done to deserve that, then realize it's actually me behind them. But then I think that really it's only a matter of perspective. She tries to slide them open but they're locked.

'Hey,' she calls out to someone further down the corridor. 'Hey, why's this locked? You know who that is in there?'

A guard saunters into view, unhooking a large key chain from his belt. He takes an age deciding on the key. It's got to be some kind of record. Finally he selects one, holds it up for a final inspection, then slips it into the lock.

He shrugs. 'Just following orders.'

The key turns, the bars slide through each other like an optical illusion, and for a moment I feel on the verge of being catapulted back.

Vermeer steps into the cell. 'C'mon, let's get you out of here.'

They'd found me in Amsterdamse Bos, a call from a concerned citizen alerting them to my whereabouts. The panic was starting to subside as the two uniforms approached me, but I was still a long way from being coherent. That was hours ago, how many I'm not sure, but the dark undercurrent is still there, still pulling at me, sucking me down. I need cannabis, and quick. Or I risk going back.

Vermeer stands with me whilst the duty sergeant fetches the box and pulls out my keys and phone. No wallet. I query that. The man shrugs, hands me a bit of paper I don't recall signing, relinquishing one set of keys. Nothing else. No vape. There's a memory of it disappearing in water.

I turn to go.

'Hey, what about your keys?'

I stare down at them, a single latch key and a Chubb, both shiny and worn from use.

'The door they unlock no longer exists.'

He looks at me like I'm crazy. Which given my state when I was brought in is probably not surprising. I suddenly remember I had two sets, though, and Sabine's aren't here.

'Where are the other ones?'

'There are no other ones; these are the keys you had on you when you were brought in.'

'No, that can't be right. I had another set.'

I try to think back, remember what's happened to them, but it's hopeless, my memory a confusing jumble.

'Why don't you just take these?' he says to me like I'm clearly unhinged and will regret it later.

I must've lost them. Fuck. I'm going to have to tell Sabine. I look at the keys to my houseboat. They're vibrating, though no one else seems to see it.

'No, really. Chuck 'em.'

It's no longer raining when we step outside and I suddenly wonder just how long I was out. A few hours, longer? The darkness is still sucking at my back.

'I need to go to a coffeeshop.'

'Rykel, you were found sprawled on the grass in Amsterdamse Bos mumbling incoherently, jumping at shadows. You tried to fight off two of the officers and they had to restrain you, which is why you ended up in that cell. I *really* think you need to lay off.'

'You don't understand.'

'You're right, I don't.'

She's a bit ahead of me now, something righteous in her bearing. I can hardly blame her. I was the same once. Only what I've gone through has changed me. I'm no longer the same person I was even six months ago. And something I realized during that period when I started to finally get better is that, really, it's not the world – it's how you look at it. Only looking at it differently is not always so easy on its own. Sometimes you need help.

'You're not hearing me. I need it right now or it'll happen again.'

'What you *need* is to take a real hard look at yourself,' she says, spinning round, her eyes flashing. 'You're standing in the street, with *no shoes on*, telling me you need a psychoactive drug.'

When I look down I discover she's right. Okay. I get that it's not ideal, but neither's my life right now. And really, if she had a headache I'm sure she'd pop a pill. What's the difference?

'It won't take long.'

In the end she actually waits outside Barney's Lounge on Reguliersgracht whilst I have to deal with a bud-tender who harbours a bottomless pit of contempt for humanity before I'm finally hitting a dab rig. I don't normally like dabs – highly concentrated cannabis extracts are not the same as vaporizing flower – but in this case I need the quickest way to get the stuff into my system. Afterwards, as the anxiety starts to melt, the sucking darkness finally receding, she takes me to a store and buys me a new pair of shoes. I catch her looking at me in a mirror as I lace them up.

I'm pretty sure the look is one of pity.

Everyone is on eggshells at the station. Creeping round me as if I'm going to blow up. Or they might catch something, as if bad luck's an illness, a vector for infectious disease. I'm at a desk in the incident room, work going on behind me, my first footstep across the threshold killing the usual banter stone-cold dead. It's been over an hour since Vermeer got me out of the drunk tank, and I've been feeling better, the dab I'd had really calming things down, though maybe it's taken me a little too far in the opposite direction. Dabs can do that; they can blanket the pain, but sometimes that blanket's too thick.

Now I'm in the canteen, the same table overlooking the intersection I'd sat at with Jansen three days and a lifetime ago, wondering just how it's come to this so quickly. Homeless, jobless. Probably responsible for putting an innocent man in prison, definitely responsible for Kush's death.

'Fuck, man. I'm so sorry.'

I look up to see Jansen. He slaps me on the back, massages my shoulder.

'Seriously, I only just heard. That's so fucked up,' he's saying.

I look at him. For some reason I find the expression on

his face, the personification of earnest concern, strange. Then I start to find it amusing. It must be the effects of the dab, I realize, a second wave swelling up inside me, blossoming in my head like some kind of weird jungle flower. I start to laugh. Hard. Tears stream out of my eyes, collect with a tickle under my chin. From there they drip down on to my still damp top. I'm finding it all hilarious.

He looks at me as if I'm mad.

'Get me a coffee, will you?' I ask when I've managed to stop laughing.

He returns with two cups, a *stroopwafel* balanced on the rim of each. He hands me mine, I can see the caramel centre is already starting to go sticky, and then sits down opposite.

'You all right? You seem a little . . .'

I think he wants to say crazy, but doesn't quite manage to get it out. I take a bite from my *stroopwafel*, I'm suddenly hungry as hell, and it disappears in no time. Jansen looks at me like I've turned into a monster, but then hands me his *stroopwafel*.

'Listen, I've got to . . .'

'Go for it,' I tell him. 'And thanks for this.'

He nods, then takes his coffee and starts to walk away before stopping and turning back. I demolish his *stroopwafel* just as fast.

'By the way, that info you asked for on DH Biotech? You want it still?'

I think about what else I could be doing right now. Don't seem to have a lot of options.

'Yeah. Might as well take a look.'

*

In the incident room he hands me a massive stack of papers. It must be well over 200 pages of assorted papers and looks like it must've taken Jansen a significant chunk of time to pull together. Luckily the caffeine's synergizing nicely with the dab and I feel motivated. I find a desk and settle in for the long haul.

The background to the company I already know; I'm more interested in the years when Muller and Kleine were both on the board, and I quickly narrow it down and focus my attention there. After a good hour of solid reading I'm beginning to get a picture, a company with financial difficulties which had pinned its hopes, and dwindling resources, on an experimental drug simply codenamed FAA673. I have to skip some of the more intense pharmacology. I realize that Joel would probably be able to help with that if needs be, but in essence FAA673 was a compound targeting a specific set of receptors in the brain implicated in appetite control, and it was hoped this could prove a preventative to obesity and therefore to all the other associated problems: diabetes, heart disease, cancer. Basically, reading between the lines, they were confident that this could become a first-line treatment, a drug that every doctor could prescribe to patients at risk. Which is probably just about everyone. I'm starting to see why they believed FAA673 could be so lucrative. One executive had noted in an email that FAA673 could be bigger than statins.

Joel had once told me about statins, a long rant demonstrating that not only were they not necessary, but they were actively screwing with you. I don't remember the details, but he was pretty plausible. It was things like that which made him switch sides, as it were. Google gives me a rough global market value of over 30 billion dollars a year.

If FAA673 could come even close to that, then no wonder they were excited.

The animal trials had gone well, and they'd had approval from all the regulatory bodies to progress to a phase-one trial, which from what I read means the first trial on humans after it's been tested on animals. But after that the information starts to become more sparse, and just over a year and a half later the company posts an enormous loss in their accounts.

I turn back, trying to find out what had changed. It takes a little while to piece it together, but it seems likely that the human trial had not delivered the results they'd been expecting. With their finances in such a perilous state the failure of FAA673 seems to have given a significant mauling to DH Biotech's bottom line. But in the end I'm not sure what any of this means. I'm just about to give up when I notice a mention of legal action buried deep in the index of a board meeting several years ago. But when I flip to the relevant part of the minutes there's no mention of it at all, at least that I can see. I flip back and check the page reference again; it *is* there in the index, but not in the document itself. I do what anyone does in this situation, turn to Google. I try 'DH Biotech Legal Action' and get no results. A little disclaimer at the bottom of the screen tells me that pursuant to some obscure EU regulation some results may have been removed due to privacy issues. Hmmm.

I go back to the stack of papers. The minutes were from the first meeting after the trial, so I try to delve into that. The trial itself had been scheduled to happen at the AMC in a private ward. There were to be twelve volunteers, and the trial was going to be double-blind, meaning half of them would be getting FAA673 and half a placebo, but crucially the staff administering the two wouldn't know which was which either. The compound had a half-life of just six hours, so the patients would be monitored for twenty-four, then allowed to leave. But that's where things end. Because I can't find anything else on the trial. Surely there'd be notes on the results, something to say why the drug didn't work? The company had its financial future pegged to the outcome, so I'd expect to at least see something.

They're headquartered in Den Haag, but I don't feel like the drive right now, so I pick up the phone. I start at the bottom, and after working my way up through increasing layers of bureaucracy, I'm once again listening to a ringtone, waiting for someone to pick up.

'Joost Beltmann.'

His voice is light, a tenor I'd guess, but confident. I explain what I'm after.

'How did you get this number?'

'It's taken me quite a while, no one seemed able to help, and I've been passed around from –'

'I'm sorry to hear that, but I'm afraid I'm unable to help either. Not sure why you got put through to me; it's not my department at all.'

I feel like I'm going to crush the phone in my hand.

'So who do I need to be talking to?'

'Give me your number. I'll get someone to call you back. Someone who can help.'

I give him my mobile and hang up. I'll give it an hour. In the meantime I turn to plan B, dialling the AMC's switchboard. It's working hours so I know Nellie will have her mobile phone turned off. It takes me a few minutes but I'm finally connected to Dr Nellie de Vries' line. She only started her clinic at the AMC after the trial took place, but at least she might be able to point me in the right direction.

I'm only expecting her answer machine, so it's a surprise when her voice comes on the line. We spend a few minutes talking, though I neglect to tell her about my houseboat. It would take too long, and frankly I want to forget about it for a bit. Using work to avoid my personal troubles? Well, yeah. Me and the rest of the world. I explain what I'm after and she promises to look into it. She does mention that there's unlikely to be much, as the trials are highly guarded. The pharmaceutical companies don't want anyone to know what they're up to, so it's likely that any AMC staff involved didn't know much, if anything. I hang up and turn back to the papers, trying to see if there's anything I've missed and I'm caught up in it all until the thought of Kush burning to death hits me out of nowhere.

I burst into tears.

Ash lifts lazily into the air each time I put a foot down. I breathe in the residue of my incinerated life. Right now I could be inhaling part of the washing machine, the kitchen table, a CD of Bach's 'Magnificat', hydrocarbons from any number of objects I'd owned or obscure parts of the boat's construction seeping into my lungs, and from there travelling throughout my body until they cross the blood–brain barrier doing who knows what damage. Or Kush. Kush could now be there, inside my head. I feel a deep wave of nausea.

Once it's passed I tune in to the fire investigator, a tall man with a neat grey moustache whose hands were freezing cold when we'd shaken earlier. Currently he's crouched down where I calculate my sofa would have been. The whole top deck is gone, so the space which was below deck is now open to the sky. The hull, being made of some kind of metal, has stayed mostly intact, enough to keep it afloat at any rate.

'It was the electrics,' I tell him. 'They'd just been fixed but something went wrong with one of the circuits yesterday.'

'Where was the consumer unit?'

I take him there and let him get on with his work. And I walk back through where the bedroom wall once stood to the main space. The devastation is total. I don't see how this can ever be repaired. I find myself over by the bathroom, where Kush would have been. The bath is still there, about a third full of ash. How long would he have lasted? I wonder. Maybe he'd already passed out from the smoke before the fire itself reached him. In many ways that would be the best option. A wave crashes down on me. It's not canal water, it's guilt. And sorrow. Possibly shame as well.

'Not the electricity.'

I find I have to wipe my eyes before turning to look at the fire inspector, who has managed to walk up behind me without me hearing him.

'What?'

'The fire wasn't started by electricity.'

'You're sure?'

'Yeah. And I'm also sure it wasn't an accident either. Come and have a look.'

He takes me round and points out what he claims are four separate ignition points.

'Four?'

'At least. And that doesn't happen by accident. No way.'

On land a van's trying to parallel park, accompanied by a loud series of beeps and a recorded voice. *Stand clear, vehicle reversing. Stand clear, vehicle reversing. Stand clear, vehicle . . .*

'Someone set it alight . . .'

'Yeah,' he says over the noise of the van, 'and whoever started this wasn't taking any chances. They wanted it to burn.'

He's getting ready to leave, and says he'll have his report written up by the end of the day. I find I'm still standing in the exact same spot.

'You got any enemies?' he asks as he steps ashore.

Sometimes I think the world is nothing but.

I step ashore myself and sit on the canal's edge. Some-one wanted my boat to burn. This is what Joel would call next-level shit, and I can feel the dark undertow swelling beneath me again. I pull out the tin of five pre-rolled joints I'd bought as a take-out after the dab and light one. Why would anyone want to burn down my houseboat? Just the random act of some lunatic? That's bad enough, but what if it wasn't?

What if it was something personal?

You got any enemies?

A shudder snakes down my spine.

*

Joint finished I get up, thinking I'd better drop in on Leah, when I spot Rashid's place across the canal. Flashback to Kush chasing the man who'd been trying to get on board. A jumble of thoughts fall into place. I start running, my footsteps echoing off the houses over the canal like rapid gunshots. People turn and stare. I startle a seagull as I turn onto the bridge taking me over the canal. It dribbles a thin line of shit as it rises fast, flapping wings and screeching. As I'm nearing Rashid's I glance up, and yes it's there. I burst in, hoping against hope that he'd actually turned the thing on. I find I'm panting hard as I explain what I need to a startled Rashid.

Ten minutes later, with a coffee in hand – Rashid wasn't doing anything until he'd plied me with a steaming mug – I'm hunched over a laptop in the back office. It's tiny, more of a broom cupboard really with a flickering light I'd been forced to turn off for fear of an epileptic fit, and stacks of paper invoices in dire need of a bookkeeper. The focus of the CCTV is obviously the front door, the way the original thieves had got in, but given the angle, in the top right-hand corner of the screen the aft of my houseboat is just visible and the canal side beyond. I watch myself appear briefly. Kush is with me, though the camera only just caught the end of his tail. I pause it for a few moments before hitting play again.

Rashid's head pokes round the door. 'Anything?'

'Not yet.'

He disappears again and I carry on until I see the first wisps of smoke and the flicker of flame initially reflected on the water. So whoever it was came from the other end. I'll have to check if there are any other cameras along the canal, but somehow I doubt it. The blaze is getting bright fast and I watch it intensify. Suddenly there's movement on the shore and I have to rewind. I inch the footage forward slowly until I catch a glimpse of an odd figure twisted out of shape, one arm trailing behind him. It takes me a moment or two to work it out, but once my brain's locked on to it it's clear as day. The figure is a man running away from my houseboat. *He's wearing a hoody.* The man who'd been poking round the houseboat the other day. The one I thought was a simple druggy, trying to fund his habit with a bit of light burglary.

Only he came back, torched my houseboat, killed Kush.

I'm starting to think he wasn't a simple druggy at all.

Familiar

'Not you again. I'm pretty sure your clearance was revoked.'

The desk sergeant's a charmer. No doubt about it. He scans a list with his finger, lips pursed, eyebrows furrowed like he's pondering a difficult question.

'Yup, there you are,' he says finally, pointing out my name, then sliding his finger across to the next column, which is coloured red. All done with an air of supreme satisfaction. 'Permission revoked. See?'

'That's not why I'm here.'

'No?'

'No. I'm here to report a crime.'

He dips his head and looks at me over the rim of his glasses, his eyebrows riding high.

'Well, at least you left the mutt at home today.'

The rush is like a raging torrent. I grab the clipboard from him, toss it away and grab the guy's shirt front, hauling him forward. His eyes shrink down with fear, his mouth open but no words coming out. My right fist is up in the air ready to strike. On the way down a hand grabs my wrist and just stops me making contact.

'Steady on, sir,' Jansen says.

'You all right?'

Canteen, drink in front of me. I breathe out. The rage vanished as quickly as it came. Now I just feel like crying. Jesus.

'I'll be fine,' I say, hoping that's the truth. 'Good catch.'

'I was kind of torn to be honest. You're not the first to feel the guy could use a bit of a slap.'

Once I've convinced Jansen I'm not going to try and hit anyone else I go off in search of Roemers. I find him at his desk, signature audiophile headphones on, colossal over-ear pieces which look pretty ridiculous, and so he doesn't hear me as I walk up behind him and tap the back of his neck.

'Fuck –'

I hold out the USB with the footage on and explain what I'm after.

'Yeah, well. First off, I'm going to have to recover from the heart attack you just gave me, then I've got some other things I'm working on for various *real* police officers so I'll get round to it when I'm ready. In an hour or three. When I can be arsed.'

'Okay, I'm sorry. But if I was to tell you my houseboat burned down last night and there's video of the man that did it?'

'Really? That's rough. What happened?'

'Like I said, someone set it on fire. The man you'll see on there. Killed my dog as well.'

He swivels round in his chair, his face hardening fast. 'You're fucking with me?'

'Do I look like I am?'

He takes me in for a moment. Chews his lip, nods a few times.

'Fuck man, a dog . . . I'm on it now.'

He's been eyeing me up for a while, and suddenly sees his chance. I'm in the waiting area for Nellie's clinic at the

AMC and a trolley with soiled bedding moves between us, but the second it's past he slips off his seat, one foot finding the floor tentatively, then the other. He moves quickly across the space, all the while his eyes staring at mine. He reaches me and I can hear his breathing, heavy and laboured. He has something in his hand and he raises it slowly and then stabs my leg over and over again. A grin cracks his face open and a long line of drool spills out of his mouth. Snot-crusts round each nostril.

'Darling, darling, don't do that,' says a woman's voice in English.

She hustles over and tries to stop any more crayon damage, though this kid's got the kind of persistence that makes global CEOs. Or serial killers. And maybe it's just my mood, but I don't like the look in his eyes. It seems cold somehow, like there's a dark intelligence in there, watching, waiting. The woman gives me a weak smile and an even weaker apology, which somehow seems to convey the message that it was actually all my fault anyway.

Perched on her hip is another child, who, from the way she's cradling her, is the reason they're here. She looks like a nice kid, a little shy maybe, and I feel bad for her, the situation she's in, even though I know Nellie's going to be able to help her quality of life no end. The woman eventually manages to drag her son across the waiting area and gets him to sit back on his chair, where he sits and stares at me, a colouring book open but untouched in his lap. He's still holding the crayon aloft in an overhand grip. I look at the marks on my jeans and decide the crayon-slasher could do with some psychological screening for the good of society.

Suddenly the young girl makes a strange strangled gurgle. I watch as she shakes, before all her muscles go rigid. Her mother holds her, rocking slightly. Saliva bubbles into a foam at the girl's mouth.

After a few moments, the seizure lessens and her muscles become less rigid. I'm no doctor, but I've been round Nellie long enough to know that she has Dravet syndrome, a severe form of epilepsy which occurs very early on in a child's life. And one for which, up until now, there was no cure.

'The doctor will see you now.'

I look up to see the same nurse who'd deposited me in this zoo twenty minutes ago. I'm relieved to see she's talking to me. I follow her down a corridor painted in Faint Apricot Vomit and start to feel a little queasy myself. And I'm sure I can feel the kid's gaze on the back of my head, boring into me all the way till we stop outside Dr Nellie de Vries' office. The nurse knocks for me – maybe I don't look capable? – then disappears back down the corridor.

Nellie's at her desk, sitting in profile in front of a tall oblong window overlooking a courtyard. She types a few more sentences, then gets up and walks over and we hug. Maybe I hold on a little too tight because afterwards she holds me at arm's length and asks me if I'm all right. I toy with telling her about the houseboat and Kush, but I'm not sure I can stand going over it again. And anyway, it's the last thing Nellie needs. So I skip it, and lie.

'Just a headache.'

'What happened?' she asks, pointing to my jeans as I take the seat she offers me.

'There's a kid out there who wanted to kill me. Luckily the only weapon he had available was a crayon.'

'Let me guess, boy, five years old. Black hair. Snot running down his nose?'

I nod.

She shakes her head. 'I saw them waiting out there earlier; they're my next appointment. They've come over from the UK. Can't get what they need there. She got into trouble with the law for helping her kid. Pretty barbaric really. Luckily I'll be able to help, but only as long as they stay in the country.'

'That's gotta be tough.'

'Hard to get a job unless you've got at least some Dutch, so really I don't know how long they'll be here. Anyway,' she says, stretching her arms over her head and yawning. 'Sorry, been a long one. But . . .'

She reaches over to her desk, sorts through a small pile of paper and locates what she's after.

'Here, this is all I could find. Not much to go on.'

I take the sheet. It's A4, and has passport-sized photos of twelve people, each one assigned with a number.

'Who are they?'

'These are the people who took part in the trial, the volunteers. This was just for the staff on the ward at the time to keep track of who was given what.'

I look at the faces: twelve men. The photos aren't great; it's clearly a photocopy of a photocopy, the original of which had been fished out of a bin and unscrunched. But still, there's something about one of them, a man, age hard to tell as his face is largely taken over with a thick beard, who is strangely familiar.

'That's not all. One of the nurses who was on the ward that night still works here.'

'Can I speak to her?'

'She'll have had to sign a non-disclosure agreement, so I'm not sure what she'd be able to tell you. What's this actually about?'

'It's probably nothing. Just something that came up in a case.'

'Well, okay, be like that then. Anyway, I've got my next patient.'

'The nurse, where would I find her?'

'You're so predictable. Luckily I already found out for you. She comes off shift in just over –' She checks her watch. '– an hour's time, in the radiology department. But I wouldn't hang out there.'

'No?'

'No, they claim it's safe and all, but really.' She drops her voice. 'Really it's not. Trust me, I'm a doctor.'

'I was thinking maybe I'll go across and sit with Hank.'

'I had lunch with him.'

I know she did. She does every day. We stand up and hug again.

'Have you heard anything yet?'

'Tomorrow. They'll tell me tomorrow.'

Out in the waiting room the freaky kid stares at me as I go past. There's actually something lizard-like about his eyes. He slowly sticks his tongue out. I check no one's watching and do the I'm-watching-you-two-fingers-at-my-eyeballs-then-point thing. Take that, you little fucker. Then I turn to see the nurse who'd walked me up the corridor stepping out of a room just ahead. She's watching me with a look of pure disgust on her face.

'Talk to him,' says the male nurse who's brought me here as he opens the door. 'It helps.'

I step into the room. A balloon inflates inside my throat. Truth is, seeing Hank has never been easy. I'd been there when it happened, and it just as easily could be me lying there with tubes to pump food in and tubes to pump shit out and a ventilator forcing air into my lungs and then releasing it. The machine measuring his heart rate beeps softly and I suddenly wonder if he can actually hear. *Talk to him*, the nurse said. But really, if he can hear people talking to him then he can hear the *beep beep beep*. And that has got to be driving him insane, each reiteration a reminder of the life he's not living, the things he's missing, the way it's all turned out. The balloon in my throat's getting bigger and I'm starting to have trouble breathing. There's a window just beyond the bed, and I step over to open it up, taking a few gasps of air before pulling up a chair. When I've visited him in the past I've tended to just sit, hoping that somehow he can feel my presence.

But with the knowledge that Nellie's decision to turn off life support has been approved and that all we're waiting for is the date, I suddenly feel I *need* to talk to him.

'Hank, it's me.'

The words fall dead into the room. No resonance, no response.

I suddenly realize how much of our world is based on

communicating with each other. So many ways to do it now as well that we're almost constantly communicating, the barrier of space a barrier no longer. We can talk to people all over the world, send messages that arrive instantly, but there are some barriers we've yet to break. And Hank's behind one of them.

I grasp his hand, as if that will make it easier for him to understand me, and start to talk, and soon I'm telling him about everything that's happened to me since he was injured. About Tanya and me, about how, unknown to her, unknown to anyone, I had to kill Station Chief Smit. He'd not only been guilty of some of the most disgusting crimes imaginable, he was also blackmailing me to keep quiet by threatening to reveal a secret about Tanya's past which would have destroyed her. I tell him about how our relationship went south after that because every time I looked at her all I could see was Smit's dying look. How I forced myself on, how seven months later the PTSD hit, how I've somehow come through it all and was on the cusp of getting out for good and yet here I am once again. I also tell him about my houseboat, how someone torched it and I don't know if it was just an act by a random lunatic, or something more, something aimed at me.

When I've finished, drained, nothing left to say, I sit there with the beeping machine.

I've told him everything. But it doesn't feel cathartic. I give his hand a final squeeze and then let go. I'm at the door when I realize there's one thing I didn't tell him.

I hesitate, then walk back, lean down and whisper in his ear.

*

I've missed her. I'd been with Hank longer than I'd thought, and by the time I get down to the radiology department and request to see her I'm told she's just left. I race through the hospital hoping to catch her before she leaves. Someone at the main entrance who knew her said she'd walked out a few minutes before me. I'm panting as I rush outside, trying to guess which way she'd gone. I catch sight of a woman in a nurse's uniform heading towards one of the many bike racks by the parking garage. By the time I get there she's bending down, unlocking a fold-up bike.

'Stephanie Dekker?'

She looks up, a soft enquiring smile on her face and dimples on her cheeks. Her brown hair is cut short, streaked through with blonde accents. There's a red patch of skin on her neck which she absentmindedly scratches, then catches herself and stops abruptly.

'Yes?'

'Nellie de Vries gave me your name.'

Clearly the name doesn't mean anything to her. She starts unfolding the bike.

'Dr de Vries, she works in Paediatrics?'

'Oh yes. She's the one whose husband . . .'

'That's the one. Have you got a minute?'

'Depends on what it is,' she says, tightening up the last hinge clamp with a grimace. 'I've got to pick up my son from school in twenty minutes.'

'It's about a clinical trial you were involved in a few years ago. Run by DH Biotech?'

Nothing changes, her expression is exactly the same, her posture is exactly the same, everything is exactly the same. And yet something's different, like a light behind the eyes is suddenly shut off. It's a reaction I like to see.

'Who are you?'

'Police. Inspector Rykel. And we really do need to chat.'

'I don't remember anything.' She turns her back to me, does a final check on the bike and starts to wheel it away.

'I'm afraid I'm going to have to insist. I'll give you a lift to the school?'

'Do I have a choice?'

'You always have a choice. But all I'm asking is for a quick chat. Please, it could really help.'

'Okay,' she says after a long look at me. 'I've been on my feet for hours; I could do with a lift. But that's all.'

I can work with that as a start. The Stang had been parked far enough away from my houseboat that it hadn't sustained any damage from the fire, and I'd driven it out here. It's up on the sixth floor. Stephanie folds up the bike again and we hit the stairs. I offer to carry it for her but she refuses. It just fits in the back and soon we're corkscrewing down through the levels and out onto the road.

'So you remember the trial I'm talking about?'

She nods, but doesn't exactly gush information at me. I'm about to prompt her again when she speaks.

'Yeah, I remember.'

'So what happened?'

A few more streets go by. We stop at a light.

'It . . . it didn't go well. There were twelve men signed up for the trial. I was just finishing my training and was shadowing the resident matron. She was the one who was administering the drug. We went from bed to bed and injected the numbered vial that corresponded with each volunteer; the point was that we didn't know which was placebo and which was real. Once that was done we had to draw blood from each one every hour, and monitor vitals, things like heart rate, body temperature. We also had to administer some coordination tests, so by the time you'd finished with the twelfth you had to start back with the first one again. Anyway, it was during the second hour when the first volunteer started to complain of a headache. It got worse and worse, and then another volunteer also said they had a headache. By then the first one was screaming in pain and . . . Well, you can imagine how everyone started to freak out. It was chaos. That was when the first one started to bleed out of their nose.'

She shakes her head and looks out the window. Her hands twist in her lap. A cyclist wavers out in front of me with no warning. The brakes bite hard, and the man yells at me with the kind of deep righteousness only found in urban cyclists. The kind that makes my foot itch on the accelerator.

'Then what?'

'We were taken out of there.'

'That was it?'

'For us, yes. I heard several volunteers were taken to intensive care but I don't know any more than that.'

'You never heard how they ended up?'

'No.'

'Isn't that a bit strange?'

'I did ask, but was told nobody knew.'

There's an uncomfortable pause. I get the feeling she's wrestling with something.

'And?'

'And the next day I was told to go to a room to draw some blood from a new patient. There was a man in there, but he didn't look like a patient. He was in a suit, not a hospital gown, which was a bit odd as it was an inpatient ward. He knew my name and told me to sit down and that he wanted to talk to me. He said that he was sorry that I had to be put through what was such a traumatic thing to witness. He also said I didn't need to worry about the volunteers any more, that they'd all made a full recovery.'

'That's all?'

'Those were pretty much the words but . . . I got a sense that he wasn't just letting me know; it was more that he was letting me know that he *knew* I'd asked about them. If that makes sense?'

'You mean he was warning you off from asking any more questions.'

'That's what it felt like. But he was so polite, and seemed not friendly but . . . concerned at any rate. So afterwards I convinced myself I was being silly, that I was imagining things.'

'Did he give you a name?'

'I don't remember, no. I would have remembered. I'm great with names and faces. Helps with the patients if you learn their names quickly.'

'Do you remember what he looked like?'

'What's this all about?'

'Right now I'm not sure.'

We're getting close to the school. I'm hoping for more red lights.

'He was tall, very neat blond hair. And he had a suit on.

I remember thinking it was a very expensive suit. Dark with light pinstripes. There was just something about it which made me think it most likely cost more than I earn in a month. Probably several months.'

'And you never saw this man again?'

'No.'

'You think you'd recognize him now?'

She doesn't even hesitate. 'Yeah, I'd remember him.'

The traffic's thickening, more and more SUVs with blacked-out windows are cruising the streets. Which either means we're heading towards a wannabe-gangsta convention, or we're getting close to the school. I've noticed pick-up time is like a military operation in itself. An old friend had done a tour of duty in Afghanistan, but he said that he'd never been so scared as when he'd started doing the school run. There were women screaming at each other, literally *screaming*, he'd told me with a haunted look, and then they'd go and stand next to each other at the school gate like *nothing had happened*.

The road ahead's clogged up now and I spot a clear side street.

'Mind if I drop you here? I think it's going to be quicker for you.'

I find a spot to hover and she reaches for the door handle.

'Just one more thing. Could you look at the photos of the volunteers and tell me which ones were affected?'

The look on her face says she doesn't want to, but she eventually nods.

I shift up in my seat and pull the folded photocopy of

the volunteers out of my back pocket. She takes it and stares at the images. Then she points out six of them.

'You're sure?'

'You don't forget stuff like that.'

I'm thinking I should mark them but I don't have a pen. I take the sheet back and get her to point them out again. I score under each one with my fingernail. She gets out of the car, flips the seat, and reaches for her bike. I can tell she's hesitating.

'Go on,' I tell her.

'It's just . . . the next day I was asked to fill out a patient death form for a man who'd died the week before. I'd filled out a report at the time but it had got lost. So I did it again and took it down to the office where they record all the deaths. I didn't want it going missing again. Just before I went in I heard one of them talking about the extra deaths from the ICU.'

'Wouldn't you expect that from an ICU?'

'No, it's about the only department in the hospital which runs under capacity most of the time. I've been working here for years, and the most I'd ever heard of being in there at the same time is four. And of those you'd expect roughly half to survive.'

Once she's gone I glance at the sheet again. DH Biotech's trial ended with the deaths of some of the volunteers who'd received the experimental treatment. That much seems clear, but what I can't believe is that DH Biotech have been able to keep it quiet.

I think of the fire investigator's question.

You got any enemies?

Could it be that DH Biotech are already aware of me, know that I'm on the scent which could lead me straight to their door? It can't be. That's just crazy. Isn't it?

I push it out of my mind and look at the photos again, at the man with the thick beard. I'm sure I've never seen him before, I've not seen any of them, but there's something about him, something so familiar. I note that he is one of the images with a score underneath. Which means, if what I've just been told is true, that he probably died as a result of the trial. But still, he looks so familiar.

Volunteer Number Six

To speak to sales, press one. To talk to us about a change to an existing policy, press two. To make a claim, press three. Thank you. Unfortunately all our claims specialists are helping other customers at present, but please continue to hold and one of our agents will be with you shortly.

Bunch of fuckers. And honestly I'm dreading speaking to them. Because whilst I assume my policy covers me for arson, I can't check because even if there was paperwork somewhere on board, and really I don't recall seeing any, there's precisely zero chance that it escaped the blaze.

The only other person in the incident room is the guy who'd grassed me up to Beving about Jansen's shoes, so I put the phone on speaker and slide it away from me across the desk. The music's probably the headline track on a compilation called *Tunes to Hang Yourself By*. Just what you need on an insurance line.

I try to shut my ears off and pull the sheet of photos out. I want to have another look, especially at the one who seems familiar. There's definitely something there, something I just can't place. We need to find out who all these people are. But I'm not sure how we're going to be able to do it. DH Biotech will know of course, but we're not at the warrant stage yet, and there's nowhere near enough evidence to request one.

And yet it's crucial we know who died, and, more

importantly, who survived. After more staring I'm no closer to an answer so I push it aside and, with the music showing no sign of giving way to an actual human being I can talk to, I get on the desk phone. The woman who answers tells me that Nellie is seeing patients, so I ask to be put through to the records office. My thought process is this: Stephanie was sure several died, and there must be a record of their deaths. Not even a large pharma company can cover that up, can they?

After a bit of wheedling I'm finally hooked up to someone with a nasal voice and a clipped turn of phrase which suggests he believes he has better things to be doing. I explain what I'm after.

'I'm not sure those can be given out to just anyone.'

I disabuse the man of his erroneous notion that I'm just 'anyone'.

'In that case I'd have to speak to my manager,' he says.

'Great, I'll hold.'

'Actually, she's away until next Wednesday. So if you'd like to call back maybe on Thursday when she's had a chance to catch up –'

'Christ, what's that music?'

I look up to see Jansen in the doorway. I tell Mr Nasal to expect me and hang up.

'You know what this reminds me of?' Jansen asks loudly just as Vermeer walks in behind him. 'It reminds me of a desperately sad handjob.'

'Is there any other type?' Vermeer asks, flopping down on a chair and putting her feet up on a desk. She closes her eyes and rubs her temples. I'm tempted to tell her that's what cocktails do, but instead I just kill the call and the music stops, leaving us with sweet silence. They both seem pretty morose, though. Which considering everything I've been through in the last twenty-four hours seems unreasonable at best. True, Huisman being put out of the picture's a major blow to everything we've been working on up until now, but still. At least neither of them had their house burn down.

I turn back to what I'm doing. I should get going to the hospital. But even if I get the death records that's not going to tell me who the survivors are without knowing all of their names. And it's the survivors I'm interested in. I pull up Google and punch in FAA673. To my surprise I get a few hits. The first being a government database of all clinical trials, current and past. With my heart beating a little faster, I click on the link for FAA673. It brings me to a detailed page which outlines the original proposal, the date the trial was set for, and eventually the fact that the trial was abandoned. It doesn't say why, though. But there's more, a copy of the original advert, with contact details.

They're not those of DH Biotech, but another company.

I quickly find their details online, and their website boasts of a proven track record in finding and screening suitable candidates for all sorts of clinical trials. Their address is less than fifteen minutes' drive away, close to the AMC itself. This might cheer Vermeer and Jansen up. I call them over and am just about to take them through what I've got when they both get up and flit away like small fish scattering when a shark enters their stretch of water. The shark in this case is Station Chief Frank Beving. A few minutes later I'm standing across from the desk in his office, listening to his condolences about the fire. All delivered with the sincerity of a menopausal supermarket checkout clerk. Duty done, he gets on to the good stuff.

'Obviously, I've heard that subsequent to the fire you weren't that well?'

'I was a little upset,' I concede.

'Yes, well. The report I have here makes it sound a bit more serious.'

'I wouldn't pay any attention to that. You know what patrol are like, drama queens the lot of them.'

He stares at me, but somehow I'm immune to it. It's weird, a few hours ago I was deep within the dark wolf's clutches, now I feel like that Sarah Jarosz song which talks of green lights, open roads and skies of endless blue. Which makes me remember that particular CD, along with everything else I owned, is now gone.

Beving picks up a couple of sheets of paper. He spends some time on the first, then peels it back to look at the one underneath. His eyebrows rise. Dear god, spare me the theatrics.

'No shoes?' he says. 'You were found wearing *no shoes* and mumbling incoherently.'

Why is everyone so hung up on shoes all of a sudden? It's not like bare feet are illegal or anything.

'My feet were hot. And I was reciting poetry; you can't expect patrol to know the difference.'

'All right, enough horseshit. The point is you were only allowed back on to this investigation because –'

The door bursts open behind me. Roemers, headphones

round his neck, a laptop clutched under his arm. 'Been looking all over for you.'

'How strange then that you find me in *my* office.'

'Not you, him.'

'What have you got?' I ask.

He reaches across the desk, roughly shoves a pile of papers out the way, and opens up the laptop. Beving, after pulling a can't-believe-he-just-did-that face which we both ignore, reluctantly gets up and steps round so he too can see the screen.

'There you are,' Roemers says, pointing to the image.

I peer at it. It's exactly the same as the one I showed him earlier.

'Yeah, that's what I gave you.'

He hits the enter key with a flourish worthy of a camped-up stage magician. More theatrics.

The image changes. It's a close-up of the man's head. It's pixelated, blurry and only really his mouth and nose are visible, the hoody low enough to cover his eyes. But nonetheless it's a partial face. Of the man who burned down my boat.

'This is the man who torched my boat,' I tell Beving.

'Whoa, hang on a moment. I thought it was an accident, something electrical?'

I can't believe he hadn't heard. Then again I can't actually remember who I've told about the fire investigator's findings. Things have been a little blurry recently.

'No, the fire was started deliberately. At least four ignition points.'

'Says who?'

'Says the fire investigator. I can't remember his name, but he was adamant. He showed me them. No question, according to him.'

I don't usually like weather metaphors, but Beving's face really is like thunder.

'And this is the man who did it?' he says, stabbing his finger into the screen so hard the laptop moves.

'Yeah, most likely.'

Or maybe a volcano is a better description, one that's vibrating just before it explodes. Jesus. It makes me think of my own Volcano.

'Rykel,' he says, turning to face me, 'we've had our differences, but this is *not* going to go unpunished. We are going to find this man and we are going to make this motherfucker pay.'

He gets on the phone, starts shouting orders, and in a matter of minutes has assigned four teams to comb the area starting on Bloemgracht and working outwards from there. Their brief is to find and requisition any CCTV, to question residents, business owners, tourists and anyone else they find in their path. They are to be a marauding army of righteousness; nothing is to stand in their way.

'Get this photo to them,' Beving instructs Roemers once he's finished shouting orders down the phone.

'Will do.'

As I leave, Beving reaches out and holds my arm. He looks right at me. 'Don't worry, Rykel,' he says. 'I will not let this stand. We *are* going to get him. I promise you that.'

I've clearly misjudged him. I always thought he was an asshole, but now, when it really matters, he's putting aside our petty differences and pulling through for me. I nearly choke up and have to walk away. As I'm heading down the stairs back to the incident room I think how strange it is that kindness can be harder to take than hostility.

I'm staring at my face, the reflection of toilet stalls behind me. The alarm's so loud in my head I can't hear anything else. I find I'm washing my hands in the tepid water. My body freezes but my heart still pumps. How did I get here? I don't remember coming here. I'm sweating hard, trying to piece it together. I'd been talking to Beving. But then the memory stops. I don't recall what happened next and yet here I am. A toilet flushes, a stall door opens and a female officer steps out. I see her look of shock register in the mirror.

I'm only just recovering when Vermeer catches me in the corridor.

'You look terrible.'

'I'm fine,' I tell her. I've been on this slope before, and it's slippery as hell. 'What have you got?'

'Figured we could take a ride out to see Klaasen.'

'Why? I already saw him. He's in no state to tell anyone anything.'

Plus, I'm still feeling fragile. I'm not sure I can handle going back to prison again. Especially after what happened last time.

'So you say. But we've now got nothing. Huisman's a bust and Kleine's killer is still out there.'

'I've got something.'

'What?'

I tell her about my talk with the nurse, the sheet of

photos and the possible threat she'd been given when she asked a few questions. I then fill her in on the recruitment agency.

'Why didn't you say that before? Jesus. Let's go.'

Which I take to mean she's interested. Down in the car pool the sergeant slides a key over. Whilst Vermeer's signing for it I pick it up.

She turns to look at me. 'What are you doing?'

'Thought I'd drive.'

'I saw the size of that . . . what do you call it?'

'Dab.'

'Right, I saw the size of that dab you took, so if you think I'm letting you get behind the wheel of a car, far less getting in beside you, then you've clearly got fewer brain cells left than I'd given you credit for.'

'Whatever, I'll let you drive then.'

'Damn right you will.'

I toss the key over. She snatches it mid-air.

Soon we're off and I stare out at the streets, the cars, buildings, the people that make up this city. It'd always felt like home, until everything went wrong. Then it felt like an alien landscape, a place I'd somehow travelled to with no purpose, and no way back. Until, after months of medications and doctors and therapies, which hardly made a dent in it, Joel persuaded me to try a different approach. I resisted, but eventually things got so bad I decided I had nothing to lose. I remember that first time. Really, it was amazing. I'd had an alarm going off in my head for years, constantly putting me on edge, priming my already exhausted body for action even when it wasn't needed. No wonder I couldn't sleep, no wonder I'd broken down and they'd diagnosed me with PTSD. And yet that one simple thing, a few puffs from Joel's vaporizer, and that alarm shut off, like it had never been there. I still can't believe it. I've come to see that the alarm is the black wolf. That's what I'm fighting against, that's what cannabis helps me with.

'You do know that production is still against the law, don't you?' Vermeer finally says.

I never thought I'd say this, but . . .

'Fuck the law.'

'You're a police officer.'

'Yeah, and, I say again, fuck the law. No one has the right to tell you what you can and can't ingest. Least of all a plant.'

'Hey, chill, man,' she says in her best stoner-stereotype voice. 'Loosen up.'

'Well, we can't all be little miss perfect. And anyway, what about the drink?'

'What about it?' she snaps back.

'You sank two high-strength cocktails in quick succession and then stormed a building where there was possibly a madman on the loose. And you didn't even look tipsy.'

She looks across at me, raises her eyebrows as if to say *oh really* but stays silent.

'Let me ask you this, how many times have you been called out to a disturbance where alcohol was involved?'

She doesn't answer.

'Hundreds, right? Probably thousands. And then ask yourself how many times you were called to a disturbance caused by cannabis?'

She still doesn't answer. Well, fuck it. She can sit there on her little high horse. Maybe she can come back to me when she's been in this game as long as I have, see what she feels like then, when the sheer volume of bad shit has seeped into her and is festering inside, threatening her very core. Who knows, she may find moral judgement's trickier then.

We cross the bridge on the tree-lined Spaklerweg. An old man shuffles through his own gravitational field, twice as strong as our own. A kid on a scooter is nearly sucked into his orbit as he goes past. Ahead and to the left the Bijlmerbajes prison's six dismal towers poke the heavy sky and ten minutes later we're parked by an anonymous concrete building with a corrugated-iron roof painted bright red. Amongst the anonymous cars parked there is a silver-grey Maserati with red-leather seats.

A man's leaning against the wall next to the only door having a conversation on his phone. 'I swear, if he makes me work on that again I'm going to walk. I didn't do a fucking degree to end up doing this kind of menial shit.' He listens for a few moments before speaking again. 'No, seriously, I think I'm going to hand in my notice. Let's see how that old prick gets on without me.' His eyes flick towards us as we pass, before he dives back into his rant.

Inside, the receptionist has never had anything so exciting as the police turn up. Soon we're being ushered through an open-plan office towards a door in the far wall, leaving a trail of intrigue in our wake. Beyond it, we discover, is a corner office which has no windows, no ventilation, and no one inside. The receptionist promises that Sven Hertogs will be there shortly. You can just tell she's itching to rush around and tell everyone that we're here.

Shortly after, a man steps in, looks at us as if in surprise, then sits down behind his desk. He's fifties, slightly overweight, and is wearing a shirt which has seen better days. As has his face, which is liver-spotted to quite an alarming degree.

'You're the police, are you?' he asks somewhat redundantly.

'A man of true perception,' Vermeer says, flashing her badge. 'He's with me,' she adds, jerking a thumb in my direction.

'I'm with her,' I say, jerking a finger back.

The man looks between us, like a marriage counsellor facing his most daunting challenge yet. His tongue swipes his lips.

'Sven Hertogs. So what's this about?' He addresses himself to Vermeer.

'He'll tell you,' she says, and I wonder about the wine broker soon-to-be ex.

Hertogs turns to me and I lay out exactly what this is about. He listens, fiddling with his nose as if we can't see what he's up to. When I've finished he says, 'I'm not sure how I can help. I can't give out the volunteers' details without our client's permission. Data protection.'

I'm about to tell him that I don't much care for data protection but Vermeer beats me to it.

Hertogs shrugs. 'Sorry, nothing I can do. You need to speak to whoever the trial was done for. Which company, out of interest?'

'Listen,' Vermeer says, leaning forward, 'we're investigating a very serious matter. We would really appreciate your help.'

'Hands tied. I'm sure you know that. So unless you have a warrant . . .' He shrugs.

Vermeer starts to help him understand the situation, but I can tell Hertogs is going to be stubborn. I make going-to-find-the-toilet motions and head out, leaving Vermeer to it. In the outer office I notice the I'm-going-to-quit guy is back at his screen. Maybe he's just waiting for us to finish with his boss. But really, if you're going to quit, you just walk in and do it regardless. He looks up when I approach.

'Can I have a word? Outside.'

The office stares at us as we walk out, their minds spinning at all the sudden drama. Once we're in the car park I tell him what I need.

'Why would I do that? I'd get fired for starters.'

'I thought you were going to quit?'

'Well . . . I –'

'Was this what you wanted to do, with your life I mean? Work for a prick at some menial tasks just so he can afford that?' I point to the Maserati.

He looks affronted at my question, but then lowers his eyes and shakes his head. 'No, not really . . .'

'So I think you should quit, and do what it is you want. You've only got one life, live it. And, just as a parting gesture, a little fuck-you to Mr Hertogs, you could get me those names.'

He stares at me for a few seconds, then his face slowly breaks into a grin.

Once it's done I walk in on Vermeer and tell her she's wasting her time. She glares at me but is smart enough to read between the lines. As we're leaving I see the young man walk into his boss's office. I feel a slight tinge of guilt. So I leave out the part about me egging the man on to quit his job when I tell her what I've got. We sit in the car and stare at the list: twelve volunteers, some of whom, according to Stephanie, would have died.

From the looks of it two men share the same surname, presumably brothers. As Vermeer drives I get Jansen on the phone and dictate the names to him, asking for background on all of them. I'm just finishing when we pull into the AMC car park where I'd accosted Stephanie. It takes us over twenty minutes to track down the records office, buried deep in a basement corridor which seems to stretch out forever. If it wasn't for the detailed instructions the strangely jovial man at the front desk had given us I don't think we'd have made it.

The nasal guy I'd spoken to on the phone isn't quite as brave in person. He tries his best, but Vermeer just steamrolls him and soon we're sitting down at a desk with the promise of the papers we'd asked for landing imminently. He disappears into a locked room with a double-glazed porthole and returns a few minutes later.

'Here,' he says, handing over a light blue folder.

Vermeer takes it and opens it up. Inside are three sheets of names, and a time and date next to each one. The period starts at midday on the day of the trial and ends forty-eight hours later. Another column has a reference number made up of two letters and four numbers.

'I thought hospitals were supposed to try and keep people alive.'

'Based on this they're not doing too well.'

We scan through them, circling each name on the original list. By the time I put down the pen any exhilaration we'd felt on finding their details has faded away.

'So many?' Vermeer asks. 'So many ended up dying?'

I stare at the list again. I can't believe it either. I pull out the photos. Stephanie had said six of them had been given the experimental drug.

And it's starting to look like FAA673 killed five of them.

It's now hours later and we've just visited five of the seven people who'd either received the placebo or had been the lucky one who had survived the drug. The way it's worked is this: by the time we've finished with one Jansen's generally managed to track down the name and address of the next. And he's just given us the name of the sixth; we're heading there now.

So far none of them have wanted to speak to us, beyond saying that it had been a terrible experience and that they'd put it behind them. We'd been unable to force the issue and had left, crossing off faces from the sheet as we go.

The sixth is called Bastiaan Polman and we try his home, only to be told by the woman with a podgy face who answers the door and claims to be his wife that he is working late today. She's in the middle of putting the kids to bed, but she gives us the address of a company out in Westpoort, where massive ocean freighters stacked with shipping containers glide overland via the North Sea Canal before reaching the Amsterdam docks proper.

'I did get called to a disturbance involving cannabis once,' Vermeer says as she turns the engine on.

I'm still angry at her holier-than-thou attitude, so it's my turn to stay silent.

'Turned up to find this guy had got really stoned but didn't have anything to eat in his flat. He called us because he was desperately hungry, thought we might be able to help.'

'Yeah, it's dangerous stuff.'

She looks across at me and shakes her head, but doesn't say anything more.

The drive out there is industrial, painfully so, the horizon dotted with mournful wind turbines that aren't moving, even though a series of tall oblong flags lining the car park are fluttering dramatically on their poles.

The warehouse is busy, despite the hour. One whole side of the structure itself is open loading bays for large trucks to reverse into. Once in place a swarm of electric forklifts appear to unload the shrink-wrapped pallets and deposit them somewhere deep in the building. It could be a nature documentary on an unusual species.

We park up and go through the motions only to be told that Bastiaan Polman had been due to be working the last shift today, but that he called at the last moment to say he couldn't. As per company policy this was possible, as long as he arranged his own cover with another employee. Which he has. We get that man's name and ten minutes later he appears. He's short, with a rounded belly and face to match. At first he doesn't want to tell us why Polman wasn't able to make it, but once we've made it very clear to him that if he doesn't tell us we'll just have to go and ask the wife, he spills his not inconsiderable guts.

Turns out Polman has a deficient home sex life and is

sometimes forced to supplement. And tonight he's supplementing at a brothel located a quick and convenient twenty minutes' walk from his place of work. Soon we're back on the road, hoping that we can catch Polman, quite literally, with his trousers down.

'You ever been to one?' Vermeer asks me.

'Really, you think I'd be the type? What about you?'

'There are times you've just got to put yourself in the hands of a professional.'

'Sometimes I just can't read you,' I tell her.

She smiles but doesn't say anything else.

We arrive at the address. It's a classic brothel above a dry cleaner's and we're in quickly and talking to the surly Eastern European with a face like a blade. Then we're moving down a badly lit corridor. We stop outside the last door on the right and listen. There's a kind of groaning going on, a rhythmic creaking, the occasional soft gasp. I push the door and we walk in.

It's far from sexy. A single bare bulb hangs from the ceiling. Along one wall is an assortment of bondage gear. On the bed is a man, ankles bound, wrists tied above his head to the metal bed frame. He's lying on his side so that the fat Asian woman sat on a wooden chair next to the bed, dressed only in panties and a bra, can slowly jerk him off whilst reaching over and giving him the odd whip. Pink lines in pale, hairy flesh. Like I said, it's far from sexy.

'Jansen was talking about a sad handjob,' I say, and the man jumps.

'I'd say this is a classic example.'

We walk round so the man can see us. I pull out my phone and snap a photo despite his verbal protests. The fat Asian woman doesn't seem to get the situation; she's just carrying on, not bothered by the audience as if the world's a bewildering nonsense to her anyway. Which it must be to anyone whose primary mode of employment is the use of her hand to rub a man's cock whilst the other whips their backside. This was probably not a profession mentioned in those well-meaning career advice lectures you had at school. Mind you, nowadays you probably need a degree even for this.

'Who the fuck are you?'

'Police,' answers Vermeer, 'and assuming you're Bastiaan Polman we need to ask you a few questions. And, you, stop that and get out.'

The woman stops.

'This is legal, so I don't have anything to say. And who told *you* to stop? Carry on.'

She starts up again, her expression neutral, like it's all the same to her.

'Get out,' Vermeer tells the woman.

She stops again and stands up.

'Sit down,' Polman tells her before directing himself at me. 'I'm not talking to anyone until I've come.'

He's on coke; you can see it in his eyes, and from the aggression and false bravado.

The woman's caught between authorities.

'Just go,' I say to her.

She makes her decision and starts to leave.

'Hey, come back,' he yells. 'Come back and finish –'

Last night I lost my boat, and my dog died a horrible death. Today I'm standing in a brothel where the man lying on the bed in front of me potentially has some information that I need to know. Only he is refusing to speak until he's been jerked off by someone. I grab the whip off her as she walks past me and crack it hard across his buttocks.

'That's police brutality,' he gasps once the scream dies down in his throat.

'You'll have a hard time proving that.'

I show him the photo I'd taken.

'Wife like to see this?'

He shrugs.

'Maybe your colleagues, your boss? Maybe we'll put it on the internet and it'll go viral somehow. You'd like to be famous? I'm sure your kids will love having a famous dad.'

Polman hears his future; it's filled with laughter and mocking voices. He tries out a death stare but in reality we all know he's beaten.

'So given that this is as unpleasant for us as it is for you, how about we just get on with it? Sound like a plan?'

Vermeer kicks things off. 'We have reason to believe you took part in a clinical trial at the AMC. Is that right?'

His eyes flit between us and a quick flick of the tongue moistens his lips. Good.

'I was,' he says cautiously. 'But it turned out I just got the placebo.'

'Yes, we know that. But we want to know about it, about what happened during the trial itself.'

At this stage all the previous volunteers we'd spoken to had said pretty much the same thing, namely they didn't want to talk to us. No amount of cajoling had made any difference, and we weren't in a position to legally force anything.

'I don't think I'm allowed to talk to you. I signed a

298

non-disclosure agreement. We all did. And they said if we ever spoke to anyone then we'd be sued for everything we had.'

'You got an Instagram account?' I ask Vermeer. 'Or maybe Twitter's the best place for this . . . Let's see.'

'Don't be a fucking prick.'

The whip cracks again. If this was standard police issue, getting information out of people would get a whole lot easier. And quicker.

'Ah . . . fuck that hurt. Do it again, baby.'

'You want a go?'

Vermeer takes the whip.

'You *are* going to talk to us,' she says. 'So why not do it now?'

'I'll talk to you once I've spoken to my lawyer.'

The whip whistles and cracks.

'You have a lawyer? You do shift work forklift driving for a living. What do you need a lawyer for?'

He clears his throat and spits something onto the floor.

'Honestly? It's to protect me from people like you.'

A Very Dangerous Game

'You're sure you don't need somewhere to stay?'

We seem to have reached an uneasy truce, maybe as a result of our success in finding Polman. Vermeer's pulled the car over on Marnixstraat, the famous mechanical bridge just visible down the Brouwersgracht. Polman contacted his lawyer, but given the time nothing's going to happen before the morning. So we'd left, making it very clear that if we don't hear from him first thing tomorrow then the photo will be going to his wife. Jansen was still struggling with locating the last volunteer and Vermeer had told him to call it a night.

'Yeah, I'm fine. Call me as soon as you hear.'

'Will do.'

I get out and start down the canal.

'Rykel?'

'Yeah?' I turn back.

'You don't think Polman's the sort to kill himself over this, do you?'

As it stands we have no legal reason to detain him, so I'm not sure what option we have.

'Think we'll have to roll the dice on this one.'

'Thanks, that's comforting. See you tomorrow.' She hesitates as if there's something more to say, but then she nods and the car pulls away from the kerb.

I walk down Brouwersgracht towards Joel's flat. The alarm/howl has been steadily increasing over the last hour or so, and it's already strong enough to set me on edge. The moon rises above the rooftops, spilling milky light onto the ink-like canal waters. A moped buzzes over the bridge and I step into its exhaust plume before a soft wind rushes towards me, clearing the air. But I can't enjoy it. Almost exactly twenty-four hours ago I was watching my life go up in flames. No wonder I'm keyed up, exhausted, but running on adrenaline all the same. And all the while the ringing in my ears, the alarm, which is really the black wolf, increases, narrowing down my world.

'You look like absolute shit,' says Joel when he opens the door to find me actually leaning against the frame. We Dutch are known for plain speaking, and Joel likes to keep that tradition up. But he ushers me inside and soon I'm shoeless, flopped on the sofa with a Volcano bag in my hand and an energy drink in the other.

'You're gonna love this one, just arrived from the farm today. We based this on some really amazing genetics I got hold of from the US. Crossed it with an old-school plant I've been keeping cuttings of until I found the right partner. I'm thinking of calling it Night Queen, after Mozart. The top Fs in the 'Queen of the Night' aria,' he adds when I look blank. 'As in, this will get you higher even than those.'

I take a long inhale, then blow it out slowly to fully get the flavour. Rinse. Repeat. This is what I needed earlier on, this would have meant I didn't lose time. I shudder when I think what I did during those lost moments.

'So, what do you think?'

'What do I think?' I wait for it, should be only a few seconds more and . . . there it is. The alarm's turned off, like it was never there. I sometimes get scared that one day it won't work any more. So far that day hasn't come. I hope and pray it never does. I think back to the two episodes where I lost time. It's because I hadn't been keeping my cannabinoid levels up, I need to be careful. I find my head tipping onto the back of the sofa and I stare at the ceiling as I submit to the Night Queen's rule. A huge breath swells in my chest then escapes into the room.

'I think it's fucking awesome.'

With the alarm shut off muscles in my body start releasing their tension, and they melt away over the next few minutes whilst Joel fixes some food and I just lie here, absorbing the music Joel has put on his vintage hi-fi system, all silver fronts with twisty dials and polished hardwood cases. The track's one I recognize, 'Lost Dog'. Which makes me think of Kush. My mind starts singing along, substituting 'lost' with 'burnt'. For a moment I panic I'll not be able to make it stop, but then my brain shifts and it's gone.

By the time Joel brings over a white platter with what looks like a huge amount of cheese, all different types, I'm calming down. And even getting a bit hungry. The platter has four indents which are each filled with a different style of mustard, ranging from light yellow to mahogany brown. Cocktail sticks abound. The only thing missing is miniature flags on each one.

'Good stuff,' he says, clearing some space on the table and placing the platter down close enough for me to do hand-to-mouth without any extraneous movement. 'But she's a hungry tyrant; we're definitely gonna need all this.'

'Long live the Night Queen,' I say. I skewer a bit of cheese, dab it in the darkest of the mustards, and hold it up in the air. Joel does the same. 'May she reign forever and ever.'

Then I cram it in my mouth. I can't even remember the last time I ate. The deep caramel notes of the cheese and the spicy pungent hit of the mustard seems like the best combination ever. Time slips by, and when the platter's clear and we're on our third bag I finally feel relaxed enough to tell Joel about the boat, and everything that's happened since. He listens quietly, only getting up to start the fire about halfway through, though obviously thinking it was maybe a little insensitive he sits back down again without lighting it. Joel's never been the best listener, he just can't help getting into the conversations himself, but tonight he's quiet, taking in what I'm saying. By the time I'm finished – how long has it been? – my throat's rasping dry so I crack open the can he'd handed me earlier and finish it in two long draws.

'Fuck, man, that's rough,' he's saying as I crush it in my hand.

He's been relaxed, lying back on the sofa. But now he shifts upright.

'You know cannabis doesn't make me paranoid, right?'

'Me neither, why?'

'Because all this stuff you've been telling me, about the Biotech company . . .' He pauses and bites his lip. 'Okay, it's like this. You know I was in that world for a while, and frankly the longer I stayed in it the more spooked I got.'

'Why?'

He picks up a used cocktail stick and rolls it between his fingers.

'What is it that any drug company needs? Sick people, right? But not just any sort of sick people; if you die of a heart attack, you're no longer any use to them. But what if you get some disease which only kills you much slower? Now *that's* what they want, because that gives them something they can work with, possibly years and years where you can be consuming medication. Expensive, patented medication. Doesn't cure you. In fact, most of the time it just gives you other problems, though thank God in heaven they have another pill for those as well. You go to the doctor because your knees hurt and in two years you're taking ten different pills and you've basically become a cash cow. And you've probably laid down the foundations of a *real* problem.'

'You don't need to tell me that. I'm flushing my whole prescription each month. Must be costing the health service a bomb.'

'Exactly. And some of the things you're prescribed have extremely low efficacy, as you found out. The bar of proof for a drug to be approved for any condition is so low as to be pretty much meaningless; placebo is about as effective. But no one tells you that. They dress everything up in complicated trial data and routinely ignore studies which didn't have the outcomes they want because they need to make money. But it doesn't stop there. Once they have drugs approved they're forever lobbying to have the criteria for prescription lowered to widen their potential market. All damaging side effects people report are pretty much swept under the carpet as being statistical anomalies, until the thirty years on their patent is starting to run out. *Then* they start crafting a narrative where the odd study shows that Drug A wasn't quite as effective as previously thought. More and more of those build up until a few years before the patent finally expires and they release Drug B, which is significantly better than Drug A. Look at aspirin, hailed as a wonder drug, prescribed liberally for pretty much anything, then demonized when the patent was up and they introduced paracetamol. Paracetamol was much safer, they said; aspirin was really bad. Only now there are studies starting to creep out which show that in actual fact paracetamol is far worse than aspirin, and causes all sorts of damage to the liver. So, yeah, maybe at first I thought I was being paranoid, but I saw enough evidence, over and over, that this is exactly how they operate.'

I take a few moments to try and absorb it all.

'If this is all true, then how come no one else has brought it to light?'

Joel does his best *Really? Are you serious?* face.

'People've tried, believe me. But they're always silenced somehow. We're talking a multibillion-euro industry here; they can buy whatever they want. They'll rake up stuff from your past to discredit you. If you're a doctor, they'll find an old patient who "remembers" you touching them inappropriately. If you're an ex-employee, they'll come at you with whatever they can, threaten you with whatever they think will make you back down. People have had their kids watched, and some woke up to find dead animals on their doorsteps. And the thing is, you've been poking around, and then your houseboat mysteriously gets torched. How many arson cases do you get a year in central Amsterdam?'

I don't know the figure, but I do know it's extremely low compared to rural areas where it's more common. Torching someone you don't like's house when it's in the middle of a field is one thing, doing it in a city as compact as Amsterdam, where the houses are jammed together so tightly, is quite another. But still. Was it a warning? I suddenly think of what the nurse Stephanie Dekker said, about her visit from the man in pinstripes. And that makes me think of Muller. He'd been trying to warn me off as well, though I'd thought it was for another reason. What's more, I realize with a thud of my heart, the description of the man Dekker had given could actually apply to Muller. I'm feeling less calm all of a sudden, the Night Queen losing her hold over me.

'I'm just saying that you need to be really careful, okay?' Joel says finally. I suddenly hear the fire investigator's question: *you got any enemies?* 'Poking round a company like that, particularly if they had a bad failure and are already hurting, is a very dangerous game.'

Bloemgracht is not on the route between Joel and Sabine's, and yet I find myself here anyway. I've texted her to say I'd be there soon and that I didn't have my keys. Hopefully she doesn't mind staying up a little longer. There's a lingering sooty smell as I near the burnt-out wreckage. With each step the air becomes more dense, and the houses on either side of the canal seem to stretch up and curl in to loom over me, blocking out the sky. The street lights are out, they must have been damaged in the fire, and it feels desolate and empty. I sit right on the edge of the canal, feet dangling over the water, and stare at the hull. I'm right in the centre of one of the most densely populated cities in Europe, and yet I feel totally alone.

My thoughts are jumbled but eventually twist round to what Joel had said earlier. Could this have been a warning to stay away? Why else would someone want to burn down my houseboat? Earlier I'd managed to brush it off, clear it from the forefront of my mind. But pushing things away like that seems to be counterproductive, because it had lurked, waiting for its moment to push its way back. And just to add to all this, hadn't Muller told me to go back to my houseboat? At the time it'd struck me as odd. Now it's looking downright sinister.

I reach out, just able to touch the hull across the short gap. My fingers come away black with soot. I trace a diagonal line with my forefinger right across my forehead. I do another one. And another. The reality settles in. Joel was right, this *was* a warning. And the only people who would want to warn me off are DH Biotech. The question is, what are they hiding that they're so scared I might find out? It's looking like people died because of them; is that it, is that what they're afraid I might find?

'What are you hiding?' I ask the night just as I get a sense that all of a sudden I'm not alone. There's a presence behind me. I tense, fully expecting a blow or a shot.

I slowly turn my head. There's something there.

It's . . . a black wolf.

My heart's hammering in my chest before I realize that . . . it's Kush. Standing there. Alive.

He's looking at me as if trying to figure something out.

I'm up and moving towards him and his tail starts to twitch gently, then he moves forward, maybe deciding that he does know me after all.

Which is when I see he's limping badly; he can't use one of his front legs. He's holding it up, and as I get close I can see fur ripped open to reveal a fleshy gash.

In the end I carry him all the way to Rozengracht where the first two taxis refuse to take me but the third tells me to hop in whilst he looks up emergency vets on his phone. Kush is in a bad way. He's barely moving, the wound worse than I thought now I can see it properly in the cold light coming from a spot by the rear-view. But he's alive. He's alive and I've found him. Or rather, he found me. The taxi driver decides the best place is the animal hospital on Leuvenstraat and soon we're plunging south through the city, the traffic light. Kush is panting hard now, his tongue hanging like limp fabric. It's only when we pull up outside the place I realize I have no money. The driver waves it off. He has a dog himself he says. Least he can do. I thank him and lift Kush out.

Before he was panting hard, now he's hardly breathing, his body slack. I burst through the doors and a woman in scrubs looks up from behind her desk. She comes round and quickly inspects Kush, who hardly seems present.

'It looks like he may have a broken bone,' she says. 'And he's lost a lot of blood. We'll need to operate. Can you carry him through to the back?'

I scoop him up, afraid suddenly that it's too late, and follow her quickly through to a room where she instructs me to lay him on the table. She's called another vet, an older woman with hair like Leah's, who listens to the first woman whilst doing her own quick assessment.

'We've got it from here,' she tells me. 'But I'm not going to lie to you, it'll be touch and go. Leave your details at reception and we'll get back to you as soon as we know more.'

'How long?'

'It's going to be hours before we really know anything.'

I reach out and stroke his head, smoothing his ears down. He twitches slightly. I follow her back to the reception where she takes my details. I write down my number, and what is now my old address, but stop when it comes to the credit card details.

'I've got a bit of a problem. I came out without my wallet.'

She looks at me as if trying to make a decision.

'Just bring the details with you when you come back tomorrow. You will be coming back for him, won't you?'

'If you can save him, I will.'

She puts a hand out onto my forearm. 'If anyone can, she can.'

It's only as I leave the building I catch sight of my reflection in a dark window.

Three smears of black right across my forehead.

Day Zero

Junk

The ginger and white cat freezes, tail shooting for the clear sky. Its back arches, fur rising like there's a force field of static electricity. I follow the aim of its gaze along the roof's spine and spot another feline, black with a white bib, holding the same pose. It's like Goya, the two felines in an immortal stand-off. They're so still now they might as well be statues.

Coffee's brewing, toast's in the toaster, radio hosts are still discussing the acid attack, and I'm sitting by the window at Joel's getting my insides acquainted with a Red Bull. As soon as I woke I called the animal hospital and left a message. I've been checking my phone compulsively ever since, but I'm not exactly getting swamped with callbacks.

'So you went there and she wasn't in?'

Joel's one of those annoying people who sleeps like a rock and then wakes full of positivity for the day ahead. Mind you, he's flying to Berlin for a trade fair where his company has a stand for three days, and then he's heading down to the farm in Spain. Maybe that has something to do with it. Contrast that with what I've got planned and I'm starting to see why he can whistle whilst preparing breakfast.

'Thing is, by the time I'd left the animal hospital it was near enough midnight; she must've got bored and gone to bed.'

Though it's strange, because she hasn't answered any of

my texts. Maybe she's pissed that I managed to lose her keys. Maybe she just decided that she doesn't like me. At this stage I can hardly blame her. I tap out another message but then delete it.

'Busy day?'

'Interviewing someone, trying to work out who burned down my houseboat, also trying not to think about all that stuff you told me last night. You're not serious about how dangerous they are?'

'Jaap, listen to me. You are nothing to a company like that. Nothing. And if they feel threatened they will act accordingly.'

'So far, though, I've not got anything on them.'

'You said that several people had died in a clinical trial they'd run and they covered it up? That news getting out equals a full-blown day-after-a-curry-shit in the mouth as far as they're concerned. That's more than enough.'

I think about that and know that he's most likely right. Which makes it even more important we get something out of Polman when he presents himself at the station in just over two hours' time. Assuming he presents himself, that is. I really hope he hasn't run overnight, or hooked himself up to his car's exhaust.

'Oh, by the way. I gave that stuff you gave me on the compound, FAA673, a glance. From what I can tell they were trying to target serotonin receptors in the brain.'

'So it should have made them happy?'

'Not as simple as that. And anyway, with things like this you can never predict what's going to happen.'

My phone rings, making me jump. It's the animal hospital.

'Mr Rykel?'

Female voice, soft and low.

'Yeah,' I say, mentally constructing a picture of her face.

'Is that a Dutch name? I've never heard it before.'

Not this again. If I had a cent for every time I get asked that, I'd be thousands of euros richer than I am now.

'It's a seventeenth-century surname, very uncommon nowadays. How's Kush?'

'Some bad news I'm afraid.'

My heart goes off like a depth charge. Nausea pulses in my stomach.

'He . . . he's dead?'

Joel's been fiddling with the coffee machine. He stops and looks across at me.

'Dead? No, no, nothing like that. The surgery went really well and he's up and about already. Someone should have left a message for you earlier?'

'They didn't.' My heart slows down to around 200 beats per minute. 'So what's the bad news?'

'The bad news is it looks like he's got fleas. We've given him a treatment so he'll be fine, but most likely you'll have them all over your house. You're going to have to get that dealt with quickly. A flea infestation in the home can be devastating.'

I think of thousands of fleas getting incinerated, maybe some jumping ship like sparks only for them to drown in the canal. I can't help it, I start laughing. One hundred beats per minute, getting there. The woman on the phone clearly thinks this is a little bit crazy.

'When can I pick him up?' I ask, wiping my eyes on my sleeve.

'Probably not until tomorrow, but you can come by to see him now if you want. And also . . . if you'd like to bring your credit card so we can settle the bill at the same time that would be great?'

Once I've assured her I'll be there soon I hang up and have a little conversation with Joel.

'You need money to help treat your sick dog?' he asks when I've finished. 'You've only been homeless a day and you're starting to act like a bum already.'

'It's either that or sell my body for sex.'

'Yeah, that may take some time. Even the girl you were giving it to for free has bailed out on you.'

Ouch. He pulls out his wallet, selects a card, and tosses it over from where he's manning the toaster.

'What's the pin?'

'1620'

Of course it is. 4:20, should have guessed that myself. Some inspector.

'So how much do you reckon it'll be?' he asks.

The toaster clicks and he grabs two slices as they fly into the air.

I actually have no idea. The woman hadn't said. But it can't be that much.

'About a hundred or so.'

A primeval scream outside. The cat's bluster didn't work. One of them must've blinked and they're now a screeching tornado of claws and fur.

'That's fine, just don't go crazy. No offence.'

I finish up my Red Bull, scrunch the can and throw it at him. Fresh from his triumph with the toast his skills are honed. It's an easy catch.

'None taken.'

'So, given your current situation, stay here until you're sorted. I've got some spare keys somewhere. Just one request.'

I'm relieved that he's offered without me having to prompt him.

'Sure, what is it?'

'Just make sure no one burns it down, will you?'

'Would you like to see him?' asks the young man with glasses and an air of super-bright keenness that's sweet but almost unbearable at the same time. There's no trace of the woman who'd called me earlier. The waiting room smells of bleach and a strip light in the ceiling is humming to itself. He leads me to the back of the building and we pass through currents of animal scent into a room with at least thirty cages. About two thirds of them are full, dogs of all shapes and sizes. Many of them seem to be trying to out-bark all the others. Kush is at the far end, lying with his snout pushed up against the metal bars. Round his neck is a large plastic cone, which I'm told is to stop him chewing at the bandage covering his leg. His eyes are closed but he opens them as we approach. In a flash he's up, his whole body wriggling, his bandaged leg held awkwardly. The man opens the crate and manages to stop Kush from exiting like a bullet before clipping a leash to his collar. He hands it to me and points to a door. Kush is jumping up at me. I can feel his claws scratching through my top. I try to calm him down. He seems frantic.

'You can take him into the yard if you want. Don't let him off the leash, though, as he's not supposed to run on that leg for a little while.'

The yard itself is covered with fake grass and is being hosed down by a worker in rubber boots. It smells of dog shit. Once they're done hosing they give the okay and I walk Kush round the fake grass. He seems happy, though he does try and get the cone off a couple of times. His limp gets more pronounced, though, and he seems tired so we head back. I give him an ear scratch and entice him back into his crate. He starts barking as he sees me leave. I turn back to him and he stops, and somehow makes his eyes go all droopy and hunches his shoulders. This is the worst sort of emotional blackmail. And it's working. I feel terrible.

'Tomorrow, okay?'

Which does nothing to calm him down. He starts barking again as soon as I walk away and I can still hear him over the other dogs back at reception. In the waiting area an old man sits with a carrier perched on his lap. Something hisses as I walk past and I catch a pair of suspicious eyes glaring out at me.

'He'll be fine,' the young man says. 'Says here he should be ready to leave tomorrow. Would you like to settle up now?'

Seems like I don't have a choice. He prints off an invoice and hands it over as I'm getting Joel's card out. The old man's cat has started a high keening sound; it's almost alien. I slip the card across the surface and glance at the bill. Errr . . . what the fuck?

'I don't think this is mine,' I tell him as he picks the card up and is about to slip it into the machine. 'It seems quite expensive . . .'

He takes the paper back and checks something on the computer. Glances at the paper again. Nods.

'No, this is the one,' he says, giving it back to me and

positioning the card machine so I can enter the pin. 'Seems a lot, but your insurance will cover it. You'll need to get a claim form, fill it out and send the invoice in. Just pop your pin in there.'

My insurance. Damn. I should probably call Joel. Then again, I've no other immediate way of paying for it, and I'm pretty sure they're not going to let me take Kush home until it's been settled in full. The light's now humming a little louder. I take a deep breath and type in the four digits. I'll give Joel a call later.

Back at the station, I find Vermeer in the incident room and tell her about my conversation with Joel, how it could frame the attack on my houseboat in an entirely different light. She listens intently. When I've finished she just sits there. A biro in her hand goes *tap-tap-tap* on the table.

'So what do you think?' I finally ask when it's clear she's not going to offer anything.

'I think all that stuff you're smoking is making you paranoid,' she says when I've finished.

'Easy for you to say. No one's burned down your place.'

The biro falls silent.

'That's exactly the point. We're both doing this investigation together, so what's so special about you?'

Well, when she puts it like that . . .

'Change of topic. Huisman doesn't matter any more but –' She tosses over a sheet of paper. '– out of interest, look who's a member of the rehab's parent organization.'

I look. Ex Judge Muller. I wonder if he found 'religion' after his daughter's death, or he'd already been part of what some might call a cult.

'You think he was the one who blocked the warrant?'

'But why would he? Doesn't make sense.'

She's right. But the more we discover the less any of it seems to be making sense.

'Maybe not.'

Still, the fact remains someone *did* burn down my houseboat, and I'm finding it increasingly hard to believe that it was just a random act, regardless of what Vermeer thinks. Something about DH Biotech's not right, I can feel it, and I'm hoping that Bastiaan Polman is going to help us find out what it is. I check the time. Ten minutes until the deadline expires. Vermeer's put down the biro and has moved on to ripping up a sheet of paper into little bits. Once done she piles them up in a heap and starts on another sheet.

I put my feet up and stare at the ceiling, wondering how I can let Joel know that I had to pay well over a thousand euros for Kush's medical bill. I make a note to myself to look into pet insurance. Then I think that maybe if I take out a policy today and ask the vets to change the date on the invoice to some time next week I could get it covered. Not sure they'll go for that, though. Not least because technically it's insurance fraud. But damn, a thousand euros? I pull out the bill and look at it closely, wondering if I could just change the date manually with a black pen. After a while I decide that it's not going to work. I'll have to think of something else.

'You think he's gonna show?' Vermeer finally asks, once she has five heaps on the desk in front of her.

'He'll show. If not, he's going viral. Actually, I think I

caught you on video whipping him, maybe I'll post that one too.'

Which earns me one of Vermeer's favourites, the sweet smile with the middle finger. To distract myself I turn my mind to worrying about Sabine. I tried to call her earlier but she didn't answer. I'm pretty sure she must've simply gone off me, absurd as that sounds. The door opens again – disturbing a new heap Vermeer has been painstakingly working on – and a different uniform informs us that a Mr Polman's lawyer had called to say they've been delayed, but they will be here in an hour and a half.

'Okay, so he didn't kill himself,' Vermeer says. 'At least there's that.'

Jansen bounces past in his running gear. I notice he's wearing the shoes I bought him, despite the colour.

'Tracked down the next one?' I ask.

Jansen shakes his head.

'But you've got time to go for a run?' says Vermeer. I'm not sure if she's joking or not.

'Yeah,' he says in not the most friendly tone and jogs off.

Vermeer looks at me and shrugs.

Flames are roaring around me. And then they're not. I'm standing on the station's roof, looking west, the sky vast and oppressive at the same time. I don't remember coming up here. A moment of deep panic. The urge to step forward into space almost overwhelms me. I try to calm down. Work it out, what was my last memory? I was downstairs in the incident room, and now I'm here. I check the time. I've lost well over an hour. I turn and walk towards the door leading back into the building on legs which feel like glass. I tell myself it was just a little episode, an after-effect of the one I'd had earlier. As I descend the stairs I sense half of me is still up there on the roof.

Twenty minutes later, minutes in which I've managed to calm myself down, I open the interview-room door and watch as Polman and his lawyer file past. Polman defin-itely looks better with his clothes on, and I'm glad to see his whole body language has none of that coke-induced-false-confidence-bravado bullshit he'd been exhibiting yesterday. His lawyer, on the other hand, is strutting around like a cockerel at dawn. He's young, and this is clearly his first time in a police station, his act an attempt to stamp his authority on what he imagines is going to be a long and glittering career standing up for the little man against the big bad authorities. Loss stabs me out of nowhere. Am I going to miss all this too much? Then a thought, another explanation for Sabine's absence. Could it be that her ex – what was his name? – found out where she was staying . . .? I push it away. I can't think about this right now.

'Please take a seat. Least the state can do in return for your cooperation.'

The lawyer pulls out a chair and sits. Polman hesitates.

'You too, Mr Polman.'

'As you well know, my client sustained some injuries yesterday at your hands, injuries for which he is very gen-erously, and against my counsel, willing to overlook. So if he doesn't want to sit then he –'

'Sit down,' I tell him.

Polman glares at me, but in a hangdog way, and pulls out a chair. It's clearly a painful manoeuvre, so we watch him with friendly, welcoming smiles as he gingerly lowers his whipped backside onto the seat. Sometimes Vermeer and I are perfectly in tune. I wonder if I'm going to miss that too. The lawyer goes through his drivel about all information being given willingly without prejudice *blah blah blah* and we set out the ground rules before starting proper.

'Tell us about the trial. How did you get involved?'

'I saw an advert in the local paper. It said people were needed for an overnight stay in a hospital and that there was a fee. I was broke at the time, and I thought, why not? So I called the number and spoke to someone who took my details and said someone would call me back. And that was that. I didn't hear for weeks and I'd pretty much forgotten it when I got a call saying I'd been picked. So I met with them, and they ran a few tests just to check I was healthy. A couple of days after that I got another call asking me to come in and go through the paperwork. Which is when I had to sign the initial non-disclosure agreement.'

'And what did this non-disclosure agreement cover?' Vermeer asks.

Polman looks at his lawyer who takes over.

'The agreement covers everything, all dealings with the company. It's the most comprehensive one I've ever seen. Just by being here my client is putting himself at risk.'

'Maybe, but non-disclosure agreements don't protect criminal acts.'

'Has there been a criminal act?'

'That we are not able to discuss at this stage,' I tell him.

'So it looks like our hands are tied.'

'Except your client is, generously and selflessly, going to help us, isn't he?' I address that last to Polman.

'I take it you're referring to the photo you have of my client? Threatening to release it would be classed as blackmail, as I'm sure you're aware.'

'What photo?' I ask.

'The photo you took of my client.'

I turn to Vermeer. 'You remember either of us taking a photo?'

'It was a photo-less encounter,' Vermeer says.

I smile at Polman. He glares at me, but then nods to his lawyer.

'Very well. Despite all this, and against my counsel –'

'– you've said that bit already –'

'– despite all this my client will answer questions about areas covered by the agreement.'

'Great, maybe we can just get on with it then.' I turn to Polman. 'What happened next?'

Polman licks his lips. He starts talking, addressing himself to the table in front of him.

'We were given a date we had to turn up and be prepared to stay for twenty-four hours. There were also check-ups scheduled once a week for the three weeks afterwards. So we turn up and we're prepped for the trial itself. It was in a ward at the AMC but they'd put beanbags and stuff in there, tried to make it not look like a hospital. There was a TV, a couple of PlayStations, even some board games. Everyone was nervous, but a few people started talking and it got a bit better. Then the nurses came, and we were each given an injection in turn, and we settled in for the long haul. An hour or so later the first guy who'd got the injection, he was this blond guy whose neck was as thick as his head, started complaining of feeling weird. We'd been playing each other on the PlayStation, some racing game, and he'd kept on winning. Then he started crashing, driving into things, going the wrong way round the track. I thought he was just being a dick but when I looked at him I could tell something was wrong. You could see it in his face, this kind of tension like he was in pain or something. About ten minutes after that he got up and went over to one of the nurses who were doing tests on us. He looked drunk, the way he was walking, and everyone noticed. He reached the nurse and said he had a headache and she'd got him to sit down and drink some water. We all just tried to ignore it, pretend nothing was happening, but you could tell the whole room was a little shaken. But when someone else also complained of a head-ache and then collapsed I knew there was something seriously wrong. The nurses were doing their best but they looked as scared as we all felt. The first guy was now lying on his back moaning, hands over his face. Each of us was thinking *Am I next?* It was terrible. But that was nothing compared to what was coming.'

The room's silent. Each of us imagining what it must've been like. Then again, is it so different from how many of us live our lives, waiting for the hammer to fall?

'So what happened next?'

Polman's been staring at the table the whole time he's been talking, but now he finally raises his eyes and looks straight at me.

'Next was when stuff got really fucked up. The first guy

started complaining of being too hot, but I heard the nurses talking to each other, saying that his body temperature was really low, dangerously low. So one of them left whilst the other one tried to stop the guy from undressing. But he was acting weird, ignored the nurse and stripped down naked. You could see he was freezing – he was shaking hard, and his skin was turning a strange blue colour. The second person who'd got a headache was now starting to complain of being too hot as well, which is when the door bursts open and several men come in. By now there are just six of us who haven't come down with whatever it is, but we're all hyper-paranoid; every second you wonder if that little twinge in your head is the start of it, the little pain in your arm a symptom. I tell you, it was fucking terrifying. The men are bringing trolleys into the room and putting all those affected onto them and strapping them in. I saw the blood first. I was watching the first guy whilst he was waiting to be hoisted up, and this little bubble of blood appears in his nostril. It grows quickly, then bursts. Then the other nostril does the same and soon blood's streaming out of his nose and starting to dribble out of his mouth too, and all the time I'm scared that this is going to happen to me as well.'

I'm pretty good at telling if people are faking it or not, and Polman is not. His delivery isn't melodramatic; it's held in, like if he was to let it go something deep and horrible might be unleashed. He was traumatized by the experience. I can see it in him, his own private version of the black wolf.

'Then what?'

Polman shudders. His hands are in a jumble on the table, and he's picking at a bit of skin with a fingernail.

'Then nothing.'

'There's more, I can tell.'

Polman glares at me. I hold his gaze. Finally he lowers his eyes.

'Then they got them all out and we were left in the room until a man came in and told us that by process of elimination we'd all received the placebo so we'd be fine. We'd have to stay in overnight, just for observation, but that was it. We were each given a room and I'm pretty sure they sedated us because I slept like I'd never slept before. Next morning I woke up and there's a man in the room and he asks me how I am and how do I feel and blah blah. It all seemed so fake, like he didn't give a shit at all but was just asking the questions because he'd been told to. First thing I do is ask about the others, the ones who got hauled away and he said they'd all been stabilized and that although it had been horrible for them they were now recovering and no lasting damage had been done. He also said that the company would like to compensate us for our trouble and he had some money he could give me. He brought out a briefcase and pulled out a couple of really thick envelopes. He opened one so I could see it was full of notes. He told me it was ten thousand euros and that I could have it. I'd just need to sign a bit of paper.'

'Did you?' Vermeer prompts once he's fallen silent.

'Yeah, of course. What would you have done? He handed over the envelopes and the papers. I signed. Before he left he leaned over and said that if I ever told anyone about what I'd seen I'd be breaking their agreement and the company would sue me for breach of contract. Then he leaned closer and whispered in my ear that the legal case would ruin me but that would be nothing compared to what he'd make sure happened to me.'

'This man you talked to, did you get a name?'

'No.'

'Description?'

'Just some corporate guy. Nice suit, clean shaven. He seemed sort of anonymous, like I can't fully picture him.'

'What sort of age?'

'Probably forties, maybe older. He was one of those people where it's really hard to tell.'

'Hair colour?'

'Blond, I think.'

There's more. I can tell. But for some reason he's not going to offer it up. Time to force it.

'Okay, that's some useful information you've given us. But there's something else, isn't there?'

Polman looks across at his lawyer and nods. The lawyer reaches into his own briefcase and is soon sliding a few sheets of paper across the table.

'What is this?'

'The document Mr Polman was asked to sign in the hospital that day.'

Vermeer and I give it a quick once-through, but it's not what we expected. It's an agreement between Bastiaan Polman and a company called Global Solutions BV, not DH Biotech, and is a blanket ban on discussing anything, just as Polman had said.

'Who is Global Solutions BV? A subsidiary?'

'That's the thing.' The lawyer leans forward in his chair

and drops his voice. 'I've checked it out and it doesn't exist.'

'What do you mean?'

'Exactly what I said. There isn't, and never has been, any company called Global Solutions BV.'

'So this agreement here is junk then.' Vermeer taps the paper.

'The one with Global Solutions BV is, yes. The original one with DH Biotech is still legitimate. But regardless, my client feels that the threat made against him was serious.'

As we finish up, thanking Polman for his time and assuring him that we'll keep him updated, my brain races through naked bodies, blood and someone desperate to keep a lid on it all.

A lid which I am going to blow sky-high.

I think of the part of me still up on the roof. It's like it's trying to tell me something.

Just Like the Others

Strategy meet. Beving, Jansen, Vermeer, myself.

I present my case. I'm persuasive. Vermeer's now coming round to my way of thinking. Which is DH Biotech is at the heart of this. Beving's more cautious. Wants more details. I give him naked bodies and blood, victims and volunteers. I give him a company desperate to keep its name clean. I give him mysterious men who threaten all those involved. I think he's starting to get it.

'The problem I think we're going to run into in prosecuting this is that presumably DH Biotech's original contract with the volunteers would most likely have mentioned death as a possible adverse outcome? We'll have to check with legal on this, but I can't believe they'd be allowed to run these trials without a clause like that. And if that's the case then what do we get them on?'

Which is what I've been worried about too. We've got a killer, but we've also got a large company that seems culpable.

'Probably get bumped down to some kind of financial impropriety,' Vermeer says pensively. 'They hide the result from potential investors. Pretty toothless. They'll probably get a fine and a slapped wrist.'

'And to even prove that you're going to have to link the fictitious company with DH Biotech. Given Polman was handed cash that's going to be pretty difficult. They can just deny.'

'Unless we can find the man who gave it to him,' I say.

Right now Polman's sitting with a sketch artist trying to conjure up a face he'd seen years ago right after a traumatic event. I'm not exactly pinning my hopes on it. Maybe there's another way.

'Get down to the AMC and see if by some miracle they keep security footage from that long ago.'

Jansen nods and heads out.

We're getting close, I can feel it. It's like being on the edge of a black hole, the pull becoming stronger and stronger. Only we don't know what we'll find right at the centre.

'We also need to go back to the other volunteers. They have to talk to us now we can prove the second agreement's not legally binding. If we can build more detail from them, we might just get lucky.'

More ideas are tossed around, some swatted down like flies, some more persistent that can't be got at. Meeting adjourned.

'Keep me updated,' Beving says.

He stands to go but looks like he's about to say something to me. I know what it's going to be. Yesterday he'd been about to take me off the case and by rights he should be doing that now. But at the last moment he decides against it. Instead he tells me about the search for the arsonist.

'The teams are still out there, but we're getting to the stage of diminishing returns. Realistically I can probably only keep them on it for a few more hours.'

What happened to all that we'll-find-him-and-we'll-break-him stuff which had me choking up yesterday? But I just nod, like it's fine. He leaves and Vermeer and I ready ourselves. A quick refuel and a toilet break.

On the way out the desk sergeant I managed not to punch yesterday calls out to me.

'Phone call for you.'

I take the receiver. It's Stephanie Dekker. She sounds nervous.

'I think I may have something?'

'What is it?'

'It's to do with what we talked about the other day.'

'I'm listening.'

'I . . . can we meet? I'd rather not say on the phone.'

Once I've got her location I hang up and explain to Vermeer. We agree to split up.

'Rykel,' she calls out as we head in different directions, 'you okay to drive?'

I don't even respond. Down in the car pool I'm assigned a small unmarked. Drives well, fast, tight. Nothing like the Stang, though. Ten minutes of blurry windows and I'm standing outside a house in Amsterdam-Zuid. Stephanie practically tears the door off its hinges as soon as I knock. She ushers me inside, and I catch her checking out the street as she closes the door. I decide not to tell her my houseboat got burned down. Through a corridor strewn with kids' toys and photos on the wall of modest holidays on windswept beaches with grey skies. I don't see a father in any of them, just two kids. The kitchen is heavy with the gluey scent of last night's pizza. A cereal packet stands on the surface like a sentinel. Stephanie turns to face me, clutching the worktop behind her for support. She'd sounded nervous on the phone, now it's kicked up several notches.

'I found this,' she says, handing me a few sheets of paper she pulls from a drawer next to her. There's a smudge of eyeliner by her right eye.

I check the papers. Pathology reports for the volunteers who died. Not all of them, though. There's one missing.

'Where did you get these?'

'I can't tell you. But you didn't get them from me.'

She's edgy, something inside forcing her to do the right thing but now she has she just wants me gone. I get that. What I don't get is why, again, there are only five, not six. Six people got the placebo, the other six people got the drug, but there are only five reports. I start to wonder what happened to the sixth. Did one survive the drug? Is that possible?

'That's all there was. See these?' She points out each report's number in the top right corner. 'I checked the numbers either side and they were for different people.'

'Not the missing volunteer?'

She shakes her head.

I pull out the list of names, check them. It looks like one of the two brothers didn't die after all, the one lacking a pathology report is Rein Benner.

'So you reckon this one, Rein Benner, didn't die?'

'I don't know, but there's no pathology report and there would be if he had.'

I suddenly feel like a wave's swelling behind me.

'One last thing.' I show her a photo. 'Was this the man who told you to keep quiet?'

I hold up a photo of Judge Muller, the same one I'd seen at his house of him and the mayor. I'd found it online, an article about a fundraising event both men had attended. In it, Muller's wearing his pinstripe suit.

She stares at it, face furrowed, but finally shakes her head.

As soon as I'm outside I get Jansen on the phone.

'No footage,' he says. 'They don't keep it that long.'

'There's something else.'

I tell him what I need him to do. He promises to get right back to me. My thoughts have been shaken up. I let them settle out until I can see clearly. Two goths walk past, hooded and brooding, listening to music on their tinny phone speaker. Chains clank on black jeans.

My phone's alive in my hand. Jansen.

'You were right, a Rein Benner was discharged. It was three weeks after the trial.'

I get into the car and sit, not aware of my surroundings. My mind's shifted gear; it's like Tetris in there, different parts all sliding into place, getting faster, stacking up. Trial gone wrong, people dead. A man, who I'd thought might be Muller but wasn't, threatening Stephanie Dekker to keep quiet. Another man, Rein Benner, who may have been the only one to have been given the drug and survive.

And Klaasen. He'd always protested his innocence because he *is* innocent. Because I fucked up he went to prison and got beaten into a vegetable.

I check the pathology reports against the images I have of the volunteers.

Somehow I'm not surprised to find that, by process of elimination, Rein Benner is the photo which has been bugging me, the one who is so familiar.

'Who are you?' I ask the photo.

I get no response, just a pair of eyes staring back out at me. Eyes which I'm starting to think could be the eyes of a killer.

Ignition on. Foot down. Amsterdam slides into a blur.

Back at the station I'm told Beving has left for a meeting down in Den Haag with the police commissioner. In the incident room I try to get hold of Vermeer but her phone's off. I find the desk that has the file on DH Biotech Jansen compiled and dive in. By flipping back and forth between multiple sheets I work out who was on the board when the trial actually happened. Unsurprisingly Muller and Kleine are there, and three others. I scribble down their names and hit Google. My existence narrows down to the screen. I've plugged into the Matrix, part man, part machine.

The first died four years ago, and his only daughter is a mildly successful beauty blogger who moved to the US three years ago and, according to her Instagram feed, was only yesterday at a beach party in La Jolla, California. I think she's pretty safe for now. The next also turns out to be dead, a legit-looking car accident on the A15 between Dordrecht and Rotterdam. His son lives in Singapore. Also pretty safe.

Which leaves the third, Stefan Zeeman. Still alive? Check. Offspring? One daughter, one son. Son Dirk lives in Amsterdam, daughter Jill in Maastricht. The alarm's ringing in my head, faint, but persistent. Vermeer's phone's still dead. Jansen's off. Beving's out. Time's speeding up. Fuck it.

Dirk Zeeman works at the Philips head office. I get on the phone. Several layers of bureaucracy, each requiring a new connection. Finally get him.

'Dirk Zeeman? I'm Inspector Rykel and you need to listen to me very –'

'Sorry, I'm not Dirk. He hasn't come in today.'

'Did he say he wasn't going to be?'

'No, we actually tried to call him a little while ago to see if he was okay –'

'Did you speak to him?'

'His phone just rang out. We were just talking about maybe calling his wife and –'

'Home address. Right now.'

As soon as I've got it I'm in the car, dialling Vermeer. Nothing. Damn. Jansen's phone is now on but goes to voicemail. I leave one and flick on the siren and lights. It takes me ten minutes to get to Plantage and I skid to a stop outside a house on Henri Polaklaan, completely blocking the road. The car's blue lights flicker everywhere in the narrow streets. People already at windows. The house I'm looking for has window boxes with spiky grasses. Black paint on the front door glistens like it's still wet. The door itself is open. Heart rate through the roof. The alarm in my head's turning into a whine. Toe the door open. Quiet inside.

'Dirk Zeeman?'

The house gives me nothing. I step in and check the downstairs: two sitting rooms, kitchen and a bathroom. A single white orchid in a slender black vase. My face in the mirror behind. Up the stairs. The seventh floorboard creaks, the rest are silent. Landing, choices. A grandfather clock – sprayed bright pink – ticks. I don't have long. I pick a bedroom at the back.

The door's ajar.

Toe again.

The whine's now a full-blown howl.

The door swings open.

It's just like the others.

Burn

It's quiet. Peaceful almost. The bed's made, the curtains hang in thick folds either side of the window, the glass filled with the contorted branches of a large elm. The bed's a double, flanked by side tables. Resting on each one is a book. The first looks like an original copy of *Storming Heaven* by Jay Stevens, the other is a translation of Gabriel García Márquez's *Love in the Time of Cholera*. A piece of artwork hangs above the oak headboard, a wide canvas sliced vertically by silver birch trunks, some close, some further away.

I've made the call, and soon the place will be crawling but for now it's just me and the body. The clock's ticking on the landing. I realize the fact I can hear it means the howl has subsided. For now. It does that sometimes, disappears, makes me believe it's gone before it comes back louder than ever. I need to be prepared. Buddhist initiates often sit with dead bodies to unlock the key to impermanence, so I sit now with Dirk Zeeman, a man I didn't know, a person I never will. A man killed not because of anything he did, but for his father's sin.

He's kneeling, his body slumped forward, forehead on the carpet. Which is soaked with blood. The soles of his feet are facing me; they're slightly dirty, as if he's been walking around barefoot. He has a tattoo on his right ankle. I can't work out what it is. His toes are curled in and his arms are sprawled out, not quite as neat as the other two victims. Both hands are on pristine carpet, the depth of the weave soaking up a lot of blood, limiting the pool. I crouch down. There's something under his fingernails. I can smell his aftershave, a heavy musk curdling with the scent of death. I lean in closer. It's blood caught in his fingernails. Could well be from his attacker. I can't get Rein Benner out of my head. Could it be him, could he be the one behind all this?

I wonder what it was the dead man in front of me wanted from life, what it was he feared, what made him laugh. What he thought about in those last seconds before life slipped away. Whether he'd be satisfied with the life he lived, or had regret flooded his system for all the little deaths he'd endured along the way? Or was he hoping right up until that very last neuron winked out that somehow it wasn't the end, that he still had a life to live?

All of this, because seven years ago I made a mistake.

Outside, sirens coming. One, two, three . . . I lose count, unable to distinguish each individual one as they cross over each other, weaving together into a chaotic tapestry of sound. I should be down there, but I find I can't move, as if my body's imitating Dirk Zeeman's. For a single moment of blinding panic I wonder if I *have* somehow died in here, that when the police come in they'll find two dead bodies.

'Rykel?'

Vermeer's voice downstairs.

'In here,' I call out. Not dead then, as I can hear her taking the steps two at a time. I stand up just as she steps into the open doorway.

'Oh fuck,' she says.

I take her through what led me here, and she listens whilst staring at the body.

Forensics are already moving in, their gloved hands like little creatures scurrying over the victim. Flashbulbs flicker. Measurements are taken. Fragments of microscopic stuff are plucked with pliers and dropped into evidence vials. The odd bit of banter proving that, in the end, there's nothing special about death. Or at least not of those we don't know. We move outside, away from it all, away from the aftershave and the smell of death.

My phone rings, Maastricht area code. Maastricht's about two and a half hours away by car. It's just about possible Benner could have got down there. I answer, expecting the worst, but a woman informs me Jill Zeeman's been taken into protective custody. I'm told she's asking about her brother. I tell the woman calling me to stall, but that someone will get back to her soon with news.

I hang up and get Vermeer up to speed.

'So this wasn't about a man killing women?'

'No, I don't think so.'

This wasn't about a man killing women; it wasn't about the actual victims at all. They were just pieces in a larger game, the intention of which was to hurt the people who'd hurt him, make them feel what he'd felt at the death of his brother. I think about the need we humans have for wanting others to feel what we feel. Where does it come from? What purpose does it serve?

'We need to get on to Benner. Let's leave this lot to it.'

The car I brought is jammed in, so I toss the keys to the

uniform wheeling out crime-scene tape and tell him to make sure it gets back to the station later. Vermeer's car is parked further down and we walk there to find a police forensics van parked next to it. The back doors swing open and two forensics start unloading a large heavy-looking box. They're being directed by a third man who seems to be giving a lot of instructions for what really is a simple lift-and-put-down job. As we get closer I recognize the one giving the spurious orders as Max Bakker. Last time I'd seen him had been on the island of Vlieland, up in the North Sea.

He jumps out of the van and walks over.

'Thought you'd moved out of town.'

Bakker strokes his grey moustache and takes an enormous pull of the cigarette he's had in his hand since I met him back at the first autopsy I ever attended all those years ago. I think by this stage if the man breathed in just air alone his system might go into panic.

'Yeah. After fifteen years in Amsterdam I decided I needed a change, get some solitude into my life. Some peace.'

'So what happened?'

'Turned out peace and solitude are overrated. Anyway, what about you? Last I heard you'd gone batshit crazy.'

'Yeah.' I can't deny it. 'But it turns out going batshit crazy is also overrated. Way, way, way overrated.'

A crunch from behind him tells us the men have managed to catch the box on the van's door.

'Hey! That's nearly three hundred grand's worth of kit you've got in your hands. Bit of respect.'

'What is it?' Vermeer asks.

'Rapid DNA machine,' Bakker says. 'Gets results in ninety minutes.'

These had been talked about before I'd left, but I wasn't sure they'd been proved reliable enough to be given the green light. Things have obviously changed in my absence.

'Impressive.'

'When they make it something I can plug into my phone, *then* I'll be impressed. Mind you, I don't have to carry it, so maybe it doesn't matter. Makes my job easier at any rate. As soon as we're set up I'll run whatever juicy stuff they're no doubt scraping off the floor inside.'

'There's blood under the victim's fingernails,' I tell him. 'Make sure you check that. I'm sure you'll find it's not his.'

'Turn here.'

'What? Why?'

'I need to go to the prison.'

Vermeer glances across at me, but then hits the indicator and we turn. Soon the Bijlmerbajes towers poke into view. The sky behind them is criss-crossed with vapour trails. We clear the first security checkpoint and drive towards the parking area in front of the towers, the car pitching and yawing over a series of speed bumps until I start to feel sick.

Vermeer asks, 'How many have you put in there?'

'Got to be over twenty. Haven't felt the need to keep count.'

'I've put eleven. I remember each one.'

I do of course remember. I just choose not to. How many others did I get wrong? Or was it just this one? Final bump, then we're into the flat of the car park.

'How many of those have been innocent, though?'

She hasn't got an answer for that. There's a space between a beat-up old Audi and a brand-new Tesla electric car. Vermeer eases us in.

'You don't have to do this,' she says. She hasn't turned the ignition off.

'Give me five minutes, then we can concentrate on Benner.'

Ignition off, the car settles.

'All right. If it'll make you feel better.'

I doubt that. How can it? How can it erase the biggest mistake of my career, a mistake that put an innocent man into prison where he got assaulted and permanently brain damaged? And yet here I am, about to do it anyway. I step into the reception area to find it oddly empty. A radio's playing, a talk show with animated voices. Out of habit I check the CCTV cameras in each corner to see they are flashing their little lights. The airport security scanner is unmanned. I'm just thinking I should call someone when one of the toilet doors opposite the reception desk opens and a man carrying a magazine steps out and sees me. He walks over like there's something delicate inside his head that he's trying not to break and eases himself into the chair behind the desk.

'Sorry 'bout that,' he says. 'Lads' night out . . .'

'Inspector Rykel, here to see Sander Klaasen.'

My stomach's been invaded by demented butterflies. The lighting's harsh. The prison's ventilation system has a high-pitched whine slightly off-key to my own. When I sign the sheet my signature's all over the place. Security checks, then through to the inner sanctum where I make my request.

The man here sorts out the paperwork and then I'm shown into the same room as last time. I step over the threshold into the weirdest feeling. It's like an echo of last time's panic, waiting for me here all that time. I've always assumed emotions were formed in the brain, but suddenly I wonder if they're just a force of nature? Maybe they can hang around places waiting to be picked up? If so, then this one's strong. I try to keep hold of my breath, not let it get away from me.

I sit down in front of the screen. For half a second I can see blood dripping down it, but thankfully it's just a trick of the light. Or my head. *Nnnnnnnnnnnhg.* What am I going to say? The door on the prisoner's side opens inwards. But the man who steps into the room is a prison guard. He sees me, shakes his head, then leaves. A few minutes later the door behind me opens and a prison warden steps in.

'Inspector Rykel?'

'Yes.'

'I'm the duty warden. Could we talk in my office?'

I look around at the room we're in.

'It's just the two of us,' I tell him. 'Let's talk here.'

'Yes, okay.' He clears his throat. 'I'm afraid that there's been a mistake. You should have been told when you checked in, but for some reason our system hasn't updated properly and the person who signed you in hadn't heard about Klaasen.'

'Heard what?' The room's tilting ever so slightly.

'Sander Klaasen's dead. He died shortly after you visited him.'

'What of?' Still tilting. Soon we're going to be sliding down towards the Plexiglas.

344

'Stroke. As you know, he'd got agitated and hit his head against the screen there. He was treated at the time, but he died suddenly a couple of hours later. There was nothing anyone could have done.'

Back at the car I find Vermeer on the phone. She's spread papers out on her lap and across my seat. I scoop them up with a shaky hand and sit down. Sounds like Vermeer's on with Jansen, working on locating Rein Benner. I feel stunned. Unreal. I pull out another pre-rolled joint. I know she's not going to like it, and I should get out of the car, but I'm not sure my legs are going to hold. I wind down my window. Vermeer breaks off what she's saying and holds her hand over the mic.

'Rykel, this is a police car, you can*not* do that in here. You shouldn't even be doing it in front of me.'

I stick my head out of the window and take a few pulls.

Vermeer's back on with Jansen, but she flashes me a look. Easy for her. She hasn't just found out she was responsible for putting the wrong person in prison who, out of desperation, finally killed himself. More pulls. It's starting to work.

But then I think about how long he'd been there. And I'm responsible for every second, every second of his wasted life inside. How much pain is that? How much suffering? If karma's real, then I'm fucked.

The black wolf isn't howling now. He's retreated, but I know he's still there in the darkness, stronger than ever, his lips pulled back into a ferocious grin.

I inhale a few more times until it starts to burn.

Vermeer hangs up on Jansen. 'You done breaking the law?' she asks.

'I've been upholding the law all my career. And it's just got an innocent man killed. So no, maybe I'm not done.'

'Who? Who's been killed?'

I tell her about what I've just learnt. I expect her to say something, maybe even tell me it's not my fault. But she simply turns the engine on and reverses out of the space, drives through the car park and back over the speed bumps. This time she hardly slows down at all. I hit my head on the roof. I get the feeling that's exactly what Vermeer wants to happen. We drive in silence all the way back to the station.

And still the glistening grin.

Is This a Joke?

Rein Benner. The man of the moment. Or ghost of the moment might be more apt. Because Vermeer and I have been at this for hours now, as well as four returning members of the team who had been poached for the acid attack, plus Jansen, plus a few others who are chipping in, and we still have pretty much nothing on him.

Born in Haarlem, he then moved to a flat in the ill-fated Groeneveen estate where he grew up with his younger brother and their father. Mother was on the birth certificate but seems she split early on. Went to the local school and then got various low-paid jobs as a waiter in central Amsterdam, enduring drunk tourists night after night. It was during this period he, and his brother who was starting an apprenticeship at a bodywork place out in Weesp, signed up for the trial. Given neither of them were earning much it must have looked like easy money. These things always do.

The last time we have any kind of official documentation was the hospital discharge papers Jansen had found earlier. After that, nothing. His last known address is his childhood home, and although it was years ago Vermeer and I decide to head there, leaving the team to carry on working.

The drive's short and we're soon parked and walking into the apartment complex itself. These were the buildings an Israeli-owned Boeing 747 crashed into shortly after take-off from Schiphol back in 1992 and many lost their lives in the impact. Many more subsequently lost their lives to a mysterious auto-immune disease. At the time there was no information on what the plane was actually carrying; it was a freight not passenger flight, but conspiracy theories flourished. The official view was that El Al Flight 1862 was carrying computer chips, perfume and fruit, and therefore there was nothing that could harm anyone.

The most persistent of the various conspiracy theories centred around chemicals destined to be used in the manufacture of chemical weapons, especially given the dire health effects those exposed to the aftermath suffered, a theory which turned out to be true. Six years after the crash it was finally admitted that the flight had actually been carrying nearly 200 litres of a chemical used in the manufacture of sarin nerve gas. But it didn't stop there. It was further discovered that Boeing used depleted uranium as a counterweight in the tails of 747s. Anyone there that day received a massive dose of radiation, alongside the sarin precursor.

Despite that, the place has been rebuilt and we walk past the Flight 1862 Memorial with the names of the known victims. Known, because the buildings housed so many illegal immigrants that the death toll that day was definitely higher than the official numbers.

We find the flat on the third floor of the second block. Current occupants know nothing about anything. Decision made to split up: I work left, Vermeer goes right. We're both armed with a blow-up picture of Rein Benner which is mostly met with blank stares. On the fifth, though, I get a result. A man in his late fifties opens the door. He's wearing jeans and a loose woollen jumper which is untangling at the cuffs. He has a full head of white hair and a beard to match. Stick a cap on him, give him a rugged polo neck, jam a wooden pipe in his mouth and he could captain a shipping vessel in the North Sea. When I show him the photo and ask if he'd ever seen the man in it he nods.

'What, Rein? Yeah, I knew him.'

I invite myself in and soon I'm sitting in his living room, which is surprisingly light, and looks out over well-tended gardens with tall trees and a large curving pond. Music's playing quietly. I recognize it but it takes me a few moments to pin it down. Beethoven. Symphony. Can't remember which one. The man invites me to sit and then eases himself into what looks like an original Eames chair, the tan leather worn and smooth. The walls are covered with tiny woodcuts, all the same size, and they all seem to be of the same scene, which looks familiar, though I can't work out what it actually is.

'The National Monument,' he says, catching me looking at them. 'Been cutting it for twenty-five years. One per day. And I've only missed four days since I started, and *that* was because I was in hospital. Those four missing days still bug me.'

'That's a lot of days,' I say, looking at all the works. I find myself wondering why anyone would want to make images, even if they are overly impressionistic, of the most ugly monument in Amsterdam? I mean, Rembrandt did his own face over and over again, but still.

'This is nothing. I've got a lock-up I rent down the road. I keep them there. Every day I take the oldest one down and drop it off on the way to work. Then the new one goes up in its place. Helps give me a sense of progression.'

'You don't sell any of them?'

The man seems to contract. It almost looks like disgust.

'Sell? I'm not selling these. That's not the point. I work mornings stacking shelves at the Albert Heijn on Stadion-weg, have done for the past seventeen years. Badly paid and tough work, but it gives me the afternoons to do this. I don't have a lot of money, but I worked out early on that time is so much more important. At least it is to me.'

He shrugs, though I'm not sure why. I haven't contradicted him. Maybe it's some ghost of his own he's still fighting. I remember Leah saying that artists should be pitied; they can't get on with their lives like normal people because they're driven to create by some inner demon. I suddenly realize they must have their own black wolves. Creating art is what feeds their white wolf.

'Anything else?' the man asks. He's looking at me and I realize I've been staring out of the window.

'You said you knew Rein Benner?' I ask, trying to get back into the swing of it.

He breathes in through his nose and leans back in his chair. Beethoven crashes and judders to the end of a fast moment and then eases into a timorous slow one. Three? Seven?

'Oh, I knew Rein all right. Him and his brother grew up here.'

'What was he like?'

'He was all right, bit of a handful, but then a lot of the

kids round here don't have the best role models. Rein and his brother didn't either, truth be told. But there was something about him. He was . . . smart somehow. I found him in the garden once. I'd gone out for a smoke at night and heard someone crying in the bushes, just over there.' He points to a cluster near the water's edge. 'I didn't know what to think, so I tried to entice whoever it was out and eventually Rein appeared. He'd had some argument with his father, and from the look of things he might've been bashed around a little; he had a bruise on the side of his face. Wouldn't admit it was his dad that had done it, though.'

'Did he say what the argument was about?'

'Yeah. He knew I was an artist so I think he maybe felt a bit more comfortable talking to me. He'd told his dad he wanted to be an actor and wanted to go to acting classes. Reading between the lines I think the father saw this as some affront to masculinity and showed him what real men do. His dad was, what do the kids say nowadays, a class A dick? In case you hadn't got that already. Their mother had probably worked that out early on and left, leaving him with the kids to fend for themselves.'

'What did the father do?'

'Dealer of some sort. I don't actually know that for sure, but that's what he looked like to me. They used to spend the summer holidays up near the coast somewhere. Bergen, I think. I remember Rein telling me about all the spiders they found in the log cabin they slept in. Pretty much the only people around here who can afford holidays are dealers.'

'So what happened to Rein after that?'

'I saw him around but we never really talked again. Pretty sure he didn't get into acting class, though. Shame, he would have been good at it. He had that thing where he could imitate people just by changing his posture. When he was younger you'd see him walking behind people, copying their movements. He was pretty good at it. It cracked his brother up, but, like I said, don't think the dad saw much point in that kind of thing.'

'Was he close to his brother?'

He thinks before replying. 'He seemed protective of him. I guess their father didn't really look out for them so Rein took on that role for his younger brother. Only natural really. So what's he done that you're here asking questions? Must be bad.'

'I can't go into that, but if you know where I can find him it would be very useful.'

The man pulls a thread from his sleeve and wraps it round a finger until the tip goes pink, then white. He releases it.

'No, can't help. Sorry. Last time I saw him would have been ten, eleven years ago. The brother died I heard, and then Rein left. Not long after someone else moved into their flat.'

Beethoven moves things up a notch. It's still slow, but it's got intense all of a sudden.

'Seven?'

He smiles but shakes his head.

'Three. "Eroica". Dedicated to Napoleon. Then undedicated when it turned out he was just as much a tyrant as anyone else. Way of the world as far as I can see.'

A plane rumbles overhead. I can see its reflection in the window.

'Were you here when the plane hit?'

'No, luckily I was out. Heard about it when I was riding back on the tram. Rammed that block over there.' He points out of the window, across the garden. 'Helluva mess. Had to be evacuated until they were sure the other buildings weren't going to go.'

My phone goes off. I let it go to answer machine.

'I stayed with my sister for a year afterwards. I think that was crucial. Many people who came back straight away got sick. I didn't.'

I spend a few more minutes with him, but there's nothing else he can tell me. Outside I stand for a moment and look up as if the answer to it all is up there, written on the sky. Then I spot Vermeer exiting a flat at the far end of the walkway. I call out but the wind's picked up and it funnels my voice elsewhere. I head in her direction, listening to my message on the way. It's from Nellie. The board have given her a time. Hank's life support will be turned off at six tomorrow evening. She asks me to be there.

'Bad news?' Vermeer asks as I reach her. She's chewing gum and smells minty.

For a second or so I wonder about telling her. But then I think I might just start crying.

I shake my head. 'Just some personal stuff. You get anything?'

'Blank stares mostly. No one who seemed to know him. Mind you, it would have been years ago. You?'

I relay my conversation.

'Doesn't really help. Station?'

'Yeah. Just let me make a call first.'

Nellie. But she doesn't pick up. I don't blame her.

*

353

Back at the hub. We have a probable perpetrator, we have a motive, we have strong links to the crime. The only thing we haven't got is any idea of his whereabouts. After the trial he seems to have disappeared into thin air, so at the very moment when an investigation would be running at speed we're now stuck in a crawl.

'He must've planned it.'

Vermeer's back to tapping a pen on her desk. I agree with her assessment. He disappeared so that he could plan the killings out in detail. But there are still so many questions. Why, after killing Lucie Muller, did he wait all this time until killing Marianne Kleine? So we wouldn't make the link? But if he was that careful, then why follow Kleine's death up with Dirk Zeeman's straight away? Why not wait like he did before?

'You think he could be sick?' I ask. 'Maybe he's only got limited time left and had to do it now?'

'He was the only one who had the experimental drug and survived, wasn't he?'

'Yeah. Maybe it didn't kill him but damaged him somehow. Like those people at the Groeneveen; it took some time after exposure for them to get sick.'

'The problem is, there are basically two cases: the murders, and DH Biotech's cover-up of their failed trial. Given the lengths they went to it was more than financial expedience; they must have been worried about a criminal prosecution. Which means they might have known the drug could have had the effect it did.'

Tap tap tap goes the pen.

I find one and start doing the same. Vermeer gives me a look and stops.

This all centres on DH Biotech, but we don't have anywhere near enough evidence to go after them. They'll have lawyers crawling all over us the second we make any sort of move. Or start burning down Vermeer's place. I decide not to tell her this. Her phone rings and she answers it whilst I realize I've made a mistake. I asked for Dirk's sister to be put in protective custody, but what I should have done is sprung a trap for Rein Benner, made sure a decoy was in place. I check the time then get on the phone. Once I've sorted it out I hang up and wait for Vermeer to finish. Judging by her face whatever she's hearing isn't good.

'Yes, we'll be right there.' She hangs up. 'That was Beving on the phone; he says we need to get back to Dirk Zeeman's right now. They've found something.'

Back in the car I find the piles of paper we'd left there earlier and I sift through them as Vermeer drives. One of her finger's tapping on the wheel the whole way. I'm starting to hope she's all right. Just as we're pulling into the street I start reassembling the papers when one slides over the photos of the volunteers.

And suddenly it all comes into focus. The lower half of Rein's face is partially covered, hiding the beard and allowing me to see what I'd not been able to see before.

The reason he looks familiar.

My stomach feels like I've just jumped off a cliff. Fuck.

'Look at this.'

Vermeer glances over. 'What?' She seems annoyed, distracted.

'This, Rein Benner. Only it's not Rein Benner. It's Sander Klaasen. They're the same person.'

She glances across, then shakes her head. 'I don't really see it.'

But then she'd not known Klaasen. I had. I'd sat opposite him in interview rooms. I'd watched him during his trial. I was there when the judges sent him down and he looked across the courtroom at me with hatred in his eyes. How did I not see this before?

'It's him. It's definitely him.'

'Impossible. He was in prison. And you said he's now dead.'

I think back to the day I'd visited him. I hadn't recognized him. The injuries and the panic attack I'd had made sure of that. More bits fall into place. Rein Benner disappeared after the DH Biotech trial. He must have changed his identity to Sander Klaasen then. More stuff: Klaasen had no background, he'd been like a ghost, we couldn't find anything on him at all. Fits in with Benner's disappearance. So what next? Klaasen kills Lucie Muller but I catch him. He goes to prison. But he beats someone into a pulp and then takes their place. I think of what the artist had said. Benner was good at imitating people, mimicking their posture. And the reason there's been a gap between Lucie Muller's death and Marianne Kleine's is that Klaasen probably got out of prison recently and decided to carry on with his plan.

I lay it out for Vermeer.

'Wait, hang on. How could he have taken someone's place? Surely it would have been noticed?'

But would it? Prison guards have a lot to deal with, prisoners transferring in and out all the time. If Klaasen was smart there might be a way.

I get the prison warden I'd spoken to earlier on the phone.

'Who was the prisoner who fought with Klaasen the day he was transferred to prison?'

The warden says he'll check and tells me to hold. We sit in the car in silence. Vermeer seems agitated. I don't blame her.

'The prisoner was called Klaas Blok,' the warden says when he comes back on the line.

'Has he been released recently?'

'Yeah, he was only in for seven years. Released two months ago.'

I hang up and am relaying this to Vermeer as a uniform knocks a knuckle on the window next to me. It makes me jump.

'Beving wants you both upstairs, now.'

We get out and I run it through in my head again, testing it, trying to see any faults. At first I'd thought pulling a switch like that, in a high-security prison, would be impossible. But the more I think about it, the more I realize it could just happen. In the end they're all just prisoners to the guards, maybe someone wasn't paying attention that day? And if he had pulled it off . . . Still seems unlikely.

There are two uniforms by the door, as if there's a prisoner inside. Beving himself opens the door as we approach.

'Follow me.'

'We've got something,' I tell him. 'We –'

'Not now,' he snaps. 'Just follow me. You two as well,' he says to the uniforms.

My phone starts ringing.

'Inspector Rykel? I'm leading the team looking for the

man who torched your boat. Think I've got a possible suspect so wanted to come back to you straight away.'

'I'm listening.'

Everyone is standing waiting for me. Beving looks impatient. Vermeer . . . I can't tell what Vermeer's thinking.

'Long story short, one of my men was talking to someone at a medical centre on Tuinstraat. They said they'd treated a man who smelt of solvents. The doctor treating him thought it was odd, said the guy seemed jittery as well, particularly when he was asked about it. Gave some story which the doctor didn't think much of. He got treated anyway and left. They didn't think any more of it until my man was canvassing the street.'

'Anything on him? Name, details?'

'Gave a false name but we got a photo from the medical centre's CCTV. Looks like he was trying not to get noticed but they have a hidden camera which he didn't pick up. I can get the image over to you if you'd like?'

'Send it to my phone.'

'Will do. We're stepping up our efforts to track where he went next. I think we're on to something.'

I'm just thanking him and about to hang up when a question pops into my head. 'What was he being treated for, burns?'

'He had a little burn on his arm, but the main thing was a dog bite. Pretty bad according to the doctor.'

I think back to the image we had of the man from Rashid's CCTV, the way he looked like one of his arms was trailing. It's because Kush was defending the boat from him, probably got hold of his arm with his teeth.

'Rykel, we need to go upstairs, now.'

We go up the stairs, the two uniforms following as Beving had commanded. The seventh floorboard creaks. Past the ticking clock. Into the room. The body is still there. Max Bakker is as well.

The uniforms are close behind us, jamming up the doorway. Vermeer's moved away from me now, closer to Beving. I get an odd sense of being alone.

'What's going on?'

'We got a DNA match,' Beving says. 'Bakker, tell him.'

Bakker coughs, stares at the body, as if his script is written there. Which in a way, it is.

'We checked the blood under the fingernails. It's not his, so we ran it through the system.'

'And? Whose is it?'

Bakker coughs again, shuffles his feet. Vermeer's face is drained. Beving's unreadable.

My phone buzzes, the image finally arriving. I glance at it, then double-take. There is no air in the room. It's impossible to breathe. Because I'm staring at an image of the man I'd known as Sander Klaasen. Somehow he'd managed it. He'd made the switch in prison and done his time as someone else. Then on his release he'd killed again.

'What is it?' Vermeer asks.

I turn the phone round so she and Beving can both see it.

'Sander Klaasen. Or Rein Benner, whichever you prefer. This is the man who torched my boat. The same man who killed Lucie Muller, Marianne Kleine and Dirk Zeeman.'

Silence drapes a blanket over us all, making the clock in the hallway louder.

Eventually Beving speaks. 'I'm not so sure.'

'What do you mean?'

He steps forward and hands me a sheet of paper. It's the DNA results.

I look at the name. It jolts me. Because right there on the sheet in black and white is a name I know well. The room starts spiralling. I look from face to face. Beving, Vermeer, Bakker. Colleagues, the good guys. I have shudders down my spine, and my legs feel too weak to hold my weight. I look down at the body, a person who I didn't even know existed up until a few hours ago.

'Is this a joke?' No one's catching my gaze. 'Seriously, what the fuck is going on?'

'Jaap Rykel,' Beving says, adopting the bland, disinterested tone of authority. The uniforms are right behind me; I can feel moist breath on my neck. The clock ticks. Someone shifts and the floor creaks. 'I'm arresting you for the murder of Dirk Zeeman.'

Schizo

The paper's snatched out of my hand and the two uniforms behind me grab my arms. I hear the ratchet mechanism of the cuffs, feel the cold metal tightening round my wrists. They check my pockets and one of them pulls out the tin containing the pre-rolled joints. He hands it to Beving who turns it round in his hand before giving it a sniff. The look he gives me is hard to decode, but it's shiny with hate and loathing and fear and maybe, just maybe, a little triumph as well.

'Get him out of here.'

'Wait, this is crazy. I –'

'Shut it!'

I'm dragged out of there like a common criminal. I should be protesting, I should be appealing to their reason, telling them that there's some mistake. But I can see from the looks on their faces it won't do any good. The chances of a DNA match being wrong are so small as to be impossible. Maybe the new faster machine is prone to more mistakes? But that'll be for my lawyer to explore later on; there's no point raising it now. The clock ticks as we walk past. I feel it's ticking just for me. The seventh floorboard creaks again as we descend. At the bottom of the steps the whole thing becomes a walk of shame. Uniforms stand aside. Shocked eyes, disgusted eyes, and eyes which are greedy for the unexpected drama of it all. The fall of one of their own.

And all the while my head chases its tail, trying to work out how this has happened. I'm marched down the road towards a waiting patrol car. Faces pop up in windows, desperate to know what's going on. I feel like ducking my head, hiding my face, but I try and force myself to stand tall. The noble hero being abused.

But just before we reach the car I have a thought so terrible it feels like it's stopped my heart.

What if I did do it?

What if it *was* me who killed Dirk Zeeman? Or rather a different part of me. The part that I've called the black wolf. What if all along the cannabis wasn't really feeding the white wolf, it was actually nourishing the black? Made it strong enough to fully take over, without me even noticing?

I try to think, imagine how that could be.

I remember coming here, to this street, the house where the body lies. I remember working out the chain of logic. Dirk being the son of the last remaining board member at DH Biotech when the trial took place. I remember it all, so none of this makes sense. Unless . . .

Unless that all could be leakage between the two parts of me. False memories, disrupted realities to cover what I'd done?

I'm shaking badly, and even though I'm freezing cold sweat is seeping out of my skin. It's true I'd not been able to get hold of Vermeer or Jansen on the way. But maybe I hadn't really tried, maybe I was living between worlds and only pretended to call them, pretended that they didn't answer. Was one side of my brain fooling the other? Spinning stories to cover its tracks, keeping part of me from knowing just what the other part was up to? I've interviewed people like that, people who seemed genuinely confused about what they'd done. Have I become one of them?

Has cannabis, just like the authorities have always claimed, made me schizo? Am I the copycat?

The thought's like a thunderclap.

In the vacuum of its aftermath my mind speeds up. What else could I have done, what else isn't as it seems? The houseboat fire. Could I have started that, done it to make myself look like a victim, show I wasn't just being paranoid? Had I hurt Kush in the process? A wave of nausea hits me. Is Kush even real? The first time I saw him I thought he looked like the black wolf. Had part of my mind conjured him up? And then, further back, could I have been the one to kill Marianne Kleine? And if so, why, why would I do it, what reason would I have other than some kind of psychic echo from the original Klaasen case, something the black wolf has been feasting on inside me for years? I'd broken down; they called it Uncomplicated PTSD, and I thought I'd got better. But what if it wasn't a breakdown, more like a change of form, a dark metamorphosis?

I feel like crying. I feel like laughing. It's coming, I can sense it. They took the tin off me. I need it. I need it now or it's going to get worse. Or do I? Maybe that's the problem. Maybe that's what's causing this . . .

I let my head fall back and from out of my throat rushes an ear-splitting, all-consuming scream. Only to part of me, part of me that's rapidly disappearing, it sounds more like a howl.

I'm on the ground, pavement pushed into my face. Or the other way round. It's hard to tell.

'What happened?' Vermeer's voice.

'He went fuckin' nuts. Had to restrain him,' says a voice close to the back of my head.

'Get him in the car.'

I'm hauled up, the car door is opened and one of the uniforms uncuffs me. The other grabs me by the upper arm, guiding me roughly into the back seat. His grip's tight and I can feel the wound reopen on my arm. Vermeer gets in the driving seat and one of the uniforms takes the front passenger seat. The third gets in beside me. I stare forward through the safety cage. A caged animal. Nobody says anything, and Vermeer starts driving. I can tell we're heading back to the station. The panic's not far away. I can sense it, almost toy with it, but for the moment I appear to be in control, my rational mind trying to make sense of the situation.

The only thing I can see linking me with Zeeman's death is the DNA evidence, my own blood found under the victim's fingernails, but it's impossible to refute. I can't believe it. I can't believe it's true. My arm's throbbing now, the uniform's rough treatment causing it to bleed. We stop at a traffic light. Vermeer seems to be taking it slower than she usually does. The light turns green. We move off. How can something be true and not true at the same time?

Heart accelerating rapidly. The interior of the car shrinks in around me.

Full-on paranoia alert.

I'm trembling to even think it.

What if someone planted my DNA there?

If that's true, then who? Who would have access to my DNA? Someone in the police?

Or could it be . . . No. No no no nononooooooo.

It can't be. I can't believe that. And yet what else makes sense? How else could it have been done? My houseboat's been torched, so they couldn't have got it from there. Or . . . We're turning on to Marnixstraat now, the station less than two blocks away.

It can't be.

But unless I'm to believe that I did kill Dirk Zeeman, that I've been running around these last few days unaware that there are two of me in my head, this is my only hope.

One block now.

I clear my throat to speak.

Sour Hound II

'Listen, Vermeer?'

'Don't talk to her,' the uniform next to me snaps.

'Vermeer, you need to listen to me. You know this isn't right, and I think I can prove it.'

We're now parked outside the front of the station, and I know that as soon as I'm over that building's threshold things are going to get a hell of a lot harder. This is my last chance.

'Prove it how?' she says, turning the engine off. 'Your blood was found under the victim's fingernails. I don't see there's anything to prove.'

'It was planted there. By the killer. He wants to frame me for his killing.'

'Even if I was to entertain such a crazy idea, how would whoever the killer is get your blood?'

This is where it gets tricky, because it's the only thing I can think of, the only way it would be possible. I need to make it sound plausible enough that Vermeer actually listens.

'I think he followed me somewhere, somewhere I changed the dressing on my arm. Look, it's bleeding now.' I glare at the uniform beside me. 'If they got hold of the dressing I threw away, then they could have scraped my blood off it.'

A lorry speeds past us, and the car rocks in its wake. I

sit in the silence, waiting for Vermeer to make a decision. My arm throbs, pulses. It's angry.

'Where would this have been?' she finally asks.

I tell her about Sabine. About how I haven't been able to get hold of her. I tell her my fear that Klaasen may have hurt her, or worse, if he did indeed go there to harvest my DNA. And whilst doing so I can't help but think of the worst possible outcome, the real reason Sabine hasn't been answering, her body lying naked in her flat just like Dirk Zeeman.

'Check my phone,' I tell her. 'There's an image there of the man they think burned down my boat. Compare him with one of the volunteers, the one with the beard.'

Reluctantly she does.

'Cover the beard. You'll see it's the same man.'

'Why would Benner want to burn your houseboat down?'

'Because Benner *is* Klaasen. And he wants to frame me as revenge for catching him in the first place.'

I take her through what I'd discovered, and she stares at the screen and the photo. She shakes her head. I think I'm losing her, despite what she's just seen.

'We should take him in now,' the uniform next to her says.

If I could reach through the safety cage I'd kiss him. Because I know how Vermeer's going to react to that. She turns the ignition on.

'When I want to hear from you I'll ask,' she tells him as we pull out into the road.

I give her Sabine's address.

'We're going there, and then we're coming straight back, understood?'

'Understood.'

'If we find something, then you're still under arrest until Beving says so.'

'Yeah.'

'Understood?'

'Understood.'

'Good.'

Five minutes later we're outside Sabine's building.

'You stay here,' she says to the uniform who'd given her advice. His face is impassive, but he's boiling inside from the rebuke. 'You're with us,' she says to the one next to me.

'Cuffs?' he asks.

Vermeer's eyes appear as a strip in the rear-view. 'You need cuffs, Rykel?'

'I'm not running,' I tell her.

She stares at me then nods. 'Keep close to him,' she tells the uniform.

The bell doesn't summon anyone. Vermeer knocks a few times and calls out but still Sabine doesn't come to the door. I'm starting to fear just what I'm going to find inside.

'This definitely the one?'

'Yeah, this is hers.'

'Knock it down,' she says to the uniform.

It takes him two well-aimed kicks, then wood splinters and the door swings open, crashing into the wall and bouncing back shut so he has to open it again.

'Sabine,' I call out. 'Are you okay?'

Nothing. No movement. I need to swallow but there's something blocking my throat.

We step into the flat, and three sets of footsteps on the wooden floor echo through the place.

'Are you sure this is the right one?'

Because it's empty. Not just empty of Sabine, empty of things. No personal possessions at all. The TV's gone, the cardboard box the photo of her had fallen from, all gone. It looks exactly like what it is, a rental between tenants.

'I need to check the bathroom, that's where I put the dressing.'

Vermeer nods to the uniform who comes with me. He's standing in the doorway as I reach down for the bin, dull metal dented with age. I already know what I'm going to find. It's empty. Cleaned out like the rest of the flat. I can feel the panic lodge in my throat, seep into my chest. I glance at the window. Then I shift my grip on the bin.

'Look.' I point into it.

He moves closer, bending to see what I'm pointing at. Which is when I swing it round. It smashes into his face and he staggers back. Before he can react I shove him hard in the chest. He steps back again and catches his heel on the threshold, toppling out of the room and hitting the floor with a loud crash. I slam the door shut, lock it and rush to the window. It's stuck, jammed hard and my fingers scrabble at the wooden frame.

Someone's banging on the door.

'Rykel, open this door right now!' Vermeer's voice.

I haven't got much time. I swing the bin. The glass shatters into a hailstorm of glinting shards. Blows on the door behind. I hear the lock give and Vermeer's in the room. I turn to look at her. She's drawn her weapon and is aiming it right at me.

'Drop it,' she says.

Bin vs gun. I drop it.

'On the ground. Now!'

'Listen, you've got to believe me. I'm being –'

'On the ground now or I will shoot.'

'No you won't. I don't have a gun. You can't shoot me.'

She switches her aim to my leg. 'I will shoot. And I'll tell them you grabbed the uniform's gun so the rules of engagement will be on my side. So just fucking do it!'

I look at her, eyes ablaze, but the rest of her cool, in control.

'Okay,' I say. 'Okay.'

I kick the bin towards her, scooping it up so it flies between us, and launch myself through the window and onto the tiles. I slide down towards the lip of the roof, just managing to stop myself before I go over the edge.

Below me a car is parked. I'm high, but I can probably just make it. I have to make it.

'Rykel!'

I twist my head round to see Vermeer at the window. She's pointing her gun at me. Again. Somehow I think this time she really will fire.

'Come back. We can work this out!'

'I didn't do it!' I yell back. 'I'm being set up.'

I can tell she doesn't believe me.

'Don't run,' she says. 'You know it'll only make it worse.'

I slip off the edge, out of her sightline. The shot rings out as my feet hit the car's roof. The metal crumples. Pain shoots from my left foot all the way up to my hip. I roll down the windscreen and slip off the bonnet. Blood's pumping. People are staring. A young couple walking a tiny dog, an older woman on the phone with her mouth frozen open, two workmen turning round from the pipe they're fixing.

I start to run. I reach the corner when I hear a noise that can only be Vermeer following, landing on the indent I'd made in the car's roof. I run even faster, trying to lose myself in the city. Though that's only going to solve my immediate situation. I need somewhere I can hide out, because every cop in the city will be on the look-out for me very soon. They probably are already. I think of going to Joel's, but that's too easy for them to work out. The thing is, I'm without a phone, without money and without any way of getting more. And each time my left foot hits the ground pain screams up to my hip.

Then it comes to me, a place where I can go. A safe place.

By the time I reach the lock-up I'm drenched with sweat and my lungs are burning, as is every other muscle in my body. I limp-jog up the row to mine and when I get there double over for a few seconds, hands resting on legs, try-ing to suppress the urge to throw up. Then I hear voices, Mark Liu's and someone else. They're just round the corner, and it's clear he's with a prospective customer. I cannot be seen. I straighten up and fumble the three little dials on the lock, thankful I'd bought this one, not one that opened with a key. The lock clicks open, I slip it off the rings and haul the door up just enough for me to scramble under. Once inside I lower it into position. I lean my back against it, trying to catch my breath. I can hear them, closer now, and I hope Mark doesn't notice the lack of lock. I move to the other end of the space so they can't hear my breathing, which is still out of control, and inch along the wall, trying not to stumble against anything in the darkness. I reach the pile of paint cans, put my back against the concrete blocks and slide down into a sit.

As my breathing starts to settle I become aware of the fact my mouth is utterly dry. I need liquid. My head's pounding. Limbs shaky. As soon as Mark's moved on I explore with my hands. There's a torch here some-where, which I used to peer deep into the Stang's engine cavity. If only I can find it. I'm on my hands and knees, starting to feel faint, and I sweep the ground like I'm looking for landmines. The floor's rough; there's grit, a metal bolt, unknown objects. As the search goes on I become bolder, until something jabs right into the fleshy end of my finger. I just manage to muffle my cry of pain and surprise. Finally my fingers clasp the cold aluminium case, it wasn't where I thought I'd left it, and I flip it on. I have light. I check what it was that punctured my finger. The sharp point of a one-handed saw.

Next up, stop the dehydration. I hunt down my two remaining cans of Red Bull and crack them open, down-ing one, then the other. The voices are coming back now, and I hear them agree on a price as they walk past. It's considerably less than what I pay. I think I should take this up with Mark next time. Then I see the absurdity of that thought. I have far more pressing concerns than Mark Liu's flexible pricing structure.

I flip the torch off and sink into the darkness, hoping it will help me think. I try to go over everything, right from the start, and tease out anything which will help me find Klaasen. Because that's the only way this ends.

What it comes down to is him or me. I'm not ready to roll over. Not yet.

What feels like hours later – though I've no real way of telling; darkness seems to hold its own kind of time – I give up and flip the torch on. I rove around the space, my breathing starting to speed up. There's got to be something. I remember the rent money I'd stashed in the old paint tin and, with nothing better to do, try and locate it. I find it and prise it open. The money's there, but so too are a couple of joints I'd rolled ages ago and then not smoked. I'd put them away and then totally forgotten about them. I pocket the money and look around for the blowtorch. I find it over on the other side and pick it up. Then I hesitate. I try to put it down. But before I do I bring it back up again. Part of me is saying no, don't do it. Another part is whispering sweetly that it's the only thing that will help. I'm caught between them, like an innocent bystander. I have no say in this. I'll simply do whatever the winning voice commands.

Soon I find my finger pushing the button. The blowtorch blazes into life. The flame's bright blue and heats my face as I light up. Ahhh . . . this is Sour Hound. I recognize it straight away. Torch off. Darkness. Just me and the Hound, its glowing tip dancing in the dark. By the time I've smoked half of it my brain is freer, less tethered. I pinch out the joint and stop trying to think. I need to let my mind free, free to do its own thing. It darts around, chasing idea to idea in a sequence that seems unrelated. But I start to sense something, a shape almost, a possibility. Random facts, connections, the THC firing up my lateral thinking, allowing me to see what I couldn't see before.

I've lost all sense of time here in the dark, so I don't know if it's taken me minutes, or hours. But I've got it now. It's there. I can see it all.

I pocket the half-smoked joint and the unsmoked one, the money and the torch. After a little thought I select a couple of tools I can carry with me easily, a screwdriver and a small wrench.

I breathe in a couple of times, then head towards the door.

It's time.

It's time to make this right.

Moonlight

Schiphol airport. Long-stay car park. I'm standing just outside, pretending to have a conversation on a phone I don't have. I'm waiting for a suitable car but so far everything's been way too modern for my needs. Just as I'm thinking I'm going to have to come up with an alternative plan a red Ford Mondeo sails round the curved road and heads right for the barrier. It slows, the window rolls down and a hand reaches out to take the ticket. The barrier rises in a series of jerks and the car moves. I finish up my imaginary phone call and walk in through the pedestrian entrance, trying to keep track of where the car is going. In the end it finds a spot between a boxy SUV and a maroon Mazda on the third floor.

I hold back, reigniting my imaginary conversation on my imaginary phone. People spill out: man, woman and two children, the perfect family. The man hauls a collection of suitcases out of the boot and ferries them one by one down the narrow channel between his car and the SUV next to it. The kids are excited, the mother stressed, the father even more so. Soon they've each been assigned a case and are disappearing into the walkway which will lead them into the terminal.

I walk back down to the ground floor and press a button on the ticket machine, requesting assistance. It takes a few moments but a crackly voice comes on and I explain that I've just come in a few minutes ago and one of my kids was playing with the ticket and lost it and that we're late for our flight so I need another one and could he do that and did I say we're really late for our flight and I'm taking the kids to Disney Land in Florida, which has been their dream for years, and I'd be really grateful if he could help us out because if we miss this flight we won't be able to afford another one and –

'What car? When did you come in?'

'Red Ford Mondeo.'

He's obviously rewinding the entranceway CCTV.

'Licence?'

I give it to him. A few moments. C'mon, c'mon.

'All right, ticket's coming out of the machine now.'

I thank him, tell him how much it'll mean to my kids, but I think he's already rung off. I grab the ticket, head back to the car and get it open quickly with no alarm going off. The wires spark and the engine comes to life. I ease out of the space and down the ramps to the ground floor. The ticket slides into the machine. Bonus, nothing to pay as I've been here less than an hour. I make myself promise I'll return the car before they're back. A yellow smiley face dangles from the rear-view, the scent it's releasing already giving me a headache. I rip it off and toss it out the window.

Soon I hit the A9, heading north, destination Bergen. The desire to put my foot down, to get there as soon as I can, is strong, but I rein myself in, driving conservatively. I stay within the limit, I indicate when changing lanes, I keep a safe distance at all times. I do everything possible to avoid being noticed.

Just before Alkmaar I pull off the motorway and stop at a light and a police car pulls up beside me. My heart detonates in my chest. There are two of them, uniforms, and the driver has dark glasses despite it not being that bright. He turns to look at me and for a moment I can see myself reflected in his lenses, my face distorted by their curvature. For a split second I glimpse a wolf. Then my face is back. I imagined it. Must have. The stress.

The light turns green and they pull away, unaware that the Netherlands' most wanted man was, for a few short seconds, in the car next to them. Now I'm on the N9, a smaller road, and the landscape opens up around me, flat fields on either side and the Kanaaldijk's waters snake along beside the tarmac. There's less traffic, just the odd lorry hauling goods, and I overtake a tractor with a baler attachment at the back. I pass a field with black and white cows, their long bodies resting on the ground. As darkness deepens I see the odd house dotted along the road with lit windows, the outline of rough agricultural buildings. I turn off again, a swollen misshapen moon swinging into view, casting its light over the tips of the trees ahead. The forest is dark and impenetrable.

Soon I've reached the point where I have to ditch the car. I'd stopped off at a petrol station and bought a pre-pay phone, then used the last of my cash to buy food and drink and a cheap rucksack. It's bright orange so before loading it I find a ditch and rub it in the soft mud at the water's edge. The moon ripples on the water's surface as I work. Once it's covered I take the four cans of Red Bull, a packet of sliced Gouda and three chocolate bars out of the car and stuff them all into the rucksack. I check the phone. I've got two bars. I can see the place I'm heading to on the phone's map app, but I just hope that when I'm in the woods I'll still be able to use it to navigate.

And the forest ahead, now that I'm here, seems several times darker and larger than I'd thought it would be. I raise my nose and sniff the air a couple of times before setting off. It smells like rain.

Off on the hunt.

The trunk had probably come down in a storm. Or maybe its roots had been damaged by insects or fungus, or perhaps it had just reached an age and, tired of this world, had decided to keel over, taking as many of its neighbours as possible. In any case, it's right across the path I'm on. I sit down by it, the huge girth partly sheltering me from the rain which has begun to fall. A cluster of mushrooms sprout from the wood like little umbrellas. I check the phone and see I've been going for just over two hours. Rucksack, Red Bull. The can hisses loudly into the night. It's almost flat by the time it's finished fizzing over. But I'm grateful for the energy it gives me.

I think back to all the crimes I've been witness to, how all of them were really nothing more than the almost inevitable conclusion of some earlier action, some chain of events whose outcome would have, despite their inevitability, been hard to predict. Invisible strings play us like puppets.

I'm here because of two bits of information that had come together in the lock-up, teased out by the Sour Hound. The artist on the Groeneveen estate had said Benner spent the summer holidays in a log cabin in Bergen, and

I remembered the note in the file on Lucie Muller's death, the officer from Bergen who'd said they'd seen a man fitting the description we'd sent out. And he'd been living in a log cabin deep in the woods. Two little bits of information that are going to end this once and for all. And to it I now add a third: Klaasen had worked on a building site in Alkmaar, which I'd passed to get here. I don't know why I didn't think of that before.

Then I think of Benner and his brother signing up for the trial, the lure of easy money overriding the danger that it actually posed. By some chance of fate both Rein and his brother were given the drug, and both fell ill. But Rein survived, and having watched his brother die wanted to get revenge. But then the question: would Rein have flipped, would he have killed at all just from the grief? Or had the drug done something to him? Had his brain been rewired in a way that made him more likely to kill, that made it easier for him to transform from Rein, frustrated actor working as a waiter and labourer, to Sander Klaasen, a stone-cold killer? Had he made the transformation out here in the woods, sitting in the building I'm searching for as the change occurred? Had it been gradual, or had it struck like lightning, the switch happening from one moment to the next? At what point did Klaasen decide he wanted to get revenge on me as well? And, the question I'm not yet willing to face, what part did Sabine play in all this? Because I'm starting to feel that meeting her that day can't have been a coincidence. Or maybe that's just paranoia.

It has to be.

Sabine upped and left, that's all. She has nothing to do

with this. She doesn't. I hear her whispering *I'm sorry* in her sleep. My throat dries up.

A noise somewhere behind me. It's like a twig snapping, distinct from the softer dripping of the rain. I'm fully alert, muscles tense, hairs on the back of my neck standing proud, ears primed. I hold my breath and turn my head slowly. Darkness, trunks standing sentinel, moonlight spikes through the canopy. I can smell pine resin, earth, something fungal. But I can't see anything moving, and the sound doesn't happen again. After a few minutes I slip off the trunk and continue on my way.

Only now I've got the feeling I'm not alone.

Reception had slipped down to one bar before it disappeared totally. I'm on the right track, though, as I'd tried to commit the rest of the way to memory; the path ahead is going to bend round towards the edge of the trees and there'll be a field. I'll need to skirt that, before diving back into the forest, following a small path that should lead me right to the property whose roof had just been visible on the phone. I move forward. The path does bend and I step into a field flooded with moonlight, almost too bright after the dark of the forest. It takes a moment for my eyes to adjust. I pick out a pale structure off to the right.

It's a ribcage.

I move towards it only to see it's not human. Given the size it most likely belonged to a fallen sheep. I spot the skull lying a few metres away. There's no way of telling if the head had been detached before it died or after. The bones are clean of flesh and glow eerily in the moonlight. My lip twitches. I move on. I'm suddenly worried that I'm wrong, but there's a feeling inside, a kind of animal sense, that tells me this is right, that I need to carry on. There is no other option.

I give in to it, picking my way along the path, slippery with dry pine needles and roots which course across it at random, ready to trip me up. At first I'm tentative but I gradually find a rhythm and soon I'm moving with a confidence and fluidity I didn't know was possible. I'm slipping in and out of it more easily now, the transitions aren't so jarring; it's almost like I'm both at once, me and the wolf.

The question is, am I the black one, or the white?

On the path again I break off to investigate a tree, before pissing against it in a hot gush illuminated by a sliver of moonlight breaking through the dense canopy. It starts to rain again, softly.

I find it. I'm crouched by a large pine tree with the wooden hut up ahead. The forest drips around me. I take in the structure. You probably could just about fit a family in it for a holiday, so it's easily big enough for one person. It's quiet; no lights on, though that's hardly surprising as we're probably not far off dawn. It's made of rough-hewn planks, both the walls and the sloping roof. There's a crooked drainpipe which leads to a water butt on one side. The front door looks sturdy. I sniff the air before creeping forward.

I do a circuit of the place, stopping frequently, but by the time I've done a full circle and am standing by the front door I've noticed nothing that would lead me to believe Klaasen is inside. I reach a hand out and place it against the wood before applying very soft pressure. It starts to open, and it seems, despite the rustic nature of the place, to be on well-oiled hinges. I step in quietly and try to let my eyes adjust to the even darker interior. My breathing's slow and quiet, controlled, ears pricked for any movement inside. Anything that might hint at Klaasen being here.

The dim interior starts to take shape. A metal sink is attached to the wall, the plumbing exposed underneath. A couple of basic shelves display a few glasses and cans of food, too dark to make out the labels. There are a couple of mismatched armchairs, though both are in competition to see which can sag the most. There are thick cross-beams at intervals and above the internal triangle of the roof. To my right there's a wall with a door. It must be the bedroom. I slip towards it, staying as close to the wall as possible, hoping the boards will be less likely to creak than walking across their middles. There's a mustiness to the air.

I pause by the door, my ear up against it, primed for any noise at all. But after a minute or so I'm sure there's no one on the other side. I push it open slowly. About halfway gravity takes over and it swings away from me, creaking loudly as it does.

Stock-still, ears primed.

Nothing.

I step inside. There's a bed with a bare mattress, and a crumpled sleeping bag on top. It looks old, worn, but when I put my hand on it I feel warmth.

Which is when the figure suspended on one of the cross-beams drops down and hits me hard, slamming me into the wall. Before I can recover I feel the cold touch of a gun against my neck.

'Nice of you to join me.'

I recognize the voice. It's Klaasen.

Make Them Pay

He slips cable ties round my wrists and pulls them tight. They bite into my skin. The floor creaks. Something scuttles across the roof. There's a strong smell of damp and kerosine and something else I can't place.

'Shall we go for a walk?' he whispers in my ear.

I have no choice. He keeps the gun jammed against my neck. We walk out of the bedroom, out of the house and into the trees, through thick undergrowth which gradually transforms into brambles. Klaasen pushes me hard, and soon my shins and knees are ripped and bleeding. And still we march on, rain prickling my face.

'I know why you did it,' I tell him. 'I know about your brother.'

'So you know who the real bad guys are then. Why aren't you going after them?'

'I *am* going to go after them. I've got enough evidence to make them pay.'

Which is a lie. Because there's nowhere near enough. It's no longer raining.

'Beat you to it. My version is better.'

'The people you killed didn't deserve that.'

'My brother didn't deserve that! He didn't deserve to die face down, naked, screaming in pain with blood filling up his lungs. He didn't fucking deserve any of that, not after the life he had. But he got it. He got it because of them. Their greed. And I didn't deserve to see it happen. I didn't deserve to survive when he died.'

He starts making a weird choking sound. It takes me a moment to realize he's sobbing. The victim's postures now make sense. It was a message, one only the people he meant to hurt the most could understand.

'No, neither of you deserved that. And that's why I'm going to make them pay. But I need your help to do that.'

'And what, I'll just go to prison?'

'There's no way to avoid it, you know that. But we can still hurt them; you can hurt them from prison. You can help me expose what they've done, what they're most likely still doing, but I need you to –'

The gun smacks me on the back of the head. Through the pain I think of a bell being rung.

'I'm going to make them pay, but I'm going to do it without you.'

'Just tell me one thing, what did you do with Sabine?'

He laughs. 'Every word you speak from now on just means I'm gonna do it slower. You get that, right?'

Up ahead I catch a glimpse of the treeline, another clearing perhaps, or maybe the edge of the forest. As we break through I look up to see the candyfloss smudge of dawn . . .

He puts the phone down. This time, instead of locking it in his drawer he opens up the back, takes out the SIM and removes the battery. In the little canteen area at the end of the hallway he drops the SIM into a ceramic mug and puts it in the microwave. It fizzes and pops and thirty seconds later he removes the cup and rinses it in the sink, what's left of the blackened SIM disappearing down the plughole. Back in his office he sits, wondering what to do next. When he'd received that call from Rykel he'd acted calm, despite the fear rampant inside. It's only a matter of time now, *he thinks. The question is, how long? He's been instructed to clean up his operation, leaving no trace. Including the man who'd been doing the work for him. He's due to meet him later this evening, ostensibly to pay him off. Only the payment's not going to be what he expects.*

Bite

I'm on my knees. Naked. A gun at the back of my neck and also a knife in play. Not a lot going for me.

Except for one thing.

The knowledge that I hadn't been making all this up. I hadn't killed the people the police think I killed. I hadn't made myself schizo.

I take in deep breaths, the air's never seemed so sweet. Painfully sweet. The sky lightens by the second, stars blinking out, and the world rebirthing around me. A clearing hemmed in by trees. There's grass, probably millions of blades of it, and on each blade tiny droplets of dew are glistening as they come alive in the light. A bird starts a long warbling melody, complex and simple and one of the most beautiful things I've ever heard. There's a stillness to it. It's like a key to another place, another time, which is nevertheless right here, right now. I feel deep pangs of regret. I've made so many mistakes, so many things that I could have done better.

Most of all I think of Tanya. But even that slips away and I start to sense this place is different, that this place is better. This place is –

'You know what I'm going to do, don't you?'

Klaasen's voice. I don't want to hear it, the ugly intrusion into where I'm heading. I just want to die here peacefully, taking in the world that I'd never fully appreciated before.

The sheer beauty of it all and my failure to see it before more painful than anything he can do to me with his knife.

Klaasen leans in and whispers in my ear, his breath hot and rancid. 'I'm going to cut your throat and watch you bleed to death.'

I'm leaving this world. It suddenly seems so simple. Like I was destined for this all along. I breathe in again as Klaasen shifts behind me and I feel the knife at my throat. The metal's cool, but then turns hot as it slices into my flesh.

The pain's like a switch. It ignites me, electrifies me, jolts through every cell I have. Thought is gone. Thought is nothing.

I slam my head back and to the side, away from the knife. I feel Klaasen's nose crunch. I throw myself down and roll several times, my hands still bound at the wrist. The world spins, grass, trees, sky, *grass, trees, sky. Something's happening. I feel different.*

I turn to face him. He's standing now, grinning at me, gripping the knife. *Nose to the wind.* I also see that I've been tricked. In his other hand, the hand that I thought was holding the gun, is a very short piece of metal piping. He holds it up, taking aim. He pretends to fire it, and then grins even more.

The world drops away. My stomach lurches. I can feel a huge swell inside me, rising up and gathering strength and speed and power. Up and up and up until I can control it no longer. I'm taken by its sheer magnificent intensity.

As I launch myself towards him, a terrible cry coming from my lips, I know that I'm not me.

Everything's easy now, everything's slow. I dodge the swing of the knife, and throw myself right at him, slamming into his chest, knocking him backwards. He takes a few stumbling steps, then catches a heel on something. It takes forever, his arms windmilling, but still he goes down. The earth vibrates as he hits. I leap forward and stamp on his wrist. The knife drops from his fingers. With the other hand he swings the metal rod up and round into my knee. The pain feels amazing. Clear, pure. I stamp on that arm as well and he drops it. He's still grinning but it's fixed now. There's fear in his eyes. There's fear in the air. I can smell it.

I drop down, knees pinning both his arms. I shove a hand under his chin, exposing his neck. It's unprotected, stretched out in the gathering light.

Something shifts inside me. Our teeth are bared. Saliva drips.

We itch to bite. Bite the neck and shake it till the crunch that tells us it's finally broken and he goes limp.

Tremors. Trembling. Bite. Bite. Bite bite bitebitebitebite . . .

I pull back. It's got me this far. But I'm in control. I'm still trembling. The desire to bite a blazing fire in my head, my whole body. I force myself to breathe slowly.

I *am* in control. I start to speak, the words *alien sounds at first, odd shapes in my mouth. But they begin to come into* focus. I'm breathing hard, the desire is *fighting back*, and wants to take control, to deal with this situation as it should be. I force it down, force myself to be the one in charge. I start to speak again, and this time the words make sense to me right from the start.

'Rein Benner, I'm arresting you for the murder of Lucie Muller, Marian—'

His scream of rage drowns out the rest. A bird, startled in a nearby tree, flaps up into the air.

Epilogue

An early frost crunches under my feet as I weave my way up the gentle slope. Kush is ahead, nosing around the gravestones. On top of one of them a crow perches, wings shimmering like a petrol spill in the low sun. My nose feels like it's dripping, but the back of my hand comes away dry. Kush reaches Hank's grave first and turns round, baffled by my comparative slowness.

'All right for you,' I tell him as I get close. 'I've only got two legs.'

He ignores me, now entranced by the stone itself, sniffing intently. Nellie's scent, most likely. And all of a sudden I'm back with her in that room with Hank lying in bed and the thin doctor with the purple birthmark on his neck asking for permission to switch off the life-support. I found Nellie's hand in my own, and it stayed there as we listened to the beep from the heart-rate monitor ping and the silence after it sounded for the last time. Hope's important, but sometimes it can become a trap, a trap Nellie's now free from.

I've seen her a few times over the last few weeks and there's a change already, a subtle shift in her which she might not even be aware of yet, but one that I'm glad to see.

My toes are freezing, and I'm due to meet Beving and Vermeer in less than an hour, and I'll have to drop Kush back at Joel's before that, but I stand for a while longer, not wanting to rush. On previous visits I've gone through memories of times I had with Hank, but today my mind's quieter, content to just be here.

I take that as a good sign.

Beving and Vermeer are all business. Rein Benner has been officially charged and is awaiting trial, and I've been called to this meeting to hear that all charges against me are being officially dropped. It's a formality, and normally I wouldn't bother, but there's something about the prospect of watching Beving squirm that made me turn up. So far, though, there's not been a lot of squirming.

Because there is a loose end, one which Beving is still tugging on. I'd met with my lawyer, Pieter Roskam, before going into the station where we were shown to the conference room on the top floor. The table probably seats fifteen; today there are just four. A plate in the middle has a small pile of individually wrapped biscuits. The packets are coated in a thin layer of dust.

'There's still the problem with the DNA,' Beving says.

'I've told you, Benner killed Dirk Zeeman.'

'But Benner says he didn't. He admits killing Muller and Kleine but not Zeeman; he was very clear on that. He said it was women he wanted to kill, not men.'

'He's just bullshitting, you know that.'

'But there's no forensic evidence to suggest he was even there. And your blood was found under the victim's fingernails.'

'With respect –' Roskam takes over for me, probably sensing my nascent frustration. Frustration that can all too quickly lead to anger. 'This has been gone over to death and –'

'Ha ha. I thought you were a lawyer, not a comedian.'

Roskam glares at him and continues. 'My client has consistently stated the facts, that the most likely explanation is that Benner had followed Rykel to the flat being rented by Sabine Wester and took a dressing he'd discarded there from the bin.'

'And yet the agency that rents that flat out has no record of Sabine Wester ever renting it. And, in fact, we can find no trace of Sabine Wester at all.'

'Apart from the report filed, by one of your officers, stating that she was attacked by a man and rescued by my client.'

'Yes, but that doesn't prove that your client then formed some kind of loose relationship with this mysterious woman, and went to stay at her flat, which, as we've already established, was in a void period when no one was renting.'

I've thought a lot about this. I can't work it out either. But I didn't make it up, I'm sure of that. Cut to her whispering *I'm sorry* in her sleep. It makes me shiver.

But Roskam's continuing, an unstoppable legal steam train. 'There's also the fact that Benner had burned down my client's houseboat, which proves he knew where he was and was actively targeting him. Has not Benner stated on the record that he wanted to punish Jaap Rykel for putting him away before he could finish what he'd set out to do?'

'He has. I have the statement here. He fully admits to

that. But what he categorically denies is that he placed the evidence on the body, and he denies following Rykel to a flat where he subsequently breaks in and retrieves a used dressing from the bin. That's a bit odd, isn't it?'

'Not really,' I say. 'It's his final fuck-you to me. That's all it is.'

And yet, what part did Sabine play in this? Why did she disappear? Time seems to be strengthening these questions, not weakening them. I've tried to find her as well, but she seems to have vanished into thin air. It suddenly strikes me that Kush didn't like her from the start. I thought he was just being weird or jealous. Now I wonder if he wasn't trying to tell me something after all.

Beving sighs, leans back in his chair and folds his arms. I reckon he's just pissed off because I didn't get him any dirt on Vermeer.

'Okay, this is where we're at. Benner is awaiting trial for the murder of Marianne Kleine. In addition he has been charged with Arson with Intent to Kill, and Attempted Murder in the case of Klaas Blok. But the decision has been made, and at a higher pay grade than mine, I might add, to leave the murder of Dirk Zeeman as open. As of now your client is no longer an official suspect, but that may change as we pursue this case. It would be wise not to book any foreign travel in the foreseeable future. Any questions?'

I glance across at Vermeer, her face unreadable.

'No. No questions.'

Outta here.

Sliding the key into the lock sets off a crazy scramble. He skids round the corner just as I get the door open, slides into the wall and then launches himself at me, front paws on my chest, claws like nails, tail whacking the designer radiator. Note to self, I need to figure out how to clip his claws. The vet had done it last, but that was a while ago and they seem to have grown. I'd got out of the shower the day Joel was heading to the airport and he'd asked me who the foxy female was who'd scratched up my chest.

I get some food from the cupboard and it's obviously a religious experience for him. He becomes still, rapt, following my moves with an intense stare. Once the bowl's on the floor, though, decorum goes out the window. He has his snout in it fast, chomping and crunching, eyes open but unseeing.

My phone buzzes on the kitchen counter, a message from Vermeer asking if we can meet later. In the aftermath of Benner's arrest and my release we'd discussed going after DH Biotech. We'd assembled everything we'd got and taken it to the prosecutor. She'd taken one look at it and called in her legal advisers. We went back the next day when she told us the advice had been, basically, no way. We'd need so much more than what we'd got.

'Let's say for a moment that everything presented here was the work of one individual. They'd set up an experiment in their own house, advertised for volunteers, made them all sign disclaimers and then administered a compound which, although it had been designed as a cure for a specific disease, killed half of them, would we have a case?' I'd asked. Not because I didn't know the answer, but sometimes in the face of the insurmountable the only thing we have are questions.

Yes, she'd confirmed, in that scenario we would have a

case. But with a company as large as DH Biotech we wouldn't stand a chance.

So there it is, one law for the people, quite another for companies with large enough reserves.

Kush has finished his food and is looking for more, sniffing round the kitchen just on the off-chance that I've somehow left another couple of full bowls around. The day stretches out ahead of me. There are so many things I could do it's almost overwhelming. I eventually decide on a drive. Kush snaps to attention when I grab the Stang's keys out of the bowl on the kitchen work surface, and soon we're heading out of the city towards the coast.

We've taken to walks on the beach at Zandvoort, for me to feel the air on my face and watch the ever-shifting muted colours of the North Sea, for Kush to run around and bark at the seagulls. He's quite far ahead of me when I notice him stop dead. He sniffs something, then tentatively puts a paw onto whatever it is that has caught his attention. He paws it a few more times, then, with a swiftness that is startling, dives onto it, rubbing his neck and shoulder along the ground. As I get close he's still at it, though now he's moved onto his back and is wriggling around, paws in the air, tongue hanging loose, a kind of ecstasy in his eyes. Once he's done I glimpse what he's just rolled in: the rotting carcass of a seagull.

I text Vermeer back.

The phone rings as soon as I pocket it. Jansen.

'There's something you should see.'

The white van had skidded off the road and nosedived into the ditch, back wheels aloft. I park up and a uniform lifts the red and white tape for me to duck under. Jansen's talking to someone on his phone, so I take a closer look at the van. It's just a white van, nothing special about it. And yet I get the feeling I've seen it before.

'Vermeer reckoned you'd want to see this.' I turn to see Jansen.

I follow him as he scrambles down the slope, hops over the thin trickle of water at the base, and onto the other side. From here it's possible to see that the van had two people in it when it left the road. Oddly, neither had been wearing seat belts, their foreheads hitting the windscreen as the front end of the van crunched into the solid earth. A halo of dark blood round each head. I get closer. The driver's face is familiar, but I can't place it. The whole scene reminds me of an old school friend of mine; she and her boyfriend had lost control in fog and ended up in a ditch very like this one.

'Foggy out here last night?'

'Not according to the local station. Said it was as clear as can be.'

I walk further down so I can see the far side of the van. Scraped paint and a series of dents. The whole van's a little beaten up, but this looks fresher.

'Run off the road.'

Jansen nods. 'That's what we thought too,' he says just as it comes to me, why the man looks familiar. He was the courier I'd seen outside Nellie's and then after interviewing Patrick Wust.

'He was following me.'

'Really?'

'Yeah, saw him twice. Too much of a coincidence.'

'What about the other man?' Jansen asks. I get the feeling he's leading me along, that he knows something he's not telling me yet. Normally I'd be impatient, but today I just play along and take another look. His face is harder to make out, squashed against the glass which is ready to crumble into a million tiny pieces.

'I give up.'

Jansen whistles to one of the uniforms who walks over with something in his hand. He tosses it over the ditch, Jansen catches it, then hands it over. It's a leather wallet. You can tell it's expensive. I open it up: credit cards, a few receipts and a driver's licence. I pull it out. I don't recognize the face, but the name I do, Joost Beltmann.

'I looked him up, seems he worked for DH Biotech,' Jansen's saying as I hand it back.

'He did. I spoke to him on the phone. Looks like they've started cleaning house already.'

He's thin and frail but there's the unmistakable air of a man who has come through something and beaten it. The real question will of course be whether he needs to beat it again. But for now Robert Huisman's off the heroin. One thing I'd missed during the investigation was that the money he'd paid for his rehab had seemed like a lot, and I'd not questioned how he'd got it. When I got Roemers to check further back in Huisman's financials we found the source of the money, one which had really surprised me.

'Good to be clean?' I ask. We're meeting on the bridge spanning the gap of water by the NEMO building. He's a different person to when I'd interviewed him years ago.

Then he'd been full of arrogance, puffed up with his own self-importance. Now he seems more humble.

'Honestly? It's hell,' he finally says. 'Needing that next hit makes things easier in a way. Nothing else matters. When you're clean everything else matters, and that's harder to cope with.'

'Lucie's death?'

'I know I did some terrible things when I was with her. I cheated on her and I'll never forgive myself. But despite all that I loved her, you know? I loved her and she was taken from me. Heroin made me do such stupid things. If I could have those days back again, I'd do things differently.'

I wonder if that's a universal constant, the wish to go back and do things differently. I know there are things I'd change given the chance. Big things. Things that matter.

'Did you approach Koen Muller, or did he reach out to you?'

'I called him up. At first he wouldn't speak to me. I guess he partly held me responsible. But about a month later he called me back and I went out to meet him at his house. We're never going to be friends, but we talked, and it was good to clear the air, spend some time with someone who also loved Lucie. I think in the end he felt like I was a kind of link back to her. That's why he suggested the rehab I went to and gave me the money for it.'

Koen Muller was an enigma to me. I couldn't work out if he was simply the angry grieving father, or his involvement with DH Biotech meant he'd been playing another role. In a way I'm not sure I'll ever know, but I decide that's all right. Certainly his move to help out Huisman, a man he'd despised and had at one time believed responsible for Lucie's death, takes a lot. In the end people are very rarely all good or all bad. If they were, then life would undoubtedly be easier.

Huisman leaves soon after and I'm left staring out into the IJ's waters, the light glinting off the choppy surface a language just outside of my comprehension.

Later I'm staring at the wreckage of my boat. We're in that moment between light and dark, just before the streetlight sensors kick in. Kush's lying at my feet, exhausted from the day, and the intense scrub-down he'd been subjected to post-dead seagull. I'm not sure the smell's entirely gone, though. It's cold, the air crisp enough to frost again tonight, but I'd borrowed a jacket from Joel which is fit for a Russian winter. The insurance company had called earlier, the chirpy representative bursting to give me the good news that they *will* be footing the entire cost of rebuilding the boat. For some reason I should have been elated, or at least relieved. But I'd found myself asking if I could cash it in instead, maybe buy somewhere else with it. The rep had told me just how much the rebuild was going to cost, a sum so small in comparison to house prices I'd be lucky to find a kennel in central Amsterdam, far less a flat big enough for a human. I'd agreed to the rebuild.

The evening's deepening, Vermeer should be here soon, and I reach for my vape before remembering what happened to it. I will have to get another one, but for now I'm going old-style. I crumble some of the white bud I'd raided from Joel's humidor earlier into a paper and start rolling, the feel of it between my fingers its own kind of therapy. I baptize it. The saliva will make it burn slower and more evenly. Kush perks up, but when he figures that whatever it is I'm doing seems unlikely to immediately yield anything edible he loses interest. I hold the joint up in front of me and guide the flame to it. For a second it looks like my houseboat's burning all over again. Across the water a light flicks on in Leah's houseboat.

'Medicating again?'

Vermeer sits down, Kush between us, and scratches his ear. Kush responds with a long low groan. I'm almost jealous. The dog seems to get so much pleasure from life it's unreal.

'Only for the trouble that's coming,' I tell her. It's a quote from a song, only I don't reckon Vermeer knows that.

'Either you have a poetic turn I didn't know about, or your taste in music is better than I thought.'

Huh, Vermeer's a dark horse indeed.

'So, here to rearrest me?'

'If Beving had his way I would be. He knows it's not you, though. He's just being a dick. Forbidden me to carry on looking at DH Biotech as well.'

Which is hardly a surprise.

'Given what they do to their own people, that's not a bad thing,' I say, thinking of the two men in the van.

'Maybe you're right. Jansen showed Beltmann's photo to the nurse, and she confirmed he was the one who'd visited her that time. She wouldn't testify to it, though. And I spoke to Roemers earlier.'

Somehow I thought she might. She has a mind as suspicious as mine.

399

'He said you'd been asking him how best to leak information anonymously online . . .?'

'Just a theoretical question. Fascinating thing, the internet.'

'Yeah, well, be careful.'

'Don't worry, I'm not going to do that.'

Because tomorrow morning I'm meeting Cheryl Kleine. There are some things best left to the professionals. She's a journalist with an intense personal interest in what I'll have to say. I take a pull and the tip glows. I notice Vermeer has a bottle of beer. She lifts it to her lips and takes a long sip.

'So, about when I shot at you. Sorry –'

'No worries, I didn't leave you much choice.'

'– sorry I missed.'

'Kush, kill.'

Kush flicks an ear, but otherwise does nothing. Nice to see where his loyalty lies.

'What's next?'

Which really is the question. One I've been trying to avoid for the last couple of weeks. Joel's not asked me about his proposal, maybe sensing that I need time. Though I'm not sure that's really what I need.

'Dunno.'

'You're sure you won't come back to the police? Once you're cleared. I could use a good partner.'

'I bet Beving would be thrilled. Tempting, just to see his face. Talking of Beving, you need to be careful of him.'

'Anything specific?'

I tell her about him asking me to spy on her. She doesn't look all that surprised. I take another pull, then Vermeer surprises me. She reaches out, and I hand her the joint. She inhales, long and hard, and I wait for the coughing fit. But she's clearly used to smoke of some sort because she holds it in before blowing out the biggest smoke ring I've ever seen. She hands back the joint, finishes her beer and gets up. 'See you around then.'

I finish it off, and, feeling comfortable, decide on just one more. Just to help me think. I've been thinking a lot since my experience out in the woods, trying to tease out what exactly it was. Did I lose it, even if only temporarily? But what would have happened if I hadn't been able to slip so easily between states? At first I'd been scared it was going to be a return of all my troubles, another break-down, this time more serious.

But over the last few days it's all started to settle.

And it comes to me in a heady rush exactly what I need to do. I can't get rid of the black wolf because in the end it's not some external thing invading me, taking over – it's part of me. I just have to learn to live with it, control it enough that I can unleash it when needed. And, really, it's not like the black and white are opposing each other; it's more that they are complementary in some way. It's just a question of having the right balance between them.

Kush yawns and rests his head on my thigh. His eyebrows twitch a few times then he closes his eyes. He stays like that whilst I finish the joint. Once I've got down to the end I flick it off into the darkness, the tiny luminous tip spiralling down towards the water. It hisses as it makes contact.

'C'mon,' I say, getting up, stretching my arms over my head. 'Let's go get something to eat.'

I turn round to see a figure standing a few metres away

watching me. I didn't hear her arrive, and don't know how long she's been there.

'Hey,' Tanya says.

Hearing her voice again brings everything into focus. I've had so many days stolen from me that I can't imagine losing any more.

I step forward and pull her into my arms.

Acknowledgements

My thanks go to Joel Richardson at Penguin who inherited this book but took it under his wing nevertheless, and applied his thoughtful and insightful editing throughout. My agent, Simon Trewin at WME, for sage advice and clandestine garden centre meet-ups. Jennie Roman for an extremely sensitive copy-edit and Sarah Kennedy for the final polish. Trevor Thrower who advised me on technical aspects relating to car repairs. Mary Jain for her continued support and guidance. To the people who have to remain anonymous because they've been forced to break the law in order to treat their conditions: what you've suffered is appalling and nothing short of a travesty. Here's to the change being swift and decisive.

And to Zara, who continues to amaze and inspire.

I now have absolute proof that smoking
even one marijuana cigarette is equal in brain
damage to being on Bikini Island during
an H bomb blast.

Ronald Reagan

The illegality of cannabis is outrageous,
an impediment to full utilization of a drug which
helps produce the serenity and insight, sensitivity
and fellowship so desperately needed in this
increasingly mad and dangerous world.

Carl Sagan

WELCOME TO AMSTERDAM

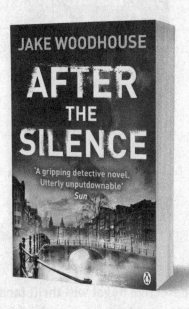

'Utterly enthralling . . . looks set to be one of the key sequences in modern crime fiction' *Crime Time*

'This is a great debut' *Crime Fiction Lover*

A body is found hanging on a hook above the canals of Amsterdam's old town. In a remote coastal village, a doll lies in the ashes of a burnt-down house. But the couple who died in the blaze were childless. Did a little girl escape the blaze? And if so, who is she and where is she now?

Inspector Jaap Rykel knows that he must halt a clever and brutal murderer. And the investigation reveals two dark truths: everybody in this city harbours secrets – and hearing those secrets comes at a terrible price . . .

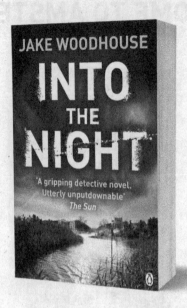

'**This gripping detective novel will thrill fans of** *The Girl with the Dragon Tattoo* **and bears comparison to** *Fatherland* . . . **Utterly unputdownable**' *The Sun*

'**Complex . . . intriguing . . . keeps the reader hooked**' *Euro Crime*

A body is found on a rooftop, the dead man's hands blowtorched, his head removed.

The man tasked with tracking down the killer is Amsterdam Inspector Jaap Rykel. But as he searches the headless body for clues, Rykel finds something which makes his blood run cold: a picture of himself on the victim's phone.

And then a message from the killer reveals the location of a second mutilated corpse. It's another day in Western Europe's murder capital . . .

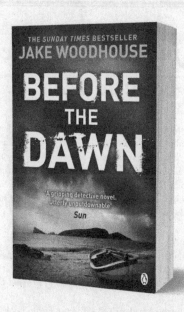

'A strong sense of place matched by storytelling that keeps the plot accelerating' *Daily Mail*

'Taut, expertly woven and beautifully written' Craig Robertson

A body is found, the victim's head wrapped in cling film, hands tied behind her back. The small island's police force needs help from Amsterdam's Murder Squad's veteran Detective Inspector Jaap Rykel.

A suspect confesses, but the killer has no history of violence, no motive and no connection to the victim.

Across the country, a similar murder is reported and Rykel wonders if these are random senseless acts, or something far darker . . . ?

Rykel walks a thin line between spotting patterns no one wants to see, and a sinister, sprawling case which will consume everything in its path . . .

He just wanted a decent book to read ...

Not too much to ask, is it? It was in 1935 when Allen Lane, Managing Director of Bodley Head Publishers, stood on a platform at Exeter railway station looking for something good to read on his journey back to London. His choice was limited to popular magazines and poor-quality paperbacks – the same choice faced every day by the vast majority of readers, few of whom could afford hardbacks. Lane's disappointment and subsequent anger at the range of books generally available led him to found a company – and change the world.

'We believed in the existence in this country of a vast reading public for intelligent books at a low price, and staked everything on it'
Sir Allen Lane, 1902–1970, founder of Penguin Books

The quality paperback had arrived – and not just in bookshops. Lane was adamant that his Penguins should appear in chain stores and tobacconists, and should cost no more than a packet of cigarettes.

Reading habits (and cigarette prices) have changed since 1935, but Penguin still believes in publishing the best books for everybody to enjoy. We still believe that good design costs no more than bad design, and we still believe that quality books published passionately and responsibly make the world a better place.

So wherever you see the little bird – whether it's on a piece of prize-winning literary fiction or a celebrity autobiography, political tour de force or historical masterpiece, a serial-killer thriller, reference book, world classic or a piece of pure escapism – you can bet that it represents the very best that the genre has to offer.

Whatever you like to read – trust Penguin.